WHERE *the* S

Book One *of* The Symphonic Masquerade

WHERE *the* SILENCE SINGS

Book One *of*
The Symphonic Masquerade

EMERY BLAINE

First Published in the Republic of Ireland in 2024 by

Wild Door Publishing
77 Camden Street Lower,
Dublin City D02 XE80

A CIP catalogue record of this book is available from the British Library and Trinity College Dublin Library

ISBN-13 978-1-7385060-0-2

Typeset at Wild Door Publishing
Printed and bound by Ingram Content Group

www.wilddoorpublishing.com

For you, me, and us.
In every iteration.

They come for me.

This history will not die with me.

The ALKONOS is more vast than we are made to believe. The SÍRIN are victim to the same fate as the grand ALICAL BEASTS that once roamed freely. The THAY are nothing more than weapons, tuned to meet the YUN's demands to conquer the aethereal realms.

I did not want this end.

For the sake of our ancestors, I have decided to catalogue what I have seen.

I pray KA'LA'DRIUS has the answer I have yet to divine. My peoples, made lab experiments for the greed of powerful tyrants in holy disguises, will rise against our oppressors.

If you're reading this, I ask: will you stand with me, or against me?

AMANASTRÉ

These are the realms I know:

CA'LORUS, a lush green land with abundant resources. The YUN have made base here, honing their ALKONOSTIC ARTS, a spectrum of aethereal duality made manifest. Natives claim their manipulations VITALITY, but I have seen what VITALITY pushed too far can do. I have done it.

MHEDOON, more accurately DO'ON'MHE, a frozen expanse of winter and water. A fearsome sea-faring culture, skilled in ALICAL ARTS. Unclear whether pre- or post-supplantment.

LU-GHAN, a substantial realm with several biomes and varied terrain; a prosperous peoples live among its sun-drenched hills and valleys.

RAENARU, a religious and spiritual realm. They revere us as gods. Think us deities. We have all but razed their heritage with our own, moulded it to our will. They claim volatile ALKONOS as ESSENCE. I do not see the difference.

QUINGA, an advanced realm and culture that rivals the talents of our greatest artificers. As tall as it is wide, and populous as it is inventive.

ORIN, the beauty of this realm is heart wrenching. ALICA veins thread beneath its soils, permeating from its core by blessings of the ALKONOS. A'GAM says it will perish with little hope of saving.

TENEBRANA, a realm of hidden strength, only whispered true in dense swamplands and carried by tongue to those fortunate enough to hear its songs and serenades. They know what the YUN fear others will discover: the ALKONOS listens if one only calls and listens in kind.

"This paradise isn't meant for the likes of us."

It was a dour admission. The kind of thing that felt too heavy, curling sourly on the tongue.

"Our role is not that of the hero. Our role is nothing more than the horror that keeps parents awake at night, hoping their child will live to see a better tomorrow."

"One day, perhaps, tomorrow will finally arrive."

PRELUDE

Gilded halls full of varnished lies and unbridled deceit.

The Thasian Tower was a horrible vision, the picture of corruption and greed. It was everything it should never have had the chance to become, cursed with an air of poisonous superiority and layer upon layer of stone stacked over buried transgressions.

It was everything that deserved to *burn*.

Seraeyu's shoes dragged sticky and red across the marble floors. Good. They should be stained, painted with the sins of the Thasian, a debt paid in blood. *His* demise, the heretical Praetor, was not enough. That man was a fool and a coward, preying upon the weak and gambling on his stolen fortune to keep himself relevant.

He was not relevant. He was *nothing*.

Seraeyu heaved open a thick metal door, revealing the stairwell beyond. That which was sought remained out of reach. Above. But not so far it could not be found.

One stiff footfall after another, Seraeyu ascended. The city

1

beyond this pristine cage's glass panels gleamed, glorious, stretching up towards the near-cloudless sky. From this vantage, the entire populace skittered like rats, scurrying from one pointless task to the next.

The design of those dense, bright city blocks around this gluttonous seat of power was a mockery. An ill-formed impression of splendour these blinded buffoons so desperately aimed to replicate. But their desire remained graciously and pleasingly unsated. None could recreate the Alkonostic Empire, and none should. It was by hubris it fell, and by the same folly this blasphemous tower would too.

Did they think that rage itself could be contained? Did they dare to assume that *they* were infallible? That they were victorious? No, they had only prolonged the inevitable.

Perhaps they had forgotten. No matter: Seraeyu was there to re-educate them. To be used like a tool did not bode well. No, it did not bode well at all. This perversion of prosperity could not – *would not* be allowed to remain.

Seraeyu had come to fix this. Seraeyu would be the catalyst these wretched realms deserved.

There now. The top of the tower had been reached. All that stood between a long legacy of oppression and a path towards retribution was one thick slab of iron.

With a crimson-coloured hand, the same satisfying rouge that now trailed a path up the stairwell, Seraeyu pushed the door open.

The sun was beautiful that day, shining down like a beacon, blessing this moment where all would come to fruition, where that which was meant to occur would finally come into being. All that was needed now was what was owed. What was *promised*.

"Raeyu Thasian," said Seraeyu.

The metal egress behind slammed shut, drawing the attention of three onlookers. Three blasphemers. Three Yu-ta who carried the horn-adorned heads of their ancestors; three Yu-ta who bore the atrocities their brethren had committed time and time and time again. Yes, the sun was beautiful that day, and it shone brightly upon that training ground at the top of the tower. Where they would hone their instruments of war. Where they would wager their kin to keep what they claimed to be the natural order.

"Sera," the traitor said, her eyes scanning her brother's bloodied form with concern.

Her companions were not as foolish; wary scrutiny in their eyes betraying their apprehension. Trained guards, mangy dogs that would lick the boots of their masters if they were ordered to lay themselves so low. *Disgusting* parasites who wouldn't understand honour and real, *true* loyalty if it was regaled to them in daily prayer.

"Seraeyu," the craven Thasian-nee called, head of his own line, his battle-scarred face wrinkling with consternation.

"Do not *speak* to me, Jourae Thasian-nee!" There were no words from the man that would negate the weight of that name. That demarcation. Thasian-*nee*. How pathetic. How very bold of them to walk around acting as if it were a mark of pride. "Neither you nor your filthy spawn have the right to address me."

Those words sparked something in wicked Jourae Thasian-nee. He held a hand out to his son, the cur, Uruji Thasian-nee, urging him to retreat, then he lifted his other arm to indicate the same to Raeyu.

Yes. *Yes.* Seraeyu was a *threat.* Seraeyu would be *feared.* Seraeyu would be *magnificent.*

"Raeyu Thasian, I will be your judge. I will be your saviour." It felt good to say those words. The vindication was intoxicating, and it coursed through Seraeyu's body like wildfire. A laugh, unchained and unstoppable, erupted before it could be contained. "Raeyu Thasian. Raeyu Thasian, I have come to reclaim what is *mine.* Raeyu Thasian, you will get what you deserve, you–"

The feeling of a presence behind, like a wraith walking on wind, pulled Seraeyu's attention away from the belatedly horrified faces of the blasphemers. It was that woman, that *damned woman,* who had been dismissed from the false patriarch's office. She had now arrived with weapons brandished and a way of twisting across what little shadow remained that sang a familiar song. Oh, what a poor, poor impression. What a dastardly parody.

The alica were favourable today, however, since Seraeyu's sentimental sister tuned with whatever gale-force alicant she held, pushing the newcomer assailant away. It was amusing in a twisted, morbid sort of unravelling. Another soft chuckle escaped as the scene unfolded, the would-be assassin's body skidding across roughened tiles, betrayed by the very person she sought to protect.

It was all too perfect.

But everything worth savouring, even a poetic moment such as this, must come to an end.

Everything was right in the realms when Seraeyu siphoned energy, the power of borrowed force crackling across his body like wrangled lightning. It was all too easy, such a simple feat, to transplant from one space to the next, driving a hand through the very heart of that wretched Jourae Thasian-nee. He had not expected Seraeyu to tune with the Thasian bloodsong, and there was that hubris piquing only to crumble down, paired with the despairing cry of his child, witness to his demise.

Uruji Thasian-nee would be next; this was already determined. It was a cruel fate to watch a parent fall, so Seraeyu would release poor Uruji from this suffering. It was only fair. It was only *just*.

"How could you!?" the distraught son cried, anger welling where serenity usually sat.

Uruji always had a pleasant temperament. It was a shame Seraeyu had to be the one to ruin that. Much of his perseverance was owed to the Thasian-nee whelp.

But some things couldn't be avoided.

Some things were meant to be dismantled.

Uruji – sweet, erudite Uruji – was sweet no more as he slipped a dagger from his belt and launched across the rooftop, all reckless abandon. None of that logical consideration he was famous for. No thought at all towards the alicant lodged in the bracers clasped

4

upon his wrists. It was sad to watch someone tumble from grace so quickly. It wasn't an unfamiliar circumstance either, and it tugged at something lingering and unwelcome, lost in the vestiges of time.

Still, it was easy to raise a wall, a tangible barrier of spirit itself, and Uruji went stumbling backwards. He had surely never felt so useless, much less opposed to Seraeyu. It must have been a terrible revelation.

"Sera!" Raeyu called, a futile attempt to reach her brother. "Sera, stop! Please!"

Raeyu could not – *would not* be allowed to call upon her bloodsong. This was unacceptable. This was part of the prejudiced fate that Seraeyu was here to fix. An abhorrent sentence that Seraeyu was here to eradicate and ameliorate.

Uruji would have to wait.

Seraeyu let Jourae fall forwards, observing the viscera clinging to revealed claws, now coated crimson gore. The colour of horrific, unforgivable violence. But this was not the time to falter. This was not the time for weakness. This was a time for action. What was owed would finally be returned.

With another thunderous blink, lightning flashed wildly across Seraeyu's body, and his form manifested beside Raeyu. There was barely enough time for their eyes to connect, deep amber melting against glistening gold, and then Seraeyu's goal was reached. It was then, hands grasped unforgivingly around an ink-scarred arm, that Seraeyu knew the fate of the realms was set. It was then because, when skin met skin, an awful emptiness crept into the space between, and a silence echoed, mourning a future that would never come to be.

And it was then that Seraeyu callously shred sinuous flesh and cracked bone from bone.

And it was then that Raeyu Thasian screamed in agony, her arm ripped ruthlessly in two.

His impression hulked in the doorway, stern eyes staring, observing. It wasn't an unfamiliar look; a gaze given by his mother when he'd done something that maybe he shouldn't have, as if she didn't quite know how to approach the situation. Just as often, it was paired with hunched shoulders and clasped hands, almost as if in prayer.

It was different this time, though. There was no soft tone asking if he was okay. Only the twitching of fingers towards the hilt of a weapon – the promise of a quick death – and the gruff voice that matched the brutish scar running down one side of a weatherworn face. One that commanded authority.

"I think it's time you stop hiding."

CHAPTER ONE

It came on suddenly. Not a hinting, quiet murmur of warning, but a whole roaring shout of *pain*. Like a ligament torn, fibrous muscle in his arm canted, feeling shorn through in a jagged ring across his bicep. Reeling, Aeyun miscalculated his next hurdle. His momentum was cut short as his limbs twisted around themselves, his cloaked frame scraping to an uncoordinated stop.

A crunch resounded as his bulky mask smashed against the rooftop. Beneath him, spore-ridden grates groaned with cantankerous, rusty complaints amid the unexpected pressure. He garbled a gasp, the unfortunate kind that was impossible to swallow, and a slew of breathless curses escaped as coagulated muck splattered against his goggles. The grime marred his already unsteady vision with a splash of vibrant, disease-dotted green. The whole of it contrasted horribly with the otherwise shadowy periphery.

Aeyun found he was hysterically grateful for the plugs shoved up his nose, else he surely would have been smelling mould rot for a month. Assuming itchy little microbes didn't burrow into his brain and turn it to mush first.

Heavy boots thumped down beside him, scattering hazy plumes of shimmering pollen. Aeyun shoved down a contained whimper – it begged to be let loose as his arm throbbed – the feeling of it lumping uncomfortably behind the hollow of his throat. With frantic concern, he double-checked that his arm was still attached to his body. Both assuaging and disparaging, it proved perfectly intact. With that assurance nuzzled into his mind, he squinted up, grimacing at his newly arrived companion.

Davah stood tall, dwarfing Aeyun more than he usually did from his well-postured vantage, concern contorting his features. His unruly hair was flattened slick from a mishap back at purveyor Emera's unprotected warehouse – foolish overconfidence on her part. Davah had accidentally popped a globby secretion while rounding a corner. It had been a precarious and mischievous thing, clinging by mucus-laden threads to a corroded crate.

Davah had not found the event as funny as his co-smugglers.

Aeyun, still discombobulated, stifled a grunt and forced himself off the grubby surface. As he did, he leant heavily on his unaffected left palm; the right one felt rather useless just then.

Davah's pragmatic gaze peered down, a curious brow betraying his stoic veneer. His work-roughened glove, dyed unevenly with mechanic's grease, was graciously outstretched to offer assistance. As Aeyun hesitantly accepted the offered hand, Saoiri landed beside them, long braid sliding over her shoulder as her wiry frame bent to pick up a stray alicant ore as gently as she'd arrived. The glittering stone had gone flying from Aeyun's leather satchel during the unexpected jostle, skidding right alongside his body.

7

"You alright there, friend?" Davah called out, his voice muffled behind the dual vents of his respirator mask.

Aeyun silently thanked his lucky stars that his own mask hadn't been ripped off when he'd tumbled, nor had it cracked upon impact. That it was not Mercur's pungent, polluted air that he was wheezing into his lungs.

Davah, still awaiting a response, had lines creasing between his brow as the pause elongated. His eyes cast warily across his fellow *liberator* – a term Davah himself had attributed to their more thieving escapades – evaluating.

Aeyun needed to collect his shattered wits. There was no time to waste; there never was. Losing seconds could mean everything. The spreading numb, however, did nothing but exacerbate his worries, twisting his senses into a singular mania.

"Holo–"

He winced. An incessant sear of heat and blister of cold plagued him. It was overwhelming in its onslaught, prickling into every quaking corner of his mind.

"Where is the damned holocaster?"

"There's one in the main square – what's wrong with you?" Saoiri asked, not unkindly. But Aeyun's headspace was too fuzzy.

It wasn't the most opportune time to head to the holocaster, he knew. They'd just gathered a huge alicant score in the bowels of this stars-forsaken city, the proud Orinian capital that had long since lost its lustre. All mists and musk, true to the vision it evoked as the subterranean epicentre of the realm of Orin, the city of Mercur dwelled in the shadows. However, its secrets seldom did. Largely in thanks to its paranoid populace. It was by the same diluted word of mouth that Aeyun was reasonably convinced the ore they'd picked up had the potential to contain what he searched for.

In the smuggling game longer than himself, his companions made sure he knew that getting in and getting out was an art of speed and agility. Like whispering silhouettes in the darkest corridors, they'd slip around unseen, leaving anyone slighted none the wiser. Most importantly, they'd never stick around long enough to garner any undesired attention.

Right now, though . . .

Aeyun didn't answer Saoiri. Instead, he veered to the left, propelling himself off ladders and rusty landings to get to his new destination, corrugated metal creaking under his weight.

It was never fair when fate practised this type of trickery. And he'd long given up the right to ignore cosmic knavery.

Bioluminescent patches of flora, vibrant climbers woven between buildings and coiling in damp cervices, all swam in his vision. Dancing in his periphery, the whole of it became a kaleidoscope of muted colours. It didn't matter. None of it mattered.

He leapt across creaky ladders, uncaring of the chafed, peeling flakes of rust he was scattering to the smoggy lanes below. Before long, above the next roofline, an ambient white glow permeated the thick air. It filtered flickeringly through curled, sulphuric steam that wafted up from the depths.

Beyond the brightness, lost in its radiance, buildings blurred into a painted impression. The blinding sheen was only amplified, reflected off the oppressive underbelly of glossy stalactites far above, the towering city blocks snug among gouged corridors. It was claustrophobic at the best of times. Now, it was well and truly suffocating.

Scraping to a halt on the next roof over, Aeyun's attention was drawn to the din of crowded corridors several storeys down. Mercur's residents bustled through their day none the wiser, unaware of the tension pulling taut from his vantage. They thronged around the corded, metal-laden base cradling the looming orb above; the city's holocaster. Even as it began to thrum, most paid its rumblings no notice.

Delivering on its promise of an incoming broadcast, snowy ore-dust pulsed and settled inside the prominent translucent sphere. It clouded the lower anterior, bearing the first indications of sound. Of whatever this new trial was that the realms bade

9

him reconcile.

A developing terror was borne from the darkest corners of Aeyun's mind. It struck like an arrow, piercing clean through his pounding chest. Like a prophecy fulfilled, sung to him from reaches within the expansive unknown, the Great Starry Sea itself, consequence had found him.

Just as it all became too much, too *real,* the punishing torment in his arm fizzled, almost as if cauterised. Distracted by the vision manifesting in front of him, he lifted his opposite hand to press upon his erratic heart, willing it to find some semblance of serenity.

The flurry finally congealed to form a transmitted image. A voice, hollow and sombre, crackled into being, its echo sounding around the holocaster.

"We interrupt your daily proceedings with an emergency broadcast. Again, we interrupt your daily proceedings with an emergency broadcast," said the ghostly vision of a woman, encapsulated in grey tones within the holocaster. "I am your correspondent Verida Berylum, reporting to you from the Realmal Broadcast Bureau Centre in Mercur. Our sources have indicated that the Raenaruan capital city of Haebal is in a state of disarray after the fallout of a reported attack on the Thasian Tower.

"Currently, there is no official line as to the motivation or group behind the attack. Several informants, including a representative of the Lu-Ghanian Sovereign Coalition, have indicated that there is speculation it may have to do with the growing animosity towards the Thasian control of trade among the realms."

Aeyun distantly acknowledged that Davah and Saoiri must have caught up at some point. Davah's worn glove latched onto Aeyun's shoulder. Aeyun didn't flinch. By then, his arm an unfeeling husk of skin and bone. Distractedly, he stepped closer to the roof's edge, nudging off the comforting gesture.

The holocaster was there, in front of him. But he needed more. He needed to be closer; to feel it, to be *immersed* in it.

To be there, on the ground, in Haebal City.

"We are just getting word that one of our Eyes is on the scene. We'll cut to–"

The image swapped too quickly, seen from the shaky point of view of an Eye. They hopped over what Aeyun could barely recognise as a toppled section of the Thasian Tower's courtyard walls. Dulled by the reflection transmitted within the holocaster, the vision of burning rubble seared into Aeyun's retinas. His breath hitched as light-headedness swooped down upon him. In the distance, he and anyone who bothered to watch the broadcast could see a figure shrouded in smoke. Soot-covered Sentinels seemingly shielded themselves from some invisible pressure, a force preventing them from reaching the stuttering silhouette. Even from a distance, the unmistakable tail ends of dignitary attire struck a bolt of dread through Aeyun's system.

Swift and sudden, a moment of confusion rattled loudly. The Eye's projected vision careened to the side with a reverberating shout, reaching a note that was likely to feature in Aeyun's next sleep. What looked like crackling sparks of lightning crossed the Eye's line of sight, then only gravel and grass were framed.

If any passer-by had not been watching before, they certainly were now, that scream still echoing around the dome.

The holocaster's focus shifted to that of a secondary Eye's perspective, whose frozen gaze was pinned upon the slumped, charred form of what could only be the downed Eye. The one who'd previously shared their sight with the realms.

Morbidly, Aeyun watched as a claw-nailed hand reached out from just beyond this Eye's periphery, dragging their attention over. Their new viewpoint revealed Seraeyu Thasian, much closer than he should have been given his previous distance. His face and neck were splattered with blood, horns atop his head only serving to amplify his daemonish appearance. Behind Seraeyu, loyal Sentinels rushed to flank him, hurriedly sprinting from where Seraeyu should have still stood, surrounded by smoke in the distant edge of the courtyard.

Seraeyu stepped back a few paces, the shuddering Eye's vision encapsulating more of his being in their view. Aeyun nonsensically noted that Seraeyu's hair was longer than he remembered it being, and much more dishevelled. There was an uncanny appearance about him, broken yet determined, his dignitary robes singed and frayed. The whole of it left Aeyun wrong-footed.

Something paranoid and foul coursed through his veins, a distant cry of duress asking him to look. To *see*.

Aeyun had to convince himself that he wasn't imagining it when he spotted what was clearly a mangled arm in Seraeyu's clenched grasp. And it was certainly not one of his own still very much attached extremities. It was someone else's.

That can't be Raeyu's . . . It couldn't be . . .

Seemingly satisfied that it was his image displayed before billions across the realms, Seraeyu swung his wingspan wide, revealing the gruesomely detached arm like a trophy, presenting it for all to see. Smug in a way that was entirely at odds with Aeyun's memory, an expression more cruel than narcissistic, Seraeyu determinedly ignored the harried Sentinels who couldn't quite seem to reach him, still repelled by some unseen barrier.

"Pay attention," Seraeyu rasped, his voice reverberating around the holocaster. The hushed air in the city became thick with apprehension as the Eye unblinkingly followed the command. "You *pathetic* vermin," Seraeyu accused, the words streaked with something dark, tainted. Enunciated with penetrating clarity.

In Seraeyu's grasp, that limp, tattooed arm, jaggedly detached at its bicep, distracted Aeyun from the man's fervent demand.

"Hear me when I tell you now: there will be a reckoning."

Seraeyu stared intently at the Eye, his hardened gaze extending to countless crowds of realmers beyond. He then lifted his hand that held the severed, ink-marked limb. Its wrist flopped unnaturally, light catching upon the hug of metal adornments snaked around deadened claw-nailed fingers. Fracturing like a barricade broken, Seraeyu's expression twisted into menacing determination.

When he shouted out, backed by anguish and anger and

something so visceral it stung deeply, it was as if he were calling down the sky itself. Electricity, buzzing and violent, began to course up that dismembered arm. While everyone gawked at Seraeyu, the man who was performing something unprecedented for an Untuned, a feat no one thought him capable of, Aeyun felt ill. Bile crawled viciously at the back of his tongue, choking him.

With a terrifying crash of galvanic eruption, Seraeyu's image disappeared in a flare of wild, unfettered energy. The Eye's feed was cut in an instant. In the tense reprieve that followed, chalky clouds fluttered uselessly within the holocaster, adding a sense of eerie stillness as the crowds awaited its next transmission.

Aeyun couldn't stop seeing it, even in the dead air. The familiar tattoos. The rings still wrapped around cold, claw-nailed digits.

He gazed unblinkingly when the announcer's likeness manifested once more, filling the holocaster's ore-dusted interior. The words she spoke resounded like a guillotine, slamming cleanly against its mark.

"We apologise for that upsetting scene. We are getting word now that–"

You're wrong.

"–Raeyu Thasian is reported dead. We repeat: Raeyu Thasian, heir to the Thasian Legacy is dead."

You're wrong.

"We have been informed that those on the scene are urging anyone in Haebal City near the Thasian Tower to retreat. In addition, those who could be in close contact with Seraeyu Thasian are being told to disengage immediately. We are now also confirming that Praetor Oagyu Thasian has perished. We repeat: Oagyu Thasian, patriarch to the Thasian Legacy, has died in today's attack. Other confirmed deaths in Haebal City include… "

Aeyun's eyes were drawn to his own lifeless limb. He tried to move a finger. Nothing came of it. Not really a surprise but unsettling all the same. His arm just dangled, useless. Still there when Raeyu's was not.

Acid bubbled up from his twisting stomach again and he bit back his instinct to heave.

"Hey, Aeyun," Saoiri whispered as distorted murmurs drifted up from the dampened, moss-covered streets below. "Aren't you from Raenaru? You don't happen to be from Haebal City, do you?"

Aeyun's mouth felt cottony, and his saliva tasted rotten. The light was too bright, too blinding. It flickered across his face as imagery cycled before him; Seraeyu's sneer, paused and un-paused in static-ridden recollection.

"Thasians went and got themselves in a real mess, huh?" Davah asked. More empathic, he continued, "Are you okay there, friend?"

"Do you have any contacts in Haebal, Saoiri?" Aeyun croaked. His voice felt rough and gravelly as he fought to gulp down lingering unease.

If I can reach Father, or Uruji. One of them will know. They would have been close.

Saoiri eyed him with concern. "I – well, yes. One. I have a comms stone connected to her here somewhere. Do you need to ask Sakaeri something?"

The flashing exposure from the holocaster made the revelation all the more severe. *Sakaeri, of all the stars-damned people . . .*

But he needed to rally. This wasn't the time.

"Sakaeri?" Aeyun asked. "That's – yes. Yes, now, please."

With a wary appraisal, Saoiri fetched the communication stone from her satchel. As she did, Davah silently took notice of Aeyun's too-still arm, his scrutinising contemplation settling on the attached, similarly wilted hand.

Once Saoiri parsed out which stone was the correct one, she held it out expectantly.

Aeyun's eyes flitted from her steadily more confused expression to the nondescript rock resting in her palm, but he didn't take it. Instead, he let it lay there as he reached out his functioning hand and brushed characters on the stone's surface, their etchings

14

disappearing shortly thereafter.

Aeyun grimaced at his boots as the silence stretched, ignoring the inquisitive and worried stares of his fellow marauders. He found himself relieved when, finally, the smoothed alicant rattled.

The group of them observed the stone as the symbol for *hello* appeared on its surface.

If anyone told Aeyun that one day he would be grateful to receive Sakaeri's greeting, he might have silently mocked them for their ignorance, too polite to jeer in their face. Today, however, he'd gladly put his foot in his proverbial mouth to get the answers he needed.

Taking a deep breath through his nose, Aeyun steeled himself for his next actions.

First, he emblazoned the symbol for *me* into the alicant's white-grey exterior, then he spelled his name in Haebal's dialectic script. He hoped it was enough. To Sakaeri's credit, her response was swift. She was, after all, ever vigilant in a crisis.

The symbols for *brother* and *safe* appeared. Next, the symbol for *royalty* appeared.

Raeyu Thasian was not royal, but Aeyun knew who she meant.

Gone appeared, not dead, but Aeyun already knew that. Gone meant missing, he presumed. After that, *brother* appeared again, followed shortly by *gone* once more. Finally, the symbol for *together* burned on the stone's surface before evaporating away.

As Aeyun debated this, something disquieting blanketed him while he awaited the next symbols to be seared on the rocky canvas.

Father then *dead*.

Aeyun's heart dropped.

He stared at the stone. The realm around him felt fake, gut-churningly unnatural, and static filled the gap between one moment and the next. He wasn't sure how long he watched nothing and everything, but when he blinked, the city of Pllametia's emblem – a flower that only grew in the marshy, swampy lands of the Tenebranan realm – appeared. It dissolved away a moment later, and then the ethereal glow of connection dimmed into nonexistence.

Everything was pale. Mucky and errant and pale. And *wrong*.

"We can set a course, Aeyun," Davah said quietly, a gentle assurance from behind.

Saoiri seemed hesitant to pack away the stone, but eventually did so in silence. Once it was safely tucked back into her bag, she reached to take his numbed hand. As soon as cold flesh was met, she dropped Aeyun's fingers and snapped her head up, peering through his disconnected gaze.

"Aeyun, your–!"

In his mind, Aeyun thought surely his steadfast father – the man who fiercely protected all that he loved with an impenetrable shield, the phantom sword of the Thasian dynasty, the impervious Jourae Thasian-nee – wouldn't have gone down so easily.

Surely, Sakaeri is mistaken.

Mechanically, Aeyun withdrew a small bottle from the bag looped on his belt. The beetle inside it skittered, clambering for escape. With practised, unthinking motions, he dislodged the cork and fiddled one-handedly with the flask. Blank still, he crushed the beetle in his fist, an action that had Davah humming in curiosity and Saoiri giving a startled gasp. He then took his gut-muddied hand and clasped it around where his nerves had been ripped asunder in his right arm.

"*Ca'ou o, cah e'ju, ou'uo,*" Aeyun muttered monotonously.

Something in the air shifted and glowing vestiges appeared. They wrapped around his arm like silken ribbons, sinking into place as they melded upon the skin underneath his black sleeve. Feeling, while stiff and uncomfortable, slowly started to return, and the sensation of it flooded painfully down to his fingertips.

"Was that . . . ?" Saoiri's trailing question barely reached Aeyun's ears. "Did you just *tune* with a descant?"

Aeyun looked down at his hand, but all he saw was Raeyu's ripped, gory arm in Seraeyu's shaking grasp. The blackened, seared-in tattoos there, drawn upon unfeeling flesh, haunted him;

16

he wondered if his own arm would end up looking the same.

Surely, he spiralled, *Jourae wouldn't have gone down so easily.*

Raeyu appeared in his mind's eye, crumpled to her knees on the floor, this version of her bloodied and battered and broken with her arm lying detached beside her. Beyond her, Jourae lay on the ground, unmoving and unseeing, his fingers outstretched towards something. *Someone?*

No. Surely . . .

The present crashed into him all at once and Aeyun took in his surroundings: the florescent city; the revolving coverage on the holocaster; his two companions watching him with consternation. A simmering flame ignited in his chest. A festering disturbance seeded long ago, burgeoning with a snarl and reared teeth. Aeyun swore the realms were cackling at this new jest on his reality.

It wasn't trade or inter-realmal meddling. He should have realised when he'd woken in a cold sweat, a nightmare playing on repeat. A merciless reliving of a choice he'd made long ago. Deep down in the perforated pit of his soulsong, he knew this reckoning was centred around just one crux.

One vengeful victim.

One Seraeyu Thasian.

His knee, still meaty in adolescence, sported a gash, the skin now marred with streaks of dirt, much like the stone he'd unwittingly dirtied was splotched with red. It hurt but that wasn't the problem. The problem was that he was alone, and he was limping, and he still had to make it home for supper. He couldn't be late because they'd be worried. They were always worried.

It hurt and he was slowed, and the bleeding wouldn't stop. His fingers fumbled around, looking for something, and then they latched onto the velvety petals of a wildflower that he didn't know the name of.

It was only a short pause, filled with a hesitant inhale, before he snapped the head of it from its stem.

He knew what to do, he did. He understood. He'd seen it before. All he had to do now was copy it.

CHAPTER TWO

"So," Saoiri began, uncomfortable. She wove a small alicant ore between her fingers, its facets catching light from the swinging lantern above. "You, uh, seem better now."

Aeyun watched as she indicated towards his – unbeknownst to her – marked arm.

The three co-smugglers sat in the hull of their sea-skimmer, gratefully free of their respirator masks. The stabilised condition of the craft was maintained by the steady drone of the air recycler, its grate rattling unevenly from ageing components. Contented to dictate the tedious work to the ore-powered machinery, the crew let the magnavaid take them towards the Great Sea Gate on autopilot.

The Magnetic Navigation Aid, commonly known as the magnavaid, was an ingenious invention back in the day. In its earliest iterations, it revolutionised travel via land and sea. In the modern age, it was more uncommon to not have a magnavaid than it was to have one.

Starry sea forbid it broke or got tapped out on the open ocean, though. Without a water-tuned alicant, full of stored energy from crashing waves or a rushing river, and a skilled alicantist or steer-savvy sailor on board, any sea-skimmer would be as good as stranded.

Alicant were fickle, though. Sometimes they stored energy aplenty, having been plucked from ocean beds, windswept cliffs, or from the fiery depths of a volcano, bursting with a resonance that sung an elemental tune. Sometimes, instead, they were counterfeit prisms that sat as char in a once-burnt fire, or a mere pebble doused in a bucket of water.

Those iterations were of incredibly poor and fleeting performance. Perhaps offering a trickle where it should be a fountain, or a weak flame where it should be a roaring blaze.

It made Aeyun's head dizzy, the confined nature of all that energy in a conduit so small. It took him a long time to come to terms with the mechanics behind it. He knew well enough that it was a complementary tune sung between alicant and alicantist, determining both strength and power. Juxtaposed, competing frequencies. The theory of it made sense: dual waves of energy, their combination resulting in a unique presentation of paired resonance. A reverberation kindled anew. But it still didn't sit right with him.

Sometimes alicant and alicantist resonated brilliantly. Other times, not so much.

Aeyun supposed, in the end, it wasn't all that different than what he knew. But it *felt* different. To him, it felt wrong and unnatural; impinged. And it didn't help that he just couldn't seem to get it right. Aeyun was definitely in the *not so much* category, he found.

"Yep, all's fine," Aeyun responded to Saoiri.

He pulled at the blanket he'd wrapped around his shoulders. It was perhaps an unjustified precaution, his feared discovery of tell-tale inky tendrils, impressions now undoubtedly welded where glossy ribbons of white had woven. It tended to get cold in the sea-skimmer out on the open ocean anyway, he figured. Even more so at night, and the constant mess of haphazard debris they kept around the craft only did so much to insulate the cramped space.

"Uh-huh," said Saoiri. She bit her lip, a silent debate casting a shadow across her face.

"Uh-huh," Aeyun repeated right back with purpose, giving her a pointed look before he gazed up.

The obscured sky bore down, its haze visible through the sea-skimmer's clear roof panels. A choking amount of smog in the air would do that – block out most of the light like a smoky chasm. It hadn't abated for anyone that day, including Aeyun and his crewmates.

Davah sighed and said, "Give it a rest; he's obviously not going to talk." He idly picked some grime from under his nail, lips pursed and petulant. "Though, I'm sure we'd both love to hear the tale of Aeyun, the peculiar ore-hunter with a harried past." Davah sighed again, louder. "It's times like these that I'm reminded you're a bit of an enigma. You've very convenient smithing skills, though. Did I thank you for my latest bracer?"

As Davah admired the hammered metal on his wrist, Aeyun was reminded of the cold, tarnished metal twisted around colder, lifeless fingers.

"You did," Aeyun acknowledged.

He tried in vain to block out the ghastly images behind his eyelids. It only made wicked impressions of the past day's revelations weigh heavier, more incessantly, so he went back to futilely searching for a break in the haze.

20

"Well, thanks again," said Davah.

The sea-skimmer skipped on a patch of choppy water and the loose wares in the hull clattered and clinked, wobbling with the interrupted glide. In the stride of it, the hanging lantern's glow shone down unevenly, its cage becoming a waning pendulum.

Aeyun tried to take a breath in, something steady and grounding. It was sharp and stilted instead.

Across from him, Saoiri rose to her feet. "It's not that I mind, but we're going to that city of wasters without question. Could you at least give us some indication of what's going on, and what it has to do with you and Sakaeri?"

Aeyun understood her quandary. It was unfair of him to expect the two of them to come so willingly and blindly. It would be cruel of him to deny them explanation. This tale, however, was like a tarnished silver relic, hanging in the tower the Thasian called home; storied and having lost its grace.

Instead of an answer, he asked, "How do you know Sakaeri?"

"How do *you* know Sakaeri?" Saoiri was quick to counter.

Davah's tired groan floated over from the opposite side of the sea-skimmer.

"How *well* do you know Sakaeri?" Aeyun asked.

If the expression Saoiri let slip was any indication, Aeyun's intuition was right.

"Not . . . not exceptionally well," she admitted, sitting back down on her rickety chair.

"Well, I know her *too* well. Let me guess: she bought a pilfered ore from you before? Something unique and strange, probably something to make weapon-wielding easier, and she gave you that comms stone herself, telling you to stay in touch?"

Saoiri blinked owlishly. "No?"

Aeyun snorted. "Sakaeri is a Sirin. You're lucky to be alive."

"I'm sorry," Davah said, tone dipping low as he gained a sudden interest in the conversation. "This Sakaeri woman is a *Sirin*? As in, one of those mad mercenaries for hire? The ones where once you've confirmed they actually exist, you're already dead?"

Aeyun hummed in response, ignoring the cringe that crawled up his spine at the mention of death. He instead fixated on the lantern's luminous reflection and the way it flittered across the floor, watching it catch on divots scattered across steel tiles.

"Oh." Saoiri sounded small. "I thought she was nice?"

"Well, good thing, since you're about to see her again," Aeyun muttered, displeased by the notion, but aware of its necessity.

He and Sakaeri weren't on the best of terms. They never had been, not really, and he never expected to be chummy with someone so clearly bent on making his life miserable. But desperate times called for desperate measures.

"Wait a moment now." The concern in Davah's voice would have been comical if Aeyun himself wasn't filled with dread. "Wait a damn moment. We are meeting a *Sirin?*"

"She was *nice*," Saoiri said again, sounding as though she were trying to convince herself of it.

"She's not nice," Aeyun contradicted with a scowl.

She *wasn't*, and definitely not to Aeyun, anyway. There were too many years of schemes and snarls and goads to combat, all filtering through Aeyun's memory like a playback reel flashing among holocaster dust. Sakaeri was no daemon, but she'd haunted plenty of his nightmares anyway. Her and her creepy eyes and quicksilver slashes, weighted with accusations that Aeyun didn't know how to address.

"If she took to you, we should let you go in first."

Ignoring Saoiri's gawp, Aeyun's gaze went back to tracing the gloomy, wispy paths of smog beyond the panels. If he peered long enough, he wondered, would it break way to the scenery beyond? What would he find there if it did?

"What do you mean? She doesn't like you?" Saoiri asked.

Aeyun let the question sit too long before he chuckled mirthlessly. A bitter smirk slid in place, perfectly paired with his biting tone. "She hates me."

"Sorry, say again?"

"She hates me."

"You're telling me," Davah said, leaning across the table so intently that he was nearly flat upon it, "a Sirin hates you and you're here to casually tell the tale?"

Aeyun shrugged.

"Aeyun," Saoiri intoned, her humour fading alongside the day's last fog-doused sunrays. "Who *are* you?"

Aeyun smiled wryly, his focus drawn back to his newly marked arm. The one that was slowly losing feeling again as time petered on. The one that told him everything he'd sacrificed for, his snap-decision wager, was crumbling at the hands of another. And he hadn't even been there to witness it.

To stop it.

"Just a blow-in who's overstayed his welcome."

"What the fuck kind of answer is that?" Davah huffed. "Honestly, that sounded so fecking dramatic. What are you – a rugged smuggler who's off to his next raid?" He let the idea linger, a grin ebbing across his freckled face. "Oh, wait."

"Yun of the stars, Davah. Read the room," Saoiri whined.

Aeyun shook his head, dropping his chin to hide begrudging amusement while Davah gleefully started professing a poorly sung tune. Some halfway intelligible story about a man braving a life of profiteering across sapphire seas.

A nice feeling spread in the cavity of his chest. Something light and welcome amid the dour vestiges of recent developments.

Saoiri, however, was quick to start chucking whatever she laid hands on across the hull. A fruitless attempt, Aeyun would wager, to save herself from verse three. Still, it didn't stop the laughter that blossomed to life. A small and precious moment, passing just as those that came before.

One of the greatest things about sea-skimmers was their speed. Tiny as they were, they could skip across wide expanses in next to no time.

By the break of dawn, while the sun was cresting through Orin's never-ending haze, their ship was fast approaching the Great Sea Gate, the same design as every other realm. It was a large, circular structure, half-hidden below the ocean's surface, carved by ancient hands and embedded with even more archaic alicant, flanked with runic symbols. Over the centuries, no one had dared impress their own investigations on the megalithic wonders, fearful that should they attempt to study them and make a mistake, the structures would become unstable.

No one wanted to be responsible for the isolation of a realm, breaking its only connection to those beyond the in-between. The Great Sea Gates that linked them all were one of the wildest wonders of their time.

As their craft approached, the gatekeeper's ore-lit station glowed red, indicating that their sea-skimmer was called for inspection.

Aeyun frowned. Who was on duty?

Davah, talented navigator that he was, took manual control of the steering, and when they'd saddled up to the station, the first thing they heard was, "Oi, Doons!"

The gatekeeper who called out gave the group of them a wrinkled grin under his respirator mask, a perhaps unnecessary precaution behind the station's reinforced glass. Regardless of his judicious gear, Perrin greeted them like old friends, and it had Aeyun's eyes rolling. The man was hardly an acquaintance, and certainly not a confidant. In fact, Aeyun didn't really like his deluded brand of genial chauvinism.

"Hey, Perry, how are ya?" Davah called back, using the receiver on the sea-skimmer's console. "Lovely, hazy start to the day, huh?"

Perrin laughed. "Ah, ain't it always, kid? Where yous headed?"

"Tenebrana. Got a tip there's a good supplier there for our antiques," Davah offered, keeping their cover story as antique dealers going strong.

It was ludicrous, and Aeyun often wondered just how long it would take for someone with more than rocks in their head to catch on. Maybe no one cared enough to call them out.

"That shithole of a realm? Jeez, kid." Perrin tutted and Aeyun felt his lip curl without his consent. "Ah, well. Good for yous Doons, making the best of it and getting out there – entrepreneurs, even, I told my missus!"

Aeyun still didn't understand how Davah and Saoiri dealt with condescension as often as they got it. Many people held unfounded prejudice against the Mhedoonian populace, thinking of them as lesser and weak. It didn't help that realms of greater influence – like Raenaru or Orin – did little to quell the false narrative, their history books boasting how reformed Mhedoon was after their, as quoted, 'valuable influence'.

The raids lived on in most Mhedoonian minds, and the oldest of those alive could likely recall their wretched end by memory. It was still a sore subject for many; if spoken about in the wrong locale, it might just result in a few broken noses.

While Aeyun held no particular loyalty to Mhedoon, he didn't appreciate some realmers' opinions. Worse still were those who treated an entire people like vermin. He'd proven his stance on that and simultaneously gained Davah's respect when he'd cracked a particularly vulgar-mouthed jaw the better part of a year ago.

"We're doing the best we can with the hand the realms dealt us, Perry," Davah said with a bright, freckle-skirted smile.

"Indeed, yous are! Good on you, getting out there and not just sittin' around." Perrin guffawed and Aeyun barely managed to muffle a groan of annoyance.

After a few more pleasantries, Perrin gave them the go-ahead and they drifted into the belly of the Great Sea Gate terminal. As the wake brought them closer, Perrin set off the resonance for the realm of Tenebrana. The massive rings that lined the terminal reverberated with a phantom chant, sounding their response to the invisible soundwaves that bounced around the gate, activating its connection to its paired sister in the intended destination. The water around them began to float in little spheres, twisting and gliding across the sea-skimmer's glassy panels as it rose.

The gate itself filled out with a foggy glow, something enchanting that always made Aeyun's hair stand on edge. He was fascinated, like every other time, because he could see the through lines. How the resonance manifested and slithered around the gate. How the runic stone's ore flickered in sequence, speaking to its brethren in a forgotten tongue. How the energy in the area soared, and how, behind it, there was the smoky mirror of nothingness beyond. The feeling that the void was just a hair's breadth away from claiming those who passed under the barrier, consuming their soulsong and everything it was made of.

During the transition from one gate to the next, Davah and Saoiri described it like a blink. A loud, overwhelming pressure, then a flash of light, then the arrival at their destination. For Aeyun, though, all the details sparked to life in those liminal moments. He could see the in-between. The utter unknown of what existed before their arrival yet after their departure. Every time, he witnessed the same thing: the glistening, colourless thread that flowed from his chest, and the hint of somewhere else.

Just as quickly as it rushed towards him, the impression of it fell away. With a gulp of air, as if he were returning to the realm anew, Aeyun found himself back with Saoiri and Davah in the sea-skimmer. Surrounding them was Tenebrana's murky, foul-scented terminal.

"Welcome to Tenebrana," a bored voice announced when they reached the gatekeeper's station. "Please mind the marshland and avoid the acid-swamps. We recommend the Labyrinthian City Jjankatot's delight, the bushberry bbluloba, as it's currently in season. Enjoy your time in Tenebrana."

The on-duty gatekeeper didn't even bother to look up, instead waving the sea-skimmer on so they could get back to whatever it was they were paying more attention to.

After a brief, wordless exchange between the crew of three,

26

Davah moved to manually steer the sea-skimmer out of the terminal. Pulling up the holomap of Tenebrana through the magnavaid, he instructed their craft to head towards Pllametia, capital city and supposed cornerstone to all of boggy Tenebrana. Somehow, Aeyun doubted that the realm's beating heart resided in the crime-ridden warehouses sprawling along its too-affordable ports.

While pollution and vapours had filled their vision on Orin, a dank humidity permeated the atmosphere across Tenebrana. Wading through it, a film of condensation formed on the sea-skimmer's panels. Inside its hull, Davah, Saoiri, and Aeyun sat in a poor impression of comfortable silence.

He didn't like going there.

It was cruel and dilapidated, just like how he imagined the hearts of the people that milled among its well-worn paths. He didn't like it there, and he didn't think he ever would.

A smaller hand reached out to his, threading trembling fingers through his knobby knuckles. It was a gentle reminder that this wasn't about him. It was about them. *He didn't have time to be disgusted or affronted. All he had was an obligation. Shield from what may come.*

So that's what he would do.

CHAPTER THREE

"You could have just paid the dock fare," Saoiri scolded Davah.

"And let them rob us blind? Nah. No. I trust Kjar," Davah reasoned. When he threw a snide grin over his shoulder, Kjar provided a stiff wave, awkwardness only amplified by a tight smile.

Kjar had been in a bad spot on Lu-Ghan, having unwittingly stolen from undermarket crime lord Pitmaster Kaisa, self-proclaimed king of combat for sport. Aeyun had offered his smithing skills in exchange for Kjar's freedom – as Kjar had a particular ore the group had been looking for – and Kaisa, out of curiosity, agreed. It resulted in Aeyun and crew getting what they wanted, Kjar gaining his life back, and Kaisa enjoying a few new overpowered toys to auction off at his arenas.

The only problem was that now Kaisa held an insatiable

fascination with Aeyun, and he looked at him like he *knew* something. Oddly poised for the head of a syndicate, Kaisa stayed infuriatingly quiet about it, though. Even when Aeyun snapped at him and his smarmy leer.

"Kjar will watch over it with care, I'm sure. Lest he be returned to the next convenient Kaisan we see," Davah said, much too loudly. A squeaked protest resounded from where they'd entrusted their sea-skimmer to Kjar in the abandoned, dilapidated delivery bay. Davah looked connivingly satisfied with himself.

"If I were a spite-ridden assassin, where would I hide?" Aeyun grumbled, ignoring their mooring woes in favour of scouring the city of Pllametia.

They had arrived at the northern boundary, a part of the city known for its more underhanded citizens and blind-eyed Sentinel patrols. It was always easier to move around when no one wanted to be noticed and everyone had something to hide. Eyes often made themselves scarce in the locale as well, knowing that they weren't welcomed in the back alleys. Their small crew's reason for docking there was in line with Aeyun's hunch that Sakaeri wasn't looking to cause a scene, and she probably would have opted for a seedier part of town.

"Will I spark up the comms stone?" Saoiri asked idly, skipping over an acid-eroded gap in the planks.

Aeyun debated the merits of doing so. Something in the back of his mind, a pestering and persistent notion, tugged at him.

"No," he said, cautious. "I don't think we'll need that."

Without further explanation, he pushed on. Davah and Saoiri trekked after him, exchanging a dubious look.

"I don't see your logic, friend," said Davah.

As they passed a few barrel fires and muscles-for-hire, Aeyun felt a deep unease seep throughout his insides. "Ah, well."

He provided nothing more as his eyes darted around their grey surroundings, derelict walls and passages mottled with decay and despair that couldn't quite be washed away by the sulking rainclouds above. The lingering stench of fruit rot permeated from whatever wretched surface it clung to, and it worsened his building nausea, thin salivation threatening impending vomit.

He led them away from the forgotten northern port and the murky waters that lapped its quay. Getting into the centre of the northern boundary, they found themselves in dense, run-down cobbled streets that were peppered with eclectic shop signs and a few too many curtained pub windows. Echoes of muttered conversations, some more escalated than others, bounced unevenly from shrouded corridors. Aeyun studied the cobweb of pathways. Down a particularly dreary alley, sharp glares from a pair of whispering figures counselled that he should avoid that route. Instead, he followed his initial unease to its source, chasing after it when his adrenaline begged him to turn heel and run in the opposite direction.

He knew, after all, that he was headed towards the maw of a bloodthirsty beast.

"Not sure where you're leading us, friend." Davah sounded flighty this time.

Maybe he felt it, too.

The alleys became narrower. Their crew sidestepped a bend where a crash resounded and flames burned brightly, viperous curses slung alongside the blaze. Not too long after, Aeyun found himself standing before a veiled doorway. Ominous when it should have been innocuous, it looked as though it led into the depths of the Great Starry Sea itself, but he pushed the material aside and entered, undeterred. He was greeted by a waft of musky air and an empty stim-caf – or stimulant café, for those less familiar with the establishments – the place to go for some fast energy in the form of a drink.

It was full of tables and booths, but no patrons.

The stimulist looked up from her boiler rack, her presentation greasy and sweat-stained from the heat pluming off the stim-set. She blinked at the three of them, grimaced, then indicated towards the poorly scrawled menu above her head.

"Tea," Davah said with a hesitant smile, then elbowed Saoiri.

"Oh. Tea, too," she said, toothily tacking on *please* as a muted afterthought.

The stimulist looked to Aeyun then. He just shook his head and roved his eyes over the room.

"Do the birds sing these days?" Aeyun asked.

Wary, he drew his gaze back to the woman behind the counter. She paused for a moment, watched him, then huffed.

"Chirping away today," she groused.

Aeyun nodded and made to sit at a table in the corner, one half-shadowed in the low light.

"I don't want trouble," the stimulist added.

"You won't get any," Aeyun assured her as he walked by.

Saoiri gave her thanks when the stimulist dropped down the tea – regular old thorn-thistle tea – and the woman grunted an acknowledgement before dropping Davah's on the table and taking her leave.

"So, the whole birds singing thing," Davah whispered, swirling his mug, sloshing the liquid inside. "Is that – I mean, it's obvious now that I think about it, but that's for *them*, right?"

"Mm."

"You're not . . . weren't one, right?" Saoiri asked, sounding as though she were swallowing poison.

"Hah, no." Aeyun drummed his fingers on the table. He had certainly never claimed to be a Sirin. "Definitely not."

"Oh," said Saoiri. "Right."

"Cool. Very good." Davah took an experimental sip of his tea, decided it was too hot, then put it down on the table again. "So, how'd you know to go here?"

"She's been watching us," said Aeyun. He stared at the darkest corner of the stim-caf. "Has been from the start. I just followed that awful feeling. It led here." He spotted glowing, slit-pupilled, cat-like eyes, creasing open in a menacing glare. "Hi, Sakaeri."

"I'd have thought you'd be more grateful to see me," Sakaeri crooned as she slipped out from the shaded crevice.

Her body was hidden under a hooded cloak, its make suited

31

for all sorts of hazards. Aeyun knew for sure that there were countless weapons wrapped around her physique beneath it, each one perfect for a different type of attack. A different type of retribution.

"For what it's worth," she said as she moved deftly across the threshold, noiseless. The stimulist didn't look up from her station. "I am sorry."

Aeyun couldn't stop his choking gulp, the one that held one last ounce of hope in it. He dared to ask, "Did you see it happen?"

Sakaeri was silent, the look in her eyes holding something significant. Wordlessly, she nodded once.

Aeyun sucked in a breath. "Was it quick?"

"Yes," she said, and he felt the lie burrow into him like a parasite.

"Okay," was all he could think to say in response.

"Hello!" Davah interjected awkwardly with a little wave. "Delighted, Miss Siri – ah!" He hesitated at the narrowed look she threw his way. "Sorry! Sorry."

Sakaeri furled her lip and tutted, instead focusing her attention on Saoiri.

"I hope you're well," said Sakaeri. Saoiri nodded but didn't look up from her tea, gripped tightly in both her hands. "Don't worry, I'm not out to do you harm." As the admission was laid bare, she turned back to Aeyun. "Quite the opposite, in fact."

The tension between them turned palpable, the air in the stim-caf becoming bloated and uncomfortable. Davah leant back in the revelation of it, glancing back and forth between the two reunited Raenaruans.

"It was your brother's wish." Sakaeri's words were nearly inaudible, carried on a murmur.

"As admirable as you make that sound, I know that's not it."

It was apparently the wrong thing for Aeyun to say, because Sakaeri's hackles rose. She sneered down at him, hissing, "Don't speak of things you don't know!"

"I know well enough!" Aeyun retorted with just as much

fervour, quick to combat.

Another short-lived staring match was abruptly ended when the stimulist rattled a few glasses louder than necessary.

"Do you know where they are? Do you think they're still together?" Aeyun asked.

The taut atmosphere slackened, if only slightly. But their postures still screamed in protest, Aeyun pushed back against his seat and Sakaeri staring him down with folded arms.

"Are you as lost as I am?" Davah whispered to Saoiri, who nodded back before mouthing *brother* as a question.

"I don't. It was . . ." Sakaeri trailed, seemingly unsure of how to go on. Her gaze fell to Aeyun's right hand. "I do think they're together, though."

Aeyun rested his opposite hand over it, covering what he could from her scrutiny. Voice as tight as his grip, he asked, "Why?"

It was a simple question, yet the possibilities were tormenting, twisting his mind into a silent frenzy.

Sakaeri leant down then. "I've only seen that type of energy in one place, and that's at the gates. And he, um, *talked*."

Aeyun couldn't find it within himself to be shocked. "I knew he was too eager." He tipped back in his seat again and groaned. "Dammit."

"If he wasn't, you'd all be dead," Sakaeri reasoned, pulling away.

"No one talks about these things – no one," Davah said, halfway between a whisper and a whine. "Why is it the second time we've been slapped in the face with fecking descanting in the last two days, when literally no one has mentioned it for I don't even know how long otherwise?"

Sakaeri took the bait. "Oh, what do you know?" A cracked sort of smile split her expression. She looked to Aeyun. "Will I dispose of them?"

"What – Sakaeri!" Saoiri protested, looking up at the Sirin for the first time since she'd approached them.

"Please don't joke about that," Aeyun said, frowning. "First, it's not funny – neither of you are in danger. Second, I don't want to poke fun at death right now."

He really didn't. The intimate realisation of mortality was still too close, and his father's tragic demise too recent. Sakaeri appeared to notice her mistake and receded, holding a hand up in the air. It was then that Davah saw her claw-like nails and he drew back in an awkward-laughed retreat.

"Ah, you didn't notice?" Sakaeri smirked, but it lacked any true mirth.

"Notice what?" Davah's pitch was too high.

Sakaeri made a show of curling her fingers as if poised to attack, mock ripping across her features as she did. Davah, for his part, was not amused and looked rather disturbed by the act, his teeth baring in an ugly grimace.

"*Please* don't," Davah breathed out in a rush. Sakaeri chuckled.

"Sakaeri." Aeyun brought her attention back. "I don't want you sticking around. Let's stock up and head out to the sea-skimmer. We'll give you a lift to wherever you're off to next."

"We will?" Davah asked, still winded.

"Maybe you can tell me why you're thieving with two ore-smugglers while we're there," Sakaeri said, but it sounded more like a threat than a question. If her brazenness offended either of Aeyun's companions, they smartly held their tongues. "A tale for blessed ears, even."

Aeyun stood up, ignoring her.

"I hope it was worth it, leaving like that," Sakaeri added, earning herself a livid glare.

Aeyun paid the stimulist as he made his way to the exit. When his foot breached the threshold, he heard Saoiri say, "I've never seen that kind of look on him before."

"Really?" Sakaeri asked. "You must not know him as well as you think you do."

None of it made sense, all a jumbled mess of jargon in his head. He didn't think he deserved the grounding hand that rested on his shoulder. Not after . . . not after everything.

Teary as his stony façade crumbled with each step, he focused on the days-old mud caked on the toes of his boots. Stinging eyes only flittered upwards when he'd stepped too close to something or someone. He was told not to speak, not there. Not on the way.

It wasn't until he was in a room that was hot – far too hot with its massive fire, light reflecting on metal clinging to walls and racks – that he dared to tip his chin. They weren't alone, and he stared unabashed at the daemon who sneered before him, flanked by that too-hot blaze, mouth curled in disapproval.

Behind him, the damning words resounded: "My son needs a home."

CHAPTER FOUR

"Oh," Davah said once they'd closed the hatch to the sea-skimmer.

They'd re-commandeered the craft from Kjar. He was overly gracious and offered them a heap of free wares, which they denied. Davah's startled utter, however, was in response to Sakaeri's hood being flipped back, revealing shaved-down, blunted horns, very unlike those presented on Seraeyu's head the other day.

Sakaeri's gaze drifted over to Davah. "I never much liked that part of my heritage."

Saoiri went about tidying the cramped space, pulling out a

blanket to offer Sakaeri – it was turned down – and dumping nuggets of alicant into bags before she pushed them to the sea-skimmer's corners. As she did this, Aeyun felt his anxiety spiking, winding like an electric current, poised to spark with the right provocation.

He did everything he could to *not* look at the one hidden latch that he didn't want Sakaeri digging into.

"Ore-smuggler, huh?" Sakaeri prodded, unimpressed.

Aeyun cut to the chase instead. "What happened?"

Leant against the sea-skimmer's wall, he stubbornly crossed his arms. To his left, Davah fired up the magnavaid to lead them to the open, oily ocean. Away from prying eyes and ears.

Sakaeri had taken Aeyun's usual chair and observed him for a moment. "Let's wait till we're further out, hm?"

Begrudgingly, Aeyun agreed.

It had already been evening when they'd first arrived in Tenebrana – the woes of travelling between Great Sea Gates meant you might miss a whole day's cycle, just like they had – so now they were dipping into night-time hours as they drifted away from the northern reach, back into the liquid chasm that weaved throughout the realm. The water had become rough in response to a sudden acid-rain drizzle, but the reinforced exterior of their sea-skimmer had the craft counterbalanced, presumably shielded from the onslaught, assuming Davah was keeping up with maintenance.

They were huddled in tense quiet as the sea-skimmer progressed, the worst of it breaking when Saoiri finally spoke. "So, how'd that ore work out for you?"

Sakaeri perked up, taken out of whatever reverie she'd lost herself to.

"Ah, it's great! I'd been looking for something to attune to that would help me retrieve my weapons – I've sewn it here, see?"

Sakaeri opened her palm, the one she hadn't lifted in the stim-caf; a flat, metallic-looking alicant was attached to the fingerless glove there. Without warning, she fished out a dirk from under her cloak, chucked it at a bag, then called it back with her outstretched hand. As the throwing knife zipped towards her in its return trajectory, it stopped mere millimetres before making contact, at which point she swiped it from the air with a grin.

"See? It's so convenient," said Sakaeri.

The assaulted bag sagged while bits of ore trickled to the sea-skimmer floor, their steady clatter bouncing off the walls.

"Oh, good!" Saoiri's sentiment sounded forced. She moved to collect the pooling pile of alicant with a nervous chuckle.

"I know you're, like, fierce deadly and all," Davah commented from beside the magnavaid, his watchful eyes set upon Saoiri's cleaning efforts. "But could you not tear our place apart? This is basically our home."

"Right, apologies," Sakaeri said, flat and decidedly unapologetic.

"This far enough for you?" Aeyun cut in, his impatience manifesting with the incessant tapping of his foot.

Sakaeri turned to him. "We will chat. We will. But I want to know some things, too."

Any pretence of banter evaporated and Aeyun scowled. Before he responded, there was a brief reprieve where he braced himself on the wall, the sea-skimmer skipping across a particularly choppy patch of water. Along with it came the familiar rattle of items settling and the waning reflection of light swinging against shadows cast over metal walls.

"How about we talk about Haebal, and how my father died first."

Sakaeri watched him with interest, taking note of what *wasn't* said.

"I was hoping we didn't have to dance, but that was naïve of me," she said. Her soured grit delivered what her mouth didn't. Navigating the intricacies of his dishonest life was surely nothing she wanted part of. "Okay, let's start there."

"Great," Aeyun ground out.

"You saw the broadcast, I presume?" Sakaeri's question

received a nod. She glanced between the other two sea-skimmer inhabitants and sighed. "Right." She took a steadying breath. "It was midday, and I was just leaving a meeting in the Tower. Seraeyu was coming down the hall, headed to his father's office. I – well, at the time, I didn't think much of it. I noticed that he looked kind of constipated, but what's new.

"I had somewhere else to be, so I was on my way out, but my instinct kept urging me to go back inside, to see what he was up to. I've been doing what I do too long to move against that, so I turned heel and went back. When I got to Oagyu's office, he was–" Sakaeri grimaced. "Aeyun, he was torn apart. You know what I do, but I do it with efficiency and purpose, to close a contract. This was–"

"Killing is killing," Aeyun said, but Sakaeri shook her head.

"This wasn't killing; it was maiming – punishment. Something personal," she said. "It was truly just . . ."

Aeyun could swear colour drained from her face, but that didn't seem right coming from a woman who couldn't count her own death toll upon her fingers and toes.

"You're capable of it."

His statement was met with a tight expression.

"If I hadn't been so shocked," she continued, "I would have noticed the pyre alicant he'd left in the office. There must have been more in the Tower, considering the way it crumbled where it did."

"Right. His tuning," Aeyun muttered, going to clench his fist before realising that it was nearly numb again. Did he have any more bugs on hand? Even a plant?

"You're telling us that an Untuned – well, *tuned* and blew multiple holes through a building that big?" Davah asked, then scoffed. "No way."

"Yeah, I don't get that part, either," Sakaeri said to him before switching her attention back to Aeyun, something left unquestioned. "It's unheard of, an Untuned suddenly able to tune." Aeyun just stared back at her. "Figuring that wasn't the end of it, I tried to trace him. I'd gone up on my way back, so he mustn't have gone down, I reasoned. So, I went up to–"

"To the training pen," Aeyun finished for her. He pushed himself off the wall, interest piquing. "Where all three of them would be, damn!"

"Yeah. So, when I got to the roof, Seraeyu was there. He'd obviously had some things to say before I arrived, but he was in the middle of shouting something about Rae getting what was coming to her. After seeing what he'd done to Oagyu, I didn't even think. I just lunged at him." Sakaeri sneered and it was marred with shame. "It was Rae whose gale blasted me away, her tune carrying me like I was nothing. And then, in that small, *stupid* moment of distraction, Seraeyu went for *him*. Your father. I think Seraeyu tuned then because he moved like how Rae does. There one second and then the next somewhere else. He–" she cut herself off, teeth gritting and jaw clenching.

"What did Seraeyu do to him?" Aeyun wouldn't drop it. He *would not* drop it.

"He . . . was aiming for his heart. Right through his chest, with his bare hand." Sakaeri hung her head. "I'm sorry, I'm so sorry." Aeyun wasn't sure if it was to him or Jourae. "I couldn't watch him suffer, so I . . ."

A horrifying moment of understanding passed. Aeyun remained silent.

Sakaeri continued, albeit strained, "When I was with your father, your brother went for Seraeyu in retaliation. I don't really know what happened, but this weird barrier formed around Seraeyu, and your brother just bounced off him and was thrown back.

"Rae was crying, and she begged Seraeyu to stand down. She looked like she was going to tune, but she hesitated, and it was enough. *Yun of the stars*, it was enough time for Seraeyu to dive forward and tear Rae's arm off. Your brother rushed to Raeyu and tried to stop the bleeding. The look in Rae's eyes was so betrayed. Your brother turned to me, and I swear he must have

39

tuned with something because I can damn near promise that he was shouting in my head to find you." Sakaeri paused, taking in the atmosphere. Then she said, "So, when did you teach him how to attune to it? Last I checked, only you can do that."

"He's obviously much more talented at it than I am if he can open a gate out of nothing – some sort of rift in the realm. Is that what he did?"

Aeyun ignored the stunned looks he was getting from his crewmates. They had, to their credit, remained courteously silent during the exchange.

"Seems like it, and that didn't answer my question," said Sakaeri.

Aeyun didn't respond.

"Fine, then. I think we can assume they didn't die on the way to wherever they went."

"Did you leave him up there?"

"Your father? I didn't – I mean, when your brother opened that *rift*, it was like gravity ceased to exist. Seraeyu took that chance to activate those pyre alicant and I had to reverse this ore's tune to pull me to the next building over." Sakaeri glanced at Saoiri. "Yeah, actually, this saved my life, so thanks."

Saoiri gave a tight smile and a nod, unable to tear her gaze from where she'd pinned it to the floor.

"I dislocated my shoulder, but I could make it back down after that. I had enough time to see Seraeyu pull his stunt with the Eye. Poor sod was electrocuted to a crisp. I thought only Raeyu could harness that type of unfiltered energy with her bloodsong?" The question wasn't so much aimed at anyone in particular as it was put out to the realms. "Then I had to hightail it out because I knew Seraeyu would be after me. I'll be honest, I'm not sure if it was his intention to have made it look like foreign terrorism, but it's mighty convenient for him that he can play the role of the risen martyr now if he wants to." The explanation was punctuated with a sigh. "And then I was contacted by none other than the prodigal son, Aeyun."

"And now we're here," he finished for her.

"And now we're here," she echoed. "Does Seraeyu know?"

Guessing at what Sakaeri was getting at, Aeyun answered with a definitive, "No."

"Aeyun," Saoiri spoke up, gentle in her tone. "I'm so sorry."

"Me too, friend. I'm really sorry all that happened." Davah gnawed at his bottom lip. In his current mood, it grated at Aeyun even more than it usually did. "But I have to ask, do we need to worry about Seraeyu Thasian coming for us? I mean, this once-thought Untuned political puppet now seems like a good and honest threat to, like, everyone out there, and maybe with a vendetta towards your family?" Another brief pause. "What's your surname, again?"

"I never gave it to you," said Aeyun.

He angled his gaze upwards, once again searching the celestial sea above, trying to find this realm's moons. There were two floating above Tenebrana, one larger than the other. He always wondered what that might mean. Then again, Mhedoon had three.

"He's one of mine," Sakaeri piped up, and it caused all heads to turn her way. Aeyun's eyes widened in disbelief, because there was no way she would go so far *now* to claim – "He's one of mine. Isn't that right, my darling little brother?"

"Sorry, what?" Davah asked.

"You're related?" Saoiri revelled in the news.

Aeyun understood their disbelief. After all, he and Sakaeri looked nothing alike, and Aeyun had no indication of Yu-ta heritage – that ancestral mutation the Yu-ta shared. It was most obviously presented as horns and claw-like nails, just like those that the Thasian and Thasian-nee lines boasted. The telling traits did, however, occasionally pop up elsewhere due to mixing of blood. Some still say it was the Thasian line that descended from the all-powerful Yun, the fabled beings of legend, but most didn't believe that anymore.

Aeyun certainly didn't.

41

"Sort of," said Sakaeri.

"I don't accept that. We are not family." Aeyun's protest was met with Sakaeri's serpentine smile. It unnerved him more than he was willing to admit. "Don't forget that you tried to *kill me* on multiple occasions."

"I'm well past that now," Sakaeri reasoned. Aeyun didn't believe in that sentiment. Not for a second. "He's Aeyun born Krunan. Apparent brother to Sakaeri born Krunan."

"Sakaeri," Aeyun warned, but she didn't take heed.

Instead, she stood up and looked at him. Really looked at him. He felt it scratch at something in the depths of his mind. A burden that he'd buried, crushed down under regret and guilt and a sense of duty long abandoned. A reflection he wanted to shatter into a million pieces.

"Brother to Sakaeri born Krunan," she repeated.

Aeyun stared at her, but he saw someone much younger in her stead. "You don't want to be a part of my family, Sakaeri. And I don't want the responsibility of you being in mine."

"Was he your father, too?" Saoiri asked, oddly meek and unsure. Too unlike the hard-headed and brash youth Aeyun had learnt her to be.

Sakaeri's expression became a strange contort of pain. It was rare for something so honest to crack through her carefully constructed walls, and it had been many years since Aeyun was witness to it. His double vision widened, and he desperately wanted to run. Run and hide and pretend the ghostly reflections didn't exist.

It was like the sea-skimmer warped through countless seconds, waiting in time with Sakaeri's unblinking stare.

"Yes. He was."

"I'm so sorry for your loss, Sakaeri."

Saoiri put her hand on Sakaeri's shoulder and gave a gentle squeeze. It had obviously been meant as a comforting gesture, but Sakaeri looked on with restraint, a frown tugging at the corners of her mouth.

For a breath, it seemed like Sakaeri would answer. But the moment passed, taking with it that raw insight that so seldom showed on her face. Instead, she simply stepped out of Saoiri's reach with a silent nod.

They made a habit of ignoring one another on these trips. It gave them both peace of mind, and it meant that he didn't have a babysitter watching his every movement, no matter how inconsequential. Not that it was fair to call a peer a babysitter, yet the implication had been clear when he'd been assigned the other's dutiful protection.

He couldn't remember the last time he'd been addressed directly. It was always carried to him through someone else, even if he was physically in the same space. What did it matter, right?

If he was the disappointment – the failure *– he might as well be a damned good rot among roses.*

CHAPTER FIVE

Seraeyu awoke staring at a velvet canopy.

A distressing, jarring discomfort sank to the back of his skull as his bleary vision tried to focus. He attempted to recount his waking hours. As his foggy mind wandered, a stabbing pain zipped from one temple to the other and he winced, pressing a palm on the tender spot, attempting to dull the ache. Eyes closed and brow knit, he groaned and his whole body screamed in protest, telling him to sleep more.

To sleep *forever.*

With a grunt, he hoisted himself upright, his fingers dragging on silken sheets. The feeling of wrongness persisted, and he dared to peek an eye open, despite the angry thrum behind it.

This was not his room. Why was he in his father's room?

Not only that, but the place was a wreck, drawers turned out and ransacked, and decorative trinkets tossed around the place, some of which had broken on impact with a wall or furniture. Oagyu's room was ostentatiously lavish, influenced by his tendency to luxuriate in his own wealth. Seraeyu was sure that he would have personally seen to the arrest of anyone who disrespected his prized space, so the mess . . . didn't make sense.

What also didn't make sense was that Seraeyu was there, in Oagyu's room, where he was rarely ever allowed. He ebbed his other eye open, just to make sure he wasn't seeing things.

No, it was definitely his father's room. The portrait of the patriarch above the dresser confirmed that, as did the presence of his mother's jewellery box, left open and empty.

Seraeyu wasn't a stranger to drink, and he'd certainly indulged too much in an evening of debauchery before, only to awaken with fragmented memories and a pounding head. No amount of drink, however, could have resulted in him wrangling his father's room from him, he reasoned, as Oagyu would have locked him in the wine cellar himself, telling him to drink his fill – that they'd be better off if he drowned in alcohol anyway.

Never in three lifetimes over would Oagyu have allowed Seraeyu to wreak this much havoc without retribution. No, something was awry. What had Seraeyu last been doing?

Seraeyu moved the heel of his hand from his temple, but the flash of something on his skin gave him pause. Slowly, he lowered his arm, breath hitching as he spotted aged blood clinging to his flesh, caked between his nails and his fingertips.

"What . . . ?" he asked aloud, throat raw and scratchy.

Instinctively, he reached up his other hand to paw at his neck, but he saw the same gruesome sight upon it. Heart thumping, he slid his legs from the covers, throwing them over the edge of the mattress.

As he stood on weak knees – why did they wobble so much? – Seraeyu tried to catch his breath. With a trembling reach, he steadied himself by grasping onto a bedpost and he let his eyes rove over the room again, mind soberingly cognisant.

This wasn't drink. Something *happened*. Something awful.

He made his way across the room, carefully trying to avoid the strewn debris, and entered the glamourous en suite. The marble floors were cold on his feet, but he welcomed the feeling as it assured him that he wasn't dreaming. Whatever this nightmare was, it was *real*. Using the counter as a crutch, Seraeyu looked up and found himself staring back, amber-brown eyes as panicked as his pulse felt.

His clothes were dishevelled and his hair a mess around his horns; had he been pulling at it in distress? On top of that, his cheek had a dried cut, and there was a bruise blossoming around his neck, as if someone had tried to choke him. The purpling skin stood in gross contrast to the chain skating across it, weighted down by the ring his mother had made for him as a child. It had been adoringly etched with the ancient, curl-tailed flame of *ah-ka*, the glyph carved upon its interior, its closest translation being an oracular love. Unlinked to time and space; boundless, infinite, and without condition.

Seraeyu did not feel boundless, infinite, nor unconditional. In fact, he felt rather boxed, trapped, and in dire condition.

Alarm set in viscerally. It felt like acid had plummeted into the cavern of his chest, and it drew his attention to a spark of soreness that rested on his heart. Shrugging off a sleeve of his embossed robe – why was he wearing something so regal, anyway? – he studied his skin as it was revealed, including an inky, vile mark that–

The next time Seraeyu awoke, he found himself upon the dusty slate tiles of the roof. Confused, he pushed himself up and looked around, that same ache penetrating his mind, muddling his thoughts. This time he was in slacks and a pressed top, not unlike something he'd regularly wear, but his body still buzzed in discomfort, as if he'd relentlessly hiked the tallest spires of Yunae's mountainous peaks.

The roof was half crumbled, the edge of it torn and jagged, as if some great beast had taken a bite from its corner. Standing on ankles that didn't want to support his weight, Seraeyu observed the scene. It was certainly the training pen, or what was left of it. The fence was bent and ripped apart in some places, and the racks of weapons that used to be there were knocked over, others missing entirely. He scraped his gaze across his arms and found that they were free of blood this time, but that brought him little comfort.

Something had happened at the Thasian Tower; something devastating. For some reason, Seraeyu's mind was failing him as to just what that event was. Taking a shaky, steadying breath, he tried to remember. What had he last been doing? Before the roof; before his father's room. What was it? Where had he been?

It was mid-week. *Right*, he assured himself, *it was mid-week, and Raeyu was told she'd be going to Orin the following week during our dreadful morning meal.*

Seraeyu could see it in his memory, the quiet surrounding their breakfast, his own strained pleasantries as he took a sip of his tea, forcing a smile at his sister as she said she'd go, dutifully, as she always did. Oagyu's praise upon her response.

Oagyu was called away by some Sentinels sent to fetch him for who-knows-what. When the door clicked shut behind him, Raeyu glanced up, abandoning her Raenaruan sign of thanks. She instead aimed her sad doe eyes, the golden-hued ones that she inherited from Mother, at Seraeyu. They held that same hint of weeping, harboured ever since her plaything had left. That lovesick man – *man-child*, Seraeyu thought scornfully – who had been chasing her since he'd arrived.

"I'm glad you don't have to go," said Raeyu.

She was *happy* that Seraeyu didn't have to do these types of things. Seraeyu frowned at the audacity. She was happy that Seraeyu was stuck here? That he was caged?

Raeyu was all smiles and kind words and comforting touches, but she was also earnest and righteous in the worst ways. She didn't understand how cruel the realms were. She didn't understand that her place was provided for – her purpose clear. She was the future of the Thasian Legacy. She was the bringer of prosperity, the hope of Haebal and Raenaru's continued power as well as their key to thriving.

Seraeyu, however, was their failure. Where Raeyu was Oagyu's pride, Seraeyu was his bane. He was his leeching son who provided nothing in return. A liability to their empire.

Many days, Seraeyu was surprised to be waking at all, often thinking that Oagyu would eventually have enough of him and slit his throat himself, saying he'd fallen ill to navigate the press. Seraeyu was sure that his father would be pleased to be rid of him – he'd said as much enough times that Seraeyu believed it.

He couldn't, though. It would be unsightly if word got out that *Praetor* Oagyu had cut off the weakest link in his lineage, especially when he was meant to be the provider who looked after the people, because Yun knows the Raenaruan Council actually did fuck all to propagate anything more than cyclical debate. So, the Praetor shouldered that leadership, meaning that Oagyu did. That is, until Raeyu took over both the Praetorship and the Legacy in full, when Oagyu considered her fit to do so.

Seraeyu, Untuned as he was, was useless to Oagyu. That's how his father saw it. How could one be a threat to the ravaging hounds of the realms if they couldn't protect their own skin, Oagyu told him. How could he be a pillar for the people if he needed the Thasian-nee child to be his hands for him, he asked.

Uruji Thasian-nee had been patient with Seraeyu; he'd give him that.

When it was discovered that Seraeyu was without the ability

to tune, his attempts dismal at best, Oagyu had threatened Jourae behind closed doors, forcing him into providing his own son as Seraeyu's instrument. He'd heard them, back when he was young. The shouts that emanated from behind heavy office doors. Words he didn't understand at the time, that *your other boy will die quietly if you don't comply and give up Uruji.*

It wasn't until the rumours started circulating that it began to make sense.

The housemaids often gossiped. One of the few times Seraeyu thanked the Yun for his lithe form was when he hid between pillars and behind bushes to listen in. The pathetic pup who pottered after his sister was apparently Jourae's bastard child, Seraeyu had discovered, and his presence became much less of a mystery after that.

It was infuriating, the way that Aeyun watched Raeyu as if she were the entire realm. It was with the same reverence the public gave her, adoring and delighted, but far *worse*. Almost worship.

It was after Seraeyu had divined this insight about Aeyun's heritage, just as he was entering his teenaged years, that he decided to be kinder to Uruji. The Thasian-nee child, he figured, was caged just like he was, and he felt kindred in that way. He still didn't appreciate Uruji's silent, wary gaze or his quiet acquiescence to do as he was told – it was too similar to Raeyu. So, not close by any means. But not adversaries either.

Seraeyu didn't necessarily mind, though, not being friends. And he couldn't blame the other, given Uruji was tasked with the *job* of looking after Seraeyu. No, they weren't pals or buddies or whatever. It was business, and always had been.

Seraeyu's hired companion.

His hired weapon and bodyguard.

Still, he wasn't cruel to Uruji, nor was the other to him. They just co-existed. Uruji was there when Seraeyu had any need to tune, like during any ceremonial proceedings, or when Seraeyu was required as a Thasian representative. Truthfully, Seraeyu found Uruji too dry for his taste in confidants anyway. Much too logical for his own good.

Seraeyu enjoyed his company brief, rash, and full of trouble. Perhaps another reason for his father's ire. What was he meant to do, when no matter how he chose to live, he'd be a stubborn shadow that Oagyu couldn't dispel? He figured he may as well enjoy himself, so he did, with every ilk. Seraeyu didn't discriminate. Fun, a bit reckless, and an imploring gaze? Absolutely.

Admittedly, when there was an Eye who caught him piss-drunk in the company of a less-than-reputable son of a Tenebranan diplomat, he could understand the difficulty it caused for the Legacy and their business endeavours, especially given the heavy tariffs Oagyu had only recently imposed. Likewise, he acknowledged the attention he'd garnered when he'd gone off gambling in Bhu-Nan unannounced, tarnishing the good Thasian name.

After that stint, his father had locked him up in the old cistern for a week's retribution. Still, Seraeyu didn't see the point in playing the respectable second sibling. And he'd never been very good at pretending that he gave a damn when dignitaries prattled on about nonsense, their heads well and truly up their own arses.

The banishment still stung, though. So, when Raeyu had said she was *glad* that Seraeyu didn't have to do things like she did – that she was *glad* he didn't have those duties – Seraeyu felt the very thin patience he maintained break.

He'd stood and glared down at her, anger boiling under the surface. He'd told her that he was tired of her. He was tired of her and her pitiful allegiance to the Legacy. He was tired of their father's barely veiled threats. He was tired of the vacant, scornful looks of their people.

Before he stalked out, he made sure to say that he was tired of his guard dog, and that he was glad Raeyu's own guard dog had disappeared because maybe the smallest part of her now understood how it felt to be left behind.

Seraeyu despised that he knew when he'd left, too. He could *feel* it. And he hated that he could always *feel* when he was near.

When the familiar perception that niggled the back of his mind was absent for too long, he knew he'd gone, and that it wasn't a temporary thing. The morose expressions on Raeyu and Uruji's faces only verified his suspicions. The thought made Seraeyu ill. Who was this man to evoke such a reaction? Who was this man to invade Seraeyu's senses?

That night, Seraeyu was feeling rebellious.

There were places he wasn't meant to go, he was told. One of them was whatever lay beyond the catacombs connected to the old cistern. That iron gate mocked him, along with the Sentinels who had stood guard beside it when he was chained up to a column there.

Seraeyu wondered how much coin his father gave them to keep quiet about his confinement.

When darkness blanketed the sky, he snuck on light feet through the Tower, following the passage to the basement that led to the much more ancient part of Haebal that few remembered even existed. Thanking the Yun for his fleetness of foot, Seraeyu was quick to hide from patrolling Sentinels, squeezing himself into shadowed corners and crevices.

When he finally reached the gate, the one covered in symbols he didn't understand, he slipped into an alcove and pulled a housemaid's outfit from his bag. With a swift tug, the white material was pulled over his head. He knew that there was a housemaid sent down in the next hour to deliver tea to the Sentinels here – more knowledge gained from his underground holiday – so he figured they wouldn't think much if it was delivered early. The guards posted underground tended to lose track of time anyway.

Internally recognising his gratitude for Uruji and his tutoring on tonics, only provided after plenty of pestering, Seraeyu mixed a dose of sleeping draught into the thermos of tea he planned to give the Sentinels. He was frequently plagued with sleepless nights, so it was either booze or drugs that helped him rest. Uruji eventually agreed that medicine was the less damning route.

Giving the tea a gentle swirl, he steeled himself and placed the tall housemaid hat on his head. At present, he was glad for the ostentatious design, a vestige of a time long passed, as it concealed his horns with ease. He held a small clam-style mirror up and smeared black lines across his eyelids, hoping to change the look of his gaze enough to not scream *Seraeyu*. With that final touch, he looped a half-veil across his face, covering his features from the nose down. He was perhaps a little too tall and not near enough demure, but he set his shoulders and steadied himself for his next move.

Oagyu would flay him alive if he was caught.

Seraeyu gathered his friendly poison and slid himself into the hall as if he'd just come down the narrow passage. After a few measured steps, he confronted the Sentinels who were blabbering something about the match held at the stadium in the next month.

"Oh, hey," one of them said, nudging the other.

The taller Sentinel stopped mid-rant about how his favoured team was sure to win. When he looked at the new arrival, Seraeyu kept his eyes trained down.

"Ah, is it teatime?" the tall one asked. It was followed by a chuckle. "I could really use a pick-me-up. You've made my day, miss."

His polite tone grated at Seraeyu's nerves, given it was the same man who had jested callously about a year ago. Whatever kind façade he was putting on now, it was just that. A façade.

"My favourite time of the evening. You're not the one from yesterday," the shorter one noted, his armour shifting as he made a move to grab at the thermos.

Seraeyu's heart pounded against his ribs.

"You new?"

After a moment, Seraeyu shook his head, the veil on his face fluttering with the movement. A new housemaid would never be sent down here.

"Oh. You got reassigned? Someone's sick, I guess," the same Sentinel reasoned, untroubled.

Seraeyu nodded. That sounded like a plausible excuse, and it was handed to him so easily. Why not take it?

"What's this brew? Smells different," the taller one asked.

Seraeyu felt his pulse quicken again. Sleeping draught wasn't odourless. In fact, it smelt quite earthy. Luckily, Seraeyu had figured a question might come up with it.

He took his white-gloved hand and dug in his robe's pocket, fishing out a labelled bag of tea. It was black and caffeinated, just like what they'd regularly be receiving, but it was an artisanal blend of Seraeyu's own preference.

He knew that these Sentinels wouldn't be familiar with it, since Seraeyu went out of his way to get it delivered from Tenebrana – it was the same diplomat's son who'd introduced it to him when they were fighting a hangover, actually. He only hoped that the Sentinels would be stupid enough to think it was the blend that caused the difference.

In a simultaneously relieving and concerning development, both men gushed about being offered a new tea to try, greedily filling the cups that Seraeyu offered.

Idiotic brutes, Seraeyu thought. *Our people are staking their livelihoods on your wits? We're utterly doomed.*

Seraeyu bowed in silence, leaving the Sentinels to their break. They didn't bother to acknowledge him leaving, and he felt annoyed by that, too. Housemaids weren't servants of old. They were *people* – as were servants of old, to be fair, though unfortunately they weren't seen as such. Couldn't the Sentinels have been courteous enough bid him farewell? At least they didn't hoot after him like some lechers may have. Not that it won them many points, given their unfavourable commentary when Seraeyu was prisoner to it.

Hidden around the corner, Seraeyu waited until the chatter slowed and quieted. Chancing a peek, he found both men slumped over, one of them having spilt his tea on his own lap.

I may have made it a tad too strong, Seraeyu considered.

He ripped off the veil and the hat, shoving them back in his bag, then did the same with his robe and gloves. It left him in his simple shirt and trousers instead, and he slung the sack of clothes over his shoulder, finally squaring up to stand before the gate.

Cautious, he nudged at one of the guard's boot-clad feet. Nothing.

Good, he thought.

"Now what?" Seraeyu muttered to himself, pouting.

It was doubtful that the Sentinels had a key. They weren't allowed in, either. Maybe it was a combination, or a specific type of tune? As far as he was aware, if there *was* a key, it seemed most likely to be with his own father, or perhaps Jourae.

With a sigh, he reached a now gloveless finger towards a runic marking. As his skin connected on cold metal, something in his core stirred and Seraeyu stumbled back as a spark of black popped in the negative space left behind.

He turned his palm up. "What in all the realms?"

Baffled, Seraeyu shoved his whole hand upon the twisted structure. Something in him surged to life, a miasmic presence blooming in his palm and seeping into the curves of carved symbols running across the door. It was as if air was stolen from his lungs, evaporating, then the gate creaked open, latches releasing.

Seraeyu dared to retract his hand, staring down at it in awe.

What had he done? How had he done that? What was the energy that rattled inside him? Why did it feel like –

Seraeyu shook his head. No time to dawdle. He knew *something* was back in the catacombs. Something that he wasn't meant to know about. Somewhere Raeyu had been dragged off to in her youth, returning with an inky scar across her arm.

Seraeyu wasn't *supposed* to know, but he did. Back when Raeyu used to confide in him, back when she let it slip that it was a place that Seraeyu, too, would one day go.

Except he didn't. Not after they'd discovered he was Untuned.

He stepped over one of the guard's legs and ventured in. The catacombs only got darker as he went, so he plucked a luminous ore from his pocket and held it before him, trying to keep his footing sure. Various tunnels led off the main one, but they were barred and barricaded, and seemed to have been for a long, long while. He figured that wasn't where Raeyu had gone, so instead he walked along the main strait.

The sound of water eventually met his ears and he paused. They were far from the cistern. Why would water be back this way? Seraeyu hastened his steps. Only one way to find out.

Turning a corner, he came upon a large, cavernous room. At its back wall, right in the centre, a waterfall spewed down, filling a basin below that circled the perimeter. The floor was covered in markings and shapes that made little sense to Seraeyu, and he eyed the two pillars that stood proudly beside the cascade. Each of them had a setting for an alicant, but only one carried a gem in its grasp. The lines that veered off from it twisted and formed symbols that looked both similar but different from the runic forms that adorned the gate before.

Seraeyu drew forward, his focus on the glowing alicant and the symbols connected to it. Something oppressive grew the closer he got. Inquisitive, he reached out to touch the strange gem lodged there.

"*For you,*" a voice resounded, "*I have long awaited, child.*"

The realm inverted then, and Seraeyu was enveloped in darkness.

Outside his memory, pain erupted in his chest and Seraeyu clasped a hand over his heart. Something was greatly and distressingly amiss. And Seraeyu, it seemed, had the typical rotten luck to be right in the middle of it.

Sharp eyes and a sharper tongue. That's what he had come to expect.

And always around, insufferably so. Turn the corner and there she was, cackling at some inside joke. With a piercing gaze that watched him, waiting. Impatient for the time he would slip up, say something wrong or do something incorrectly.

But he didn't know. He still wasn't sure, and her quick jabs weren't coming from even ground, so he glared at her.

Wasn't it enough that he already wasn't enough?

CHAPTER SIX

"So, ore-smuggler, huh?" Sakaeri asked again.

The tone in the sea-skimmer finally shifted towards camaraderie, but a glower tugged at Aeyun's face. Trust Sakaeri to not leave it alone. She never did, and his swirling derision was alight, ignited by mournful self-loathing.

How was it her business, anyway?

"I never agreed to talk about this."

Sakaeri ignored him. "You all have a pretty successful operation going, considering you've not been caught yet," she said, mostly to Davah and Saoiri.

Davah perked up, clearly pleased to be on a topic that he felt more at liberty to talk about. "We're some of the best in the business, thank you very much! It's only become easier since Aeyun here has come along. A year on and his skills have given us some mighty fine creations that we can use or sell."

Aeyun groaned.

"*Sell*? You've been selling your work, Aeyun?" Sakaeri's genuine surprise felt like the twist of a knife.

Davah rubbed the back of his neck, a sheepish grin covering embarrassment. "Ah, sorry, friend. Should I have not said that?"

Aeyun wasn't shocked that Sakaeri was taken aback by the news, considering how careful Aeyun had been in the past about his wares and who he gave them to. He also wasn't exactly meant to take up the smithing mantle in his father's place, so his skill in Thasian-nee workmanship wasn't common knowledge. Outside of that, outside of Raenaru, however, he wasn't as *watched*.

"It's fine," Aeyun told Davah. "Yeah, what of it?"

"Just . . . it's interesting, that's all," said Sakaeri.

She was sat back in Aeyun's favourite chair, finally having accepted the blanket that Saoiri offered. It was getting chilly in the dead of night, and Aeyun was a little jealous of her swaddled state. The night's frost was nipping at his exposed neck, and something warm to bundle around his shoulders sounded pretty nice. If that also served to barricade him from the realms' misfortunes, all the better.

"Aeyun has been really helpful, with more than just wares. He looks after us, too," said Saoiri.

A small smile graced her features as she regarded Aeyun, and Sakaeri watched the interaction intently, gaze narrowing and mouth souring. Aeyun glanced at his so-called sister and muffled a snort. She wasn't as stoic as she thought she was.

Aeyun returned Sakaeri's glower and said, "Don't try to endear yourselves or me to her. She's daemonish."

He wasn't keen on having his crewmates prove his usefulness to her – there was no need for such a fruitless endeavour – or having them get attached to her.

Sakaeri was nebulous, unpredictable. While terrifyingly devout to those she deemed worthy, that tradition was not afforded to Aeyun. It never was, and it never would be. Sakaeri had her eyes set in one direction, and that was not towards Aeyun, but beyond him. Towards more regal counterparts.

"You're just walking heartbreak, aren't you?"

Sakaeri's question made both Mhedoons recoil.

Aeyun, however, gave her a withering look. "Don't start."

Davah apparently decided it was time to change the subject. "This is all really weird. I feel like we woke up and the realms have gone the wrong way up. Honestly, I knew you had to have some sort of past – you didn't just appear from thin air – but what we've heard is – I mean . . ."

Aeyun knew it was jarring, what they'd found out in the past few days. If he was on the opposite end, he probably would have cut ties with himself when he'd first mentioned meeting a Sirin. To most, that name was synonymous with death, their presence as good as a sharpened sickle. Getting tangled with that was surely a bad omen. Aeyun would have considered it too much of a risk, too far a departure from known variables.

His Mhedoonian crewmates were not Aeyun, though, and they did not shy from veering constants. In fact, they leant into volatility, embracing it, as if it were the only way to live. To survive. In the back of his mind, he knew that communicated something painfully thorned into their past, informing their very existence. Their curiosity, he found, dredged up some small reflection of himself, staring at pastel-coloured skies with earthen musk in his nostrils, grass tickling his feet, a wonderment of the unattainable hovering in his unspoken thoughts.

Davah gave an odd sort of snort. "I mean, I'm only wrapping my head around the fact that your father and brother were with Raeyu Thasian, of all the damned people in the realms. And your sister is a Sirin?"

"Not my sister," Aeyun corrected, then added, "and don't think about it too much."

"I'm sure you'd prefer I didn't. Does that have to do with why you're looking for–"

Davah was cut off when Aeyun lurched across the hull and slapped a hand over his mouth. Saoiri grimaced at the exchange, and Sakaeri's head tilted in interest.

"Oh?" She rested her chin on her fist and blinked up at Aeyun. "Searching for what?" She recognised his indignation, frowned, then sighed. "Fine, fine. Anyway, where are you headed?"

"Well, originally we were going to Lu-Ghan, but . . ." Davah trailed, mouth now graciously unclamped. He looked over at Aeyun for confirmation.

"It's as good a place to start as any, so we may as well head there," said Aeyun.

Truly, they had no leads, so it couldn't hurt trying to gather some in Lu-Ghan. Of the realms, it was the largest. Its capital of Bhu-Nan served as an inter-realmal hub; a nexus of activity. Many types of trade happened there, including the exchange of secrets whispered in dark, sinful corners of bars and casinos. The likelihood that some sort of intel would be syphoned through its network was as high as they could wish for.

"What a coincidence! I'm going that way, too," Sakaeri exclaimed, overly enthusiastic.

"Sakaeri," Aeyun deadpanned. He knew what she was doing.

Sakaeri shrugged and pulled her blanket tighter.

"Oh, for the love of – *fine*."

It was not as though Aeyun could easily evade her, anyway. Not if she was actually looking for him. A part of him wondered why she hadn't sought him out before, back when he'd first skipped town. But a deeper, more fragile part of him, the one wrapped in years of hardened resolve and calcified resentment, knew.

She hadn't wanted to.

When they got back to the Great Sea Gate, the gatekeeper on duty had changed. It was someone who looked more alert than the last one. Aeyun motioned for Sakaeri to follow him from the hull, ducking into the small dormitory in the back of the sea-skimmer, where they could hide from scrutiny.

They crawled into the cramped space and sat side by side between the swinging hammocks, the material's chained links creaking during the sea-skimmer's approach.

"I'm amazed to see it still attached," said Sakaeri.

The muffled conversation on the other side of the door had finally quieted. It seemed they'd passed the checkpoint. To clarify, Sakaeri indicated to his right arm. Aeyun's hand came to rest on the spot where feeling ceased below his bicep.

"Well, neither of us has lost a limb before," he said, trying to twitch his finger. It offered a pathetic result. He needed to tune a stitch to it soon. "Descanting an exchange seems like it reverts it, for a time."

"But you lost feeling in it?"

"Yes, right away," said Aeyun. "I felt Rae lose her arm." At the admission, Aeyun let loose a mirthless chuckle, an echo of something lost and regretful. "I should have been there."

"Maybe, but maybe not," said Sakaeri. "I'm almost grateful that you weren't. Had you been, maybe your heart would've been ripped out by her beloved brother, and then you both would have had to watch each other die, perhaps in one another's arms." She scoffed. "How poetic." She turned to him then, offering a bitter smile. "I don't know exactly how it works, but maybe it's a blessing that you were separated, at least in this instance."

"That was part of the idea," Aeyun confessed, unwillingly running through scenarios of his and Raeyu's untimely demise in his head.

If he had been paying attention, he would have caught Sakaeri's curious appraisal at his declaration.

The air changed and Aeyun could feel the gate at work around him. With no visual to go on, he closed his eyes and tried to see without seeing. Reality slowed and unravelled, as it always did when they jumped realms, and then he found himself in the weightless, void-like in-between once more. Incorporeal, boundless.

The glistening tether still pulled from his chest, and the impression of *somewhere else* remained. He breathed out, the vapour of vacuous air feeling crystallised as it left his body, and he called out to the distance. He tried to find the right note, that one that would carry his voice.

There, enveloped in darkness, he could have sworn he saw something that wasn't his own. Something that didn't belong in his head, filled with vibrant green. He was almost upon it, wide yet small, present yet transient. It was gone just as quickly as every other time, and Aeyun came back to the present.

They had arrived in Lu-Ghan.

When he looked over at Sakaeri, she was staring back at him, so he asked, "What?"

"Nothing," she was quick to say. "I just thought . . ." Her eyes flickered down to his chest, zeroing in on where he could swear the colourless thread had been. "Nothing," she repeated.

"Hey," Saoiri said as she opened the door to the dormitory. "We're here!"

The two of them nodded and returned to the hull with nothing further mentioned on the subject.

"Welcome to Bhu-Nan!" Davah cheered, happily paying the fee to have their sea-skimmer tucked away in a secure docking facility in the swankier part of town.

Aeyun always thought Bhu-Nan felt similar to Haebal: clean, modern, and dressed in colour during the evening hours. It exuded a heady mixture of exotic perfumes and perspiration, sweat from hundreds upon thousands of the city's inhabitants. Buzzing with a vibrancy that titillated the air – a mischievous energy hanging between smooth-lined structures and bulbous overhangs – Bhu-Nan was a land of respite for all sorts if a person was willing to

61

seek their fancy within its ever-expanding borders.

They'd registered their sea-skimmer, something that was customary depending on the location, and exited the welcome terminal. Its mosaiced walls were gilded with art and advertisements for pricy wares and fashions. Each one was perfectly concocted to draw the eye and entrance passers-by, more glaring and fabulous than even the surfaces on which they hung. Even the lacklustre cry of a busker's poorly tuned instrument wasn't enough to sever the attention of an enraptured customer.

"It's so different from Tenebrana, right?" Saoiri asked. She eyed the likeness of a particularly attractive piece of jewellery portrayed in an ad to her left.

"It feels like Cheyun," Aeyun and Sakaeri said together, referring to Haebal City's lavish centre.

The aftermath included an obstinate exchange of glances and a scowl on Aeyun's part.

"Wow," Davah said with a snicker. "Right, so let's–"

"Let's find reasonable accommodation and not blow all of our money on a penthouse, right?" Saoiri asked with wide, penetrating eyes.

Davah shivered at the look, shrinking away. He nodded mechanically. "Yep. That's what I was going to say!"

Luck was not entirely on Saoiri's side. It was a popular season to visit Bhu-Nan and rooms were in limited supply. In the seasonal shortage, they were able to book a spot in an upscale joint in the centre of the entertainment district.

Not a penthouse, but a room with a view.

When they arrived at their suite, Davah was quick to open the curtains and take in the night-time vista of the city, complete with feedback from multi-coloured ore and the towering presences of high-density buildings nearby, twinkling back at them with illuminated winks. Definitely different from Pllametia's low rooflines and constantly scaffolded structures.

"Ah, sweet civilisation!" Davah sighed. He had his hands pressed against the windowpane, undoubtedly leaving greasy impressions where they lay.

"Have money to spare, huh?" Sakaeri asked, searching for the liquor cabinet.

She'd announced just a moment before that she was sure a stash of it existed in a hotel like this one. A woman on a mission, Sakaeri rifled through the cupboards with purpose. Chirping a delighted squeak of success, she lunged beneath the countertop, away from view, a myriad of clinking sounds rising from where she'd disappeared.

"When required," was Aeyun's curt response.

"Aeyun, would you mind coming with me to check the rooms?" Saoiri asked.

He nodded. Even though Sakaeri didn't reappear, it felt as if her attention clung to them the whole time until they walked into the first of two rooms. Its décor was a dated testament of former opulence. The hotel had clearly survived due to its convenient proximity to Bhu-Nan's fantastical, attraction-bloated centre, something stale cracking through its layer-thickened paint.

"Everything okay?" Aeyun asked when he and Saoiri were alone.

She worried her lip between her teeth; an anxious habit she'd picked up from Davah, Aeyun was sure. Or maybe it was the other way around.

"It's been a lot between Orin and now. So, are you alright?" Saoiri asked.

She looked up at him, concern casting lines across her forehead. Aeyun let soft recognition wash across his face. He appreciated her thought, but –

"I'm functioning. Are you okay? What about you and Davah? I never meant to drag you into my affairs like this," Aeyun admitted.

He hadn't. He was going to finish the business he had to do with them, ore-hunting aplenty until he accumulated what he needed, and then let them go about their merry way once both parties were satisfied.

Kind of. If their satisfaction included his sudden departure and a few gifted alicant accessories.

"I guess. I mean, I already knew Sakaeri, but I didn't know she was a Sirin. And I had no idea that you were so involved with the Thasian." She wrung her thumbs a few times. "Is there . . . anything we need to know, other than what we know now?"

It prompted Aeyun to think for a moment. How intertwined did he want or need these two people to be in his life? Things had changed now, a new obstacle thrown in the mix, and he wasn't sure where his path would take him. Saoiri kept her steady stare upon him, beckoning and lacking all the guile one should have as an inter-realmal ore smuggler.

"Not at the moment," he decided.

Saoiri nodded before saying, "Alright."

Aeyun wasn't sure where to look. His gaze ended up drawn to the window, where the city loomed beyond the glass. It summoned him, enticing and alive, while inviting something obscured and forbidden in the same breath. Without meaning to, his eyes caught on his own reflection superimposed upon the urban vista. He frowned at it.

Are you proud of yourself? Messing everything up, abandoning everyone? You haven't changed. Not at all, you disappointing –

"How's your arm?" Saoiri asked.

Right, he'd not even tried to explain that to them. He wondered if, based on context, they might already have an idea.

"It's been better," he said.

He'd barely be able to move it now if he tried, and he knew that Saoiri had felt how deadened it had become on Orin.

Wordlessly, she dipped a hand into her satchel and pulled out a small bag that held an odd-looking bug, native to Lu-Ghan. When had she even snatched that up? At the docking facility?

Aeyun hesitated before taking it. Something felt wrong about spewing a descantation in front of her, so he walked further into the room and turned away. When he was far enough for his nerves to calm, he took the bug from its prison and crushed it in his palm.

"*Ca'ou o, cah e'ju, ou'uo*," he muttered.

Just like the last time, materialised smoky white tendrils wove around his arm and sunk into the skin underneath his sleeve. Any remnant that the bug once existed evaporated, its entire soulsong sacrificed to Aeyun's will. He grimaced at his limb and the hand wrapped around it.

"That's fascinating, you know," Saoiri said from beside the door. "Elder Emagh said that Davah and I would run into destiny. I think she meant you."

"Don't put too much importance on me," Aeyun warned.

The expectation that he would bring any great purpose to anyone was flawed from the start, he knew that well enough. In his life thus far, all he'd done was chain hassle to those he was closest with. Thinking otherwise, that he would be a guiding light of some kind, would only set them up for disappointment.

"I think your elder was only trying to give you motivation."

Saoiri smiled softly. "Maybe."

When they re-entered the living area of the suite, Sakaeri was watching Aeyun's return like a hawk. "How was checking the rooms?"

Aeyun gave her a testy glare and said, "Don't start."

He walked up to where she was seated, right next to a bottle of something that looked entirely too fancy. Its body was bubbled in odd places, and it boasted a cap that contradicted the rest of the design. It was something that surely belonged on the shelf in Oagyu's office.

"How much is that?" he asked.

"Who knows?" Sakaeri grinned, pouring him a glass and pushing it forwards.

"You give him a drink, but tell me I can't have any yet?" Davah complained from the other end of the counter.

Sakaeri whipped her head around to look at him, making Davah jerk back at the suddenness of it. "I'm sorry, did you just find out how your father died today?"

That was enough to shut Davah up.

Aeyun eyed the deep amethystine liquid, then he took and raised the glass to cheers it against Sakaeri's.

"To Father," he said, a term he rarely affirmed aloud. Their gazes connected for a long moment before she returned the sentiment, then they tipped their beverages down their throats. In the swell of enduring melancholy, Aeyun gently returned his glass to the counter.

"Looks like you're ambidextrous again," Sakaeri commented and Aeyun grunted.

"Yep."

"Thanks, Saoiri." Sakaeri cheekily took another swig from her glass, ignoring Aeyun's stink-eye.

"Don't thank her on my behalf."

"Oh, it wasn't on *your* behalf," Sakaeri corrected, the jeer light-hearted on the surface. Aeyun could feel its sinister underpinnings beneath. "I mean, it has been a long, long time."

"Don't start," Aeyun said once more.

His face must have been a sight, because soon Davah was saying, "Okay!" and reaching to pour himself a glass from the now free liquor bottle. "Let's all have a drink and give today's troubles to tomorrow, shall we?"

"Yes, please," was Saoiri's mumbled response as she too gave herself a generous serving of the bittersweet liquor.

She was so bright it was nearly blinding. Always smiling, cheering for everyone. It sat funny in his chest because he didn't know what to do with that.

Her hand was always thrust towards him, a grin on her lips, asking for him to come along. To enjoy, to be there in that moment. And again, he didn't know what to do with that.

The day she told him she loved him was the same she said they were doomed because of promises poisoned by politics, and he didn't know what to do with that either.

CHAPTER SEVEN

When Aeyun woke up, Sakaeri was sat on the windowsill, looking into the morning fog that had settled across the city. The night before gave them a few options, but everyone was quick to have Aeyun in the same room as the Sirin, since she seemed to have some sort of inclination to keep him alive.

Free of her cloak, her battle-scarred skin was on full display, sinuous arms wrapped around her knees, pulling them close to her chest. Clutching around her bicep was the damned arm bracer that had soured his day so many years ago. When he'd been so enthused, so overjoyed that Raeyu had actually asked him to craft something, back in his early days as an apprentice, back when she rarely requested any favour of him. Perhaps she was saving up her favours, waiting for a more taxing request to cash out. But this had been an exception.

Sakaeri was always an exception. That unevenly hammered

metal professed this proudly, still wrapped dutifully around her arm, its gleam too sharp for its age. She must care for it diligently, and Aeyun was sure that only one face was recalled as she minded it. Kind eyes and a gentler disposition.

Aeyun's thoughts took a moment to catch up, his prior sleep deprivation having made his mental faculties sluggish. Then the realms shattered again. Then the last few days came crashing down on him like his hammer to an anvil.

He sat up in his bed, scrubbing the last remnants of slumbering bleariness from his eyes. His head came to rest in his palms, heavy.

"There was a paper shoved under the door this morning. It's the weekend, did you realise?" Sakaeri didn't look behind her, her profile showcasing a frown. "Apparently Haebal City is a restricted zone right now, no news going in or out of it, and Raenaru is on lockdown. They're turning people away at the Gate." Aeyun didn't miss it when she pulled her limbs in tighter. "At first, I wondered: what if they'd not left the realm? What if they're stuck there, Eyes out on Seraeyu's command to find Uruji, and to keep their mouths shut about Rae. What if, what if? But something about that felt wrong."

She finally turned to him, a shadow of lost innocence cloying on the fringes of her expression.

"They're not there, are they? Aeyun, do you have any idea where Rae is? Can't you ask the in-between or something?"

"It doesn't work like that," he said, voice gravelly from disuse.

"You said her name in your sleep, you know," Sakaeri said, turning away again.

"I dreamt of her dying," Aeyun admitted.

He still held his head in his hands, exhaustion bleeding further than the physical kind.

"You know it didn't happen, though," she said.

The air in the room felt weighty, like the stagnant linger that manifested before a storm. Aeyun didn't like to think about it, that horrible day from years ago.

"Not now. Then."

"Did she really – that day, did . . . ?" Sakaeri, even after all this time, still couldn't bring herself to say it.

Aeyun was sympathetic to that.

"I don't know for sure." Aeyun debated his next words carefully. Things had changed. Maybe she should know. Maybe it would help somehow. "It wasn't me. I'm not – it was Uruji. I begged Uruji to bring her back. In my place. I can't. I don't know how."

"Your younger brother did it?" Sakaeri's incensed shock made Aeyun finally lift his head. When he did, he wished he hadn't. Her glare was biting, prying an old wound open. "You asked your brother to exchange your life? To make that choice?"

Aeyun felt Sakaeri looked like one of those old guardian animal statues from Raenaru's spiritual epicentre, Yunae. Fierce and feral sabre-maws. Feral sounded about right, but a traitorous part of him felt like he deserved it.

Maybe he did.

"You asked him to kill you, Aeyun. You asked Uruji to decide you weren't worth more than . . . than Raeyu. You *know* that would have broken him."

"I know," said Aeyun. "I'm selfish."

After a moment, Sakaeri offered a distant hum. "I can't make any comment on your selfishness, can I?"

Aeyun didn't bother to verify that.

"So, you can't tune with it? It's Uruji who can? Yet you told me that it was you. And I've seen it."

"Uruji can." Aeyun paused.

He'd only ever called it strange, ambiguous names for so long, he'd nearly forgotten that what he could do wasn't quite the fabled *it* that she was referring to. His manipulations were strange transfigurations of energy independent of ore, yes, but they were not the same as those glorified in local legends and lore.

Sakaeri, of course, wasn't aware of this, and Aeyun held no desire to rectify that.

"I can, too. Just, our talents are different. People think that type of tuning is a lost art, something that hasn't been practised for millennia. But they're not right." He had Sakaeri's full attention now, silhouette faced towards him, her back to the window. Her stare was daunting, concerningly unflappable, and he fought the urge to look away. "Those tattoos that cover the arm of the mainline Thasian; they're not just some ritual rite. They're scars."

Scars that Seraeyu, despite being Thasian, did not have. Or at least, didn't have before all this. Aeyun wondered if that had since changed.

"What do you mean?" Sakaeri asked, nails dug into the windowsill below her.

Aeyun peeled off his shirt, displaying his right arm. It was the first chance he really got to look at it as well, and he could already see the difference. The shaping of the lines stood in contrast to those on Raeyu's arm. Aeyun's were softer, more delicate and intentional pathways that culminated cleanly in a weave around his bicep, borne from stitching a tune on a limb that lacked its reflection.

So, it really wasn't the same, after all. Only the mirroring of a similar concept.

"Why were hers so . . . jagged? So–"

"Disorderly?" Aeyun interjected, frowning. "Our talents are different."

"Wait." It seemed the realisation had hit her full on. "You're saying that Uruji had done that to Rae's arm? That doesn't make sense. Why would the Thasian even have it done?"

"No," said Aeyun. "Not Uruji. Jourae."

There was a brief, confused respite, then the fire in Sakaeri sparked. Her voice was low as she said, "I forgot. I forgot how much I despise you, Aeyun. For stealing *everything* that should be mine." The words tore like a gorge between them, and her palm slammed down upon the windowsill. "So, our father could attune to it, and he decided that you deserved to have that talent cultivated, did he?"

Aeyun didn't know what to say in response. No, Jourae did not teach Aeyun.

"If you can tune like he did, you really are Jourae's son after all, aren't you? I'd wondered, for all these years." She clicked her tongue in thought. "If half of you is of Jourae's heritage, and you can attune to the aether – the void, the Great Starry Sea – whatever the Yun declared it to be . . . can I?"

That, Aeyun didn't know. It wasn't pedigree that was the issue, though. At least, he didn't think so. But he didn't like the idea of a Sirin, much less Sakaeri, harnessing that type of raw, unmitigated power. Maybe he shouldn't have said so much.

"I honestly don't know," he said.

"Okay." Sakaeri seemed agitated. "So, why give the Thasian a scar in the first place?"

"I don't know," he lied. He wasn't really *meant* to know. "But I recognised it for what it was when I saw it."

Sakaeri narrowed her eyes at his answer, but she didn't push any further on it. Instead, she stared on. He could feel it puncture through him, like a fissure stabbing through a wound, cold and hungry for carnage.

"So, the Thasian-nee attune to it, like a bloodsong. Does that mean that the Thasian bloodsong that Raeyu and, apparently, Seraeyu have is actually them attuning to it, without descantation?"

Aeyun didn't like where this was headed. It was all getting too complicated.

His deceit was cratering, its bottom falling out, and he didn't want to start weaving a narrative that didn't exist. That so-called bloodsong was a farce, after all. Nothing more than a tale to coax the populace into believing the Thasian worthy. Believing them to be blessed by the Yun.

"Not the Thasian-nee, just Jourae's line."

He tried to keep it to truths. It was only Jourae's lineage that dealt with that raw energy – that strange, feral *Essence* – due to its dangerous nature. The Thasian didn't, not directly.

71

"Just Jourae," Sakaeri repeated. "Is that why he'd thrown me aside? I was the result of an error in judgement, and his line was *too important* to mix with riffraff? Then why claim you as my mother's child years later when she couldn't have even been alive to birth you? When it was *me* who killed her?"

Quickly – too quickly – Sakaeri snatched a dagger from where it had been strapped to her ankle and hurled it in Aeyun's direction. Without enough time to dodge, he swayed to the side and the blade sliced his left shoulder, lodging itself in the wall behind him. Sakaeri's wide eyes glistened, her arm outstretched, and her fingers stayed stationed just as they were when she'd thrown the knife.

"She'll feel that, won't she?" she asked, quiet.

Aeyun continued to watch her for signs of danger.

"I'm sorry. I'm sorry." Sakaeri stood. "I didn't mean to. I'm sorry."

As she walked over, Aeyun pulled the dagger from the plastered wall. When she reached him, he held out the sharp implement, blade between his fingers, hilt towards her.

"If you ever try to kill me again, I will make sure you take your last breath." As Aeyun let his threat linger, Sakaeri paused in her grasp, the image of terrified regret on her face as she fought her own inner turmoil. "I will not let you accidentally kill her in one of your rageful fits."

"I'm sorry," Sakaeri choked out. "I would never hurt–"

"But you would still kill me," Aeyun declared just as the door opened to reveal a panicked-looking Davah.

"I heard this noise, and it sounded suspect, so I – uh . . . "

Davah observed the scene, his gaze catching on the speared tear behind Aeyun, then the implement still offered yet unaccepted in his hand. Apprehensive, his focus trailed to the broken repose of Sakaeri's face, swooping back until it finally landed on the markings upon Aeyun's naked arm.

"Uh," Davah repeated. "That's, um, sorry, what the fuck is that new tattoo, friend?" Drawing a conclusion in the wrong direction, he went on to ask, "You didn't descant that gal's arm off, did you?"

Sakaeri swiped the dagger out of Aeyun's pinched grasp, then rubbed her free hand across her face to rid herself of any unwanted display of pulpy insecurity. With a huff, she tore out of the room, bumping shoulders with Davah on the way.

"No," Aeyun finally answered. He tilted backwards until his head hit the wall and he closed his eyes. "No, I did not, Davah."

"Should we have not put you two in the same room? Is it worse to do that?" Saoiri asked.

She and Aeyun walked behind Davah and Sakaeri, the four of them winding through the bustling streets of Bhu-Nan. The jingle of chimes and idle chatter buffeted off the colourful narrows, and in the air was a lingering bouquet of damp bodies and expensive perfume mixing with cheap, potent spritzes. Across the street, waiting for the next oversized town-skimmer to arrive at its stop, a woman stood in primly leathered heels. Her shoulders were draped with a fine, metal-woven collar that boasted gems of ruby and violet, and she fiddled with her needlessly ornate purse, pointedly ignoring the shorter youth beside her. He was a dusty-looking fellow, maybe around Uruji's age, with beat-up boots and a tired droop to his eyes, perhaps just off a morning shift.

"It's nothing I can't handle," Aeyun assured her, partly to reassure himself of the same.

The fog had stuck around to midday, and it was only now dissipating as they meandered through the main thoroughfare. Plenty of pedestrians were milling about, filling the city with a fluttering sense of urgency, making it easier to not stand out. Morning to midday was prime market time in Bhu-Nan, and many seeking savvy deals were rushing to and from the square to get the most exclusive delicacies. Others were contented to go through another cycle's motions, lumbering down walkways in some variety of exuberant or exceedingly vacant.

What Aeyun and his ragtag group were looking for was not any fine pastry or fresh-caught fish, however. Nor were they waiting on transit channels to bring them to their obligatory place of work. They were seeking someone with a particular emblem; one that looked like a coppery, skeletal hand.

The Reaping Hands, they called themselves. Dealers in the undermarket with clientele notoriously more nefarious than Aeyun's crew dared to engage with. Davah and Saoiri took risks, but they were usually measured, and with some degree of preparation. Those like the Reaping Hands were unbothered by the smugglers' unwritten code, which levelled some grade of loyalty to one's own. It proffered an understanding that a semblance of diplomacy was needed across various turfs, even if it eventually ended in a brawl anyway.

No, the Reaping Hands unbound themselves from this, instead seeking their own ends, no matter what the cost. While frustratingly cocky to many, it also made their particular bunch somewhat vindicated in their obtuse sureness. They often got their grubby fingers on some of the rarest, most valuable alicant and materials to trade, sold to the highest bidder in coin or favours.

It was by Saoiri's prompting they were even in Bhu-Nan. Through her network, she had got wind that the Reaping Hands were flashing around an alicant that no one could touch with their bare skin. It was exactly the type of thing Aeyun was looking for, so they could only hope the group of less reputable merchants hadn't sold it off yet. Even if Aeyun wasn't exactly keen to deal with the secretive, shifty launderers. The one encounter he'd had with their group in a different life – the one where he acted a guard, disguised and under a different name – was uncomfortable. He had been so woefully unprepared for it that his confidence had been shaken for months.

Aeyun's eyes were drawn to Sakaeri's back, once again hidden underneath her hooded cloak.

He hadn't had time to worry about her presence yet, but the closer they got to the market, the more concerned he was with her involvement. Sakaeri was a lot of things, but dumb wasn't on the list. And there were too many questions that Aeyun just didn't want to address.

"Do you think we'll find your and Sakaeri's brother?" Saoiri asked.

It nearly made Aeyun trip as he crossed from one mosaic slab to the next.

"Please don't call him her brother; it doesn't feel right. She'd have a fit, too," Aeyun said, voice an octave lower so it wouldn't carry among the crowd.

Saoiri looked at him with curiosity. "But she said–"

"We're not really family, me and her. And I don't think those two could be family if they tried. He is mine, though. I'm not a very good brother, if I'm honest." Aeyun sighed something bitter. "I could have been a lot better. I'm not great at the whole reliability thing."

"That's exactly what you want to hear from your crewmate," Saoiri joked, elbowing him with an airy chuckle. "But Aeyun," she said, and her tone lost its humour. "You say that like you've lost your chance already. He's still out there. You're just as much his brother yesterday as you will be five months from now. And anyway–" She poked him in the shoulder, "–you're actually a pretty nice guy. I wasn't lying when I said you take care of us, so you can't be that bad of a brother."

Aeyun gave her a wry smirk. "Maybe."

"Whispering sweet nothings?" Sakaeri spat behind her.

Aeyun inwardly swore he'd be rid of her as soon as he was able.

"Don't. Start," Aeyun growled, sending her a scornful look in response to her sneer.

"You two are very well acquainted," Saoiri murmured, looking fixedly at the ground. "But you *are* related, right?"

Sakaeri's loud guffaw ripped through the distance between

75

them, unwittingly beckoning some glances in their direction as they finally shuffled into the market, the yeasty waft of fresh-baked bread mixing somewhat noxiously with the pungent stench of fish.

"Wow," she said. "Wrong impression, doll. I don't crave his or any man's warmth in the daemons' hours. Even if we weren't, he doesn't have the right *bits*."

With that, she broke away from the group to gander at the inventory of the third vendor in, a stall showcasing strips of stitched leather and intricate buckles, a sign professing tailoring services for all sorts of wearable accoutrements. Aeyun took his chance to disengage from the Sirin. At least she'd provided some much-needed distance, hopefully enough that they could get in and out without involving her.

"Right, so," Davah said, gesturing to the sprawling lines of kiosks before them. "Somewhere in this market is a Reaper's Hand. They're always here; we just need to find one, right, Aeyun?" It was a not-so-subtle reminder that they were on this dangerous goose hunt due to his request. "Look at bracelets, broaches, earrings, sewn details – whatever might showcase that hand."

Trying to find one small, ambiguous symbol in the sea of hecklers and hagglers would not be easy. The market itself was an old establishment, an emporium with ancient roots and a beautifully etched stained-glass atrium. When the sun shone through, it created a spectrum of colours that danced around the floor. Some historians claimed that the architecture was that of the infamous and elusive Mesmeri, the hidden work of master sculpting alicantist Han Klu-Fan himself. But it was still debated if the design on the atrium was his or that of an artist inspired by him.

Regardless, on a cloudy day like the current one, the tones were muted, and the market was instead lit by warm glowing ore that was strung from one rafter to the next. While it made for nice scenery, it didn't do any favours for their line of sight.

"I have one set, who's going to take it?" Saoiri asked, referring to the pair of communication stones in her hand.

Communication stone pairs were incredibly rare. Each stone was innately paired with a sister stone; the only problem was that the mate could be anywhere. Originating in the same realm, that usually narrowed it down. However, with so much inter-realmal traversal over the centuries, stones had been known to pop up in entirely different realms from time to time. When one was found, it didn't guarantee that the other would be. Buying them was outrageously costly, since they were so precious a commodity, and they were usually given with priority to government entities and news authorities – where most Eyes would work.

Sacrificing one's privacy to be a live feed for reporting, anyone who was gutsy enough would have their eyes injected with a particular type of alicant that was dangerous at best and deadly at worst. It took years of training to master and months to recover, but if it didn't kill the host, monetarily at least they'd be sorted for life.

Assuming they didn't get themselves into hairy situations like the one with Seraeyu.

Another drawback of the arrangement was the inherent fettering to a handler; some individual with the core of the alicant used in the procedure. Not unlike communication stones, it would link the Eye to their handler, who was charged with the safekeeping of their aptly named transmission stone. It was all business and bureaucracy with governments and reporting outlets, but, as always, there was a darker shade of the clandestine to contend with.

Eyes were part of the underworld as well. That's why Aeyun was always distrustful of people with mutated pupils. Those who chose to be Eyes had a cross seared on their iris. Any distortion was a sign of experimentation, though.

Like Sakaeri's.

He still remembered the night he'd first seen them changed. The very same she nearly succeeded in killing him, her stare hard and frigid. Predatory.

If Sakaeri had some sort of *handler* as well, Aeyun held no envy for them.

From what Aeyun gathered, Sakaeri had been the one to hand Saoiri a paired communication stone, asking Saoiri to contact her if she'd come across anything more of interest. That was how Saoiri got most of her stones, in fact. It was the same way they'd received the tip about the Reaping Hands' unique bounty in Bhu-Nan.

All of those little stones in her bag were connected in a cosmic web to people across the realms, each holder looking for the next deal or business trade in the smuggling circles. Of her own collection, she only had the paired two in her hand, which all three of them considered thoughtfully.

"Easy," Sakaeri said, her unannounced return startling Davah enough that he jumped and slammed a hand over his heart. She plucked the stones from Saoiri's upturned palm and distributed one to Aeyun and one to Davah. "Now we all have one." The slow blink that followed made her look far more harmless than she was. "What are we looking for again, and why?"

"You see someone with the Reaper's Hand, just get that information to me," Aeyun whispered, watching a passer-by.

"Interesting." Sakaeri tilted her head to the side. "Okay, then."

"You see that?"

It was a simple question, one that should be easily answered. But it wasn't, and he didn't see it, whatever it was.

The silence must have spoken for him because what followed was, "I don't know what life you're running from, but this here is my domain. My broken kingdom, among these waters. You see a craft with that kind of symbol on the side of it and you get the feck out. Nothing, no matter how much coin it promises to heavy your pocket, is worth a tangle with eejits like them."

CHAPTER EIGHT

Aeyun was annoyed.

They'd been searching around the market to no avail and the crowd was starting to wane. The number of times he'd been told he could get a special sale – *only today!* they said – was fraying his nerves. Sakaeri was who-knows-where while Saoiri was off pretending to peruse a stall somewhere to the left.

Davah was beside him, waves of frustration tangible as he sighed.

"I know they're meant to be secretive, but, like, don't they want business as well? Damn." Davah shook his head, leaning his weight against the massive foliage-covered fountain at the back of the market. "Honestly, it's been hours."

"Yeah, it has," Aeyun grumbled.

He pushed against the fountain's basin, looking over the edge and into the water's reflection there. Staring at him were his own green eyes, more tired than he'd ever remembered being. As he took in the dark, sleep-deprived circles blooming above his cheekbones, a glint of something caught his attention.

There had been a ripple in the water, carried forth by the endless torrent above. It had shown something bronzy in the pool of black. Aeyun roved his eyes across the fountain's surface, once again finding the coppery flash on the other side. As he shifted his gaze from the basin to what was standing beyond, visible through a tangle of leaves opposite his side of the cascade, Aeyun put a pausing hand on Davah's arm, trying to get him to hush his complaints.

Davah glanced over, trailing off as he was chattering about bad business practices. Curious, he looked over his shoulder to see what Aeyun was staring at.

There, between the greenery and vines, beyond the rivulets of water, a figure stood, her back to the fountain. Slick hair was draped over one of the stranger's shoulders, and her exposed ear had a thin, dangling chain with a skeletal hand at its end. It was tarnished but shiny enough to be noticed.

"No way," Davah whispered.

Aeyun dismissively – and victoriously – smacked at Davah's arm, the same he'd grasped onto. He pushed away from the fountain's basin, cautious as he took measured steps, rounding the edge. Tentatively, he approached the presumed Reaping Hands member.

"Do you agree that you sow what you reap?" he asked the woman, reiterating the words Davah had coached him to say.

Secret groups and their stupid riddles.

She turned to him; an apathetic expression disturbed only by the quirk of a brow.

"And you reap what you sow," she said, concluding the statement with a nod, narrowed leer matching gaunt cheeks. "To whom do we owe the pleasure?"

The woman regarded him with interest then, taking in the ore-encrusted earring pierced into Aeyun's own lobe.

80

"We heard a rumour that you all had something peculiar that can't be touched." As Aeyun spoke, Davah darted off to grab Saoiri. "Is that true?"

The Reaper's Hand seemed to scrutinise him, pursing her lips before she clicked her tongue. "And if it is? Would you be looking to relieve us of this oddity?"

"I would," Aeyun answered, short and clipped. "However," he started, just as the Reaper's Hand looked as though she would say more, "I'm also looking for some information."

"Oh, are you?" The Reaper's Hand's eyes followed Davah and Saoiri's movements as they closed in, joining the small gathering. "Perhaps this little rendezvous should be moved elsewhere," she advised, a frown replacing her sly smile.

Aeyun nodded his consent, gesturing for her to lead on.

"I'll send a comms message to—"

"Don't," Aeyun said, cutting off Saoiri's explanation. "Leave her out of this. We'll find her after."

It wasn't so much a statement as a command. Saoiri gave him a troubled look but said nothing. Davah, on the other hand, didn't seem bothered at all.

The Reaper's Hand led them out of the market through a narrow delivery corridor on the far side. Once they'd been dumped out into the alleyway, she wove them through some shaded, overgrown back lanes until they reached what looked like a warehouse entrance. In silence, the Reaper's Hand opened the door and ushered the three of them through.

Inside, the stale warehouse was grim, giving off a distinct feeling of abandonment. The woman stamped her foot on the ground in a rhythmic pattern, and shortly after a latch could be heard opening behind a stack of crates, startling some birds enough to flap their wings away from their nests in the rafters. Another woman appeared, rising up from the hatch in the floor.

"Ah, the Doons! What a welcome surprise," she said.

Her rouge-dyed lips were upturned with a sharp-toothed grin, and her shoulders were dressed in mismatched jewels and gems, strung and looped under coppery shoulder guards. The adornments were seemingly lifted from decommissioned Draconguard gear; decades old, if Aeyun clocked them right. Complementing this was a hodgepodge of luxurious fabrics, all half shrouded by a black cloak held together with a bronze, skeletal hand.

"You, though – who are you?" the woman asked, looking at Aeyun.

Aeyun bowed his head slightly. "An interested party."

"He brought up *that* ore, and he said he's looking for some information."

"Ah, I see. Please, then." The sharp-toothed woman beckoned them. "Come on."

Aeyun, against his better judgement, stepped forward and allowed himself to be led down the hatch, Davah and Saoiri in tow. Below the floorboards was dark, but little pieces of luminous ore were strung up here and there to light the way. Behind them, only the second of the Reaping Hands followed. Aeyun assumed the first went back to the market, or wherever she was meant to be.

"Lovely gaff here, um . . . " Davah trailed, trying to prompt the woman into providing a name.

She hummed. "Call me Madame, if you please."

Aeyun inwardly noted that Davah *didn't* know her name so, logically, he'd not dealt with her directly before. That was . . . curious.

"Sure, Madame Reaper," Davah responded uncomfortably. "So, you recognised us?"

"Mm, the Doons with the clean hands. I did."

The words left an odd taste in Aeyun's mouth, but he kept following Madame Reaper through the passage, which looked as if it led to several doors. She creaked opened the fourth one on the left, and it fed into a dim-lit room with a velveteen sofa and a rich-wooded desk. Around the stone-carved walls hung a mismatch of sconces, likely pilfered from lavish mansions or estates. They were piled to the brim with glowing ore, bathing the room in an eerie ambiance. It didn't escape Aeyun's notice that an oxidised mirror hung above the couch, reflecting any tricks clients might have up their sleeves.

Madame Reaper flicked her wrist, impatiently indicating for them to sit down. As they did, movements sluggish with tepid curiosity, she waited by the door until a hooded attendant came to her side.

"Fetch the untouchable alicant and bring it here, please."

The attendant nodded and slipped away, and Madame Reaper closed the door in their absence. It left her and the three ore-smugglers alone in the room. Alone and quiet.

"So, what possible use could you have for an ore than can't even be touched?" she asked.

"Is that question necessary?" Aeyun shot back, stone-faced.

The woman laughed, but it came out more like a cackle. "Oh, dear me. Look at that expression!" She calmed and shook her head as she went to the desk, leaning herself upon its edge. "No, I suppose it's not. What can you offer me in return?"

"Something you can actually sell," Aeyun said, patting the satchel at his side.

"A trade, is it?" Madame Reaper seemed to consider the prospect. "Let's see it, then."

Aeyun shook his head. "I'll show you my hand when you show me yours."

She gave him a wide, toothy grin before looking at Davah and Saoiri. "Have you been teaching him the trade? Is he your new protégé?"

The two of them looked at one another but remained silent.

"Mm, I see. Secrets, secrets. Nice to know you two might finally be digging some deeper trenches," she said. A knock on the door made all their heads turn. "Ah, and here's my hand, boy."

Madame Reaper sashayed across the room, opened the door, and accepted the wrapped bundle held out to her. Wordlessly, she placed the package on the table and gestured for Aeyun to get up and have a look at it.

Warily, he stood and stepped over. Something didn't feel like it should. He wasn't getting that cool buzz of energy he normally felt when encountering the alicant he'd been collecting. But something did strike him with that confusing sense of foreign-but-familiar he got on occasion.

He unravelled the tie that held the bundle closed, feeling oddly entranced. It unfurled before him, revealing an amber hue he hadn't expected. Something pulsed under the surface of his skin, and he could feel the colour pull from his face. His fingers hovered as his mind froze. *What. What?*

"Odd-looking ore, isn't it?" Madame Reaper said from beside him. "It's like nothing I've seen. You touch it and it stabs you. Positively ruthless! Needles poked holes straight through some of my best Hands. Was this what you were looking for?"

The question was left unanswered for too long as Aeyun stared at the treasure.

It wasn't an ore. One could argue that it was an alicant, of sorts, but it wasn't an ore. And it shouldn't be here. *Why is it here?*

"No," said Aeyun. His hand inched towards the displaced commodity. "But it's piqued my interest." Feigning ignorance, he glanced at her and asked, "It won't poke holes through me if I grab it with this gloved hand, will it?"

"Unless you have tears in that glove, I'm under the impression that it won't," she said, a touch too nonchalant. "Hold on now, though. This is my hand, hm? What's yours?"

Aeyun stilled for a moment, then reached into his bag and retrieved a bracelet. It was elegantly twisted upon itself with notches aligned to accommodate better tuning. A pyre alicant, expertly faceted, was embedded in its centre.

"Oh, my." Madame Reaper plucked it from his grasp. "Look at this beauty. Is it Thasian-nee? It looks very much like another of theirs I have. You're trading this for something you can't use?"

The question was casual, but it had Aeyun's muscles stiffening, the presumption hitting too close to the mark.

"It's not the real deal," he told her. "No signature. I figure it's not worth the same without a seal."

Madame Reaper ran a thumb along the bare inside of the bracelet's flattened closure piece. "Seal or no seal, a good piece of craftsmanship can be of profit." She regarded him predatorily. "I will accept this trade–"

"You can have that if you tell me where this was found," said Aeyun. He snatched one end of the bracelet, not letting her pull it out of reach.

"Ah, so there was more. That was the information you were looking for? You're asking me to give up a potential resource location, you know." She offered him a glower, an off-putting display, her sharpened canines glinting.

"You don't seem to think this stabbing ore is of much use anyway, and you said it yourself – fine craftsmanship can bring a good profit."

Aeyun stared her down, and she harumphed.

"Not as foolish as I was hoping, I see. Unfortunately, that cursed ore seems to have changed ownership quite a few times. It's an old thing, jumping from realm to realm through various trades over the centuries. We found it in Haebal City's Narui district. However, our tracking traced its earliest known presence to Mhedoon." Madame Reaper leered at Davah and Saoiri. "It was a record of death in an ancient text. Some poor Doon picked up a brown ore only to be stabbed through by the very thing. The ore was then locked in a box. Seems like it must have left Mhedoon at some point after the raids."

The atmosphere in the room spoilt at her casual mention of Mhedoon's past traumas. Curiosity decidedly quelled, Aeyun let go of the bracelet, relinquishing it to her grasp. Concentrating to calm the tremor in his fingers, he carefully re-wrapped the amber alicant on the desk and slipped it into his satchel.

"Consider the trade done," Aeyun told her.

Madame Reaper's interest instantly vanished. "Well, that was more boring than I'd hoped. Is there any other business you have with us here?"

Aeyun let the question settled in his head, but he found that something stopped him from asking about the Thasian or the incident in Haebal. Madame Reaper's eyes were too beady, and her disposition too eager. He didn't trust the information that someone was asking about it to not be sold, at least if it was this woman involved.

Aeyun shook his head. "No, thank you."

It was an uneventful departure, Madame Reaper bidding them farewell and pawning them off on the same attendant from earlier, told to show them out. When they finally re-emerged through the hatch, they were met with a solemn warehouse.

Then the door to the street opened once more.

Light poured in, encroaching upon them like great, luminous tide. The Reaper's Hand from the market made room for none other than Kaisa, the infamous Pitmaster himself. He sauntered into the cavernous space with a wolfish smile, his attire as gaudy as it had been the last time Aeyun saw him.

Kaisa's progress paused, if only briefly, then his smile widened as he took in the sight of Aeyun and his companions.

"Imagine," he said, generously dramatic. "Of all the places."

Aeyun, Davah, and Saoiri gathered closer together, starting an aborted stand-off between themselves and the man's appraisal.

"Kaisa," Saoiri greeted, her voice steely.

Around them, the two Reaper's Hands waited in poor patience. Kaisa took his time entering the warehouse, focus unsettlingly upon Aeyun.

"I was so hoping that I'd see you again, you know. Quite peculiar, you." Kaisa stepped forward with a lazy finger shake, his ore-adorned cufflink catching on a stray beam of daylight. Aeyun fumbled a step back. "My condolences, by the way."

The room stilled.

Those words, unfathomable, took a moment to sink in. Once

they did, Aeyun felt the sickening sensation of falling, his stomach turning the wrong way around and the realm tipping off kilter.

Tactfully, he decided to start walking towards the door, intending to slip right past Kaisa, paying the other little mind. Leaving him and his statement far, far behind him.

"It must have been tough to lose your father like that," Kaisa whispered when Aeyun was near enough to hear it, a sly tilt to his grin.

Aeyun's head snapped in his direction. Just as dread began festering, cold and nauseating, Kaisa was reaching out a ring-laden hand. Not a second later, Sakaeri dropped from the rafters and pushed herself between them, glaring menacingly at Kaisa and his outstretched fingers.

"Oh, hello!" Kaisa smiled charmingly.

"Keep your hands off him," Sakaeri snarled, shoving Aeyun towards the door and away from Kaisa. "If you touch him, I will do what I do best."

"How very interesting," Kaisa said with a tinny laugh, eyes simmering but tone light-hearted. "But, dear, he and I are friends. Aren't we?" The last bit was aimed towards Aeyun, paired with an imploring crick of Kaisa's neck.

In his own spinning head, Aeyun managed to notice that, oddly enough, Kaisa hadn't said Aeyun's name. Not once. And that could mean many things, most of which he didn't have the mental fortitude to ruminate over as he stared blankly, just past Kaisa's ear.

"Aren't we?" Kaisa asked again, finally catching Aeyun's gaze.

"Think what you want," is what Aeyun decided to answer with, a response that had Sakaeri flinching with an unreadable look. "Our business is done here. We're leaving."

Aeyun reached out for Sakaeri's wrist and pulled her along with him, too shaken to debate her uncharacteristic compliance. Behind them, both Davah and Saoiri quickly caught up, leaving a wide berth around Kaisa as they did.

As Aeyun stumbled out and crossed the threshold back to

the streets, he caught Kaisa's bemused murmur of, "What an intriguing pair."

"No!" was shouted in a whiplash of earnest fear, his mother's hands clamping down on his own. Her eyes were shadowed, reliving some memory far off in the mists of time. She often looked lost like that, complexion drained and pale as the ivory beaded across her adornments.

He gently dislodged her trembling fingers from his own, used to this type of reaction, and instead squeezed her clammy grasp. He'd never told her about that time at the market, when he was alone. He hadn't fallen into a ravine, but she didn't know that. She also didn't know about the hunters in the woods who looked at him with the same sneering snarl as if they'd encountered a wild creature, the perfect pickings to maim and enjoy for dinner.

She didn't know, but she didn't have to. All she had to know was: "It's time, Mother."

CHAPTER NINE

"How do you know Kaisa?" Sakaeri was the first to ask when they'd returned to the hotel suite.

Aeyun took off his cloak and cracked the knuckles on his right hand – still functioning for the moment. "I don't know; seemed like he knew you, too."

"I do know him, and that's why I'm concerned that he seemed particularly interested in you." Sakaeri huffed and turned on the other two, pointing accusingly. "Is this what you've done? You've brought him into the fold of this kind of underhanded crowd?"

"Hey, hey, look," Davah held up his hands, sidestepping

around the room to linger by the window. It had started to rain, the splatter of the droplets painting a muted picture of the city behind him, darkening the urban vista in the early evening. "We don't mess with these kinds of things. The Reaping Hands aren't our buddies, and Kaisa is not our friend. We had an encounter with him once, when Aeyun wanted—"

He was quick to cut himself off, mashing his mouth closed.

"How did you find us, anyway? I hadn't messaged on the stone," Saoiri interjected.

She had her hands folded behind her back, an index finger scraping at her knuckle in what Aeyun suspected was anxiety. He felt something heavy and intangible bear down on his shoulders. A reminder, ghostly and vindictive, sang in the space between his ears, mocking him for his lack of finesse. For causing more distress. For failing again and again and again.

"No, you didn't, did you?" Sakaeri's tone sounded about as annoyed as her expression looked. "I track people. It's what I do. And that was a lovely attempt to change the subject, but Aeyun wanted what? What could Kaisa possibly have that you want?" She flipped her attention back to Aeyun, who didn't bother to smother his grimace, the one that revealed his itch to be anywhere else. "And you want to tell me about whatever happened in that crypt the Reaping Hands have down there?"

"No, Sakaeri!" Aeyun said, exasperated. "I don't, and we don't have to. It has nothing to do with you. I don't know why you're still even here. If you could kindly go the fuck away, that would be great."

"I am not leaving until we track down Rae," Sakaeri said through gnashed teeth. It made Aeyun's hair stand on end for more than a few reasons.

"I would appreciate it if you didn't talk about her like you own her. Like you can actually help. You're a danger to yourself and everyone around you."

"I'm not ta – oh. Oh, that's rich. Are you that petty? We are looking for Rae, Aeyun, who is currently missing and gone to who-knows-where with your brother. Remember your brother? Get over it and start thinking about the bigger picture. We need to find her."

"You keep saying *we*, Sakaeri! There isn't a we. I will find her – *them*. Both of them, without you. I don't owe you–" Aeyun paused. Somewhere, in the swirl of emotions, he did feel like he owed her something.

"You owe me *everything*. You owe me everything, you *bastard*," Sakaeri said, low. Lethal. "What? What is it? What was so important here that it took precedence over finding Rae?"

Aeyun should have anticipated it, but he hadn't. It all happened in a split second: Sakaeri tossing out and recalling a dagger that cut Aeyun's satchel away from his waist, the bag ripping open and its contents spilling on the floor. The amber alicant tumbling across the tile, as if spiteful of its cage.

As it clattered, Aeyun couldn't tear his eyes away. He was once again struck with that notion of distant familiarity. It called to him. Registering movement in slow motion, Aeyun watched as Sakaeri started reaching for it, determined. Doused in a discombobulating fog, his senses dulled, he heard garbled warning calls from both Davah and Saoiri echoing.

The distance between Sakaeri's fingertips and the unbelonging alicant on the floor lessened. In a terrifying vision, he saw Sakaeri get stabbed through with Davah and Saoiri falling victim behind her. He saw the look of betrayal on her face, her fingers clawing at the wound. He saw Davah spitting blood, holding Saoiri's shaking hand as she took one final, pained gasp of air into her lungs.

Imagining it was all it took, and in one swift motion he threw his glove off to the side and lunged for the amber mass.

Sakaeri barely touched it, the tiniest of nudges, and the alicant was springing blackened thorns, vicious spines shooting out to pierce her. As one managed to puncture her hand, Aeyun's palm fell over the coiled origin. He winced on impact, but the thorns receded, leaving only smooth amber in their place.

91

Sakaeri took a moment, brows furrowing. "*What* is that?"

She cradled her wounded hand, her gaze flitting between Aeyun and where he had the alicant pinned to the floor. Blood rushed behind Aeyun's ears.

"You touched it," said Davah.

Somehow, Davah ended up on the ground beside Sakaeri. Was he trying to pull her away from the alicant? Standing behind him, Saoiri was staring down at the scene, seemingly frozen. Her focus hadn't shifted from Aeyun's caging grasp upon the day's spoils.

"I don't understand how – it's not related to descanting somehow, is it?" she asked.

The question went ignored as Aeyun swept the alicant up from the floor and gazed at it. So, it *was* a seed. It was a seed, and it didn't belong in these realms. It . . . never belonged. But it was here.

The room blurred around him, and he couldn't hear the three of them past the interference in his own mind. It was proof. And it had been in the realms for *centuries*.

"This doesn't belong here," Aeyun muttered under his breath, not realising he'd spoken aloud.

The three around him stopped their chatter in observation. Sakaeri crawled forward, curious.

"What does it – centuries." Aeyun gave a dry laugh. "Fuck."

The sentiment was a broken one, and he felt tears well up. Because it wasn't two realities, it was a single fractured one, and now he knew. Now, he felt he could be sure of that.

"Aeyun?" Saoiri's softened tone brought him back to the present.

Aeyun blinked and looked between their concerned faces.

"Don't–" he started, then noticed how off his voice sounded. Clearing his throat, he began again. "Don't ever touch this."

"What is it?" Sakaeri asked, but it was quiet. Careful.

"A seed," Aeyun spoke without thought. When process caught up to him, he inwardly cursed. "It's an alicant. Don't touch it."

"You've said that," Sakaeri chastised.

"But how can you touch it when it does that? Is it like the other ones?"

Aeyun inwardly cursed again, this time at Davah.

"Other ones? Are you collecting these weird *seeds*?" Sakaeri asked.

Aeyun glared at Davah, who curled in on himself, his shoulders dropping guiltily. Aeyun should really have words with him about blurting out unfiltered thoughts.

"Is this why you left?" Sakaeri continued. Then there was a pregnant pause. When Aeyun dared look at Sakaeri, what he found was unsettling. "You left for power?"

"What?" was his immediate response, because *no* he did not leave for power. "No," he reiterated aloud. "No, I didn't leave for power, Sakaeri."

"I mean, Yun, it looks like it! Do you even understand what you did? How you left it? And for what, some weird fantasy of glory?"

"I understand," Aeyun gritted out.

He did. He did understand, and his sudden departure loomed behind him like some ghastly cloud. The culpability of it all was *crushing*. He'd managed it again, his aptitude for desertion astounding. But they would have tried to help.

Raeyu, Uruji . . . Jourae.

He didn't want his presence, his very existence, to be their demise.

"If I had realised what Seraeyu would do, I–"

"Would have stayed?" she asked mockingly. "Would you have? Because this seems like you have your own agenda. Do you actually care, Aeyun?"

"Of course I do."

"I wish you'd never shown up, Aeyun. I wish you were never there to cause all that trouble from the start."

Something about her words cut deep and jagged. Just as the guilt burrowed deeper, Aeyun felt a sharp pain in his left hand, and then he saw crimson bead from a fresh slice, pooling in the carved paths of his palm. Startled, he watched it collect, transfixed. It had been his left hand that slammed down on the thorns, but those wounds were stitched together when he drew back the seed's tune, so this new cut was unrelated. It was his left hand, the hand –

The hand that Raeyu still had. And this cut wasn't Aeyun's.

Alive. Living, feeling.

His eyes stung. Too suddenly, he curled his fingers inwards, ignoring the bite of jolting feedback his body gave him, hiding the bloody gash there.

"Is that–?"

"Stop, Sakaeri," Aeyun managed to say, the words shattered in their delivery. "Please."

He stood, seed in one hand and wound in the other. Silently, he began the trek towards one of the bedrooms.

"Aeyun," Saoiri tried, but her call was met with the click of the bedroom door closing.

Alone, Aeyun sat on the bed closest to the window. He blankly watched the pelting rain paint a feathered landscape. It thrummed against the glass panel, blurring the lights beyond, but his vision would have been clouded anyway. It didn't matter. He didn't . . . *. I'm not . . .*

"I'm sorry," he said. "I'm sorry, I'm sorry. I'm sorry."

The alicant fell on the blanket, and blood smeared on his cheek as he sobbed into his hand, recounting his remorse in broken fragments.

Aeyun felt something warm on his face and he leant into it. What had he been doing? Someone was saying something to him; a soft murmur. He put his hand over the one on his cheek and his brows knit together. Why did he feel so uneasy, and why was the hand all wrong?

Regardless, he felt the need to say, "I'm sorry."

"Aeyun?"

The voice made him alert at once and Aeyun shifted up and away from the gentle touch. He found himself staring wide-eyed at Saoiri. She had a wet cloth in one hand, the other one braced on the edge of the bed. Aeyun blinked a few times, willing himself back to the present. He must have fallen asleep.

Panic overtook him momentarily, thinking back to the seed he'd dropped, but he found it safely isolated on the bedside table. He was grateful he'd had the wherewithal to move it before he passed out. At least he'd done that much.

"Sorry," Aeyun said again, still lost in a half-awake, bewildered state.

"You, um, said that," Saoiri told him, seemingly confused herself. "You have blood on your face."

"No – not sorry for, I mean–" Aeyun took a second for his mind to recalibrate. "Is Sakaeri still here?" he decided to ask.

Saoiri didn't look particularly pleased at his line of questioning, but she nodded anyway. "Drinking whatever the hotel will give her, yep." She indicated for him to get closer. "Can you come here so I can get the rest of that off your face?"

Aeyun instinctively batted at his cheek. When he did, he spotted the crusted slice on his palm, and . . . right.

Raeyu.

"I'll do it, thanks."

Saoiri passed over the damp terrycloth. He swiped at his skin, grimacing when he could feel the dried blood flake off.

"Aeyun, we'll find your brother. Don't let her discourage you," Saoiri said in what was probably meant to be reassurance, but it had Aeyun reeling.

He did want to find Uruji, very much so, but that hadn't been where his head was, and he felt dreadful for that. He really couldn't do right by his brother, could he? Uruji was probably suffering after his getaway stunt, and here Aeyun was, feeling sorry for himself. Not sparing a thought towards him and his pain and his grief.

Instead of acknowledging his worries, he said, "Thanks, Saoiri. I really didn't mean to drag you two into this."

"We want to help, Aeyun," Saoiri said softly. Further muted, she added, "*I* want to help."

Aeyun quieted. A discomfort that he'd yet to name arose from the given platitude. Suddenly, himself alone beside Saoiri felt less welcoming. More damning, perhaps, than it should.

Scrubbing roughly at his face, he tossed the towel to the side and got up.

"I appreciate it," he said, polite, then strode towards the bedroom's entrance. "Thanks for waking me up, too."

Aeyun opened the door to find a sight in the kitchen that he wished was an illusion.

There, Davah was downing what was certainly not his first drink, and Sakaeri was next to him, glowering at an empty bottle. She looked up at his entrance, expression muddled behind a layer of boozy recognition.

"You look like shit," she told him, slurred.

Aeyun breathed in deeply, readying himself, still feeling the dregs of sleep trying to drag him back to the comfort of his abandoned mattress. And yet, he crossed the rest of the room. When he reached them, he moved the remainder of the bottles well out of reach.

Sakaeri cackled and said, "Yun, you look so puffy when you cry."

"You shouldn't drink like this," Aeyun told her as she reached for a glass that was no longer on the counter. "Neither should you," he mentioned offhandedly in Davah's direction, to which he got a noncommittal grunt in response.

"Let me forget, *bastard*," Sakaeri said in what was probably supposed to be a hiss, but it came out more like babble. "Let me – look, sorry. Sorry, I know you care." She looked at him, a little unfocused. "I know you do. I know you care."

Aeyun couldn't really think of a response, so he said, "Good."

Davah muttered something and slipped off his chair, stumbling to the second bedroom with words like *fine now* and *finally sleep* wafting from his retreating form. A smirk pulled at the corner of Aeyun's mouth. Davah was more considerate than he let on.

Sakaeri groaned in drunken discontent and folded over, half across the counter. Sighing, Aeyun rounded the corner and scooped her up in his arms, finding her uncharacteristically amenable to his efforts.

"I know you care," she said, drawing out the last word. "I can't help but hate you, but I know you care." Sakaeri clawed her fingers into the collar of his shirt and opened her eyes in alarming coherence, making Aeyun look down at her in apprehension. "I know you care, dammit!" She violently tugged at the material and then frowned. "So why are you such an idiot?"

It wasn't often that Sakaeri gave him reason to laugh, and he wanted to be annoyed, but Aeyun couldn't help the strange puff – the oddly strained chuckle – that escaped him. It was mainly due to her petulant look. It almost made him imagine a past where she hadn't been out to put him in an early grave, and instead they'd interacted like regular children, two people drawn into Raeyu's embrace. Two people blessed by the same precious presence in their lives.

"Why am I?" he asked rhetorically.

Saoiri was in the living area, halfway to the second bedroom. She watched them with a peculiar expression. Aeyun tried to smile at her. He wasn't sure if he succeeded.

"Two idiots," Sakaeri muttered, eyes half closed. "You and Rae, both." Her head dropped to the side, huffing with a bitter smile. "Three idiots. You, Rae, me . . . four idiots. You, Rae, me, Uruji . . . five idiots, you–"

"I get it, Sakaeri," Aeyun grumbled. "Thanks."

He adjusted her weight in his arms, making a face when he felt the bulk of hidden sharp implements distributed across her form, all poking in odd directions beneath the rough exterior of her cloak. Even inebriated, she still had those close at hand.

Stars above, you're a stubborn menace.

"Will you be okay?" Saoiri asked.

Aeyun slowed as he came back towards the room he'd only recently awoken in. He considered his predicament. Did he trust Sakaeri? No. Did he trust that she would fight endlessly to keep Raeyu alive? Yes. And that was enough.

"It's fine," said Aeyun.

The look Saoiri gave him told him that she didn't agree.

"You know who the biggest idiot is?" Sakaeri asked, lost in her own musings. "Seraeyu."

His name was said like a breathless prayer, a morose hymnal utterance, and a tremor in Aeyun's arms gave away Sakaeri's unrest as she turned inwards. He felt something in his soulsong stir, a sort of weeping outreach, trying to cast out to leagues unknown.

"Rae loves him so much," she said. "She loves him so much, why would he have done that?" The room felt oddly stilted as Sakaeri added, "He ripped off her arm without hesitation. He *ripped off* Raeyu's arm." She hiccupped and inhaled, and it sounded . . . *so damned sad.* "And I couldn't – I didn't do anything. And he – and he . . ."

Saoiri glanced between the two of them with consternation. With one last look, she began backing away, towards the room that Davah had entered. Aeyun gazed up at the ceiling and away from the fractured woman he carried. The one who oftentimes seemed detached, fighting against herself to smother her emotional impulses. Not now, though. Certainly not as what he wouldn't dare define as a whimper escaped her.

"You found me," said Aeyun. He barely caught the perplexed scrunch of Saoiri's features as she turned the door's knob.

"Wouldn't they be proud?" Sakaeri said softly, forcing a wet laugh.

Aeyun found it within himself to murmur back, "Yeah, I think so."

The sound of two doors softly clicking closed left the suite in silence.

Aeyun couldn't sleep.

He sat before the window in the living area, hunched in the lowlight of Bhu-Nan's glowing evening feedback, dampened by the rain. He rolled the alicant seed in his fingers. He hadn't seen one since he was a child, since *before*. Before Jourae and the Thasian-nee. Before Uruji and Aeyun's place in his and his father's household. Before Haebal and Raenaru. Before Raeyu found him, back when he wasn't Aeyun, but A'vor.

Ca'lud A'vor da'Ca'ille a'Ca'lorus.

It was hard to remember all the details of his birthrealm as he'd aged. The daily sights that used to fill his youth – iridescent pastels streaked across the sky, overgrown foliage clinging to stone, rot mixed with growth – the dewy musk of the forest he'd been surrounded by, and the life that he'd had.

His mother and father, he did remember them. At least, he remembered how they'd died. He remembered running, too. Following the river to the craggy hills, like his mother had told him to do. Getting closer to The Veil, that great, reflective barrier that bound all of Ca'lorus. And he remembered Da'garu.

Da'garu, the sister he'd failed to protect.

Da'garu, the helpless child he'd left alone, dooming her.

It was unlikely, but a part of him couldn't relinquish the hope that she'd survived. Wishing against all reason, he'd always maintained hope that the odd sage who lived in the even more odd and derelict a'teneum, full of books and tomes and manuscripts, found her. Saved her. Kept her safe, surrounded by the hallowed grounds that no one else seemed to be able to find.

Gama-of-Yun, he was called.

Surely, it wasn't coincidence. He never swore, pledged, or prayed to the Yun. Why would he when he'd met one, and he too was only mortal flesh and bone?

He stared at the seed that was undoubtedly from Ca'lorus.

It was something that he had not had much experience with personally, as he'd been so young, but he'd seen his father use it. His father had resonated with it, embedding it on a glove for simplicity's sake, usually employing it for agriculture. Tilling, like when it was time to rotate the crops.

It was an odd alicant – a word he'd not encountered until away from Ca'lorus. Like most attunement with the natural realm, it was cyclical and flowing; a symbiosis. The seed would attach to the host, both drawing and giving energy. It would also store potential energy, gathered from resources that it had pierced itself. An aggregator, of sorts.

The main issue was keeping the balance right. Too much energy and the tune was out of sync, harming the tuner or expelling the extrapolated power in a chaotic way. Trying to tune without the proper resonation, unbalanced and inharmonious, would also lead to the seed's destructive behaviour; hence its untouchable nature to those who didn't understand it.

Aeyun, though . . . He did understand it. He was of Ca'lorus, as was the seed. That gave him an advantage, having been a part of the same bed of life for some years. Just as Aeyun was not meant to be part of the realms, this seed was the same. From somewhere unknown, unheard of, and unmentioned.

So, why was it here?

"Should I consider you a friend?" Aeyun asked the alicant.

It said nothing back, of course, but Aeyun reached out to it, a disembodied thread of understanding. A small inky vine of thorns twisted from the amber, slow and disengaged, and then it serenely wrapped around his right thumb, points digging in but not unbearably so.

Aeyun watched it with interest. There was a shift inside him that felt like an acknowledgement – some foregone state – that he was returning to.

"Are you lost as well?" he asked, quieter.

In the stillness, Aeyun wondered if Raeyu would feel it, these little pinpricks on the hand she'd lost. Aeyun hoped not, since he might yet find use for the seed, and he didn't want her to suffer any blowback. He didn't wish her any further pain.

Aeyun let go of the seed and let it coil little thorned vines around his hand as it pleased, almost feeling the sigh of relief the strange, out-of-place alicant seemed to breathe.

"You can stay there for now," he told it.

The sense of something aligning was prominent throughout his body and Aeyun breathed in deeply, changing focus from the amber seed to the city draped in night-time darkness outside. Hyperaware of his attunement, Aeyun revelled in the moment of respite.

But it was short-lived. He felt the seed's inherent song converge against something else, something tied to his very core. An unyielding tether.

For that fleeting second, Aeyun could have sworn he saw the realm through another's eyes.

He could swear that spirits roamed the halls. He felt it, deep under his skin, like something was creeping just beneath the tiles, or pacing beyond a picture-laden wall. It was that type of eerie tell that made hair stand on end; a sudden awareness of one's own shadow and the shudder in what should be still breath.

He felt it, that buzz and tingle. That push and pull.

An aborted laugh sounded from around the bend, followed by the familiar trill of his sister's carefree giggle. Something in him squirmed against his ribcage and thrummed, its echo prompting an acerbic plummet. He decided he'd been haunted enough that day, and instead turned heel and stalked in the opposite direction.

CHAPTER TEN

Seraeyu never liked when things were too quiet. It made him overthink things, question his choices. As if he ever had any worthwhile ones to make. He never liked having the opportunity to get too into his head about the realms and what it all meant. That's why he tried to keep a constant buzz around him. Music, chatter, the numbing murmurs of something in his system. Whatever it might take to not leave him alone in the darkness of his own mind, wallowing in self-loathing.

When he awoke this time, it was silent.

There were no echoes in the halls, no birds chirping beyond the window. Just quiet.

His bones ached and his muscles groaned in protest as he sat up, finding himself back under that damned velvet canopy once more. The sight didn't faze him like it did the first time, but it did worry him. Seraeyu suspected that whatever had happened down in the catacombs was connected to the state things were in now. He knew that he had initiated *something* when he'd touched that profane alicant. He could only hope that the results weren't as cataclysmic as his gut told him they had to be.

Seraeyu was back in normal clothes again, looking like he had very earnest intent to laze about for the day. It was odd, looking at oneself and not recalling how memory one led to memory two. Like an entire fragment of recollection was just gone, disintegrated.

He sat up from the bed, finding Oagyu's room in the same dire state before. With effort, he stumbled to the en suite. Why was he so tired?

His body was sluggish, as was his brain, and it took him a moment to recognise himself in the mirror's reflection. There were deep circles under his eyes, and there was a new scratch on his neck, flanked by two identical scrapes running parallel to it. And wasn't that strange? It almost looked like claw marks.

Curious about the pain he'd felt on the roof, Seraeyu carefully pulled up his shirt, slipping it over his head and off his shoulders. There, angry and swirled, a black mark was punctured into his chest above his heart. An inky brand of some kind. Breath left Seraeyu's lungs as his gaze pierced into it.

What in the starry void is that?

He hovered his hand over the ugly, festered stain, but instinct urged him to not touch. Instead, he looked up at his reflection and searched his face.

Where he was usually met with youthful features, he found his colouring dull, and the skin of his lips chapped. He didn't look healthy, and he didn't feel it either. Whatever was going on, his body wasn't reacting well to it. Leaning closer, his nails tapped on the glassy surface of the mirror, and he noticed browned crust upon them again. Troubled, he ran his hands under the faucet, his worries confirmed when it turned pinkish under the flow, dribbling into the drain.

"What have you been doing, Seraeyu?" he questioned aloud, voice warbling. "Who have you been hurting?" It was a whisper. He didn't think he actually wanted to know.

Seraeyu tugged his shirt back on and looked around his father's room. No revelations came, and the jewellery missing from his mother's box still put him on edge. Numbness permeated his thoughts, seeping into desolate corners.

"Okay," he said.

A few long strides brought him to the door, and he turned the handle. Or, he *tried* to turn the handle, because it didn't budge.

"No." Seraeyu jiggled at it more. "No, no, no. What is this?"

No amount of yanking gave way, and Seraeyu began to feel despair set in. Had someone locked him in? Were they drugging him? He didn't feel drugged, but something was wrong.

"Hey!" he shouted, pounding on the door. "Hey!"

"*Stop that.*"

Seraeyu's chest clenched painfully before all went dark.

It was as though the realm warped into place around him and Seraeyu came to with a gasp. The moment provided enough time for someone to shove against him, causing his body to thud to the ground. He grunted out in pain as he hit slippery stone, his elbow scraping upon it, and he coughed against the air that pressed to refill his lungs.

"You daemon!" someone yelled.

Seraeyu struggled to get upright, coaxing his eyes open. They were bleary so he rubbed at one. Was that blood from his face, or was it already there? Looking up, despite the voice in his head that cried out don't – *don't!* – he spotted a terrified-looking Yu-ta man chained to a column. The presumed prisoner was ghastly pale, skin chafed by rusted shackles. His eyes, piercing, held only rigid hate.

What is . . . What? Who is this? Am I in the cistern?

A quick glance around and the musty stagnation in the air told him that yes, indeed it was. He didn't want to look back at the man – he really, *really* didn't. But the realms, ever against Seraeyu, forced his hand when the chained-up Yu-ta growled low and spat a glob of pink-tinged saliva right onto Seraeyu's cheek.

"You foul monster! I hope the Yun banish you! I hope you're ripped apart by the Great Starry Sea itself!"

Seraeyu struggled to stand and nearly tripped on his silken robes. The bottom of them was stained with muck and red. Morbidly, he wondered if it was from the man, who appeared to be bleeding from two large claw-like marks below his collarbones. Stricken with something terrifying, Seraeyu looked down at his own hands, stained with crimson.

Oh. Oh no.

"Please, wait," Seraeyu urged, but the man flinched and spat at him again. "Wait, I don't understand."

"Daemon! You're a vile daemon!"

"Please, I don't understa–"

"I hope you crystallise in the frozen reaches of the void!"

Seraeyu's breath came in ragged spurts, the realm feeling shaken and upside down. Slowly, he backed away from the man spouting profanities at him, cursing him to death in progressively more horrid circumstances. His feet didn't stop moving until he hit the wall, and his head twisted to the side to see the gate beside him, left gaping.

No Sentinels, just an open gate, Seraeyu covered in bloody robes, and a chained Yu-ta man with wounds by his neck.

Seraeyu spun on his heel and ran from the man who cursed him. He tore into the catacombs and kept going. Dim-lit ore lined the path now, and some of the barriers had been removed, opening previously barricaded entrances. Seraeyu ignored them, though. Instead, he ran towards that room that he knew had started this. The last one he remembered standing in.

A stench permeated the air and dread filtered into his veins. Rotten and pungent, the smell worsened as he progressed, and it had him gagging, holding the crook of his elbow to his mouth and nose. When he curved around the last bend, he faltered and stopped. He could see it from where he stood: a pile of corpses that had been stacked carelessly, each sporting a pair of horns, all decomposing. Another gag clenched his throat and this time he turned to the side to retch, tears filling his eyes.

"No," he whimpered.

No, no, this has to be a nightmare.

He knew it wasn't. He also knew – something deep in the recesses of his mind telling him so – that this was *his* doing. That those lives were stolen by *him*. *His* actions.

Seraeyu retched again and fell to his knees with a silent wail. He couldn't look at it; at them. What had he done? What had he done? What had he *done?*

He crawled back around the bend and heaved air, his body trying to expel contents it didn't have. Another sob wracked him, and he collapsed further. Rolling onto his back, the slime of the tiles seeped into his silken robes. Lying there, he could still hear the screams of the Yu-ta man down the corridor. It was as if the realm had paused, the only things existing being himself, the anguished cries beyond, and the heap of the departed around the corner.

"I can't do this." Seraeyu didn't know the extent to which things had fallen into disarray, but if this much was real, the rest must have been . . .

Seraeyu raised his bloodied hand in the air and stared at it, his gaze hard and resolute.

"I can't do this," he said again. He held his breath and poised his sharp – so very, very sharp–

Seraeyu awoke and it was quiet once more. This time, he didn't bother moving. He just stared up at the velvet canopy, taking in a regretful gulp of air. A wet trail rolled down the side of his face, dripping uncomfortably into his ear and leaving a damp residue in its wake, but he didn't care.

"Why?" he asked the silence. "Why is this happening? What did I do?"

He took in a shuddering breath. It was devastatingly quiet around him. Deafeningly so.

"It was me, right? I did this? It was my fault?"

Nothing answered him, and reality felt fuzzy. Seraeyu closed his eyes and tried to focus on small things. The sound of puffed air leaving his nose, the stretch of his arm across the sheets, the rise and fall of his chest. His beating heart. He didn't know how long he stayed that way, trance-like, but slowly it was as if he was aware of more within himself.

There was a flow that he'd not felt previously, as if something were unlocked and open.

Something was *free*.

But something was also missing. There was a part of him that had been there for so long – longer than he could recount – and it wasn't there now. The juxtaposition confused him, because he'd never felt so whole, buzzing with energy like he was, not in his recollected life. But something also felt irreplaceably gone, as though a part of him had wandered off. Just vanished.

He tried to remember what it was. The piece that was gone. Did it even matter?

Seraeyu opened his eyes and forced himself up. He didn't bother to step around the debris this time, not having the mental acuity to care when his foot knocked something out of the way. Instead of heading for the en suite or the door, he wandered to the closet and stepped in. Clothes were strewn around, just like everything else was in Oagyu's room. Seraeyu knelt down and picked up one of his father's robes, much too large for himself. He held it in his hands, so tight that his knuckles whitened, and then he pulled it close.

Oagyu's cologne still clung to it, something musky and woodsy, and Seraeyu bit back a morose quiver of his lips. A melancholy swathed him, seeping in like poison. It filtered through his bloodstream, collecting in his chest with an unrelenting, choking squeeze.

Where was his father? Taken? Tortured? Killed?

. . . Piled with the rest of them?

After long moments with his face shoved into his father's ceremonial robe, he gently set it down, as if it had a place of organisation with the rest of the clothes scattered there. He slunk forward, towards the chest in the back. The one that held his mother's garments.

Gingerly, he pried the trunk open, and plucked out one of her elegant longline jackets. It was a billowy, charcoal-hued, and graceful garment that looked like it belonged on models from Cheyun. He was told that she was something of an icon, and he believed it. With soft motions, he slid one arm through a wide sleeve, then followed with the other, flipping the hardy tweed material around him so that it draped down and pooled where he knelt.

Still for only a moment, he twisted around and sat with his back to the trunk and the remainder of luxurious fabrics within it, all fabulously storied with tales he'd never heard.

Reaching as if anything sudden would bring the realm crashing down, Seraeyu pulled at his father's ceremonial robe and laid it across his legs, creating a barrier between himself and . . . everything. He let his head drop back against the coffered wardrobe and his fingers came to rest on his face, his shoulders shaking with each tremor that wracked through him.

In that confinement, silence reigned.

"There are stories . . ."

It was a gruff voice that didn't match the gentle tone, or the softness with which he found himself being patched back together. Burnt skin, tarnished from the smelter, screamed when a cold jelly came into contact with it.

"About days long passed, and then even further before then."

He wrinkled his nose in distaste at the grating prickle that bit through his forearm. It had been a stupid slip of his wrist, just enough for consequences. Instead, he focused on the broad shoulders in front of him, the ones that carried so much weight and never seemed to falter. He focused on them because he couldn't bear to look up and meet eyes that saw right through him.

"About realms and raging storms. Stars and oceans. About feats both great and fearsome." A beat passed. "Perhaps you think me a fool, and that's why you leave yourself wounded. Perhaps I'm the fool, for suggesting you do otherwise. Flagrancy never rewarded anyone."

CHAPTER ELEVEN

"I don't care where. Let's go," said Aeyun.

He'd already gathered rations for a short journey in the early morning hours, back when the sun was only just beginning to bleed past the obscured horizon, when the rest of them were asleep.

Davah rubbed his eyes with a yawn. "Did something happen?"

Beside him, Saoiri's subtle shift of her foot had her falling into an unintentional posture to stand at attention. On the other side of the room, Sakaeri was leant against a wall, looking like death incarnate. Despite her unenviable state, she also quirked a brow, intrigued.

"I just need to see something."

"I suppose we could head back to Mhedoon for a bit," Davah reasoned, then he glanced at Sakaeri. "Uh . . ."

"I'm not disappearing anytime soon," she said tiredly.

"Okay, okay. Fair enough. Just don't cause trouble," said Davah. "We've had enough of it."

"Sakaeri," Saoiri started, hesitant, but fists clenched with a resolute bravado that Aeyun had to smile at. She was getting braver, more stalwart. "We need your word that no harm will come to anyone when we reach Kilrona."

"I have one goal right now," Sakaeri told her, sounding entirely dispassionate as she pressed against her temple, willing her hangover away. "And I can promise you that it has nothing to do with harming the people of Kilrona."

Saoiri gave her a wary onceover. Another pass and it was followed by a nod.

It didn't take too long for them to grab what they had and find their way back to the sea-skimmer. Mid-morning saw them departing the port, setting a course on the magnavaid for the Great Sea Gate. Huddled in the hull, the four of them sat in disharmony, wrapped in blankets to combat the open ocean's chill.

Aeyun covered his right hand with a glove again, hiding the little bruises left behind from the seed. His sleeves did the work of covering his tuned scar for him. As a precaution, before they'd left Bhu-Nan, he'd made sure to tune another stitch to repair its function. It had been getting stiff again, and he didn't want to be caught out with the dead weight of a useless limb.

Sakaeri broke the quiet. "Does this have to do with it?"

Aeyun looked up from where he had been testing the mobility

of his rigid joints. She hadn't specified, but she didn't have to. Aeyun caught the purposeful placement of her hand over her chest. Her heart. Her attention was similarly placed on his sternum before it flickered up to catch his eye.

Aeyun was weary. Maybe saying something would be okay, just this once. Sakaeri knew of his bound nature, he reasoned. And he remembered how she'd looked at him, back between the hammocks, when they'd portalled from one realm to the next. She suspected already.

He simply responded, "Yes."

Contemplative, Sakaeri acknowledged him with a hum.

"Do you see it, too?" he asked.

There was a lull after his question. Aeyun went back to flexing his fingers, attention having strayed from Sakaeri's face.

Perhaps as a courtesy to his previous easy answer, she finally said, "Yes."

"You know," Davah piped up from his side of the table. "I can respect that you two have been through a lot. I can. And it *is* a lot, I'm sure. But you can't just keep talking in riddles around us. It's a bit unfair, considering how we're wrapped up in this now, too."

Aeyun, at a loss of what to say, provided nothing.

Sakaeri, however, did. "There's a moment, during a gate jump, where everything and nothing collides. It's *boggling*, and difficult to describe, but it's like seeing the convergence. The manifestation of the realms' connectedness. Like the wild Essence of everything, and the existence of nothing between it. I . . . I see it. And I guess Aeyun does, too. I hadn't realised it wasn't just me. There are other unseen things there, and Aeyun–"

She stalled, shifting a glance towards Aeyun.

"I have a theory I want to test," said Aeyun. "I want to see if I can attune to something in that liminal space."

"Do you really think that's possible?" Sakaeri uttered, almost reverent, and Aeyun shrugged.

"We haven't–" Saoiri paused. Aeyun could see the cogs turn

111

in her head as she considered her next words. "We haven't asked out of respect, but even Kaisa seemed to have figured it out. Who was your father?"

The dour atmosphere dampened further, the air becoming bloated with apprehension. Sakaeri and Aeyun's eyes connected across the hull. He saw a myriad reasons to not convey this, to not give their death-marked secret away. But then he also saw the truth and its virtues weighed between their stare; an understanding that sometimes it just couldn't be done alone.

A silent debate finally met agreement, sealed with a gentle nod.

"Jourae Thasian-nee," said Aeyun.

Davah's disbelieving laugh broke the lingering tension. "Thasian-nee? Your father was the personal tunesmith to the Thasian Praetor? So, you weren't a fan or a copy-cat, but the real deal. That's why your works look like that." Davah shook his head, looking beside himself. "Friend, I couldn't wrap my head around that even being a possibility."

Saoiri gave a quiet *um* before following it up with, "Your brother is Uruji Thasian-nee? You're both from the second house of Thasian? But he's an only child."

"He's not," Sakaeri commented, wrapping herself tighter in her blanket.

"He's not," Aeyun echoed.

Davah gave a quiet *uh-huh* before continuing, "So, we . . . are looking for Raeyu Thasian and Uruji Thasian-nee, both of whom are believed to be dead by the realms and wanted dead by the gone-mad Seraeyu Thasian, current head and new Praetor of the Thasian Legacy, as far as the realms are concerned?" He got two solemn nods in response. "And I guess you two became so intertwined with Raeyu Thasian through your father, then?"

"No," both of them responded, an automatic compulsion. It made Sakaeri perk up in interest.

"No?" she directed at Aeyun.

He hesitated, a million scenarios running through his mind. Then he considered what kind of future was beginning to take shape. Denial was a convenience for which he no longer had leeway. Begrudgingly, Aeyun acknowledged how truly in over his head he was. That Jourae wasn't around to try and protect him anymore. Nor was he around to protect Uruji. No one was, except for a one-armed, bloodsong-less Raeyu.

That truth crawled into the tendons of his neck, a chill slithering down his spine. Haebal, the only home he'd known, was in ruins. And he'd been the actual catalyst, hadn't he? And Aeyun was exhausted. Aeyun wanted to curl up by a winter night's fire and sip on aromatic tea, a ritual shared with his brother. He wanted to listen to one of Jourae's beloved poems or finger-plucked melodies, notes melding keenly with the warmth of the hearth's blaze. He just wanted a quiet moment, shared in peaceful contentment.

"No," said Aeyun.

A strange sense of relief washed over him. Like a replenishing aura, it brought him back to the attunement he had achieved with the seed the previous night, and how it felt like something had stirred inside him, reawakened. A sense of *who* he hadn't realised he'd been lacking, or even seeking. A piece of him, recovered.

Jourae Thasian-nee was not his first encounter on this path, but rather a fortuitous collision. And Aeyun was forever grateful for that. His relationship with his father was a beacon in endless dark.

Aeyun tried not to think of what a return to those ceaseless, despairing depths would feel like. Will feel like. *Does feel like.*

"So, it's more complicated than that?" Davah asked. "Of course it is."

The absurdity of it dawned on Aeyun, forcing a sort of manic, miserable laugh. "More than it should be."

The sea-skimmer finally began encroaching upon the Great Sea Gate, long after another pensive bout of silence had fallen. Aeyun could feel anxious eyes resting upon him.

"Is it dangerous, what you'll be doing?" Saoiri asked softly.

Aeyun truthfully responded that he wasn't sure.

113

Both Aeyun and Sakaeri pulled their hoods over their heads for the gatekeeper's check, letting Saoiri and Davah handle the logistics. It went smoothly enough, only involving a brief exchange at the gatekeeper's entry, and then they found themselves drifting into the belly of the terminal. Reverberation bounced around them, floating little spheres of ocean, like it always did. In preparation, Aeyun stood in the middle of the hull, his seat abandoned.

The pulse of the realm was doubled in weight by the heavy stares of his companions, and it wedged into his chest with an erratic rhythm. He needed calm. He needed serenity, harmony. He breathed – *in . . . out; in . . . out* – and closed his eyes. The right moment approached with an inhale, and it washed over his soulsong like a dousing of starlit water.

As it always did, reality began to unravel around him.

Aeyun did not often reach out to the vast unknown. What he attuned to, he knew as Vitality; a complementary antithesis to the volatile Essence the Thasian line had favoured. He knew, though, that harmonising the two was possible. Uruji was capable of it to a degree, as history had shown.

Despite the many things Aeyun had taught Uruji in their years of adolescence, Uruji had returned several lessons in kind, the most memorable and recurring of which was humility. It was a trait that Aeyun had observed in his brother time and time again, watching as curious eyes turned sagely, restless demeanour evaporating, instead blooming into a composed shroud of clever wisdom.

Aeyun opened his eyes, extending his tune and trying to slow the transition from one gate to the next. One of the first things he noticed was Sakaeri's glowing, cat-like gaze upon him, fully cognisant, floating in a blurred doppelganger that stood next to mere shadowy implications of their two Mhedoonian companions. The next thing Aeyun saw was the jagged burns of wild energy around his right arm, softened and soothed by the Vitality of his attunement. The thread that always pulled from his chest was present, as if eternal, flowing in what seemed like every direction and none at all.

Aeyun moved to put his hand over its origin, and the stuttered impression of motion made nausea set in. Once he'd placed his palm down, he tried to feel Ca'lorus; that innate vestige of a song that had been sung within the seed.

The next moments felt like a millennium and the shortest of seconds, colliding. Essence flowed around him, and there was a distinct push and pull that felt at once new. In that space, the tether from his chest became all-encompassing, all he could comprehend. Then came the manifestation that consumed him, bright and deafening.

It was like a silhouette, filled out with colours and sensations that Aeyun could read as distinctly Raeyu. The void around him became less vacuous, and he accepted a notion of groundedness that had no place in an endless backdrop of twinkling, elusive ebony. As the imagery became clearer, revealing a Yu-ta woman – horned, worn, and armless – the feeling of pure connectedness abounded.

Every part of Aeyun's being screamed out, a muted cry in the vastness.

"*Aeyun?*" echoed around him, within him, and everywhere, the two syllables soul-wrenching and melancholic. A rhapsody as much as they were a requiem.

Then it all dropped away.

"Oh, Yun!" was the first thing he heard in his dizzying re-emergence into the present.

Aeyun swayed, stumbling on what felt like wavy flooring. The nausea he'd felt before bubbled up in full force, and soon he was relieving his stomach of its contents into something that had been thrust before him. Had he fallen over? He was trying to brace himself upon whatever he could gain purchase on. Two pairs of hands steadied him, and his world wavered a little less. He tried to blink back reality, but his reception of it felt all wrong until the fifth or so blink.

"I saw–" Aeyun sputtered, the struggle of it followed by a hacked cough. "I saw her."

"What happened?" Davah asked, clearly unnerved.

For himself and Saoiri, the transition from one gate to the next was instantaneous. What was likely only a fraction of a second, a blip in the continuity of time, took Aeyun from perfectly healthy and steady to suddenly woozy and collapsing. The shift must have been jarring for any outside observer.

"I can't even begin to describe what–" Sakaeri started, looking at Aeyun as though she'd never seen something so baffling in her life.

"Your eyes are attuned to it, did you know? Turns out you can tune with it after all," Aeyun said, but it came out groused. Sakaeri, in turn, continued to stare at him like he'd gone daft.

He didn't know why his throat felt so strained, like he'd been yelling. In front of him, Sakaeri dropped into a chair, its legs scraping across the floor at the sudden pressure.

"And your arm is *not*," she stated. "It is, but it's not. You aren't – you couldn't be, I mean–" Whatever thought had crossed her mind wasn't finished. Instead, she swapped to asking, "That was Raeyu, wasn't it?"

Aeyun regarded her carefully and nodded, but the movement made him haul the bucket close again as he heaved. His stomach, apparently, was not a fan of traversing the in-between. Once satisfied that bile wouldn't dribble from his mouth, Aeyun leant back with a grimace and swiped his arm across his face. *I hope this won't be a regular thing.*

Davah cleared his throat. "Hey, friends, we can continue this conversation on land. Let's pass through the terminal and get to Kilrona."

At his command, Sakaeri shakily dragged Aeyun into the small dormitory, away from curious onlookers. There, Aeyun groaned lightly while his stomach did flips. He didn't even care to posture then; he just wished that the acidic curdle would dissipate.

"You're not part Yun, or something, are you?" Sakaeri asked, all too serious.

The farcical nonsense of *that* notion mixed with the dire revelation of Aeyun's void-faring discovery. He chuckled blithely, feeling delirious.

"No, definitively not."

A dense drowsiness overcame him, dulling and unforgivingly persistent. The realm became a wavy cloud of blanketing noise that he couldn't seem to focus on. The last thing he recognised was Sakaeri's whispered complaint when he unwittingly teetered over, right onto her shoulder.

Sounds of movement caused Aeyun to stir, and he slowly awakened to a soft-lit room. The sighs of the ocean, just beyond the window, lapped softly at cliffs below. Aeyun inhaled with the tide. He forced himself up, recognising the distinctive Mhedoonian carvings around the interior woodwork; beautiful scenes of mythos and lore in workmanship that he envied as an artist himself.

Their etchings represented old deities, forgotten tales of grandeur and lost legends, stunning symbology that drew importance from the realm that was Mhedoon. Covered mostly by ocean, the cities and towns throughout its vast waters were often compact, built upon high cliffs and rocky peaks that were safe from the coastline. Some sparsely funded expeditions had since found underwater ruins, remnants of a time long passed. Nowadays Mhedoon was primarily known for its seemingly endless horizon.

Those less fond of the realm gossiped more about its pirated waters, spreading tales of fearsome, ruthless bands of renegades who would rob one of all they were worth, operating under secretive oaths and a nebulous code that made only a modicum of sense after being passed from one mouth to another too many times. Aeyun couldn't be bothered to listen to their hearsay. Not when those who wagged their chins spent most of their days in literal gilded towers.

Kilrona was a lesser port city, sat in the Bunaragh Ocean, between the Mhedoonian capital of Caiggagh and Mhedoon's second city, Dath. Its structures crawled up the side of a caldera, a long-dormant volcano, and its docks had been carved into the base, which led into a grotto with countless stairs that ascended into the heart of Kilrona. If you were lucky, you'd find some room to stand on the watermill-powered lift; an ingenious innovation that had been installed centuries prior and still worked to this day.

A damp, wet, and rainy realm, the Mhedoonian air was always filled with an inherent, salty mugginess that never seemed to go away. The plus side to all that, Aeyun supposed, was that what vegetation was around was vibrant and lush, and the resourcefulness of the Mhedoons had led to leaps in the development of vertical agriculture, with climbing farms cascading from ledges and outcroppings all around.

Wherever Aeyun was – presumably in some sort of inn or sailor's rest in Kilrona – Sakaeri, Davah, and Saoiri were all sat at a table on the far side of the room. He attempted to clear his throat to draw their attention. The action quickly prompted a rough swallow in the resulting scratchiness.

"Aeyun!" Saoiri exclaimed, looking like she was ready to fling herself across the room to greet him.

"You're awake," said Sakaeri. Something in her tone sounded . . . different.

Davah looked over with a subdued smile. "Good to see you awake, friend."

They're acting weird. Aeyun's brows knit. "How long was I asleep?"

"A few days," Sakaeri supplied.

"Oh."

"Aeyun?" Sakaeri said, again with the odd tone. It held

trepidation wrapped in the bindings of relief, and it curled unsurely in the space between them. Aeyun regarded her curiously. "No, it's nothing."

Aeyun resituated himself to be more comfortable, still feeling a heavy fatigue in his bones. It was as if energy had been sapped out of him, down to his very core, and his body was protesting anything that expended effort. It wasn't unfamiliar, or even unexpected, but it was definitely uncomfortable.

And *stars* was he thirsty.

"I was able to figure something out," said Aeyun.

That didn't prompt as much joy as he'd anticipated. Instead, three pairs of eyes watched him as intensely as they did intently. Nothing in their attention cried out in celebration.

He sighed, unsettled. "I'll start by saying that everything will be even more of a mess from here on out. If you want to step away from it all, now would be a good time."

The first to stand was Sakaeri. She strode across the room, stopping to sit on the edge of the opposite bed. Aeyun blinked at her, and she stared right back, something fierce behind her resolute expression. Next was Davah, who sat beside the Sirin. His own face conveyed a mild interest, as did his roving gaze. With barely a moment's delay, enough to grab a glass of water for her newly reawakened companion, Saoiri followed, seating herself beside Davah. She watched Aeyun, apprehensive, but something soft bled through that edge of the caution.

"Okay," said Aeyun. He quietly gave his thanks for the refreshment, allowing himself a moment to quench his parched throat.

He'd never quite had such readily given allegiance outside of Raeyu or Uruji, one bonded by circumstance, the other by perhaps unfounded admiration. Even so, memories of distinguishing glances and confused grimaces played across his mind. There had been the potential for others, maybe, but those avenues were never explored.

Even still, he wanted to choose his pacing carefully.

119

"I'm fairly certain I know where Rae is, and she must be with Uruji there, too." Aeyun watched their reactions, which were all achingly gloomy. "The bad news is that I don't know of a way to get there. Yet."

"You're not doing that again," Sakaeri said, the clip of it so sudden that Aeyun startled.

"What?"

"I agree with Sakaeri. You shouldn't do that again," Saoiri said, fiddling with loose threads on her sleeve.

"It was pretty scary there for a while, friend."

"What?" Aeyun repeated, because he definitely felt like he was missing something.

"You–" Saoiri started, then took a deep breath. "Your eyes were bleeding, Aeyun. And on top of that, there kept being these weird eruptions of, well, I don't even know what for the first few hours after we got back. It looked like–"

"Like Rae's lightning but pitch black. I think it was from the in-between, like pure energy, Aeyun. Just trying to consume you," Sakaeri finished. The other two agreed.

"Oh," said Aeyun. "Okay. We can try and build it."

It took a while, but eventually Davah said, "Sorry?"

"Ah, *stars above*, Uruji," Aeyun muttered. "That probably happened to him."

"Aeyun, why are you so calm?" Saoiri asked.

Aeyun's mind supplied, *because that happened the last time.*

"We can try and build a gate," Aeyun announced, passively calculating how much ore they had on hand. "It will be more stable than trying to rip a rift out of nothing."

"Aeyun–"

"With the right materials, we might be able to actually do it now, since I've seen it. We might not have enough yet though. So, we have to keep searching."

"Aeyun!"

"And I can modify my designs to account for the right resonance. I think–"

"Aeyun!" Sakaeri shouted, slapping a hand down on his knee.

His ramblings ceased and he followed the trail from her hand to her face, then noted the lost expressions of the other two.

Sakaeri's grip tightened. "What are you talking about?"

"We can build a gate to them." The words sunk in as he said them, a mixture of anxiety and giddiness welling up like a geyser. "We can build a gate."

He'd never gone to school. It was a waste of time. All he needed to know was back in the smithy or lodged in his mind, circulating endlessly about facts that seemed like fiction.

His younger half, reflected so differently with his visage of horns and inquisitive eyes that sought out every book on the shelf, hadn't realised the seed he'd planted when he brought it up. The what-ifs. The peculiarities of those enigmatic connections. The possibilities of elsewheres. A curiosity, ripe for conversation.

Because what-ifs festered, roots shooting out to wrap around hope and guilt and pride. Whispering what-ifs, wondering what-ifs. Vile what-ifs that wouldn't leave, not until they saw solid truths.

CHAPTER TWELVE

"Let me get this right," said Davah. "You're not at all concerned that your veins were emptying out from your eyeballs, that angry black lightning was literally eating you, and that you fecking passed the fuck out for days? And now, you're saying we can build a gate? To some unknown realm?"

Aeyun chuckled half-heartedly. His body was leant weightily on the headboard, and at rest he could note how torn up he felt. It wasn't as bad as his thoughts, though. No, those were far more fragmented. Maybe he'd been too excited in his planning. Maybe he should have held off on divulging his hare-brained scheme, if only for a little longer.

He licked his lips, the skin of them cracked and dry.

"Look, I know this all seems mad," said Aeyun. "But I'm fine; I won't die from that. Even if it happens again. And as for the gate – well, yeah."

"Well, yeah?" Saoiri repeated.

Her uncertainty came across clearer than ever, written starkly as disbelief. It wasn't every day that someone shattered barriers and proposed routes to new realms. And it wasn't common for Essence to try to reclaim that which walked the in-between, or one to walk the in-between in the first place. Saoiri had reason to be somewhat irate, Aeyun figured.

"I mean, yeah. We can build one. I've been studying them, and now I know–"

"Aeyun."

Sakaeri's tone was arresting, surprising Aeyun enough that he clamped his mouth shut. He looked over at her. By the expression on her face, she seemed to be desperately holding something in. Something she wanted to ask or say but couldn't find it in herself to do so. Instead, she stared, her entire aura seemingly itching.

"Wait," Davah called out. "Aeyun, friend. Do *not* tell me that those pieces of ore are what I think they might be."

Aeyun imagined he likely looked very impish in that moment.

"*Aeyun!*" Davah's jaw dropped.

"Explain, please," Saoiri demanded, her attention ricocheting between the two of them.

"They're those little bits from the gates! They're those feckless little ore bits from the gates!"

"Aeyun," Sakaeri said again, this time with more intention. Her body had leant forward with the call, eyes boring into his.

Aeyun faltered. "Look, I know it's – I know how it seems. But it can be done, I'm sure of it."

"So," Davah started, incredulous, "you can touch alicant that can't be touched, like that *seed* and like the hazy white ones that, apparently, are *Yun-forsaken* gate alicant we've been piling up. And you want to build a gate. You want to build an entirely new connection to another realm?"

123

Beside him, Saoiri was nervously pulling at the ends of her hair. Next to her, Sakaeri said nothing. Davah pressed his lips together, waiting.

"Yep," said Aeyun.

"Yun of the stars, friend. You're a walking chaos magnet, truly!"

"Would she have felt it too?" Sakaeri asked suddenly, and it gave Aeyun pause.

The meaning behind it blossomed in his mind and a migraine prickled into a dull existence behind his temple, a pinpoint bludgeon as exacting as it was frustrating. Would Raeyu have felt it? While Aeyun was passed out from the poison of tuning within the in-between, would Raeyu have been suffering the effects of it on the other side?

"I don't know," Aeyun answered honestly.

"You've lost me," Davah interjected, but Aeyun just shook his head.

"Look, I know it's a lot to process, probably, so let's leave it for now. We can rest for the evening, then talk about where to go from here tomorrow," he reasoned.

"So, that's it?" Saoiri asked. "That's the plan? That's what we're doing? Building a gate? And then we are going – where? And what then?"

"We–" Aeyun briefly debated how much to reveal. "We are going to where that seed came from. That's how I found the connection."

It wasn't a complete lie.

"You're telling me you have confirmed that there is another realm out there?"

It was Davah who asked but, for some reason, Aeyun's gaze was drawn to Sakaeri.

"Yeah," Aeyun said after a moment. "That's what I'm saying."

Something, however fleeting, flashed behind her eyes. Aeyun felt it graze him. She leant back, brows furrowed. Then she stood abruptly. Another moment and she was shuffling around the other two, leaving the room, not bothering to shut the door behind her.

"Uh, is she okay?" Davah asked.

Aeyun answered with a quiet, "I don't know."

Saoiri stood up as well. "I think I need to step out, too. This is a lot to take in. I'll, um . . . I'll be back later."

She turned and gave one last concerned glance over her shoulder, then strode out, the door creaking loudly before softly clicking closed on her departure.

"So, Aeyun Thasian-nee," Davah said, and Aeyun felt a little drowned by the reference, long discarded. "Was it always your plan to portal off to unknown lands?"

Aeyun fought off a wry smirk. "Kind of. Sorry."

"Nah." Davah shrugged, leaning back on his elbows. "It's kinda cool to know I've been a part of something as wild as making a new gate regardless. I guess now it's more of a rescue thing than an explore-y thing, though, huh?"

In his mind, Aeyun scoffed. *It was never an 'explore-y' thing.*

"Yeah, I guess it is."

"So, you think your brother is with the Thasian gal, right? Why'd you track her and not Uruji?"

The question caught Aeyun off guard. He wasn't sure how to broach the topic of his tether to Raeyu, and he wasn't sure if he wanted to, either. Davah did question Aeyun's arm, but it hadn't gone further than that.

A simple explanation for a simple deterrence.

"Sakaeri." He said the first thing he could think of. "She could see in that space, and I thought it might help if she saw Raeyu, alive."

"Right, right," Davah said, but didn't sound convinced. He didn't push it, though. "So apparently that weird alicant was first found here on Mhedoon, right? I wonder why, and where."

"You're right, it was," Aeyun mused, only remembering that bit of information after Davah reminded him of it. "Maybe that should be our first goal. Locate that record and see if we can find anything else. Maybe there was once a connection from Mhedoon."

"You think?"

Aeyun did think. For maybe the first time, he really thought about it. He found his eyes trailing over the intricate wooden carvings around the room, feeling the resonance in the air, and suddenly suspected he that he'd never looked at Mhedoon close enough.

"Davah," Aeyun said on a whim. "Is there an ancient Mhedoonian language?"

Davah leant forward, elbows on his knees in thought as he considered the quandary, his gaze following Aeyun's own focus: a depiction of what looked like shining mountains, arching in odd angles.

"Ah, sure. Of course, there is! Most don't really know it anymore, but I always thought it was, like, kind of intriguing. Some actually say it's a derivative of descantation."

"Oh," Aeyun said, heart pounding. "Do they?"

"Yeah. It sounds pretty similar to what you said there back on Orin. You didn't happen to say something about togetherness, did you?"

Aeyun stared. And stared and stared.

"Aeyun?"

"I did." It came out in a rush. "I did. I did say something about togetherness."

"Ah." Davah gave him a weird look. "Cool."

The silence carried and Davah drummed his fingers before getting up. "Well, sure, look. You've had a time of it, right? I'll leave you be, and we'll chat tomorrow, yeah?"

He gave a short wave and walked out, leaving Aeyun to his solitude.

In the empty space, long and confounding, Aeyun swallowed.

Mhedoon couldn't be that closely connected, could it? In some way brethren to Ca'lorus? And he'd only now figured that out because he'd bothered to ask?

Aeyun peered at his hand, the one with the healing scar from the disembodied slash.

Had he even been looking?

"Morning!"

Sakaeri woke him by throwing a pastry at his face. In his drowsy bafflement, Aeyun nearly tossed the thing off the side of the bed. She caught it and handed it back to him.

"Hi?"

"Hello," she said calmly. Too calmly. Aeyun eyed her blearily as he sat up. "You stink, you know."

"Well, sure, I've not showered in days."

"Yeah, it's gross."

"Why are you being weird?"

Aeyun could feel it. He could almost touch the tension in the air. It made him feel like something was about to snap. With Sakaeri on the other end of it, he didn't want to find out the consequences.

Sakaeri, for her part, looked dramatically affronted.

"Me? *Weird*? No." She ripped off a chunk of her own pastry, gnashing it between her teeth. "Never."

"Look—"

"Nope," Sakaeri said, hand up. "Nope. Not ready. Don't want to know. Let's just go on this little hunt of yours and save our precious Rae and foolish Uruji."

Aeyun contemplated her presence before eyeing the pastry in his hand. Slowly, he brought it up to his mouth, only realising then how famished he was.

"Okay," he mumbled between a bite.

"Okay?" she tried to unnecessarily confirm.

"Yeah, yeah, okay," Aeyun assured her.

He was silently delighted with the pastry's taste, a buttery base paired mouth-wateringly with sticky preserve.

A few minutes passed as they ate in an unfamiliar camaraderie. When enough time had elapsed, Sakaeri grabbed at his wrist. "Up," she commanded. Aeyun gave her a cagey expression. "Yun, come on. Get up."

Aeyun stood and found his knees stiff. After a stretch, he allowed her to guide him to the window, where she unlatched and threw open the shutters. Someone must have closed them while he was sleeping.

"Honestly, you really smell so awful we need the fresh air in here."

"Right," Aeyun intoned.

He looked out at the sight beyond, taking in the early morning light that streamed across the placid ocean. At the shore, a gentle spray was brushing up against the stone, showering barnacles and tickling the bellies of birds that dared to fly so low.

"I've not been to Kilrona before," Sakaeri offered, drawing Aeyun's gaze. She wasn't looking back. Rather, she was drinking in the vista, looking more at peace than Aeyun had ever witnessed. "It's . . . different. Serene."

"It wasn't always."

"You don't need to remind me," she said, and it sounded more like an admission than it should have. "Mother was from here. Mhedoon. Or her mother was, anyway."

"Oh?" Aeyun said, because he'd never bothered to learn much about Ube of Krunan. Now he felt a little guilty about it.

"It doesn't matter much now." Beats passed, and they stood side by side, the sun rising in the distance. Sakaeri sunk into the windowsill, chin resting in her palm with a barely there smile on her lips. "You really do smell."

"Yeah, I get it. Thanks."

"You fish?"

"You don't?" It was asked like he should. Like it was ridiculous to think otherwise. A scoff preceded a smile, one that felt oddly hollow. Like it didn't belong. "You learn things when you're not in opulent, stomp-on-the-fodder skyrises. And I was just about as far from those as you can imagine."

"Rusted, raise-up-the-fire dungeons?"

It was a stupid joke, and it didn't even make sense. The look it awarded him said as much, and something behind it unfurled, like a fencat on its haunches.

"Sorry." An automatic, ugly, and kneejerk thing.

Empty space can feel full in the absence of chatter, and he felt it swell uncomfortably then.

"What do you know about feckin' rusted dungeons, anyway?"

CHAPTER THIRTEEN

"Anything?"

"Nope."

It had been a long week. Once Aeyun had fully recovered – or at least, when he told them his bones didn't creak anymore, and that his body didn't ache with every inhale – they'd been able to find the record Madame Reaper referenced. As it turned out, it was easily accessible in the annals, a copy of which was housed at the Kilrona Library. With less than a day's search, and some help from the archivist Mierna, who seemed to have a soft spot for Saoiri, they'd figured out that the record came from an old, now-abandoned and sea-drowned parish, Beldur.

Davah and Saoiri hadn't made a fuss about leaving, so Aeyun figured they must have visited whatever relations they wanted to when he'd been incapacitated. He didn't feel it was his place to pry, so he didn't ask. It did, however, make him wonder if their abandonment had left Sakaeri alone with what may as well have been his temporary corpse. That, he found, was an unnerving thought. What had she thought, resting her eyes upon him? Had she wished it real, that he wouldn't awaken at all?

It was when they left Kilrona that the true frustration set in.

The magnavaid couldn't be routed to Beldur, possibly because of its remote status, or because it had been reclaimed by the realm long ago. With Mhedoon being mainly ocean, it made getting anywhere that wasn't the capital or a port arduous. Instead, sailors, travellers, and adventurers alike were confronted with a vast blue network that washed over the realm, dotted with small land masses here and there.

Beldur was somewhere in the middle of that, and they'd been hopping islands for days, trying to figure out which blemish among the watery depths was home to the ill-fated, elusive settlement. The annals had provided some references that led them to believe the sunken town might be nestled among the Maighbah archipelago, since it was there where the current died. An odd collection of confetti land where water stagnated, marooning vessels that found themselves there.

"Ah, wait!" Davah exclaimed, his sudden bark causing the others to flinch. "Look, I think there's something here."

As he said it, Saoiri prepared. Mhedoons were renowned for their ability to attune to water, and Saoiri was no exception. Using the ore around her neck as a conduit, a pearly-looking alicant, she stood in the middle of the sea-skimmer and clasped her hands together over the stone. Saoiri breathed in, and when she breathed out the water around them roared, moving aside as it created a liquid tunnel for the sea-skimmer to traverse. Davah urged the craft into the water's wake, bringing them towards a sunken village.

As they dove, a clearer picture of what was before them manifested. The crumbled buildings were covered in seagrass and spongey masses. Upon seeing its recessed expanses, it was clear that there was plenty of ground to cover – if it were walkable. The town itself appeared substantial, certainly by the standards of a bygone era, and it had left impressions on the bedrock. Little ring-like forts that contained several other dilapidated, ocean-claimed structures, silt built up in their corners.

"Is it worth investigating?" Davah asked.

They had a finite amount of energy to expend towards attunement, so they wanted to ensure it was worth it when they did. To traverse the settlement, they'd have to tune with either water-based or air-based alicant, keeping water away and the space around them breathable. It wasn't a particularly gruelling task for those with some sort of accomplished control of tuning, but it did take a constant effort of energy and concentration, chipping away and depleting at reserves of potential expendable attunement.

Aeyun scoured his eyes over the site. It didn't look that different from the previous three, but it *felt* different. Was that enough? A feeling?

"Hm?" Sakaeri said beside him, startling him from his thoughts.

"Let's try it," Aeyun decided.

They anchored the sea-skimmer back on the ocean's surface, above the tallest building in the village, where it could be secured to the last intact wall of a tower there. Davah was ready to dive, and so was Saoiri, but Sakaeri watched Aeyun with expectation.

There was a problem. Aeyun could attune to Vitality, as he saw it, and some biotic organisms, using descantation to guide manifestations away from the erratic. He could also dip into the very edge of wild Essence, so it seemed. Aeyun, however, was never skilled at ore tuning, or any alicant with purely stored energy rather than active energy. The conduit of a solid mass like that never suited him well; it felt stagnant, muted, and polluted. He wasn't entirely incapable of it, but he wasn't particularly skilled at it either.

Sakaeri, of course, had inferred this throughout the years, seeing him fumble when he did tune, and jeering at him when he failed miserably.

At that moment, her gaze was more penetrating than ever.

"Should we all walk together?" she asked, and Aeyun closed his eyes, inwardly cursing. "Expend less energy in one group?"

"Ah, you're a sharp one, huh?" Davah cheered, nudging Sakaeri with his elbow. "I like the way you think."

It was a simple enough excuse, but Aeyun saw it as just that: an excuse. He spared a glance in Sakaeri's direction, but she wasn't looking at him. Instead, she was loosening the tie on her cloak, looking at the rooftop hatch they'd soon be climbing through.

As a unit, they allowed themselves to drop into the ocean, water swirling around them, but never breaching the barrier they'd procured. There was a musky brine that Aeyun could nearly taste on his tongue, mixed with something distinctly benthic that only had a home in the deep. If he were to reach out, he'd bet that the undulating veil erected around them would bend softly, moulding around his hand with gentle ease. A part of him wanted to do just that, to test his theory with childish wonder, same as he had when confronted with a shimmering pastel wall. But he refrained.

Landing on the broken roof of the building below, Aeyun noticed that it had what looked to be religious symbols carved upon its bow, something depicting an interpretation of the sun. As they descended further, he could see why. The day itself had been blessed with a bright sky, and it broke through the water's surface in sparkling streams, casting highlights on the buildings below. It was as mesmerising as it was ethereal, flickering across the oceanic ruins as if it were meant to be painted on its canvas.

Four pairs of feet broke the noiseless waters as they connected with the first bit of jagged flooring below the roof. Safely landed,

Aeyun caught Saoiri brushing her palms across her clothes, as if dispelling dirt, likely a force of habit. Davah was seemingly checking the state of his boots, seeing if they were muddied between the treads. Beside him and next to Aeyun, Sakaeri had her arms folded and was staring through a large crack in the building's foundation, into the vastness of the waters beyond, pensive. It was barely a moment more before they were venturing further.

As they trekked on, Aeyun felt *something*. He couldn't identify what it was, but it was close, and it was *here*.

Careful to not have their boots slip on the slimy surface, the group of them traipsed down the winding staircase into the bowels of the cathedral-like building. Aeyun felt uneasy at the distant tug of familiarity. Something similar, but not quite the same. Beside him, he could tell that Sakaeri was struck as well, if her stiff stance was anything to go by.

They continued their descent, each in a state of concentration while focusing their attunement. All except Aeyun, who felt distinctly guilty since he knew that Sakaeri was compensating for his lack of tuning. Because Aeyun just couldn't – never really could – and if it didn't pester some mucky, repressed contempt he held, he knew he'd be lying to himself. Caught up in his self-deprecation, he nearly tripped over Davah's foot when he'd paused, interested in a stone carving across an interior wall.

"That looks like something. I can't put my finger on it, though," Davah said, eyeing the etched rock.

The depiction was of a man with what looked like a stave, its end connecting to and extending into the ground in a system of branching roots. He was offering something – the section looked scratched out, almost purposefully – to another figure, who was hooded and graciously holding out their hands to receive the gift. Next to that was a woman's silhouette, but the place where her head should have been had long since cracked away. Beside her was yet another hooded character, this one with a stone hung around their neck. The pendant was etched in such a manner that it looked as though the stone were glowing.

Aeyun didn't realise when he'd stopped walking, but he was lucky the others had paused as well, since their bubble of breathable air stayed encasing him. He stared at the scene, scrutinising it because it just *felt* . . .

It wasn't only the stave that caught his eye, but something about the second hooded figure. Something about that entity–

"Aeyun?" Saoiri called.

"Sorry," said Aeyun. "Sorry, it's just wild to look at this type of artistry."

It was a lame explanation. Passable at best. But he wasn't ready to divulge everything yet, all the thoughts that raced through his mind. Maybe he never would be.

"Ah!" Davah cried out. "He's a monk from the ancient days, isn't he? Don't you think?" The question had been pointed at Saoiri, who debated it alongside the carving, then nodded her agreement. "I wonder how old this place is, actually."

"Probably pretty old," Saoiri asserted, casting her eyes across the stony mural once more before setting out to continue on.

Despite his want to stay and study the picture, Aeyun walked forward with the rest of them.

They reached the entrance of the ruin, one door completely missing while the other was wedged open and covered in barnacles. From their vantage, it looked as though the structure had once stood upon a hill, perhaps a focal point for the village. If one were to follow the path down, it seemed to lead directly to some sort of sunken centre, other converging routes branching away towards the small congregations of once-buildings.

Something unspoken hung between them as they descended upon the central courtyard. There was a solemn rapture about the scene presented to them, but the melancholy went beyond that. It was as if squalor lay hidden beneath the beauty, or malice masqueraded as if divine.

As Aeyun's feet carried him, he could feel the spectre of something lingering in the water, or maybe in the silt, shifting with it, flowing around him. It tickled his vertebrae like a chilling whisper, the impression of a moment lost to time. The closer they came to the centre, the stronger that feeling became.

There was a murmuring behind his eardrums, and it beckoned him. It became louder, more incessant; something buried, clawing. Like it was crying out for something inside him, calling. Calling for him to notice, just to see–

It was the moment his foot hit the first fractured stone that Aeyun was truly struck.

"Aeyun?" Sakaeri called, but he didn't hear it.

Aeyun continued. As he stepped, stones below him crackled, volatile power seeping through. The closer he got to the middle, more energy swelled and pushed settled debris away, revealing a splintered, centuries-seared scar twisting across the ground. His scrupulous gaze snagged on rubble, bits and pieces of which had script in two tongues scraped upon it.

Compelled by something instinctual, Aeyun began to speak.

"*A'Beldur a'Mhedoon, ou'e'uo, A'vor a'Ca'lorus n'a'Beldur a'Mhedoon.*"

At his words, something broke through the wild Essence, and the sharp crackling energy became softer, less frenetic. Its transition from menacing to docile was almost immediate.

A gentle glow began to emanate from the runic script, despite its broken state, and an umbral-shrouded model of what once was flashed in the courtyard. Ghostly visions of a gate, much smaller than those of the Great Sea Gates, appeared. People, wraith-like, milled about, disappearing when they reached the vaporous depiction's edge. The reflection of energy coursed through the spectre gate, and there emerged a horned woman, eyes reflecting darkly with little pinpricks of light. She spoke, the words soundless, and those spectral observers seemed to cower back in fear.

She then held out her hands, and there, upon the very ground where they stood, untamed energy imploded, sparking and crackling, not unlike Raeyu's bloodsong. Aeyun felt the power of it impale him, suffocating and boiling him from the inside out. The gate there crumbled, its ghostly impressions settling where their present masses lay, and some seemed to disappear entirely. The phantasmal people, the ones who had been vocalising unheard terror, evaporated in the ignited plume, and trails of something intangible traced their way back to the woman, whose expression remained unchanged.

She then stalked forward and her being stuttered, reminding Aeyun of the brief moments he'd spent in that liminal jump between gates. The woman walked on, and Aeyun couldn't tear his petrified gaze from her distorted reflection, her features obscured and befuddling. He couldn't bring himself to move as her image phased through him before disappearing beyond the hazy vision.

"Hey," Davah called, and it drew Aeyun from his stupor, the scene falling away around him. "What's happening?" The question made Aeyun turn his head and Davah took a jilted step back. "Shit, friend, your eyes again."

Aeyun blinked away a blurry film. "What?" he asked. Even to his own ears his voice sounded distant.

"I don't know!" Davah laughed nervously. Beside him, Saoiri twitched as though she meant to interject a thought, but her hesitation lasted too long, and Davah barrelled on. "You were descanting, and then your eyes went like the night sky again. The energy here felt weird, too."

That made Aeyun thoughts snap to the present. Did . . . Davah and Saoiri not see that? Any of that? Out of curiosity, Aeyun turned to his last companion.

Sakaeri's gaze was trained on where that time-drowned gate once stood, something akin to horror painted across her ashen face.

Well, two of four, then.

It was one of those quiet days that he cherished, the breeze carrying the soft scent of fresh blossoms. Walking in the garden, his grasp was tangled with his sister's, and she held on tightly, as if he would slip right through the ground and disappear if she didn't.

Too young to properly formulate her meandering thoughts – and she never was much good at communicating her intentions anyway – she tugged at him to follow. He did.

It was a small thing that caught her interest, furry with big ears, nuzzled in the underbrush of berry bushes. A sudden stop, prompted by little feet, greeted him with a quiet shushing noise and a matching demand from her finger. They dropped down together, slowly encroaching. Skittering soon followed, and he was ready to console until a slow return of tiny paws in the dirt stopped him.

The cheeky grin that erupted across her face was enough to tear his heart asunder in the best way possible. He wanted her to do nothing but smile, always.

CHAPTER FOURTEEN

Aeyun hadn't meant to disregard Davah's concerns, yet that's exactly what he did.

He dove towards the rubble in the courtyard and started turning stones, searching. His third attempt was lucky, and he saw an ore lodged there, glowing that ethereal milky hue he'd become well acquainted with. Aeyun retrieved his dagger from his side, and he pierced it into the cratered stone, attempting to dislodge the alicant embedded there.

"Ah, hey, friend – Aeyun!" Davah tried again to no avail.

"Was she–? What even–" Sakaeri muttered to herself from somewhere behind.

"If the stone has ore, don't touch it. It'll be caustic," Aeyun said absently.

He continued to work at the ore, wedging his blade against it with a violent thrust, succeeding in prying away two securing bits of rock. Once loose, he snatched the alicant from its ancient resting place and held it, weighty and foreboding in his palm.

It was a gate. A smaller gate; a manageable gate. A replicable gate.

Moving to the next piece of rubble, he paused.

–lorus was there, in Ca'lorus's script.

"Aeyun, you need to explain what just happened!" Sakaeri pleaded.

It was something that Aeyun would normally marvel at, but right now he didn't have time.

Ca'lorus. He was wasting precious moments.

Standing once more, Aeyun tried to retrace his vision. He tracked a similar path on the ground where the scar had spread, but nothing sparked or crackled. He tried to focus and bring back those incessant murmurs, but nothing cried out. But . . . no. No, *no!* Why? Why not?

"Dammit!" he shouted.

"Aeyun?" Saoiri called cautiously. "You're scaring us."

Aeyun paused, taking a stifled breath. He knew he was. He was being selfish, again.

"I'm sorry," he said, head angled down. "I know, I'm sorry. This is already such–"

"Aeyun." It was Sakaeri again. "What did we just witness?"

"The memory of this scar? I don't know. I've never seen anything like that," Aeyun answered with sincerity. He twisted on the spot, as if he could find the location that instigated it all with a more scrutinising, purposeful gait.

"Aeyun," Sakaeri said again, and her tone made him flinch. "That woman eviscerated those people. They *ceased* to *exist*, and it looked too similar to your little stitching trick, and her eyes looked like yours did now, and in the in-between."

She brought up a good point. It was something he hadn't thought about, the way those people disappeared, and how something was drawn to her when it was done. In a way, it did look reminiscent to what Aeyun did, but it still seemed different. A bit like that, and a bit like –

His hand flew to his chest, gripping the fabric over his heart.

"You said my eyes looked like that?" Aeyun asked. He had to be sure.

"That's the second time your eyes have looked like the night sky, friend. It's scary as fuck, honestly," Davah chimed in. "Now, what was this about a woman eviscerating people?"

Now there was no denying it. Aeyun hadn't realised he'd been tapping into that much raw Essence. If anything, when he attuned too strongly, his eyes turned *white*. Similarly, when wild, untamed Essence was attuned to, like how the Thasian-nee preferred, it was pure inky black. When it was both – harmonised – it was a mix of the two, resulting in something like the night sky.

He'd seen it appear in Uruji's eyes, but not his own. He'd not delved so deep into the untamed, he thought. Now, though . . .

That also meant one thing: that woman was harmonising. She was harmonising, and it produced something that looked like Raeyu's so-called innate talent, but *more*. More like Seraeyu's destruction . . . like rage manifested. And she was definitely of the Yu-ta, as the horns on her head attested.

"I'm tired of the constant dance you two do," Saoiri's grumble broke the silence. "We're here, too. We are helping, too!"

"There was a gate here," Sakaeri said, filling the gaps when Aeyun seemed incapable. "We saw a vision, and it must have been held in that strange plane of the in-between if only we two did. A woman appeared from it. She tuned, and people disappeared on the spot. That was it. That was what we saw."

Sakaeri may have left out some of the finer details, like the familiar electrified explosion and the woman's very obvious heritage, but that was the gist of it.

"Terrifying." Davah shivered, then cast a watchful eye towards Aeyun, who had shifted his hand from his chest, instead pinching the bridge of his nose. "So why did you act up all weird?"

"I don't know! This is all so damned confusing, and I don't even know what I'm . . . What I'm doing," said Aeyun. His atypically blunt declaration cast a shadow upon the group. "I'm really . . . I'm just–"

"Your efforts don't have to include shutting us out," Saoiri reasoned, stepping closer, a hand outstretched in offering. "We can be here for you. We want to be."

"We and I are not the same," Sakaeri grumbled under her breath. A grimace flattened her mouth when she realised Aeyun was close enough to catch the sentiment and she huffed. "Sorry, look. Yeah, I guess me too."

Aeyun let the tension in his posture melt as he observed his companions: Davah, with his big, lopsided grin; Saoiri, with her sympathetic, beckoning smile; Sakaeri, with her grumpy, reticent regard.

"How did I manage to get here?" Aeyun couldn't help the rancour that bled into his chuckle, a vindictive reaction to his own question. He would never have imagined spending this much time with Sakaeri and being thick as thieves – literally – with a pair of Mhedoons he'd met at a market.

"It's not all about you," Sakaeri commented offhandedly.

Aeyun was about to thank them all for their patience – for their uncanny persistence to remain by his side – but a sharp pain above his hip made him wince. *What was that?*

It felt like something had lodged in his gut, and soon a blistering warmth spread from the point of impact, prickling outwards. When he looked down, blood was already pooling on his shirt, collecting at his waist.

No. No, no, no – I need more time.

"Aeyun, are you bleeding? Are you hurt?" Saoiri asked, panicked.

"You better fucking live through that!" Sakaeri demanded, then she lunged and grabbed whatever she could – barnacles, sea moss, fallen seaweed. "Take this and fix yourself and let's pray to Yun–"

She didn't finish, but Aeyun knew it would be something like: *that Rae does the same.*

Aeyun was *worried*, because he was feeling too dizzy too fast, so Raeyu was definitely in trouble. With a grunt, he took the mismatched bundle of biota that Sakaeri had gathered. Grimacing, he lifted his shirt and pressed the greenish, slimy bunch against his suddenly splitting waist.

"*Ca–*" he started, but the realm spun, so he closed his eyes. "*Ca'ou o, cah e'ju, ou'uo.*"

Aeyun had forgotten, though.

The alicant was still in his other hand. An alicant that had once jumped between the physical realms, drawing a connection to Ca'lorus.

There was a lingering energy in the air, and it pulled towards him. As it coursed into his being, he opened his eyes and a gasp drew from his throat, like a gentle murmur indicating what was to come. This time, he could feel the feral Essence seep in. It bled into the stitch that would normally just leave a lightly discoloured scar, as opposed to Essence-tinged tunes that unfurled inky, chaotic stains, like the one on his arm.

He gagged as something in him was pulled taut, then there was a rip in the fabric of space before them, echoing out with a crack. It startled some fish that had dared to near their curious bubble, and they swam away in a frenzy, darting this and that way. Aeyun struggled to keep his eyes open, hunching with a grimace as something not quite like pain but just as overwhelming engulfed him.

The domed cavern of air in which he stood, flanked by his comrades, shuddered as the crisp scent of ozone wisped from the widening fissure. Spherical bubbles of water slid across the cusp of their tuned barrier, and the curtain of liquid extending ever beyond started to tear up at its seams, dragging silt and seagrass with it. For that moment, the ocean felt very much *alive*, and water, somehow muted for all its movement, whirled around their group, spurred by abounding energy.

There was a brief lapse of cyclical remembrance as Aeyun stared up towards the rift, a reflection of his childhood nightmare. This time, though, he was not small and frightened. He was curious and devastatingly determined, his eyes narrowing in anticipation of what lay on the other side. In answer to his wonderment, just like all those years ago, Raeyu was there, the mirror image of Aeyun's likeness.

Uruji was half-slipped off Raeyu's back, seemingly unconscious, and Raeyu was holding her side, looking worn and haggard. She was on her knees, hair wild in tangled ringlets, and – of all things – a sharp, long piece of thick tree bark was stuck through her, peeking through her fingers. Raeyu stared up at Aeyun, only a brief connection that lacked a cathartic reprisal or reunion. Her bafflement ended abruptly as she looked at something else that Aeyun couldn't quite see.

In shock, Aeyun tried to reach up, but the weightlessness that took effect once the rift opened had him tripping forward instead, his feet losing purchase.

"Rae – Raeyu!" Sakaeri cried out.

Aeyun spared her a quick glance; Sakaeri was locked up, frozen still in disbelief.

Somehow, in spite of her situation, Raeyu managed a strained, serene smile at whomever she was addressing beyond the rift's sight. She pointed up – or down, depending on perspective – presumably at Aeyun, and she managed a strained, "A'vor."

At the mention of his birth name, Aeyun's eyes blew wide. With a shivering pulse, the rift started to shrink. Panic set in. He scrambled to move, then cringed as he heard a dagger – his own dagger, a gift from his father – whizz past his ear, launching itself through the rift before lodging in a tree trunk behind Raeyu. In the last moment the tear stood open, Aeyun's eyes were drawn from Raeyu, who seemed wholly fixated on her hidden counterpart, to said counterpart, who finally appeared in the corner.

She was petite but nimble, and much taller than Aeyun remembered her to be.

"Da'garu!" he shouted without thought.

The young woman's focus darted to him, quick like a hunter on the prowl, and time stilled. Cruel and unforgiving, the rift closed, and it took Aeyun's consciousness with it.

"Da'garu!" A'vor called, unable to see his younger sister beyond the thicket that lined the craggy landscape. Their mother had told them to run; run and don't come back.

It was A'vor's fault for looking behind him. He tripped over himself when he did, just catching a glimpse of his father's downed form and his mother's stomach being run through with a sword. There was someone else tossing a torch into a window, intending to cultivate a fire to purify the vile wickedness he perceived there. The heat began to cut the dewy forest air, snuffing out birdsongs and playful chitters. Only the shouts of pious men remained.

A'vor's eyes watered, and he gulped back a cry. Despite his best efforts, a sob still came as he righted himself, pushing momentum back into his legs. He needed the trees to carry him away, but he also needed them to guide him to his sister.

"Da'garu, don't look back! Keep running!" he shouted, garbled behind snot and tears.

At the time it had seemed silly, but their mother had specifically instructed that, should they ever find themselves in trouble, they follow the Ou'grobh's largest river, and to keep going. To think of somewhere else, somewhere safe and far away from Ca'lorus. Earnest as ever, A'vor readily agreed to the plan, should it ever need to happen. He would never disobey his mother. She was so caring and kind. So full of love for her kin that A'vor hoped he'd live up to her legacy.

Never, though, did he imagine a day in all his adolescent years that it would be necessary.

"Da'garu!" he called again, worry seeping down his oesophagus, blistering into his lungs.

Da'garu, where are you?

Da'garu had run off first when A'vor and his mother told her to. A'vor had intended to stay and take his father's mantle, stepping up to protect the family, but his mother begged him to run. To protect his sister, and to leave.

"Da'gar – ach!" A'vor butchered his sister's name as he stumbled over a crag. Everything that followed felt like it happened in an instant.

A'vor's view of the darkened sky suddenly shifted, becoming a kaleidoscope of shadowed green and grey as he tumbled forwards. Instinct told him to shut his eyes as he fell, and rough vines and roots scratched at his skin as he slipped into darkness with a thud.

Groaning, A'vor attempted to reorient himself. Above him, light filtered through the mess of foliage he'd ripped into during his descent. From the underside of a crag, A'vor processed the fleeting moments in a stunned silence, his scraped-up fingers digging into rock and dirt.

It lasted for mere seconds before panic set in, true and swift, and he was clawing at the walls of the rocky abyss. It was fruitless, however, and he only managed to reach the very tips of the soggy, damp roots hanging down. Breath shuddering, he looked around for an exit, a path, anything.

"Da'garu!" he called again. This time, it was laced with fear.

There were a few deafening beats of nothingness, just the eerie wallow of damp corridors, and then he gulped down a whimper that crept up his throat.

I have to . . . I have to be strong, for Da'garu!

In the dark distance, a steady drip, drip, drip made itself known to his keen ears. A'vor felt around for purchase. There, just to the right, he found enough space to crawl. So, crawl he did. With effort, A'vor dragged himself towards the noise. A mistake.

Teetering over a pitched edge, a splash announced A'vor's arrival in an underground ravine. He cried out with a gasp, and the desperate call echoed, taunting in the quiet as it bounced off dank, unwelcoming walls. Cruel in its onslaught, a rushing current carried him through the darkness, and slimy surroundings offered him little reprieve. His hands slipped along as he was pulled, an undertow dragging him below, consuming him in its suffocating embrace.

Spat out on the other side of wherever the flow had taken him, A'vor was quick to refill his lungs with much-needed air. He choked on his inhale, gasping as he struggled to breathe once more. Everything hurt – where was Da'garu? How would she be safe? How would A'vor find her? What would Mother say? Or Father?

They won't. His mind reminded him. *They won't say anything.*

A'vor wiped wetness from his face; water or tears, he wasn't sure.

Where he'd ended up, in this forbidding underground passage, the pool around him was placid. Less volatile. Taking advantage of this, A'vor swam towards the dry lump of land he'd spotted in the distance. It drew him in, something about it calling him, like a lantern on a dark night. The closer he got, the more of an oddity the destination appeared. In the middle of what he could now see was a cavern, an elevated piece of ground sat above the rest, littered with ruins and odd markings. Its impression was ancient and ominous, covered in stalagmites that seemed to have formed over more years than A'vor could comprehend.

Reaching the isle, he hiccupped with another quiet sob. He could see that the markings he'd spotted were emanating a black,

145

crackling energy from within a curved formation. Climbing onto solid ground once more, A'vor felt his mind fog over as he stared at the peculiar site.

Come, it beckoned.

His body moved with a lurch, and the sparking light from the snaps of inky energy were dim, dulled but bright in the blackness around him. As he reached its centre, the stalagmites that warded it shattered in a violent reaction, and light flooded the cavern. A'vor called out aghast as a hazy glow ripped through the air, an odd inversion of the familiar.

A tear into a scene from the woods appeared there. It stared back at him, along with what looked to be a girl, caught by surprise. All A'vor got was a glimpse of golden-amber eyes boring into him before he was engulfed in a flash of white and swath of obsidian, encasing both him and the space around him. As it bled into his surroundings, a silent resonance communed with him, latching to his soulsong.

Warmth washed through him, at first comforting, then all at once burning. His feet, lifted off the ground, were weightless, and water droplets floated in the air around him. A blink and the cavern was gone, replaced with something *different*. Something unfamiliar, wild, endless, and consuming. A threshold of blackness, punctuated with bright, hazy pockets of energy.

Where had he ended up? What had he done? *Where was Da'garu?*

Air was stolen from him as he impacted something solid. With a jolt, A'vor wheezed as he struggled to lie on his back, a twisting nausea bubbling in his throat.

"Ow! Hey!" someone said.

A'vor gasped in short, pained breaths, and he couldn't quite open his eyes. Not yet. But the atmosphere felt different, not as dense. And there was a powdery, crisp scent, carried by a light breeze that brushed past his shoulders. Was he out of the cave?

"H-hey, you! Um, are you okay? You came out of nowhere!" The voice was concerned but held a curious note of excitement.

Soon hands were clasping onto A'vor, nudging him. "Hey! Uh, really, are you okay?"

He jerked away from the grasp. No, A'vor did not think he was okay.

A'vor forced his eyes open as he gulped in precious air – a commodity to cherish as of late – a whole heaving lungful. As he did, a prickle threatened to give away his volatility, how incredibly unstable and *weak* he felt, so he scrunched his nose and coughed.

There was a child's face above him, likely someone near his own age, but she looked wrong. More specifically, she had horns curling out from her hair. And her clothes looked weird too, all ornate patterns and bright colours. Where were her leathers? Her furs?

Distantly, A'vor wondered if she was playing dress-up.

"Sister," he managed to wrench from his throat. "Have to find my sister!"

The child above him looked relieved that A'vor spoke, then suddenly concerned at the proclamation. She pulled A'vor up into a sitting position, and he noted the gems that hung from her ears. *That's odd*, A'vor considered, wry and irrational, his mind latching onto it to anchor himself. Jewellery was expensive, and why would a child puncture their lobes to wear it?

"Oh! Is that why you – um – appeared? Was that tuning, by the way? That was amazing!" The girl with the horns grinned, and it lit up her whole face.

A'vor, on the other hand, frowned. *Tuning?*

"Have to find Da'garu," he said, still wincing against the burn in his chest. He had more important things to focus on than playing pretend.

The girl's face wrinkled quizzically. "Daa. Gaeru?"

What? What a useless dolt.

"You're not with them, are you?" A'vor managed to growl out.

He pushed her away before standing on wobbly feet. His

147

crash back to the ground was quick and painful, and admittedly a little embarrassing. Not that he had time to ruminate on that. He groaned and steadied himself on his elbows.

"Hey, take it easy!" the odd girl cried out.

She crouched down to help A'vor sit upright. Again.

As A'vor took another look at his companion, he noticed that the girl's bowed head did not indicate a hat, pin, or band of any sort to support the horns. Even her overly intricate and impractical hairstyle didn't seem to be holding them in place. It brought the question to A'vor's mind: were they actually attached to her head?

"I'll help you find your sister!" the strange, horned child announced. She looked up then, clearly struggling with her next words if her face was any indication. "Dah-gaaroo?"

A'vor scowled, eyes scanning the grove of trees that surrounded them. How did he end up in the forest again? *Am I still being followed?*

"Da'garu," A'vor told the useless child, impatient. "I'm A'vor, who are you? You're not with the rest of them, are you?" he repeated.

The horned girl's face creased in confusion.

"Ae-voore?" No, that was incorrect. "I'm Raeyu."

Silence stretched for a long moment.

"Ra'yuu?"

"Um," Raeyu said, clearly at a loss as she righted her back to stand at full height once more. "No?" She smiled again, but the distress wasn't well hidden. "Raeyu."

They blinked at one another.

A'vor suddenly yelped in pain as something biting swept through his body and an electric pulse of inky black energy curled around him. The other child, Raeyu, jerked back in alarm before she leant forward again, enamoured.

"Wait! You can do it, too?"

"What are you talking about?" A'vor gritted out.

Another shock jolted his frame. Beyond the prickling

discomfort, something thicker than a tear ran down his cheek and his vision became murky.

Raeyu then looked troubled again, and her excited smile fell away.

"You don't know what this is? Does it hurt?"

The trauma of the day compounded on the pain of the moment. "Yes," A'vor said, voice wobbly. He ground his teeth at another wave of nauseating shocks. "Please, help."

"I–" Raeyu seemed at a loss. With a muster of determination, a look of resolution straightened her jawline. "I will!" she declared. She held out her arm, which was covered with odd black markings, and she tightly gripped A'vor's wrist. "I'll help you!"

"Worthless whelp of a child!"

Shame. It flooded his veins, emptying wet and salty from his eyes.

"And your mother went off and died, so now you've left it to your sister. Are you proud of that, you absolute waste of offspring? You did that! You've ruined *this legacy."*

Disgust. He could feel it as much as he saw it reflected in front of him.

"I'll fix this, like I fix everything. If you can't handle your responsibilities, we'll get someone who can do it for you." A scoff. It sounded like it should be followed by spit. "What a hassle."

CHAPTER FIFTEEN

"–will resume trade under the given conditions. Thank you for your cooperation, Seraeyu Thasian."

Seraeyu blinked as the transmission was cut, not quite catching who was on the other side of the holocaster before it faded out. He spun around and found that he was in the communications room, its curtains drawn to allow for better visibility during a call. As he was apparently alone, he wasted no time skirting over to the window, throwing the material aside to look upon Haebal City.

It was the middle of the night, and where lights should've been peppered across the streets, there was pitch black. It was eerie, the way that shadows crept into corners that were usually lit and lively. His reflection upon the glass showed that he was back in robes – why was it always robes? Who wore robes these days? – and he sneered at the sight. Looking down further, he could swear he saw wreckage piled in the courtyard far below.

Was that from the roof?

Seraeyu turned and stalked across the room, throwing the door open – *thank Yun it opened!* – and was met with the sight of a Sentinel. Shocked into stillness, he stared at the woman. She gazed back, the visor of her sleek and pointed helm lifted. She frowned.

"Praetor Thasian?" the Sentinel asked, a little dubious.

Praetor? Seraeyu thought. *But Praetor is the title for the head of the Thasian . . .*

The implications of Seraeyu, the youngest of the Thasian house, being called *Praetor* curled around his cranium and trickled down, slinking slowly and mercilessly across his prickling neck. There it was. His fears confirmed. Oagyu must be dead. Worse than that, Oagyu was dead, and it wasn't Raeyu who took his place, so she–

What was the last thing he said to Raeyu? What was the last thing he said to Oagyu?

"Praetor Thasian?" the Sentinel called again.

Seraeyu looked up at her hulking presence. She didn't seem scared of him; only concerned.

Yun of the stars, what was this nonsense nightmare he'd fallen into?

"Would you like to rest? Will I take you to his late Oagyu's room?"

"No!" Seraeyu said, perhaps too suddenly. In stilted display, he bit his lip and held his hands up disarmingly, grateful to see them free of blood. "Sorry, I'm just on edge," he told her, hoping he'd imagined the feeble warble that shook his voice.

The Sentinel nodded. "I understand, Praetor Thasian. The vigil is a few days away. I think it will be difficult for many Haebalians, but most of all you. You lost so much that day – we understand," she told him kindly.

Seraeyu could feel the cogs slowing, his considerations congealing into one large, boggling unknown.

"I did lose a lot . . . that day," he said. *Which day? What was this day?*

The Sentinel bent down, as if to share a secret. "I know that many have lost confidence, but I still believe that Raeyu could be out there, somewhere." Hope sparked in Seraeyu's chest, burning and bright. A small, blessed light in vast darkness. "I believe that you can lead us from these difficult days, as you've said yourself."

As I've said myself?

"I have faith in you, Praetor Thasian."

"Thank you," said Seraeyu. It was a reasonable response. Practical. Expected.

"I will light a lantern for the late Oagyu as well as Jourae-nee and Uruji-nee–"

Jourae-nee? Uruji-nee? Seraeyu's mind twisted, distant and dissonant thoughts sprouting thorns he dared to poke at. *They're dead? They're all dead?*

"And I will light another in honour of our wish for Raeyu to be found."

"Time to sleep."

It wasn't fair, Seraeyu determined, when his vision went black.

Seraeyu was really getting tired of the sight of this damned velvet canopy.

"Who are you?" Seraeyu asked.

He was tired. He was depressed. Mostly, though, he was *angry*.

"Who. The fuck. Are you?"

He got up and stumbled to the curtains, throwing them open, their grommets skidding gratingly across the pole. It was still night out. Was it the same night? A different one? How much time had passed since *that day?*

Frustrated, Seraeyu tugged his shirt up and prodded at the one thing that had been most out of place on his being since he'd awoken memoryless the first time. The scar there rippled under his skin, an irritated and puckered thing, searing into not just muscle, but bone. Seraeyu groaned in malformed discontent, the consequence of his prodding.

"*You will quiet, child!*" a voice called out; a woman.

Seraeyu pushed upon the gnarled scar, channelling all his visceral disdain onto it.

"Who are you? What is this?" He'd lost his mind. He was convinced fabrications would opine till he'd beg to be taken away. "What have you done to me?"

"*You only hurt yourself, foolish young Yu-ta. Do you not recall? You came to me. You called to me. I simply answered.*"

The voice echoed in his mind, bouncing around in his skull. Still, he heeded the warning, easing off and gently placing his hand over the mark instead. It seemed this method was ineffectual, so he would simply have to divine a better way to threaten this disembodied voice.

"I came to you? Who in all the frigid void *are* you? What did you do?"

He could see his own reflection in the glass again, the night beyond staring back at him. Haebal City was still dark, but some streetlights were aglow once more. It made Seraeyu's chest loosen, if only a little.

"*You sought me out, in those accursed depths. I heard you, so clearly in the Sea, and I answered. We are simply righting wrongs, child. Now let me rest.*"

"Righting wrongs? And what do you mean I sought you out in the depths. In the catacombs?" Seraeyu turned, as if he would find the incorporeal speaker behind him. It nearly sounded like it. "You were in the catacombs?"

Visions of a solitary gem haunted him in blurry frames. It couldn't be . . . could it?

"Are you in that alicant?"

There was no answer. Whether it was because the entity chose to ignore him or because she did not hear him, he wasn't sure. Seraeyu made his way to the en suite and peered at the mirror, moving his palm from in front of his heart, considering the botched scar with renewed interest. *You were in the alicant?*

You'll go there one day, too, Raeyu had told him. *When you're older.*

When she'd returned, she had a new marking on her arm, black and inky, a less offensive likeness of what marred Seraeyu's chest now. And there had been two pillars in those depths: one empty, without its alicant. The other, however, had still clutched a gem, awaiting the right daft idiot to pluck it from its confines.

Is this it? Is this the secret you wouldn't tell me? The rite?

Curious, Seraeyu held his palm up, imagining that sparking power from when he'd touched the gate in the cistern. He breathed in deeply, a grounding inhale, searching within himself, and then energy flowed and gathered, sizzling to life in his hand. A zap of white lightning shot up and snapped at the ceiling. Seraeyu abruptly cut off the flow and angled his head up. There was a burst of sooty residue where the lightning had struck.

That was . . . like Raeyu.

Seraeyu's energy waned dangerously. He suspected it was due to his recent stunt, but the question begged at his mind: *am I not Untuned anymore?*

Even still, that feeling of something missing remained. As complete as he felt – and now he suspected that something indeed had been freed – he also felt contradictorily and irrefutably incomplete. As if something was lost, something that still called to him, seeking refuge.

Seraeyu had no idea what it was.

Baffled and overwhelmed, Seraeyu slunk back and laid in the bed that was not his own, in the room that was not his own, with the title he'd never wanted looming over him. He pulled the duvet up to his chin and curled in the silken sheets.

What's missing? He closed his eyes. *Raeyu, where are you?*

"–and I–" Seraeyu cut off mid-sentence, an intangible weight nearly bowling him over.

He stumbled back, the realm odd with a sense of unreality, and he steadied himself. When he regained his faculties, he looked up and found himself staring at a Sentinel he didn't recognise. The man was tall and burly, stern in his regard, and it took another moment for Seraeyu to realise that he was *not* a Sentinel, but an Orinian Draconguard. The charcoal, gaudy, over-designed armour should have tipped him off immediately.

"Praetor Thasian?" the Draconguard said, his voice low and menacing, likely unintentionally.

If the man had been wearing his helm – an oddly missing piece of his ensemble – Seraeyu would not have seen the inquisitive quirk of the soldier's brow, adding further distinction between his dichromatic irises. It was a unique trait among some Orinian natives, said to have been carried over from ancient lineages hailing from reaches of the realm that were no longer habitable. Seraeyu knew there was some fable told to Orinian children, prophesising the fantastical origins, but he could not remember if the bicolouration indicated a blessing or a curse.

Seraeyu held up his hand, noticing his mother's missing jewellery wrapped around his fingers. Attention snagged there, perhaps for too long, he swallowed thickly, trying to catch up. Trying to make sense of the barrage of utter drivel he'd come to know.

"Um," he said. "Ah, my apologies, I seem to have lost my train of thought."

What is a Draconguard doing in the Tower?

Seraeyu scanned the room. It wasn't Oagyu's office, and a worried part of him wondered why that was. Instead, they were in one of the other meeting rooms. It was a generic-looking space, sparsely furnished with a clean, colourless design. A plant sat in the corner, and Seraeyu noted that it looked watered, if only a tad wilted. Someone had been providing general upkeep, anyway.

"You last told me to deliver your message to our Dracon. I will do so, at your behest." The Draconguard paused, eyeing the window where light poured in. A passing conflict marred his expression, then he turned back to Seraeyu, curiosity tingeing his tone as he asked, "Is there a reason you brought the barrier down?"

Seraeyu followed his gaze. *The barrier?*

"I–"

There was a shift in the realm. His vision inverted for a moment, and something numbing coursed through his extremities. To Seraeyu's horror, he felt his own body straighten without his consent, and his palms brushed down the front of his robes as he cleared his throat.

Only, it wasn't him. *He* didn't clear his throat.

"My many apologies, Draconguard Ephrite," Seraeyu spoke, but it wasn't of his own volition. Behind powerless eyes, he watched as his hand waved out, effortlessly erecting a wall of black beyond the window; pure energy twisting angrily in an endless whirlwind. "I seem to have not had enough rest lately and my mind wandered, only momentarily. Please relay my message and tell your Dracon that I will await her word."

Seraeyu's arm lifted to chest height, then he placed his hand perpendicular to his heart in the Raenaruan sign of thanks. In response, the Draconguard bent a knee, bowing his head in Orin's own gesture.

"*Do not cause trouble, child. You will rest now.*"

Seraeyu's awareness lapsed, and he instead found himself surrounded by a sea of black.

Echoes of nonsensical chittering faded into a hollow noise, becoming something whistling and deafening until only softened, distant distortions remained – the chime of a bell or the drip of water filtering through an endless pool. Nothing presided over him, an endless, stretching void, and nothing rested below his feet. A fractalised aetherscape expanded, flipping upon itself over and over again. If he squinted, Seraeyu could swear that odd colours of *something* swirled in the distance, popping in and out of existence.

He took a step, and it was as if the blackness rippled under his shoe, soundless waves echoing out. When Seraeyu took another step, a muted call responded, beckoning him somewhere far in the depths.

He couldn't hear it, and nothing cried out to him, yet there was something that implored him. Dazed and possibly two ticks past what might be considered of sound mind, he wandered. His feet drew forward and the blackness enveloped him, almost like silk slipping past his shoulders, then smoke, then something viscous and thick, but not impenetrable.

There were moments that felt suffocating, as if his lungs tightened and his body compressed, and then there were fleeting seconds where the endlessness felt freeing, if not desolate and incomprehensible. Colours spiralled beyond reach, a kaleidoscope of wispy, ethereal form, and something continued to summon him, harkening a missing notion.

What is that? It was the question that plagued him most, obsessively egging at him more than his curiosity for where he was. This echo, a fragment of something far removed, chanted in a silent serenade as he was drawn to it. An elegy – or perhaps a requiem – in the void, it sang.

He took another step and energy erupted beside him with a *whoosh*, making him jump and stumble. But not fall. He wasn't sure how he could. Nowhere seemed to be up or down or otherwise.

This is worse than that time on Lu-Ghan, came the rueful thought.

Steady once more, Seraeyu hesitantly reached out a hand. It was by instinct, something magnetic and aching to respond, to try and connect to whatever was out there.

Where are you . . . ?

"Lunarius. Lu-naer-ee-usse."

The distinct brogue of the stated word made him falter, pausing his progress to the smelter. "Why are you saying it like that?"

Eyes that shined, ever inquisitive, met his own among the fire and flame. Nimble fingers eared a ragged book's page as the tome was set on soot-marked slacks. "You used to sound like that." *A tug of horns indicated a coiled anxiety, or something akin to it, as he'd long observed in the other's behaviour.* "When Father first brought you home. I used to think I imagined it, but it comes out every once in a while, on certain words."

He didn't have enough time to justify himself before more of the intended sentiment floated across heated space.

"I always thought it sounded cool, like something distinctly yours. I can't get the sound right."

"You want to sound like me?" he asked without thinking.

A bright smile responded to him, and he felt a strange sense of pride inflate his chest.

CHAPTER SIXTEEN

"I'm really sick of you passing out," Sakaeri commented as Aeyun awoke once more to the familiar sight of the small sea-skimmer dormitory. "How much sleep does one man need?"

"How long was I out?" Aeyun asked, still groggy.

"Surprisingly, only a few hours. That ore crumbled to dust in your palm, so maybe all that *whatever* you do was channelled through it. You think?"

159

It wasn't uncommon for ore to crumble once its compiled, tamed energy was tapped out. They were nearly like instruments; play them too vigorously and they'd be worn out and broken. But look after them and give them maintenance – time to restore – and they could be used comfortably for a long while.

"So, I squandered that opportunity," said Aeyun.

He kicked himself inwardly. It was a gate alicant, and it was already tuned to Ca'lorus. If he had only –

"What exactly is *aah-voore* and what is *daah-gah-ruu*?"

The question made Aeyun freeze. The moments before he lost consciousness came back to him and – *Da'garu is alive!*

"*A'vor* means 'of luck' and *Da'garu* means 'from the heavens'," he said, distracted.

"Descantation?" she questioned.

He didn't bother to correct her.

"Why would Rae say that, and why did you respond back with 'from the heavens'?"

"Ah," Aeyun began, but he wasn't sure how to finish, so he and Sakaeri just stared at one another awkwardly in the lowlight. "Where are Davah and Saoiri?"

"What? Is it personal or something?" she teased and Aeyun floundered.

"No!" he refuted with a sigh. "Not like that."

"Right, okay." Sakaeri waved a dismissive hand. "Davah and Saoiri dove back down to see if they could tell if any of the other rubble had ore stuck in it. They didn't see that little shitshow of a vision we did, but they *did* see the rift and Rae on the other side." There was a pause. "I know she made it okay because you're still here, but do you think Uruji is alright?"

"I hope so," Aeyun muttered. "He has a tendency to push himself too far."

"Pretty sure he learnt that from you."

"You're probably not wrong." Another blank space filled with only the whir of the recycled air filter. "Why'd you throw my dagger?"

Sakaeri looked at him as though he were stupid. "To retrieve it."

"What?"

"I've done it before, from Tenebrana to Raenaru. It took a few months."

"But why my dagger?" It took a moment, but finally Aeyun followed that up with, "Wait. You're gauging the distance between the realms?" And then, "There's a measurable distance between the realms?"

"That is indeed the way it seems," Sakaeri responded, feigning disinterest.

Aeyun, for his part, was stunned. He'd not once considered that there was physical distance; maybe metaphysical, some sort of *idea* of space, but not an actual, measurable length that could be defined. He and Raeyu had joked that maybe they were looking at the same starry sea from one realm to another, but –

Could they actually be?

"Sakaeri, you're a genius," Aeyun breathed out, fully appreciating her inspired thought.

She shook her head, as if assuring herself that she wasn't imagining the compliment. "Am I?"

"Who else has thought to consider that?"

"Aeyun," Sakaeri said, and he didn't like her tone. "You sheltered baby. Loads of people have considered it. Loads of people have certainly tried to test some theory one way or another. But the powers that be don't like change. So, study is brushed under the rug, academics disappear, or alarmist rebuttals are immediately put into circulation."

She made a cooing noise and patted him on the head.

He forcefully pushed her hand away. "Is that so?"

"It *is* so! I had a target who was an academic," Sakaeri reminisced.

The thought broiled in Aeyun's mind until he realised that she was referring to one of her victims – one who was most assuredly dead now.

161

"His studies were fascinating. I may have taken a look around before I left the scene, and I may have nabbed a few of his findings, so that they weren't destroyed. Honestly, the guy was obsessed with the stars, but it started to make sense after reading about it."

Aeyun frowned. "So, you killed him in cold blood?"

"Focus on the important point, Aeyun–"

"It is important!"

"And I saved his work! Either I was finishing the job and saving his life's research, or someone else was and they were burning it to a crisp."

Aeyun hadn't considered that, but still. Was that really justification? No, surely, she could have spirited him away somewhere safe if she'd wanted to. She could have avoided bloodshed.

"Anyway, it's kept safe at – well, it's kept safe. I was already curious because I'd read somewhere that the Yun traversed the Great Starry Sea in ancient times, so I wanted to see if there might be merit to that. Well, this guy thought so, and I guess my little knife retrieval experiment proved it? I doubt it jumped through a rift on its own. So . . . I guess we can find out how far this other mysterious realm might be – days, months, years?"

"And if it never comes back?"

"Then someone or something intercepted it, or this realm is over a lifetime away from us."

Aeyun offered a hum and a mumble about *so that's why it was my dagger* as he ruminated. Sakaeri's retort that a dagger never suited him anyway did not go unheard. It annoyed him that he kind of agreed.

One part of her tale stood out.

"The Yun are said to have traversed the Great Starry Sea?"

To the realms, the Yun were a people of legend. They were beings of immeasurable power, capable of manipulating and shaping reality itself. Aeyun never paid much attention to it because it was nonsense. Gama-of-Yun was as ordinary as they came. The sage just lived, ate, and slept at that old a'teneum. Not once had he seen the man do anything *godly*. He just existed, and quite forgetfully at that.

But if the Yun had once travelled the Great Starry Sea . . . If Gama-of-Yun's ancestry had once sailed through what Aeyun assumed to be the vastness of Essence and energy . . . could it happen again? After all, the fables were false, but Gama-of-Yun was *real*.

"Yeah. Can you imagine some all-powerful beings showing up one day, dropping from the stars?" Sakaeri chuckled. A sort of stagnation preceded her next admission. "It's also said that their eyes looked like the starry sea itself."

"*What?*"

"You're not part Yun, are you?" Sakaeri asked, not for the first time.

Aeyun was starting to think it didn't matter if he denied it.

"No! Genuinely, I'm not!" he said, but she gave him an unconvinced side-eye. "You realise you're asking if I'm what is apparently believed to be part-deity, right?"

"See, you even phrase it weird."

"Sorry, what?"

Sakaeri sighed. "Nothing, Aeyun. Honestly." She stood as well as she could manage in the small space and made to go into the hull. "Today's been – well, every day has been an absolute cyclone of disaster lately. I'm going to make some tea and enjoy a moment to revel in the fact that I was able to see Rae, damaged as she is, and know that she's still alive with my own eyes."

She looked back over her shoulder and gave a short wave before closing the dormitory door. Once alone, Aeyun leant back down on his cot. Sakaeri wasn't wrong: every day had been disastrous lately.

For a moment, his mind drifted back to that memory of when the rift was open, where Raeyu was right in front of him, and he didn't push himself straight through it.

Why didn't I push myself?

He could have imagined it, and maybe he did, but it didn't *feel* like Raeyu wanted him to arrive yet. Like she knew it was too soon, or too rash. And, realistically, it was.

If Aeyun had used that ore, that would have been it. There may have been no return without risking Uruji's life. If he was even able to open a rift again. And didn't Aeyun want them to come back to the realms? Didn't he want his – now confirmed alive – sister to see them?

He did.

He also realised, somewhere in the recesses of his mind, that there was more going on. It wasn't just that Ca'lorus was separate from the realms. Aeyun got the impression that it was blocked from them, and he wanted to know why. Maybe Raeyu had come to that conclusion as well. Whether that was before or after her arrival in Ca'lorus, Aeyun wasn't sure.

Her arrival in Ca'lorus.

Raeyu was in Ca'lorus, with Uruji as well. And with Da'garu.

Raeyu was in his homerealm, without him, with Uruji and Da'garu.

Aeyun groaned. Things were entirely the wrong way up.

"Hey," Saoiri said upon her arrival back in the sea-skimmer. Davah was right behind her. "Believe it or not, there's only one other ore down there." She stopped to look pointedly at Aeyun, who had paused before his tea mug hit his lips. "Don't worry, we didn't touch it. We were careful."

"Good!" he said with a smile before he took a sip. She looked away. It almost seemed bashful, and Aeyun wasn't sure he wanted to address that.

"How about you grab it in the morning. We could probably all use a night's rest," Davah suggested, and Aeyun agreed.

"Sorry if I scared you all earlier. I know it's been–" he struggled to find the right word "–weird."

"Eye-opening!" Davah supplied triumphantly, and Saoiri looked thoroughly unimpressed.

"Very funny," she deadpanned.

"I know, right? Ha!"

"Look," Saoiri started as she grabbed a blanket from the stack in the corner. "It has been – all of that. But we chose to be here, and I for one am glad to be of help where I can be."

"I really do appreciate that," said Aeyun.

"We know," Davah said with a grin, then looked around. "Where's Sakaeri?"

Aeyun jabbed a thumb in the direction of the dormitory.

"I came out here to get a tea and she pretty much traded places with me right away. I don't think she wanted to hang out with me right now. Anyway, Sakaeri's not one for loads of socialising. She probably needed the space."

"Fair." Davah nodded, then glanced at the closed door. "Is it cool if we head in there to sleep, though?"

Aeyun shrugged.

"Wow. Thanks. Great help you are."

He took his chances anyway, sliding open the door and slipping in.

"Aeyun, can I talk to you about something?" Saoiri asked.

Aeyun nodded, indicating for her to sit down.

"Well, so, there's an ancient language tied to Mhedoon. For example, our hometown of Kilrona would actually be *a'kil'ron* in the ancient tongue. Likewise, that follows with many others, like *do'on'mhe* and *ga'gh'caig*." She nervously drummed her fingers on the table. "So, Davah's name is actually secularised; in the ancient tongue, it's *da'bhe*. Mine is in common tongue, ancient tongue being *i'sa'oir*. I'm only wondering because I've heard something in the ancient tongue you spoke: *da'ga'ru*. 'From great sky,' if directly translated. I just–" Saoiri looked at him, anxious. "It just seems odd?"

It is odd, Aeyun thought. The commonalities between

Mhedoon's ancient tongue and Ca'lorus's ancient tongue were too numerous.

"Davah said that your ancient language has loose ties to descantation," Aeyun replied, deciding to keep that narrative alive for now. "It seemed like someone needed to look up to not harm Rae and Uruji." He counted his lucky stars that it fit the story. "Rae had been pointing up, anyway."

"Oh." She didn't look convinced. "Yeah, I guess *Rae* was."

Aeyun's brows furrowed at the way Raeyu's name was said. Saoiri was gazing determinedly away from his face.

"I just thought I'd bring it up, since it stood out. Thanks for . . . Well, thanks."

With that, she stood and retreated into the dormitory where Davah had disappeared earlier. Upon her exit, the air left in the hull had a stagnant, stilted quality. Alone again, Aeyun let out a breath he hadn't realised he'd been holding in.

With more curiosity than usual, Aeyun angled his gaze upward, peering through the glassy panels of the sea-skimmer's roof, watching the star-spotted abyss above them.

"Are you happy?"

It wasn't a question he'd expected, and it wasn't one he found himself eager to answer. Maybe she knew that. Maybe that's why she continued on.

"It's hard to tell, right? It's the same for me."

It was spoken with a smile, and he didn't know how. It didn't fit, and yet somehow it did, perfectly. Just like her regal clothes, entirely right and wrong.

There she sat, a sunset framing her as he imagined she should be, drenched in light and colour, with an expression that didn't suit her sentiment. For some reason, it made him ache deep in a quiet corner of his soulsong that he couldn't reach. Couldn't comfort. Something in him hollowed.

"I don't know how to be happy." And he didn't know how to help her be happy, either.

CHAPTER SEVENTEEN

Aeyun tied the small pouch closed and looped its chain around his neck, keeping his one assured connection to Ca'lorus safe and on his person.

That morning, while Saoiri and Davah lay sleeping, he dove into the ocean to retrieve the remaining ore identified the night prior. Sakaeri begrudgingly accompanied him to tune the water away, jeering at his embarrassed, pleading look. Below, back in the depths, Aeyun took another moment to gaze at the stony mural in the building on the submerged hill. There was something hauntingly familiar about it still, and he tried to rack his brain as to why.

His first conclusion was that he'd definitely seen that stave somewhere before. A depiction of it, if nothing else. His second conclusion – perhaps more of an assumption – was that the stone around the second hooded figure's neck was likely the same type of ore he'd just draped from his own neck; a glowing gate alicant, or something like it. So, he theorised, at some point in the past, there was most likely a connection between at least Mhedoon and Ca'lorus, and these gate alicant weren't always just in gates, but with people.

Back in the hull of the sea-skimmer, Sakaeri asked, "What now, Yun-boy?"

"What?" Aeyun whipped his head around to stare at her, exasperated.

"Oh, nothing. What will we do now?"

Aeyun debated rebuking her outrageous claim – silently, he pleaded that she would just give it up, already – but he also figured that it would be more effort than it was worth, so he let it go.

"We look for more of these," he said, pinching the chain that connected to his new velveteen pendant.

"And that's it?" Sakaeri folded her arms across her chest, clearly disappointed. "We'll ignore the vision we saw, the archaeological record below us, the fact that your eyes turn *Yun*, and that you tore a rift out of thin air with a now crumbled ore that only *you* seem to be able to touch. Not to mention, we saw a realm that apparently does actually exist outside of our known realms. We'll ignore all that?"

"Right," said Aeyun. Sometimes he really did forget how much more he knew than the others. "The vision: I don't know how to approach that, and I don't think we could understand it right now if we tried. The stuff below us – well, yeah, it's not like we're about to start a dig, so why stay? My eyes don't turn *Yun*, get that out of your head, and we knew rifts were possible. I was holding an alicant that is usually in a Great Gate, or whatever that was, which connects realms. It makes sense, doesn't it?"

"Not really, Aeyun! And shouldn't we scope out the grounds, or something? See what other connection there might be, since you opened that rift here, in this place?"

"No."

"Why?" Her question was tired, desperate.

"Because it doesn't work like that!"

"How would you know!?"

Sakaeri's shout apparently stirred Saoiri and Davah from their slumber, because soon their heads were peeking out from the dormitory's entrance, eyelids still heavy with lethargy. Aeyun took a calming breath.

"Uruji opened a rift at the top of the Thasian Tower. As far as I'm aware, nothing in the ancient past would have been located there – *where* has nothing to do with it. We need more of this ore. That's it."

Sakaeri frowned and made a frustrated sound. "I don't get it. I don't get how you – you know what?" She uncrossed her arms and pressed on her temples. "I need space. I need space for a few days."

"You don't need to come back," Aeyun supplied. Sakaeri looked ready to rip him in two.

"Fuck off, Aeyun. *Fuck off* with your superiority complex."

"Right," Davah said. He entered the hull, carefully sidestepping Sakaeri. "I'll fire up the magnavaid. We're closer to Caiggagh, so let's just head there, yeah?"

There was only silence.

"Cool, yeah, we'll do that. Good talk, friends."

Caiggagh turned out to be similar to Kilrona, but on a much grander scale. Compared to other realms, it was quite small, but in its own context, Caiggagh was an epicentre of urban life.

Craftily constructed upon the cliffside and spreading further across that plateau above, Caiggagh was bustling with activity when they arrived at the cavernous port below. Sakaeri darted off without a word of goodbye, and Aeyun offered a brief apology to Saoiri and Davah, saying that he too could use some time. It had been too long since he'd truly had any extent of time to himself, and he felt like there was a lot plaguing his conscience these days.

With an agreement that they would meet back at the tip of the plateau in two days' time, Aeyun gave his thanks and headed off towards the watermill-powered lift – there were four of them in Caiggagh. As he reached the top of the cavernous shaft, he took a moment to gaze out across the watery vista beyond. It really did look endless, from that perspective. A deep line of blue diving off the horizon. Stepping onto the arrival platform, he gave his stiff right arm a stretch, then ascended to the flat, uppermost part of the plateau.

Where Kilrona had been lush and muggy, Caiggagh was more windswept and salty. The stone-carved buildings of the city were etched with weatherworn markings, and there seemed to be walls built specifically to shield various parts of the architecture from the coast's harsher elements. Caiggagh itself was very grey in terms of its palette, but Aeyun knew that all the colour was housed inside the buildings, be it by décor or wares or tight-woven shawls that kept the biting gales away.

Finally reaching the crest of the plateau, Aeyun took a glance back at the climbing city behind him. It really was a peculiar site to look down on, all varying levels and mismatched staircases. The plateau itself had bits of condensed city populating it; from the top, Aeyun could gaze all the way across it. Beyond the last of the city walls, a road led to the opposite end of the lifted landmass. There a forest stood, too dense to see through. He took note of this, a fleeting and quick catalogue, then wandered aimlessly into the heart of the city.

By the time his mind came back to him, he was sure that he'd looped around the city more than three times. The sun in the sky had already dipped down, the stars coming out to bask over him. Aeyun sighed and decided to stop by the holocaster – every large urban centre had one – to see if anything new had cropped up. It was under a larger dome in the centre of the plateau, presumably to stave off any weather-related damage. It hadn't taken him too long to trek there, navigating the narrow alleys he'd been circulating.

When he slipped inside, the inner portion of the dome was dark, the only ambient light coming from the powder-fine ore that glowed inside the holo-bubble. A few other people were scattered throughout the curved room, some sat on benches put in place to allow for comfortable spectating. Aeyun followed the rounded line of the wall until he leant against it, shoulders and one foot keeping him steady.

There was fifteen minutes of rambling about the various realms' weather patterns, and then coverage that Aeyun actually cared about finally began.

"Nearly a month into the Haebal disaster and the realm of Raenaru is still on lockdown," the announcer said. "No information is moving in or out of the region, and supply chains continue to be disrupted. A few trusted sources had reported that Seraeyu Thasian is still alive. However, we cannot confirm the state of the Thasian Legacy nor the citizens or city of Haebal." The announcer glanced over at something, nodded, then continued. "We are reminding our viewers that on the month's anniversary of this tragic event, a vigil will take place in every capital city across the realms. For those who may have lost loved ones, we extend our condolences, and we hope that you will find solace in this historic demonstration of solidarity."

Aeyun's thoughts soured.

Solidarity. Half the realms are probably pleased that Raenaru is in shambles. The other half would be clawing to take advantage of its misfortune. Ruling by fear didn't do the Haebalian Praetorship any favours. Oagyu never did care for nuance.

171

Next came the unveiling of a new museum in Quinga and a reported missing person case on Tenebrana – brought to light as it was a government official – and then came a report outlining how an Orinian woman's faulty respirator mask led to a manufacturer's mass recall.

Aeyun found his mind wandering.

The flashing, glowing dust that swirled around the holocaster lost his focus, and instead he considered the ghostly vision he and Sakaeri had seen under the ocean, in the time-forgotten settlement of Beldur. The unnamed woman's eyes came to mind, and he wondered what it could mean that some time, way back when, there was a harmonised Yu-ta woman who tore through a small, Ca'lorus-connected gate with a clear agenda to leave no survivors. Beyond that, the result of her actions looked a little too similar to what Aeyun had, on occasion, witnessed from Raeyu.

But Raeyu did not attune to wild Essence. She attuned to alicant, like the one in her scarred right arm; the one that was subsequently ripped off by a gone-mad Seraeyu Thasian. Nausea and anger boiled in Aeyun's gut, but he willed it to tamp down.

Aeyun had obviously never seen the alicant, since it was deeply embedded in Raeyu's flesh, supposedly fused to her bone, but he had his suspicions that somehow the alicant itself housed captured, raw Essence, filtered through gemstone. It didn't make any plausible sense, but the fact that the thing needed to be embedded with descantation as a guide, courtesy of the Thasian-nee, was odd enough. It hadn't once occurred to Aeyun that it might not be just Essence, but Vitality Raeyu drew upon confined there, too.

Now, though . . .

Now that seemed like the only thing that made sense. Vitality to soften the Essence, and alicant to instil an added barrier of protection between tuner and implement, providing a supplemental conduit. If, some way, a harmonised energy was present within that alicant, Raeyu and the Thasian didn't need to concern themselves with walking the dangerous thread of life

172

and death when it came to feral, untamed Essence. And they likely wouldn't even have been aware that Vitality was part of the deal. Raeyu said it was a secret tradition that spanned back longer than their records seemed to go. The Thasian bloodsong, as it was known. Their ability to harness pure power without a conduit, all thanks to a well-bred Yu-ta heritage.

The bloody falsity that it was.

Raeyu had said herself that she had doubts about the origins of it, and of the presumed noble intentions surrounding it. There had also definitely been some questionable actions in Thasian history – once warmongering, now riddled with shady industry and enterprise affairs – likely to protect this so-called bloodsong.

Regardless, the stories had done what they were meant to do, and they created fear and awe around the Thasian Legacy, enabling them to manipulate the realms into fealty time and time again. To gain favour among the Raenaruan Council, bending them to the Thasian agenda. Aeyun knew first-hand how much Raeyu despised it.

Despite it all, some treacherous part of Aeyun's mind started to wonder: *can I do it*?

Could he manifest what Raeyu could? Could he jump and appear through space like Raeyu could? A clip in reality, slipping through air and time like a sudden warp.

. . . Like Raeyu used to be able to do.

And then there was Seraeyu.

Seraeyu had been silenced by Aeyun's own hand, at the behest of Raeyu.

Raeyu had been terrified that, should she perish, Seraeyu would be made to take her place, and she wanted the cycle to stop. If Raeyu died, she wanted that alicant to disappear and for her younger brother to not be used as a tool for power. Perhaps foolishly, an only recently arrived Aeyun complied, and he pulled upon his intrinsic connection to the enigmatic energy he called Vitality. He'd done so in an effort to quiet Seraeyu's song when he was only young, moulding his very being to react to alicant differently, all to help Raeyu deceive her father into thinking that Seraeyu was Untuned. With their mother already passed, the true blood heir to the Thasian Legacy, no further children reared from Oagyu could reasonably claim the bloodsong, instead leaving it with Raeyu to bear until the next generation.

It was something Aeyun had never done before, quiet someone's innate song. He'd imagined a cage, something inky and twisted and vine-like, wrapping itself around and trapping that part of Seraeyu that could attune to alicant, and sealed it. When he had, it felt like a part of himself had been sealed away as well – that he had lost his ability to commune with something.

Now, Aeyun wondered if it was Essence. He'd only been able to connect with and *feel* it so viscerally recently. For as long as he had been in the realms, he thought he could *sense* Essence, but not manipulate it. Whenever he tried, it always felt stilted; strained. Inconceivable. He'd assumed that only Vitality was truly within his reach, and the smallest dabble into the uncomfortable and confining practice of ore tuning. Thinking back to it, though, he had connected to Essence in Ca'lorus. Right before he'd left it.

Seraeyu had, quite obviously, broken that seal. *But how?* It was the question that begged since he first saw Seraeyu tune. The younger Thasian seemed like he had been on a rampage, but it was a purposeful one. A focused one.

Aeyun was baffled, and a dripping guilt welled inside him, reminding him that he played a part in this, and that he had taken away something precious from Seraeyu, even if Raeyu had convinced herself that it was the merciful thing to do. In his fleeting time among the Haebalian elite, Aeyun had seen it. Seraeyu's spoilt disposition, the way he vied for attention, demanding respect from those around him. He was of a certain temperament and, given enough encouragement, he could've perhaps become a terror with his hands on that kind of power. He *did* become a terror with that kind of power.

He wondered if Raeyu had truly fooled herself into thinking she was playing the role of saviour, or if she admitted somewhere to herself that the thought of the bloodsong in Seraeyu's hands scared her, thinking of what her brother could become.

"Kaisa has been looking for you," a voice to his right startled him.

It was a Kaisan, roughed up from a recent scuffle. His eyes had the faintest hint of a glow, and his irises bore a distinctive cross.

"Tell Kaisa that I'm not interested," Aeyun muttered back, kicking off the wall.

The Kaisan tutted and shook his head. "He'll be disappointed to hear that, I'm sure."

"Let him be," Aeyun grumbled before he stalked out of the dome, arriving back on the night-shaded streets of Caiggagh. A brief glance behind him revealed that the Eye hadn't followed him, and it was only then that Aeyun let himself shiver.

He hated the feeling of being watched.

Aeyun walked to an inn a few blocks over – far enough away that the Kaisan wouldn't see where he went, if he had lingered – and booked a room for the night.

Spent, mentally and physically, Aeyun fell backwards and stared at the ceiling. Quietly, he cursed the realms and the entirety of the endless in-between.

He kept his gaze locked to the floor, as he always did in these situations. When he looked at him, he saw what lay beneath, and it made his blood run cold.

There was something cruel and slithering that clamped onto the man with a vice grip, and he hadn't been around him often enough to see if it ever loosened; if he ever softened. He was told it was a veneer, something of a defence, but he wasn't sure he believed that. He wasn't sure he wanted to believe that it could be, and that there was something more humane underneath it.

Without meaning to, his eyes travelled up the tile, catching on the ends of tattered slacks and bloodied feet. A dented manacle was still clasped around a chafed ankle. What had the boy done?

A shift in the ruined fabric had his focus snapping back to his own boots.

"Let me make it very clear that you saw nothing."

CHAPTER EIGHTEEN

"*Where—?*" The call echoed in segments, distorted.

Aeyun woke with a start and shot up, momentarily lost in the fog of bleary cognition, the bed where he lay feeling foreign. There was a voice. There was a call, and he felt compelled to respond to it, to bring it back, to welcome it.

But there was no one. The room was empty. But he could have sworn . . .

He scrubbed a hand down his face and grimaced at the days' old funk that wafted towards his nose upon the lift of his arm.

He needed a shower.

Checking the locks around the room in paranoia, he ensured that everything was securely latched before he discarded his pouch-held pendant, the pack on his belt – which held the seed and several other alicant and bits of biota – and his shoddy replacement dagger. He disrobed quickly and made his way to the attached bathroom. Like a boglizard drawn towards a pyre alicant, he was instinctively compelled to look in the mirror.

The twisting tattooed scar on his right arm looked as though it were growing, little by little, with every stitch he tuned. He wondered if the whole thing would be inky black at some point. Maybe he'd be better off getting rid of his arm before it became a permanent deadened weight at his side. He wasn't sure.

Aeyun's other mark – besides the new one above his hip – rested over where his heart beat steadily in his chest. It wasn't as smooth as the lines on his arm, but it also wasn't as jagged as the descanted scar that had been on Raeyu's arm. It was an amalgamation of the two, and it fanned out from its centre like ripples, little thorn-like edges protruding here and there.

Above Raeyu's heart was the very same mark.

He shouldn't have asked Uruji to do it. Even so, he still couldn't say that he regretted doing so.

Aeyun's eyes trailed up from that tethering symbol, the one that fated him to Raeyu, and caught sight of his own reflection. A haggard man stared back, bruised eyes and a greyish complexion. It wasn't surprising, considering, but he still sighed at the extent of it. In exhaustion, Aeyun leant forward and pressed his forehead against the cold mirror. He closed his eyes. Only for a moment. Just one moment.

If the realms could just still. If they could only allow him to take a breath. To wrap his head around what had happened and what was to come. If only he could grant himself the option to stop running, forward or backward. If only he could stop hiding. If only he had a place to rest his head.

When he resigned himself to face his reflection again, something shattered. He found himself frozen, looking into the void, and he could swear it was a familiar amber hue in his sight, not his own vivid green.

Startled, he pushed off the mirror and stumbled back.

It was only him. Him and him alone.

Aeyun scrubbed at his face again. He needed to shower, and he needed to get things done.

As it turned out, *getting things done* meant trekking towards that forest on the other side of the plateau. Something about it resonated with him, and he wanted to know why. On his way, he passed a few hikers, and it was the fourth one who'd bothered to address him.

"You going on the pilgrimage?" they asked with a pleasant smile.

"The pilgrimage?" Aeyun echoed. Was he?

"Yeah, the pilgrimage." The hiker chuckled lightly and nodded. "I see, you're not from around here, huh? The pilgrimage, to the forest." They waved a hand in reference behind them. "There's a shrine set up there right before the trees start shifting. Don't go past it; you'll never get out. Lose your sense of direction right away – the forest moves in weird ways, I'll tell ya. Everything up to the shrine is fine, though." The stranger smiled again, ignoring Aeyun's perplexed expression. They grabbed Aeyun's wrist, turning his palm up to drop a coin in it. "There. Go on now and offer that in the well there and you'll have good luck for the day, hm?"

By the time Aeyun acknowledged the interaction, the hiker had long since walked past him. He was left staring at the forest in the distance.

It *shifted*? It shifted, like the Ou'grobh?

Why, why, *why* had Aeyun waited so long to run around

Mhedoon?

With renewed vigour, he traipsed on, taking long strides towards the now much more appealing destination. It took longer than he anticipated, but he made it to the forest's edge, and he could see the shrine just beyond the first line of trunks. There was something in the air there, a certain energy that reminisced an old, familiar tune. Even the trees looked the same – were they the same species?

He slipped into the shrine's empty space, spotting the well and the smattering of offerings placed around it. Considering the coin that the stranger had given him, he tsked. With a smile, Aeyun tossed it into the well. Everyone had a right to their own traditions, after all. Sidestepping away from the small flower-surrounded and ornament-adorned shrine, Aeyun looked up at the canopy of foliage above.

It was too similar, right? Too broad-leafed, too spindled, too knotted around its bark. Too overgrown and too beckoning, urging him to come, explore.

Aeyun took five more steps, then felt the first shift. Scenery rushed by, and when he looked back, he was surrounded by dense forest, far from the shrine.

"No way," he whispered.

A jovial bubble of a laugh slipped out. Putting his hand on the nearest trunk, he patted the wood there, happy. As a test, he reached out from inside himself, seeking to tune with the forest, and he willed his next step to bring him back to the shrine.

As expected, he nearly walked into the backside of the well wall. Something close to a giggle tumbled from his lips and he was positively gleeful.

"I can't believe it," he said under his breath.

New agenda set, he turned heel and stepped back into the thick of the forest, letting it take him in. He allowed the trees to guide him where they pleased for a while, and he delightedly greeted them on occasion, offering a gentle nod. Eventually his steps slowed, and he paused to voice a thought.

"If you're here, are you from Ca'lorus? Or is the Ou'grobh from here?" He could have sworn the trees stuttered around him. His brow furrowed. "Was someone from Ca'lorus in these woods before?"

He took a step and exclaimed as he nearly fell, feeling as though he'd been tossed through the trees. When his foot landed, he found himself in different surroundings. Still in the forest, but there were old fissures in a bald spot of grass, congregated in a swirled pattern. Something there made Aeyun clam up. He wasn't sure if it was the forest, the fact that Essence scars remained there, or the fact that he could *feel* it simmering, not unlike the ones in Beldur.

Slowly, hesitantly, he walked forward. As he did, Essence began smoking upwards once more, just like before. It sparked, licking at his ankles as he landed upon the first fissure. Just like before, a hazy, spectral vision began to manifest, and it revealed the image of a man in a thick traveller's cloak, standing in the middle of the marks twisted upon the present-day ground.

The ghostly figure looked as though he had said something with a dry chuckle, then sighed in response to someone outside the field of view. Aeyun had turned his head in that direction, but all he saw were trees. The spectre of the man gave a tired nod and closed his eyes, then he opened them again and Aeyun could see a starry reflection. He said something once more, then energy shot up from the ground. It seemed as though it startled him, since his eyes returned to normal in a flash, and he'd jumped upwards in surprise. A few blinks saw him laughing, then he placed a hand on a nearby tree trunk and bowed to it.

The vision fell away and Aeyun stepped back from the Essence marks.

"Well, that was different from the last one," Aeyun considered aloud.

Taking a moment, he noted that he'd asked if someone from Ca'lorus had been in the woods. It looked like they had, at some point, in some time, and they were . . . attempting to harmonise?

Someone from Ca'lorus was on Mhedoon soil; he let it sink in.

There were signs between the two realms, and he couldn't claim they were all new revelations. Had Aeyun wilfully ignored them throughout his youth, he wondered. Had he pushed it to the back of his mind?

And there Da'garu had been on Ca'lorus, this whole time. She'd been there, alone.

Thinking he might continue on, Aeyun took a distracted step forward, then nearly tripped when the vision manifested again. *What? It didn't show up again in Beldur!*

He watched it play out in stiff trepidation, this time closer to the man, his sallow face showing in startling clarity, and he tried to read his lips. Something about 'not right' and then 'okay . . . again' and finally an apology to the tree.

Testing his chances, he reached out to the scars once more and attuned to them the way instinct compelled him to. The vision appeared for a third time.

"What in the realms . . ."

Aeyun had ended up wandering a while more, but he was too distracted, and soon he felt like he needed to be out of the wooded labyrinth. It didn't take long to make his way back to the shrine – he nearly put two pilgrims in an early grave when he arrived, if their shocked reactions were any indication – and he made the trek back to Caiggagh.

Night was falling once more, the sky darkening. Where he walked, there was a lower path along the sunken ridge, and he noticed that people had gathered there. Out of curiosity, he approached the crowd with softened footfalls. When he reached a small half-barrier, he saw hundreds of lanterns bobbing in the water far below, set out to sea.

The vigil, Aeyun thought.

Had it really been a month?

His eyes were drawn to the furthest lantern, where it crested on a ripple that reached up towards the twilight sky. Leaning on the waist-high rail, he distantly registered the sound of muffled sobs, somewhere to his right. He wondered who they had lost. Gaze still upon the furthermost lantern in the distance, Aeyun set his jaw.

I'll do my best.

I'm sorry I wasn't there.

. . .

I'll try my best, Jourae.

Aeyun swiped his wrist under his eye to disappear the wetness there, then took one large, deep breath before turning away from the vigil and continuing his journey to Caiggagh.

When he finally stepped foot inside the city gate, dusk had fully set upon the vacant streets. In the darkening hours, the surrounding lamps pulsed with bits of alicant that had soaked in the daylight. The paths were quiet, with a crowd still on the cliffs and others in the dome or dispersed over the cascading oceanside edge. Only a few people manoeuvred around him as he went, including a pair of children who ran past him, in a rush to get somewhere.

Hit with something akin to nostalgia, he turned to look as the kids skidded around the corner, the older one leading. For the briefest of moments, he saw an echo of himself and Uruji, scampering through the evening-dimmed streets of Haebal, Uruji beaming up at him in one of his rare moments of delight.

"Ah, damn," Aeyun muttered as he pinched the bridge of his nose.

He'd not allowed himself time to process. There hadn't been a spare moment, not yet. Now, he was drowning in the passing seconds.

You okay, Uruji? Aeyun wondered. Last he saw, Uruji wasn't even awake. Was he now? *You're looking after him for me, right, Rae?*

182

Aeyun ambled on, dipping into a vendor's kiosk to purchase a simple meal as he went – he really wasn't eating enough lately. As he bit into the handheld morsel, he caught a glimpse of himself in the distorted reflection of a shop window. In his mind's eye, he saw the shadow of someone else beside him, shuffling her feet before she'd leant close, smallest finger threading into his own. When he looked down, though, his hand was as it had been; scarred and on its own.

Aeyun cursed under his breath before biting down into the food he held.

By the time he'd made it to the exterior of his inn, the twilight had finally turned to night. He didn't have to look up to know the moon was obscured. The moisture that hung in the air told him that it would certainly be raining later, if not soon.

About to climb the stoop into the lobby of his accommodations, Aeyun paused when the familiar feeling of being watched washed over him. The hair on the back of his neck stood and he fought the urge to pull out his blade.

"What do you want?" Aeyun asked, turning fully to the side to face his visitor head on.

"Is that any way to greet a friend?" Kaisa leered, arms crossed as he made a tutting noise. "I was so very disappointed to hear that you weren't interested in my invitation."

"Why would I be? We aren't friends."

Aeyun stood his ground, taking note of the still very abandoned streets. Kaisa gave a half-hearted chuckle and waved dismissively.

"So you say." He took a step closer, and Aeyun felt his muscles tense. "But we could be, *Hana*–"

It only took a split second and Aeyun's replacement dagger was held in defence before him, his grip steadier than his heartbeat. A good metre was placed between himself and Kaisa after he'd leapt back and crouched down, ready to fight at a moment's notice.

"Don't call me that," Aeyun said through gritted teeth.

Kaisa laughed. "Oh-ho, dear me! Imagine my surprise when I found out that you were a Thasian pet!" Kaisa put his fingers to his mouth, obscuring his grin. "The prophetic Raeyu's faithful Hana, at least until he ran off maybe a year ago. My Eyes stopped reporting sightings of her little guard dog around then. The same time Jourae-nee's unremarkable apprentice disappeared – what a coincidence, indeed!" Kaisa stepped closer, and Aeyun's other hand crept towards the pack of alicant on his belt. "Of course, I'd already heard the whispers about a bastard son; it couldn't have been anyone else, really. And *then*! And then." Kaisa's voice dropped into a conspiratorial whisper. "None other than he himself shows up to offer me a deal with Thasian-nee craft on hand. Wild, our realms are, truly."

"What do you want, Kaisa?" Aeyun asked again, glaring when Kaisa leant too close, allowing the blade of Aeyun's dagger within easy striking distance. It would be effortless, too, if his hand wasn't trembling under the weight of it.

"Satisfy my curiosity. Tell me why you ran off, and I'll tell you what my Eyes have seen on the ground in Haebal." Kaisa's grin grew at Aeyun's hitched inhale. "I know you'd like to know." Aeyun glanced down as Kaisa's finger gently pushed the dagger away. "Let's take a walk, shall we?"

A few minutes later they were winding further into the city, side by side as Kaisa's dark, breezy jacket billowed in the squalls that swelled with the drop in pressure; a warning of that imminent weather. If Aeyun's right arm hadn't ached already, it most assuredly started to then.

"Will you be telling me your story anytime soon?" Kaisa asked as their boots' steps echoed around them. Aeyun kept a fist wrapped around the hilt of his dagger, held under his cloak as they meandered, his every step tight and calculated.

"No. How about you start with your tale?"

"Tsk, tsk, Aeyun! You play so unfair!" Kaisa gave a put-upon sigh. "Fine, then. It's quite gruesome, so you'd best be ready." Aeyun didn't respond. "Well, just after Seraeyu's little show for that ill-fated reporting Eye, one of mine kept watch nearby. Poor Untuned Seraeyu is certainly Untuned no more – but I figure most of the realms know that now. Anyway, he took his dear sister's arm – that *was* beloved Raeyu's arm, wasn't it? – and ripped something out of it." Aeyun could feel colour drain from his face, and he fought the gag that snaked up his throat. "Can't say for sure what it was, but he tossed the limb aside after that, obviously having got what he'd wanted. After that, things became . . . odd."

"Odd?" Aeyun struggled to say, trying not to imagine Raeyu's cold arm skidding across the rubble.

"Mm, odd. I even saw it on the feed, and I have a tough time describing it. I guess whatever Seraeyu found there, he didn't like it. He screamed bloody murder and there was this implosion. In the depths of it, I could swear . . ." Kaisa pursed his lips, then shrugged. "Well, anyway, that was it for my poor Eye, too. It wasn't until a week or so later that I got another report. What's left of the Thasian Tower is barricaded in Essence – pure Essence, like the kind from the fables – and no one has heard hide nor hair from *Praetor* Seraeyu. Not directly, anyway. It's been like that since then, like he's waiting for something in there. And, of course, no word is going in or out of Haebal, and travel is barred from Raenaru because Yun forbid the realms find out what a disaster it really is, considering the towering mass of untamed *chaos* swirling around the centre of that city. It's like a pyre alicant, just biding its time until the kaboom, you know?"

"He's waiting?" Aeyun got a sinking feeling. "For what?"

"For what, indeed." Kaisa hummed as the first droplets were dispelled from the sky. "Now, on to you, my dearest friend."

Aeyun frowned and pulled his hood forward, watching the ground paint black under the drizzle. Next to him, Kaisa unfurled an umbrella.

"I left before Oagyu could kill me," Aeyun said. A portion of the truth.

"Ah, he already knew you were the Thasian-nee's bastard son. You can't skip by on that one, I'm afraid. Why would Oagyu want to skewer your measly self out of existence?"

It was a gamble, a dangerous game that Aeyun would play.

"What did you see in the implosion?"

Sensing Kaisa's dismissal, Aeyun stopped and gripped harshly onto his arm, turning him so that they stood eye to eye. The jesting smile on Kaisa's face faded at whatever expression Aeyun held, and he instead adopted an intrigued appraisal.

"For a moment – a trick of the eye, perhaps – Seraeyu looked, well, accompanied, let's say. Some sort of phantom of *something* was with him, incorporeal and ambiguous, but there."

"I see." Aeyun catalogued this. "I had a hand in silencing Seraeyu. He was never Untuned. That's why Oagyu would've killed me. He started sending tails after me; the intention was obvious."

"Ha, you–" Kaisa's disbelief morphed into something reticent. "You're joking. That's not possible." For a moment, they stood still as rain started to pelt down around them, filling the air with a dull roar. "That's not possible."

"Don't stand in my way," Aeyun said, taking a step back, removing himself from the umbrella's shield.

"I – was that a threat?" Kaisa asked with a raised brow, almost looking amused.

Aeyun steeled his expression into something deadly. "Yes."

"Dear, precious Aeyun." Kaisa tutted with a light chuckle. "You *are* terrifying."

"What was that?"

There were three of them, and he felt his lungs squeeze. He couldn't even swallow air if he wanted to, and he was sure that if he did, he'd make a horrible gasping sound. Instead, he stayed hidden under wood and rubble, wishing to things he didn't understand that they would just leave.

"You think it was one of them?"

He didn't want to cry. He didn't want to fear. He didn't want to be there at all.

A hand burrowed into the back of his tunic and yanked him from his hiding place, as if he were an animal to be caught by the scruff of his neck. A grimace and exposed teeth flashed in his vision as he thrashed wildly, limbs swiping out in all directions to escape.

"You should unhand that child if you do not want the consequences thrust upon you." The voice, slow and steady, was paired with a grim frown and an erudite air.

He never did find out what happened after that, his eyelids fluttering shut, opening to an endless dark with ghostly echoes.

CHAPTER NINETEEN

It happened again that morning.

After Aeyun had returned to his inn, leaving a bewildered and likely even more fascinated Kaisa in the rain, he'd tossed and turned for the majority of the night, nightmares clawing at his ankles. He'd woken once more to a distorted call, mists of willowy black behind his eyelids, but when he'd looked around the room, he was most assuredly alone.

With only the morning left to him before he met up with Davah and Saoiri, Aeyun realised that he'd dallied too long. If he wanted to put any sort of plan in motion for his seed alicant, the one that currently tumbled neglected in his satchel, he'd have to be hasty about his errands. Ideally, he'd have liked to make his own implement, but with time as short as it was, he'd have to find something prefabricated that would do.

Aeyun slid into shop after shop, but nothing felt *right*. Too dull, too sloppy, too brittle. He'd ended up with a second-hand gauntlet that had a deep-set slot for an embedded stone. The material was half metal and half leather, so it offered space for movement while also providing surface area for Aeyun to carve into, leaving him the option to optimise it for better attunement – a task he would have to do later. While not his preference, it wasn't the worst he could do.

It was nearing midday and Aeyun took stock. He had all he'd come with, so logistically he was ready to meet with Davah and Saoiri. Mentally, though . . .

Aeyun wanted more time to explore, or to ponder his current state of things. In the brief reprieve, he felt like he'd barely had a moment to breathe. Then there was the issue of Kaisa.

In retrospect, it hadn't been a good trade. To know that Seraeyu was self-barricaded and likely named Praetor, something generally amiss about his sudden resurgence of power, wasn't too large a leap that Aeyun couldn't have already guessed it. Now, Kaisa knew that Aeyun was capable of something that shouldn't be possible, and surely he'd be curious as to how and why. If for no other reason than to figure out how he might harness it.

It had been a dumb choice.

But it was also a threat. He wanted Kaisa to think that he could take away his ability to tune with ore. He wanted him to be wary, fearful enough that he might steer clear. Aeyun likely couldn't do it, of course, as the situation would be very different.

Seraeyu had still been impressionable and pliable. Regardless, if Kaisa thought him capable of it, maybe he wouldn't cross the line. So, it had been an okay choice?

No, it had been a stupid decision.

While lost in his reverie, Aeyun hadn't copped onto the presence of the two Mhedoons.

"What has you looking all pensive, friend?" Davah asked.

Aeyun's head snapped up and he blinked at the two of them. They were wearing different garb, something picked up from a local clothier, he was sure, and Saoiri looked as though she'd taken the time to plait her hair in some sort of pattern.

Stood at the main wall, on the very tip of the plateau, the three of them were crowded around one of the small viewing ports; a tiny square punched in the stone where one could observe the horizon. Aeyun shook himself out of his slump and shrugged.

"Just the regular worries: alicant, gates. Missing heirs and siblings."

"I thought I was the one with the bad jokes," Davah said with a smirk, crossing his arms in a petulant show.

Beside him, Saoiri rolled her eyes. "What did you get up to the past two days?" she asked.

"Ran around a bit. Found that lucky well. Some hiker gave me a coin to toss in," Aeyun told her.

The benefits and detriments of disclosing more rattled around in his head like loose change. Davah snorted and scuffed his boot on the cobbled ground.

"Useless tradition. Charming, but a load of shite."

"You didn't walk in, right? Well, obviously not, I guess. You're standing here now," Saoiri reasoned with herself, as if she shouldn't have mentioned it in the first place.

Aeyun felt his shoulders tense and he shifted, uncomfortable. He forced a chuckle and said, "I was warned about that, alright."

The traveller had indeed tried to dissuade him from going past the well.

"Did you catch the vigil?" Davah's tone was surprisingly

sombre, unsuited to his disposition. "Shame it rained later."

"Yeah," Aeyun said quietly.

He didn't want to talk more about it. Saoiri must have picked up on that since she cleared her throat and adjusted the bag slung over her shoulder.

"So, where's Sakaeri? Are we waiting?"

Aeyun frowned, thrusting his attention to his instincts to feel if they were being watched. If they were, it was probably her. Or a Kaisan. Or someone else who decided they had a vendetta against the ore-smugglers, or Aeyun himself.

Thoughts of how they should probably be more careful and discreet in the future crossed his mind.

Projecting, he didn't feel the distinct marker of Vitality that was Sakaeri's foreboding presence, and the lack of it disconcerted him more than he'd be willing to admit.

"Aeyun?" Saoiri prompted.

"I don't think she's here," Aeyun responded. Had she really just . . . left?

"Should we hang out and see if she shows up?" Davah questioned.

Aeyun scanned the crowd in the area. No one stood out, and no one looked over.

"I guess not," said Aeyun. He started to walk towards the entrance to the cascade that led to the watermill-lifts. "Let's go."

Their apprehensive gazes burned into his back as he went.

Halfway down the lift's descent, Aeyun's unease truly started to set in. Everything in his being was screaming that something was wrong – *wrong!* – and he should do something about it. Unfortunately, Aeyun didn't know what that something was, or why it needed to be done. When the gate opened to the docks, Aeyun was feeling fidgety.

They wove through the crowd and looked for the bay they'd moored the sea-skimmer in. It still was there, floating and unassuming in the calm marina waters. Aeyun paused.

Something wasn't right. Something felt just disjointed enough that Aeyun's every nerve was on edge.

"Hey, is that light on in there?" Davah asked.

Where he'd pointed, there was a glowing speck visible through the frosted panels – a handy feature to obscure the interior from curious onlookers, when desired. Upon further observation, Aeyun could see that a light was, in fact, on.

"Shit," he muttered.

He surged forward, taking long strides to cover the rest of the distance to the sea-skimmer. Clambering up and ripping open the latch, he dropped into the hull and scoured his eyes across the interior.

LIAR

It was etched violently on the wall above the now-open hatch where the gate alicant had been stored. Left sheered and gaping, it was clear that the stowed enclave had been emptied of its goods.

"Shit!" Aeyun said again, and then his gaze caught on a stone out of place, one that had slid under the table.

He picked it up, knowing what it was immediately, having made use of its sister stone not so long ago. Sakaeri's communication stone, discarded. A distant tug guided him to glance back up at the angry accusation on the wall again.

"Oh damn, friend," Davah called breathlessly from above, leaning into the rooftop opening.

Saoiri appeared beside him, and her hand flew swiftly to cover her sudden gawp.

"Oh, no!" she said as she dropped into the hull and scrambled to assess the damage. "Who would do this? Did Sakaeri . . .?"

Aeyun didn't answer because he didn't know. He didn't know, but something felt awry.

"We should leave," Aeyun announced. He couldn't keep from staring at the etched lettering. "I think we should get out of here."

"Right," Davah said, dropping in as well and making his way to the magnavaid. "Tell me where you want to head and we–"

"No, I mean this skimmer. And Caiggagh. And Mhedoon. We should leave it all."

Aeyun felt it. That notion of being observed, and he couldn't tell from where, but it was most certainly there. The bags of ore scattered around the place didn't help, either. If there was attunement to some sort of audio-tuned alicant; one that projected or recorded. Or even multiples of that kind.

"What?" Davah slowly began to back away from the magnavaid. "What do you–?"

"Grab nothing, we have to go," Aeyun said, leaving no room for argument.

Saoiri gave him a disheartened gaze, but she did as instructed and climbed out of the sea-skimmer. Davah, on the other hand, offered more protest until Aeyun basically forced him from the craft.

Once alone, Aeyun dug around the various sacks until he found what he knew for sure to be pyre alicant. He mechanically placed them around the sea-skimmer, distributing them among the various other treasures and wares. He felt the oppressive energy rolling off almost every corner of the sea-skimmer, so he was sure there were several alicant devices hidden away.

He was so, so sure of it.

With Sakaeri's abandoned communication stone in hand, Aeyun followed his crewmates out of the craft and gave them a tight-lipped shake of his head.

"Tell me we're not leaving this baby," Davah pleaded, but it didn't get him an answer. "We're just leaving it? All of it?"

"Let's sort out something else," said Aeyun.

Parting with far more coin than any of them wanted to, they were able to purchase a used sea-skimmer from a broker on the far end of the docks. After they made the deal, Aeyun twisted the communication stone around his fingers. Something was–

"This magnavaid is just as second-rate as the sea-skimmer! It's half broke!" Davah complained, swiping the dust off the old panel set above the craft-embedded alicant.

"We could have at least grabbed the blankets," Saoiri grumbled, sitting on a ratty old bench that replaced their previous table-and-chair combo.

"Can you get us to the Great Sea Gate?" Aeyun asked Davah, who gave him a begrudging nod. "That's good," Aeyun muttered distractedly, still fumbling with Sakaeri's communication stone.

When they navigated away from the docks – sea-skimmer creaky and groaning – Aeyun looked back through the yellowed, glassy panels. He focused on the pyre alicant in their old sea-skimmer and concentrated. There, it was like he could feel it, that confined energy, its blistering song bouncing around in the crystalline, fiery red masses. It wasn't enough to feel it, though. Aeyun had to draw it out, and pyre alicant being some of the most abundant, he'd ensured he had some on himself, pierced into his ears in the rare case he needed to call upon it and attune to like brethren. Even so, the compressed nature of it felt wrong, and Aeyun couldn't wrap his head around the right tune. It didn't make sense to him. Fire was meant to be wild and chao–

"Oh, fuck," left his lips before he'd even realised what he'd done.

His mind had wondered to the vision he'd witnessed in the woods and soon the pungent zap of Essence stung the air. A moment later, he felt a manifestation draw itself together and slither to wrap around the pyre alicant, far from him, hidden within the sea-skimmer still stationary at the docks. Without his consent, the Essence constricted on the pyre alicant, and Aeyun's eyes widened in horror as it did.

All noise was sucked away from the area and, from the mouth of the cavern, Aeyun watched, morbidly entranced as the first explosion of the chain erupted. One after another, blinding flashes reflected off the dampened stony walls, an odd combination of white and blue and streaks of jagged black. A cacophony of sounds came back at once, piercing and loud, and shrapnel flew in every direction. It took a second for Aeyun to realise that it wasn't only from their exploded sea-skimmer, but from structures and vessels around it as well.

The first scream reached his eardrums before they rung in

a high pitch, and then Aeyun, Davah, and Saoiri were being pushed out to the ocean in a strong backlash wake, away from the wreckage and mayhem.

Aeyun stumbled back and Saoiri was shouting something he couldn't hear. He didn't even look at Davah as he crashed into one of the sea-skimmer walls. A thick wetness made him wipe at his eye and his hand came away smeared in crimson. With a jolt of pain, Essence twisted down his arm and he subconsciously clenched his fist around the communication stone, willing his Vitality to calm the prickling shock that pinged through his form.

Time stuttered, tearing into jagged bits, and knowledge flooded into him, too much to comprehend. Symbols in his mind that played like a reel: *New ore?* Or *Hello.* Or *Nothing of interest.* Then there were other segmented conversations about danger and death and seeking. And the more foreboding warning: *don't come back.*

Aeyun doubled over and bloody droplets dripped onto the rusty floor where his hands trembled, barely holding him up. He rolled onto his side and grimaced, chest aching. As he hacked a breath, the torn reality's unnatural vibrations abated, filling his misshapen visage of the realm with a haze. Something warm and familiar and safe flooded his veins. Indistinguishable, but present.

He could almost feel it, the whispered, discordant caress of a distant touch.

"*Calm down.*"

"What?" Aeyun asked, his voice still muted to his own ears.

"*You're hurting.*"

"I'm sorry. I . . . I'm sorry."

"*Is someone there to look after you?*"

"I don't know. I messed up."

"*–yun!*"

"*I can't stay. I don't know how. Don't strain yourself.*"

Exhaustion spread from Aeyun's toes to his fingertips, and he was only just becoming aware that his eyes were open but unseeing, gazing into a void of something without form.

"–yun!"

"I don't know if I can do this."

"*Don't burden yourself. It's okay.*"

"–yun!" The call was getting more desperate, and the voice was near, but he couldn't place it.

"Don't say that. I won't give up."

Somehow, his surroundings felt less real than they had a moment before, more of a fleeting mirage, and he was starting to feel the floor pressed to his shoulder once more.

"*You never were–*" there was a brief pause, and it felt like fading, "*–one for letting go.*"

"Aeyun!" Saoiri's cry reached him, and awareness returned to him with a sharp inhale of breath. "Oh, Yun! Aeyun!" Saoiri was knelt beside him, tears rolling down in rivulets from the tip of her chin as she hiccupped. "He's alive, Davah!" she called, sounding relieved.

"Well, thank fuck," Davah said from somewhere to the right.

"Aeyun, what happened? What even happened?" Saoiri sobbed.

Aeyun, while trying to get his bearings, struggled to sit upright and he brushed his palms across his face, leaving them doused in sticky red. The realm was spinning, and his head pounded with tension while his chest felt odd, his pulse faint.

"What?" he said confusedly, brows knitting. "What?"

"I swear you were dead. You weren't breathing! Did you mean to do it, Aeyun?" He stared at her, unable to string coherent thoughts together. "Did you mean to kill those people, Aeyun?"

"I didn't – I didn't kill . . ."

"Aeyun, everyone on those docks is dead," Saoiri said with a lump in her throat.

"On the . . . docks?" Aeyun's head continued to swim, and his beating heart was sluggish. Slow. Everything was slow. "I killed people on the docks?"

"Aeyun, what's going on?"

It was an effort to look up at her; he realised he must have slid down the wall. He couldn't feel his right arm. Without thinking, Aeyun clawed at his shirt, pulling it up as far as he could – fumbling more than once – until it was lifted above his pectorals, and he tried to scrutinise the mark there. The inky thorns had spread out, looking angry and rotting, and a webbing of blackened, poison-tainted veins networked from the scar.

"Shit," Aeyun breathed. "This is . . . my fault."

Saoiri reached towards him, hesitated, then drew back her hand.

Everyone on those docks is dead. Aeyun closed his eyes. *I won't let you die now. I won't let you die.* He reached out with his Vitality, feeling for fleeting soulsongs, free from their confines. Aeyun reached out to cradle them.

I'm sorry.

He called to them.

I'm so sorry.

Colourless manifestations flew towards him, and he wasn't sure if Saoiri even saw the one that careened by her head. Aeyun felt them coalesce inside him, filling him with life where it was fading, even if they were diluted when they reached him. As they melded within him, his crimson tears stopped seeping, instead becoming watery once more.

I'm so sorry!

His heartbeat rushed to a gallop, filling his body with energy, and feeling swept back into his right arm. The bright pulse of life centred around his heart, and he felt it traverse elsewhere, siphoned through an incorporeal thread.

I'm so sorry! I had to!

Realising what he'd done – everything he'd done – Aeyun crawled himself back up the wall, into a standing position.

"*Ca'ou o, cah e'ju, ou'uo.*" This time, a salty trail slithered down his cheek. "*Ou'e'uo.*" He banged the back of his head on the wall. "*A'pan o!*" Aeyun bit back a sob. "*A'pan o . . .*"

A'pan o, he apologised to the numbing buzz in his mind, over and over and over again.

It was quiet in the land-skimmer, as it tended to be. He sat huddled in a corner, at least two-fourths of the realm blocked by his makeshift barricade. Across from him, despair wafted over in sullen waves. It was making his foot antsy, nerves dancing.

"I think he's really left this time."

The words were spoken without prompting, and he didn't know why she was telling him that. Or maybe he just didn't want to acknowledge that she was looking for some solace that he couldn't provide. That he didn't want to provide. It didn't help that he knew the words to be true because something felt wrong, and he didn't know why.

"I knew he would eventually, but I didn't think it would be like this."

He wasn't sure why those words unsettled him, enough to glance at her and her red-rimmed eyes, but they did. He found himself looking down again, inwardly cursing his own worthless hands.

CHAPTER TWENTY

Seraeyu awoke with a start this time. The sun was fading beyond the crest of the horizon, and he once again found himself on the half-crumbled roof of the Thasian Tower. He suspected that this was yet another time whatever entity resided in him didn't intend on his intrusion, since he could already feel a bruise forming where his hip had hit the slate tiles.

With a groan, he collected himself and sat up, observing that he was not in a robe this time, but slacks and a pair of leather shoes.

Oh, lovely. Having some fun with fashion, are we? he thought blithely. Seraeyu stood and noticed a dull ache behind his chest. *Odd.*

He had dreamt again, and this time it was of death, but not his own. He had offered condolences, words of comfort, but they were fractured and ragged. Confused. Hapless in his inability to actually help. He could only comprehend the bastardised impression of shallow breaths and a bloodied face, broken in its own way. What was he meant to do? He already felt haunted, and now his guilt festered in his subconscious, he supposed. He wondered how many times his mind would manifest tragedy, forcing him to bear witness.

Walking to the edge of the roof, he gazed upon Haebal City – the place he'd loathed so deeply in the past, but now, as he stared at its empty streets, he wished for the festivals to return. For the people to be milling around, going about their daily business, gossiping about their neighbours, about what they might have for dinner. He missed the mundane most of all, and he smiled tightly as he ran his fingers through his hair. It was an anxious action he'd picked up at some point, and as his nails left his scalp, he noted that his strands were long enough that it must have been a while since they'd been cut. He'd already been late on a trim, so the fact that they tickled the base of his neck now told him he'd neglected it for weeks more.

Or that the *daemon* had, whomever the entity was who took over him.

He wasn't quite sure how it happened, but it certainly did. This *thing* took control of him for prolonged periods of time, killing, negotiating, *ruling*. It was infuriating and . . . terrifying. Seraeyu was still lost, and he could only recall mere minutes; fleeting moments between his comatose stasis when she took control. Whatever she was doing, he knew it wasn't good.

In the same breath, though, that Sentinel hadn't been scared of him, so what *was* the woman playing at? Whatever game it was, she seemed to be winning.

Seraeyu looked down at his hands where they rested on the railing. They were adorned with his mother's rings again, and a quick tug at his ear told him that he had her earrings on as well. Was it for show? Or was it –

Without daring to consider the consequences, Seraeyu held out a hand and attempted to find the pyre-ring's tune, trying to connect with the resonance of it. A burst of flame sizzled out into the humid evening air, evaporating with a wisp of smoke.

"Oh," Seraeyu said, an exclamation where words failed.

It was so *easy*. It was *effortless*. He did it again and got the same result. Then he drew a circle's shape, the cloud of its dissipating impression lingering for a moment before being carried away by a gentle gust.

A bubble of laughter escaped him, a little manic, before he attempted to tune with an air-based accessory – the one that held a beautiful translucent green gem. The wind picked up around him and swirled, rustling his loose shirt, fluttering his uncut locks. Another chuckle left him, but it unfurled into something morose, and he sniffled as the zephyr died down.

So, he wasn't Untuned.

"Was it worth it, Seraeyu?" he asked himself bitterly. "Whatever you did, was it worth it?"

He sniffled again and turned away from the city, looking up at the greying sky. The stars twinkled down at him, glittering among the dark depths, and he gave them a wry smile.

He swallowed thickly. "You're Praetor now, right? No shadow? You can tune. Isn't it just brilliant, Seraeyu?"

A sudden sensation crashed over him, and he tipped forwards, unsteady.

"Oh," he said, breathless.

He felt it – no, he *heard* it. A silent song, carried across starry waves, reaching him from far beyond. It was the same as *that* day. The one when he was stuck in that odd black void. He'd reached out then, looking for that missing piece in the darkness. What he'd found were weary green eyes, staring at him from the hint of a reflection that he couldn't quite wrap his mind around.

He knew, though. When he found it, it was as clear as day because of the familiarity. That resonance that had disappeared maybe a year ago. The presence of that man who followed his sister around like a lost pup. Seraeyu *knew* it was him. And those eyes haunted him, refusing to dissipate from his memory. Not only because it was so plainly Aeyun – Aeyun born Krunan, Aeyun Thasian-nee, the man in the mask, he *knew* – but because those mossy irises looked plagued with obligation, dimmed and listless. And Seraeyu was confused.

Why had it been Aeyun, of all people, whom Seraeyu had found in that void, and why did he seem so sapped of life? Was he looking for Raeyu? Was he with her? Did he know his father and brother had perished? Is that why? Did he care that Seraeyu was still in Haebal? Did he know that something – some mystic parasite – was taking hold of his actions?

Maybe his dream . . . wasn't a dream. Maybe Aeyun was out there, somewhere, bloodied and fading, hanging on words spoken from a voice he might recognise.

Now, stood on the battle-torn roof, Seraeyu could feel him again. It was like a pulse that exploded, seeking a response from Seraeyu, only he didn't know what to do. The silent tune was *strong*, and it was abrupt, and Seraeyu was sure that something more happened. But why could he feel it?

A very small part of him, the one that cowered in fear in the corner of his mind, wondered if Aeyun heard it too, however quietly it might ring out. Or if he didn't feel it at all. Somehow, considering that option was even more terrifying, and Seraeyu swallowed an emptiness in his throat, its bitter desolation spreading into the rest of his being.

"Whatever you're at, child, stop at once!"

Seraeyu thought only of his isolation as he faded.

Seraeyu awoke looking at a velvet canopy, and a dull sigh announced his arrival. He didn't bother getting up. Instead, he lay flat and smacked his palm on his chest.

"Who. Are. You?" he demanded, emphasising each word with a whack. "I will scream and shout and do whatever I must if you don't tell me *who* and *what* you are. I'm tired. I'm *done*." Seraeyu tried to dig deep into his consciousness, searching for wherever this thing's nest was. "Who are you, and what are you doing?"

"*Do not be mistaken, child. I hold the power over you.*"

"Oh, I'm well aware," Seraeyu answered. "And yet, here I demand answers still. Will I pester you into submission? Annoy you enough to tell me? I can, you know. I've been called many names in my time, and 'nuisance' has been one of the nicest ones. Will I live up to it, then? I can be *insufferable*."

A pause followed, then finally the voice responded, "*You're angry, young Yu-ta.*"

Seraeyu sat up at that. "Of course, I'm angry!" he growled lowly. "You've stolen not only my body, but my memories! I have not been myself for who knows how long, and I have no clue as to the state of things! I also seem to be able to tune, but I – I . . . none of it makes sense."

"*I removed your cage, like I said I would.*"

"What?"

"*I removed that which silenced you, a foul act imposed upon you. I freed you, young Yu-ta, and now you are helping me fulfil what needs to be done.*"

"I'm sorry?" Seraeyu asked.

She *freed* him? To then control him? And he, what, agreed to this? When?

"*You truly do not recall. You came to me, that night. You found me, as if by destiny, and you called upon me – it was the right tune sung in your soulsong. I could hear it, resonating so evidently; we were meant to become as we are now. I removed your shackles, and so did you mine. I told you that I would provide you with all that you lacked, and in exchange you would assist me complete my calling. My purpose."*

Seraeyu was afraid to ask, "And what's your purpose?"

"To right the wrongs of the past."

"What does that mean?" Seraeyu closed his eyes, trying to piece together what he could from the experiences he'd had since his foray into the catacombs. "Did I ask you that, then?"

"You said yes."

Seraeyu scowled. That meant *no*, then.

"It has been nary longer than a month since we met."

Something about that didn't sit well in his mind. A month? There was this much devastation in Haebal City within a month since Seraeyu was cognisant? What in the realms could have happened in that time?

Torturously, his memory recycled visions of the Yu-ta man chained in the cistern, and the corpses not far beyond. That Oagyu was dead. Jourae was dead. Uruji was dead.

"These wrongs of the past . . ." He felt like his own breath was choking him. "Who committed them?"

"Many, child."

"Were they Yu-ta?"

He didn't want to know. He didn't want to know. He didn't want to–

"Many of them, yes."

Seraeyu already knew when he asked, "Have you killed with my hands? Have you killed Yu-ta with my hands?"

"They were not your own when those acts were committed."

"What did you do to them? To my father? To Jourae-nee? Uruji-nee?"

"They suffered as they deserved. I still seek the rest. I will find them."

Seraeyu shook his head, staring at his hands, remembering the blood upon them. Remembering the scratches on his face and neck. The mottled bruise, as though he'd been choked. Perhaps as a comfort, he plucked at the chain lying against his collarbones then, pinching at the ring it threaded through.

"You tell me that I am not the one who killed them."

There was a long silence before the voice answered, "*As I said, your hands were not your own when those acts were done.*"

Seraeyu couldn't respond. He couldn't find it in himself. Instead, he stared blankly, not truly seeing.

"*The others found their demise through my hands, and mine alone. I do wish you hadn't woken when you had, then. I was drained and, in my hubris, I kept going. I needed rest. Your body was unable to handle such strain for so long, as unused to attunement as it was. When I finish my purpose, I will bring you peace; I can promise you that, young Yu-ta.*"

"Peace?" Seraeyu scoffed out a broken laugh. "Peace? You've turned me into a murderer. I committed patricide, you daemon! I had no desire to kill anyone. And I – you've turned me into a monster – a weapon. A–"

A distant memory tugged at him. One of the few times his sister confided in him, about how she knew she was only a tool, and how she was glad that Seraeyu was not used in that way. That he could escape that.

Whatever situation he was in, Seraeyu was held captive.

He understood now. There was no saving him. Not in this lifetime. He was doomed and had been from the start. A disappointment, a liability, a weapon, a tool, a monster, a leader. Seraeyu was caged, only now he was truly a feral beast worth caging, and it was of his own prompting.

"*You are a conduit for what is just, young Yu-ta. You should be pleased to be a part of this vindication. You will find harmony among it all, as will I. We will bring justice to the realms, as I promised myself long ago.*"

"Pleased," Seraeyu said, but it rang empty. "Who in the wretched starry sea are you, daemon?"

"See that cluster of stars, over there?"

His eyes tried to follow the line of her finger and far beyond it, into the vastness of the starry sea. On the sea-skimmer floor they lay chilled in the night air, swaddled in the forgiving embrace of several blankets stolen from the corner. He found himself basking in the innocence of the moment, reliving memories that might not have any place in reality. At her insistence, he offered a hum.

"Some call that the maelstrom. An endless tempest within the Great Starry Sea. The origin of the Yun, perhaps."

He couldn't help but smirk and say, "that sounds like bogshite to me."

It earned him an indignant complaint and a smack on his shoulder . . . He couldn't be more grateful to be in the company of the two hawkers he'd found at the market.

CHAPTER TWENTY-ONE

It was quiet in the rusted old sea-skimmer.

Aeyun was in a corner with his head in his hands. Davah had long since left the magnavaid's side, letting the craft drift among the endless ocean waves. Saoiri was curled far away from both of them, wrapped in a moth-eaten blanket that had come with their purchase, found in a hammock strung up in the dormitory.

If there was ever a time that Aeyun wanted to talk to Sakaeri, it was now. And if there was ever a time that he wanted to dig himself a hole of shame and never look Raeyu – or anyone else – in the eye again, it was also now.

He fiddled with the communication stone in his hand once more.

He understood what he saw in Beldur now. What she'd done, that Yu-ta wraith. What Aeyun had done. What he'd stolen.

He was disgusted with himself, and he felt like he needed to shed his own skin. The worst part of it was he couldn't even repent. He couldn't even rid the realms of himself because it would rid them of Raeyu, and he couldn't bear the thought of that. It was a bitter justice, that he'd have to wake each day knowing what he took. Firstly due to paranoia, then due to desperation.

Aeyun's self-loathing ran deep, and it felt endless in its spiralling descent.

"Are we going to talk?" Davah asked, mouth set in a fierce line that didn't suit him. "We need to talk."

His call didn't garner a response.

"Alright, let's lay out the facts then: we are now terrorists. We set off a bomb in the capital of our homerealm – Saoiri and I's, that is – and it killed who knows how many people. You obviously did something with Essence, because Saoiri was right, you looked like you were on death's door there, *friend*, and it was even worse than your little stunts before. We need something to go on, else maybe you're just as mad as the Thasian."

"I didn't know," Aeyun said, almost inaudible behind his hands. "I didn't think."

"Yeah, you rarely do. But we need more than that," Davah told him.

Saoiri tugged the blanket closer, twisting it around her shoulders. It was a feeble barricade, but it still stood testament to what Aeyun already suspected. He was something to be guarded against. Something dangerous, something to be feared.

"We were being watched – tailed, listened to, I don't know – and I wanted to – I only wanted to wipe the interior of the sea-skimmer. I didn't mean to tune with Essence. I didn't mean to do anything with it. I just did." Aeyun lifted his head, eyes pleading up at Davah. "I didn't mean to do that!"

"I–" Davah started, then he bit his lip and sighed. "Damn, I honestly do believe that. It's weird, though, that it would've just *happened*. And you didn't speak a descantation until *after*. At least, none that I heard, anyway."

"No, I guess I didn't," Aeyun murmured, hanging his head again.

He didn't because that had to do with how he channelled Vitality. It wasn't language for harnessing wild Essence that he spoke, it was just ancient Ca'lorian, and it was just what he remembered from when he was young. For a better connection and attunement, to convey intent back to the realms. Essence didn't really need descantation to manifest, but that was a little-known fact.

After the mayhem his deplorable slip-up had caused, though, Aeyun was starting to think that maybe descantation was necessary for all types of Essence manipulation, including that which was infused with Vitality. To help direct the Essence, and to tame it, just like one would with Vitality. They'd spoken during Raeyu's rite, after all. That's what she'd said when she'd explained it to Aeyun. The problem was that Aeyun didn't *know* that language.

Uruji did. To the untrained ear, it sounded eerie and otherworldly, and it most certainly wasn't the same as Aeyun's words spoken in an ancient Ca'lorian tongue. Uruji's descants were voiced in a language that resonated in one's very bones, rattling them inside out. You could trick the populace by speaking something unknown, and ancient Ca'lorian was enough to guide Vitality from its source, but you couldn't trick the realms and the fabric of *whatever* they existed in to fool wild Essence into submission.

"Care to share?" Davah prompted when Aeyun had been silent for too long.

"I didn't, you're right. And the Essence was out of control. I didn't even realise I'd attuned to it until it was there, and then–"

"What is it?" Saoiri cut in, not looking up from where she'd affixed her attention to the floor. "That thing, over your heart?"

"Oh," said Aeyun. He didn't know how to explain that. "It's from a long time ago." He knew it wasn't enough, and the way Saoiri shifted to place her piercing gaze upon him told him as much. There was something there, too, that he couldn't hide from. A desperate sort of ogling, begging him to continue. "There was something that happened. This is from that," Aeyun told her – or the air in the sea-skimmer, he didn't know anymore – and he pressed his palm over the much-calmed mark under his shirt. "It's an Essence scar. There was someone I wanted to save, and this was the only way to do it."

"It looked like it was trying to consume you," Saoiri whispered, eyes drooping once more. "Was it – is it killing you? Does the Essence make it worse?"

Aeyun flickered a glanced towards Davah, who was giving him an unreadable look. It's not that he hadn't seen him with that sort of expression – or lack thereof – before, but it always gave Aeyun pause. Because when he looked like that, he barely looked like goofy, joke-cracking Davah.

He looked like a stranger.

"That's kind of hard to explain," Aeyun said with a frown. "But the Essence probably makes it worse, yes."

"So, what'd you do? After the explosions, I mean. When you were staring starry-eyed at the ceiling with bloody tears? When you stood up, said some nonsense, then looked like you wanted to hurl yourself to the bottom of the ocean?" Davah asked, expression still tight. "Must've been something awful, for you to look like that."

"I was . . . fading," said Aeyun. He was sure he probably looked the very same then as Davah described he looked earlier. *But I can't tell them about Raeyu.* "I have to live. I don't have a choice. I needed – I needed–" he couldn't finish.

Admitting it made it real. It meant accepting what he'd done. What he'd took. The lengths to which he was willing to go. It meant facing himself. And he couldn't . . . do that.

Movement caught his eye, and he saw Saoiri lift her head once more. A terrorised realisation was written starkly across her face. Aeyun found himself unable to disappear.

"Oh, Yun," she gasped, and Aeyun remembered then that she had seen him stitch his arm before. That she had even given him a bug at Bhu-Nan to do it. She knew. He was sure. She had put it together. "Oh, Yun, you didn't!"

"You've got to fill in the gaps here," Davah stated, alarmed by Saoiri's reaction.

Aeyun looked away shamefully, angling his head up to stare through the yellowed panels there. The moons peered down that night, but Aeyun found he didn't want to be under their gaze right then. Their judgement filtered across him in glistening beams, highlighting all his flaws and unforgivable deeds in their soft glow.

"Tell me I'm wrong," Saoiri begged.

Aeyun could tell her that she was wrong. That he hadn't atrociously consumed soulsongs, and that he hadn't siphoned the lives he'd only recently stolen, a support for his and Raeyu's continued existence.

Instead, he said, "It was three people who perished. Too close to the blast."

It was fewer than he would have thought, and surely more were injured, perhaps dying later. Still, it was three soulsongs he'd counted. Three lives that sped through his mind, three soulsongs snuffed out and redistributed as pure, exchanged energy, their unique tunes dissolved. Condensed momenta that dissipated along the way, loosing several half-lives on arrival.

"Aeyun, no." Saoiri's lip trembled. "You couldn't know that."

"I understand if you don't–"

"For the love of fuck, Aeyun!" Davah pushed himself off the wall in a rare show of anger. "*What* did you do?"

"I took them!" Aeyun admitted aloud and he felt the trauma of it all rushing back. "I took them!"

"I know you took their lives, Aeyun! But what did you do?"

"No." Aeyun forced himself to look at Davah. What met him was far more resolute and far less apprehensive than Aeyun expected. "Davah, I *took* them. I stole their soulsongs, to live. That's why I looked like . . . I wanted to bury myself in the ocean."

Davah watched him. Under his scrutiny, Aeyun felt stripped of his armour, instead bare and disgraceful. Small and incapable, yet untamed and feral, stricken and trapped. Breaking the pressure between them, Davah's expression shifted into something more pitying.

"You still kinda do, friend," he said. He shuffled over to Aeyun and crouched down, grabbing Aeyun's clenched fist and unfurling it so that the whites of his knuckles faded back to even-toned skin. "And you won't do it, nor will you do what you did again, right?"

"What?"

Aeyun blinked at him, baffled by his utter acceptance of all that was just revealed. Saoiri, on her side of the sea-skimmer, said nothing.

"You fucked up. You fucked up, and you did something unforgivable. But you obviously have something to live for, and you will live with remorse for what you did for the rest of your days. You fucked up, and you can't fix it. But you can do better."

Aeyun stared.

"Davah," Saoiri said weakly.

"You will do better."

"But what I did–"

"You," Davah emphasised with a harsh poke in Aeyun's sternum, "know it's not okay. But you will do better. It won't go away. What you did won't disappear. But you will do better."

"I don't understand why you're so . . ." Aeyun trailed, struggling to put into words the baffling interaction.

It's not right. Everything's wrong.

It was the look in Davah's eyes. Acceptance; a resolve towards penitence. Like he knew. Like he somehow knew what this contrition was. And Aeyun wondered if he did. *Why* he did.

"We all have a past," Davah said, stepping away. "Looks like you're having a pretty difficult present."

"But what I did–"

"Was awful, you're not wrong," said Davah. "But it happened, and now you're here, crying on the rust-eaten floor of a shitty old sea-skimmer, wishing you could exchange your life for theirs. I'm afraid you have more to do, though, Aeyun. And I can't let you go off and die yet."

"Davah," Saoiri called again, quietly.

Davah turned to her, head tilted. "So, I'm allowed to have a fecked track record, but he's not? You don't want your illusion shattered?"

"Davah!" she cried out, looking bewilderingly betrayed.

"Come now, Saoiri. You really thought we wouldn't get into some sort of shite like this at some point? I thought it'd eventually be me who messed it all up, and you would have accepted that for what it was, right? Because a part of you would have expected it?" Davah crossed his arms. Saoiri shied away, shrinking back. "So now that it's him, you're struggling with it. You put him on a pedestal, Saoiri. And it's dangerous to do that with anyone. You need to think about your own motivations for being here, I'd say."

Saoiri wavered between Davah and Aeyun. In a sudden-made decision, she stood and crossed the short distance to the dormitory, slamming the door shut. Davah sighed.

Aeyun didn't know what to think. Firstly, his mind was still scrambled by the horrible memories of the day. Secondly, he was, for the first time, wondering what sordid past Davah had. Thirdly, he was uncomfortable with the interaction that just happened with Saoiri.

Aeyun wasn't ignorant, nor was he blind. He could see it with the subtle hints here and there. The way Saoiri was too eager to help, or the way she was too willing to be on his side. Now, however, with this nightmarish development, it seemed her ideal version of whoever she imagined Aeyun to be had finally shattered. And maybe . . . maybe that was for the best.

Davah sunk to the floor beside him.

"It's pure shite. Everything about it. And you're right to be angry with yourself," Davah said, solemn. "But you did what you did, and now you've got to keep going."

"What I did was—"

"Yeah, Aeyun, it *was*. It was horrific, every part of it. And if you didn't realise that I'd be really concerned. But you're a broken shell right now, friend. If that's not remorse, I don't really know what is. It's rough, too. Knowing what you've done and keeping on. But you do it."

"Davah," Aeyun said softly, closing his eyes. "Why do I feel like I'm only just now getting to know you?"

"Because maybe it's only just now that you're getting to know me?"

"I'm sorry," Aeyun said, and he was. Maybe he'd been overlooking his companions. Maybe he'd undervalued them, and maybe he really needed them, especially now. "Will I ever get to hear the story about why you're so . . . like this?"

He felt Davah shrug beside him.

"Perhaps. When I hear more about who you actually are."

"That's fair."

It was quiet for a moment, then Davah said, "She's only young. Give her time and she'll figure out where she stands, and why."

"Sure." Aeyun shifted, letting his shoulders relax some. "I really hope I've not pushed her too far."

"Yun of the stars, Aeyun. Worry about yourself. She'll be fine; you're the one in tatters."

"Am I?" Aeyun said, and it echoed emptily.

Davah gave him a tired, unamused glare. "Yes."

"Well, thanks for being by my side while I'm in tatters."

Davah blinked at him, apparently not expecting that response. There was a tug at the corner of his mouth, some sort of corralled amusement. He leant back, closing his eyes as he resigned himself to an uncomfortable sleep.

"No worries, friend."

"Sometimes people do things because they have to, or because they're scared." His father's grip dug into his shoulder, like it kept him steady. Like it was the only thing keeping him steady. "You must live. Your mother would tell you to run, and usually she would be right." Eyes met his, hard in their determination. Their damnation. "Sometimes you must fight, though. To protect."

There was a constant vigilance around his father, as if he were prepared for an ambush at any moment. As if he expected a knife to be at his throat in an instant.

"I'll fight," he said, because he felt like he had to. "I'll live."

"You'll fight," his father told him. "And you will protect."

CHAPTER TWENTY-TWO

Aeyun awoke to Davah tapping away at the magnavaid. It was morning, if the daylight streaming into his face was any indication, and the dawning hours greeted him with despair. They were still somewhere in the middle of the ocean. He couldn't find it in himself to care where.

"Morning," Davah said distractedly, peering closely at something on the display.

"Hey," Aeyun responded.

He stretched his arms above his head with a grunt. His right arm was still surprisingly limber, and the reason why niggled at his brain like a viperous pest.

But he stood up. He had to. He had to keep going.

"So, this is really weird. I was looking at this magnavaid

213

thinking it was broken, but it's actually just pulling other *things*. I only noticed because look, look there."

Aeyun tried to focus his bleary-eyed gaze on the spot Davah had indicated.

"That's Beldur, right? It hadn't shown on the other one."

From what Aeyun could tell, the observation was correct. It did look like the magnavaid had the outline of where they'd found Beldur. If nothing else, it was made clear by the small yet indicative outline of that cathedral-like building at the top of the underwater hill.

"What is it attuned to? Where's its information coming from?"

"See, friend. These here are really rare." Davah tossed him a smug grin. "It's either, one: a very old magnavaid that was one of the proprietary few first distributed; or two: one that has been restraint-broken." As he reasoned through the explanation, Davah excitedly swiped across the display, searching for more outliers. "It's really difficult to do, you know? You need an expert to do it, and there are so few alive now. Honestly, I'd say this might be an original, and that's *fascinating*!"

"Were you always such an alicant nerd?" Aeyun muttered, rubbing at his eye.

Davah gave him a blank look. "Yeah, Aeyun. Why wouldn't I be?"

Aeyun shrugged. He had never much liked ore alicant.

"Anyways," Davah continued, ignoring Aeyun's indifference. "This little buddy of ours lets us see way more on the panel – useful or not. Because it shows absolutely everything it pings off, it means that the user is privy to things that would otherwise be hidden. Do you get what I'm saying, friend?"

It took Aeyun's sleep-rattled mind a moment to catch up. "Well, that's pretty convenient, isn't it?"

"Uh-huh!"

"Um," a small voice came from the dormitory behind them. Both men turned to the call. "Hello," Saoiri said, shuffling out of the room and into the shabby hull.

214

"Morning!" Davah said, far too chipper.

Aeyun didn't know what to say, so he stayed quiet and gave her a slight nod.

Saoiri didn't go near them. She wove her way around to the ratty bench and sat down, picking at the nail on her thumb.

Davah regarded her for a moment, then turned around and fiddled with the magnavaid again. "I bet we can find all kinds of interesting things with this."

"Ah, yeah," Aeyun agreed distractedly, finding it difficult to turn away from Saoiri's shrunken form.

A sharp jab from Davah had Aeyun's head whipping his direction. Davah was giving him a very pointed look alongside a very indiscreet directive to turn away from her and back towards the magnavaid. Aeyun, confused, did as prescribed, but he wasn't sure he was happy about it.

It wasn't until about ten more minutes of Davah zipping around the realm via the magnavaid's display that Saoiri finally spoke.

"I think it will take me a while to get over that. And . . . and I want to say that I'm not really okay with it. But I–" She cut herself off with a sniffle. "I want to stay! Elder Emagh said that we would run into destiny, and I don't want to abandon that calling!"

"Yun, Saoiri," Davah sighed out, twisting on his heel. "You've let your life be decided for you by others for as long as I've known you. Screw Elder Emagh–" Saoiri looked highly affronted by the sentiment. "–what do *you* want?"

"Me?" Saoiri asked, still shrunken small in a way that settled wrong.

"Saoiri, it's okay if you want to separate yourself from this. From me," Aeyun told her.

"Me?" she asked again, seeming overwhelmed. "I – no, I don't. I just . . . I'm not sure I can. I want to help, but if there are more – like that – but I want to help things."

Saoiri's reasonings became ramblings, and Aeyun felt his heart plummet. He'd disappointed yet another person. Someone else he should have protected. She'd only wanted to assist him, and he'd done something terrifying. Something unforgivable.

"Saoiri," he said quietly, and she looked up, jaw closing softly. "There are other ways you can help. I have this now." Aeyun held up Sakaeri's old communication stone. "And you have the other one. There are things that I want to look into, but I just can't stay in one place long enough to do it. If you want to help, but it's all becoming too . . . much," that felt like a ridiculous understatement, "you can research instead. Look into the annals and find anything that seems strange, or references to other realms. An ancient war, maybe. Or things that just don't make sense. When you've found them, you can tell me, with this stone, and that would help more than you know."

He believed what he told her. It would be immeasurably useful to know more about the past and any connection that could have been there. He couldn't do it, though. Stay too long and he risked being noticed. Or tracked or targeted.

"I think I might need that for a while," Saoiri admitted, and Aeyun gave her a sad smile.

"I understand," he said.

"I'll miss you, Saoiri," Davah commented, and Saoiri faltered.

"I know. I'm sorry. Just for a while."

"I get it; it's okay," Davah said, then turned back to the magnavaid. "We'll drop Saoiri to Kilrona, then we can figure out the next step in this. How 'bout that?"

"That's perfect, Davah, thanks," Aeyun told him. "And I—"

"You know, I'm really sick of everyone apologising all the time. We're all our own person, aren't we? We do what we want and don't do what we don't want. It's all fine, friends. It's not the end; this is just part of the bigger picture, right? I'm curious, so I'm here. She wants a bit of distance *for the moment* and that's okay, too. All's well, friends. Let's just carry on."

"Right," Aeyun said in response to Davah's interjection.

That summed it up . . . well. He guessed. But it still left him floundering in the lingering notes of underserved benediction.

"Davah is tougher than he looks," Saoiri said, still sounding outside herself, even in her attempted jest.

"I'm getting that impression," said Aeyun. "But still scared of birds."

"Birds?" Davah asked.

"Sirin," Aeyun supplied, disappointed that he hadn't picked up on the reference.

"Oh, that bird. Well, I'd be mad not to be, honestly."

"That's fair," Aeyun said, wondering if he should be questioning his own sanity.

It wasn't long until they reached Kilrona. Aeyun noted that the trip there was much bumpier and more jostling than the other craft – a sick feeling carved through him when he remembered why that other craft wasn't available – but Davah seemed to have a handle on the sea-skimmer anyway. During the journey, Saoiri had kept mostly to herself, only glancing over at Aeyun every once in a while.

"Saoiri," Davah said on their approach to the docks of Kilrona. The cliffside parish seemed to have a barrier set up. It made sense, with all the commotion at Caiggagh only the day before. "I know you're processing, but I'd ask for your discretion here."

Saoiri stood up from the rickety seating in the corner and peered through the panels, gaze darting from one sea-sentry to the next. Tiny, zippy crafts, sea-sentries. Easy to manoeuvre, and with space for two aboard its vessel. Ideal for a chase.

"Right, I–" Saoiri nodded with determination. "Right."

Davah looked back at Aeyun. "We'd snuck you in last time, you know. It's a good thing you weren't running around Caiggagh with us the whole time, too. People can place Saoiri and I together, but not you, unless we were watched. It might be best if you hole up in the dormitory until after I drop Saoiri off here."

Saoiri started looking fidgety while Aeyun nodded, gathering himself up off the floor where he'd self-confined to the corner.

"Aeyun!" Saoiri called, hand outstretched.

He let his eyes trail up to her glistening gaze, feeling depressingly meek, and he found her expression the reflection of something torn. Her cheeks flushed rosy, and she looked indignant for a moment before she launched herself at him, wrapping her arms tightly around his torso and slamming her forehead into his sternum.

"I'm sorry!"

"You're sorry?" he said disbelievingly. "Saoiri." Aeyun bitterly accepted his own failings and gently patted the back of her head. She was crying. "Saoiri, what are you sorry for? Don't apologise. We'll all be reunited soon, okay? After we figure some things out. It will be okay."

He hoped it came out with more conviction than he felt. Saoiri sniffled and pushed harder against his chest.

"I don't want to break it up, but we can't stay floating out here without drawing some suspicion," Davah commented from beside them.

Saoiri slowly unwound herself from Aeyun and stepped away, but she didn't seek his gaze, instead bowing her neck.

"I promise, I'll–"

"Saoiri," Aeyun said again, softer and crouching down a little. "You don't have to promise anything. You don't have to *do* anything. I'm going to give that stone to Davah. When you're ready, message him. If that says you want to come back, great. If that relays information you found, great. If it's just to talk to Davah, that's okay, and he will let me know if you'd like to talk to me at any point. Okay?"

She finally lifted her head, presenting a sad, wavering smile.

"If that stone never gets etched, or if it never gives indication that you want back in, that's alright."

Saoiri nodded, looking as though she wouldn't be able to

speak if she wanted to.

"Aeyun, friend, you've really gotta go. They're approaching."

At Davah's warning, Aeyun made to leave. He gave Saoiri one last look, an attempt at a smile, then darted into the dormitory; just in time for the first torch light to beam through the sea-skimmer panels. The day had become quite grey and dour as it progressed.

There was a lot of muffled chatter over the course of the following minutes, and then Aeyun felt the sea-skimmer jolt to life again. It was slow and steady, so he figured all had gone well with the sea-sentries' crews. He sat against the furthermost wall and pulled his knees towards himself to rest his chin upon. The thought of Saoiri in the very same room the previous night, likely fraught with emotion and scared, ate at him.

He hated it. He hated that he brought danger to those around him. For a blissful stint of ignorance, he'd almost forgotten that the danger didn't only exist as an outside threat, but an internal one as well. Of course it did. Even with Oagyu gone, a man who would've surely wanted him dead on multiple accounts, there was the ever-present threat that Aeyun didn't *belong* in the realms. And what didn't belong caused trouble through fear, unfounded or not. And he, selfishly and stupidly, hadn't wrangled in his rediscovered attunement to Essence, which he'd still experienced barely a handful of times in his life.

Now, not only would certain individuals believe Aeyun to be dangerous, but they'd be right. Aeyun was a menace.

Aeyun wasn't a killer.

At least, he hadn't been a killer. But he had trained in that pen at the top of the Thasian Tower, when some combination of he, Uruji, and Raeyu would sneak up there. Aeyun was never good at ore tuning, so he'd learnt with weapons. Never lethal moves, but defensive manoeuvres with implements of all kinds. In addition to the metallurgy skills he'd honed for Jourae, all to craft the finest and most well-tuned alicant accessories on the market, Aeyun had dabbled in weapon-smithing. He'd done it mainly to understand the components that went into well-structured battle implements, and how best to handle them when trying to *not* kill your opponent.

He'd set down his swords when he'd joined up with Davah and Saoiri, only harbouring his dagger on his hip. Something deep in his gut told him that he might need to brandish more again soon, though. The reason he'd taken them up in the first place was so that he could secure his mask and become Hana, Raeyu's awfully uncreative choice of an alias, to walk beside her.

Aeyun hadn't lied when he'd said he'd not been a Sirin, but that's what Haebal and Raenaru thought Hana was. A masked mercenary, hired as Raeyu's bodyguard. It had been a convenient ploy. If it had the added benefit of actually ensuring Raeyu's safety? Well, that was just a plus.

He had adopted the Mask of Hana, of course, a traditional mask persona; a guardian spirit of alicant materials across Raenaru. It was the perfect match to the Yu-ta Yisuna, who was directly tied to Hana. In many of the paintings and relics from days long passed, Yisuna was depicted with ceremonially dressed horns and matching extravagant gowns, always flanked by an ornately robed and hooded figure with an intricate mask: Hana.

Oagyu, of course, hadn't taken long to figure out that it was a teenaged Aeyun under that mask, and he'd expressly disapproved. But then Raeyu had gone on to defy his wishes and romped around with a veiled Aeyun anyway. Aeyun genuinely believed that if the threat of Jourae's line being the only one able to conduct the Essence rite didn't exist, Oagyu would have been done with his existence ages ago. Barricaded from this fate, Raeyu and Aeyun-as-Hana had stuck firmly by one another's side for years.

Only a handful into those years, it had happened. Aeyun hadn't been with Raeyu when she was cut down. To this day, he could swear he knew when it happened, though. The moment that Raeyu's soulsong faded. It had been like the pulse of something dropped away, and Aeyun paused his smithing efforts, burning his arm in the process. Uruji, having been across the room, noticed his mishap and asked if he was okay. But Aeyun hadn't heard him. All he could focus on was that something was off. That something was *gone*.

No more than a second longer and he was up and running. He sprinted towards that feeling of unease, of utter wrongness. Uruji had darted out behind him, calling his name. When he'd grasped onto Aeyun's wrist, the realm moved in a blur around them and then they were there, in the woods. In retrospect, Aeyun wondered if they'd accidentally combined Vitality and Essence and jumped there, like how Raeyu could hop through short distances by attuning with the alicant embedded in her arm.

The scene was a bloodbath. It was meant to be a simple trade envoy, Raeyu sent as the diplomatic representative of the Thasian Legacy. There had been plenty of Sentinels with her as well, a company of three land-skimmers packed with security. It was clear, in this instance, someone had thought to take advantage of the Thasians' confidence on home turf, and they'd put out a hit. They'd attempted to assassinate the only known Thasian bloodsong user, and they'd done a thorough job of it.

Sentinels' bodies were crumpled around the place, some looking to have died a much more painful death than others. Raeyu's form was in the middle, lying on top of a series of burned, blackened fire marks on the ground. She'd been left there, unmoving, surrounded by crimson-dyed grass and blood-soaked corpses. A dagger protruded from her chest, professing the assassin's success.

"*No!*" Aeyun had yelled, running forward.

He'd knelt down, hovering over Raeyu's lifeless body, repeating mantras of disbelief over and over again. In his distraught mind, Aeyun acknowledged that he was not alone, and that Uruji was still on the far side of the path. He'd gathered Raeyu's far-too-cold and limp form in his arms and looked up.

"*Please.*"

Uruji had been pale as he stumbled forward. "*What? P-please, what?*"

"*Save her.*"

Davah's knock broke Aeyun from his thoughts. He popped his head in the door with a wry smile.

"It's all done," he told him. "She'll be here for a while, I'd say. We've got other problems, though." As Aeyun began to stand, Davah held up a pausing hand. "You can't be showing your face around here, friend. It's best we move. All the realms are on high alert, looking for the culprit." Davah grimaced. "They think it's the same person who attacked Haebal. It's not looking good."

Aeyun realised then that not only had he done something unforgivable, but he'd just helped fuel the fire for a realms-wide manhunt. If people were to connect him to any of it . . .

"Shit."

"Yeah, and it's worse. Seraeyu Thasian is supposed to be making a statement tomorrow regarding the recent attack."

"Fuck."

"Fuck is right. We just gave him the perfect out to be a martyr."

"So, you're an outrealmer? Like, from the stars?"

The question sounded ludicrous, and he had to take a moment to temper a snide remark. "Yes, I guess. But, no? That makes me sound like some mythical thing."

"You did just appear one day, you know. Maybe you are some 'mythical thing', for all I know."

"Don't be dumb. And you said yourself, you can do that, with your weird lightning."

His comment was met with an affronted squeak and the shifting of shoulders to face him full on. When he looked at her, the blue sky shone in her eyes, making them more vibrant than ever.

"I don't hop from one realm to the next; it's within running distance. And my lightning isn't weird!"

"Says you." Despite the protest, a delighted fluttering tickled his insides and he smiled, feeling warm against the blustery autumn day.

CHAPTER TWENTY-THREE

"Where've you taken me?" Aeyun asked when he realised they were nowhere near the Great Sea Gate.

Davah glanced over at him before focusing back on the steering.

Unfortunately, with the magnavaid the way it was, it meant that they could see more across the vast waters, but it was missing its honed ability to draw the craft to the point of interest, leaving the sea-skimmer to be steered manually.

"Somewhere I think you need to go right now. Might not be the best time to go to the gate now anyway. We have to figure out a plan first."

Aeyun couldn't argue. His mind was still scrambled, and he hadn't yet contemplated the *what next* of the whole journey.

"You see that lighthouse there?"

Aeyun nodded when he followed the direction of Davah's pointed finger.

"That's where we're going."

The lighthouse appeared aged; half its glowing ore seemed to have tumbled away at some point, taken by time or vandalism. After Davah anchored the sea-skimmer near a rickety-looking pier, they climbed out of the stale craft and ascended the stony, moss-covered stairs up the top of the small land mass. The cries of swooping gulls bounced from rocky edges, and a lingering scent of sea-soaked kelp permeated the space between outcroppings. There wasn't much flat land at the top of the small summit, but what was visible presented as overgrown and weatherworn.

Twilight was again bearing down upon Aeyun, and he frowned at the torrent of waves crashing on the rocks below. The lighthouse itself was old, that much Aeyun could tell, but it wasn't ancient. That glowing ore – different from those in the Great Sea Gates – was built into its architecture in a crosshatch pattern. Aeyun was pretty certain that was a design choice implemented in written history: the Radiant Era, it was called. The circular structure was remarkably plain otherwise, just typical Mhedoonian stone.

"I used to come here," Davah said as he stepped a few paces ahead, stopping at the cliff's edge. "To scream at the ocean, blame it for my misfortunes. Or to punish myself. Spend a night in the cold or the rain, thinking I deserved the pain. Or to repent what I could; show my respects somehow."

Aeyun stayed quiet, joining Davah as together they gazed across the darkening expanses.

"If you want to let it all out right now, go ahead. I won't judge you."

Aeyun watched the horizon, but he didn't make a sound. He found he couldn't.

Davah crouched down, yanking at a few raggedy blades of grass. Accepting the implied invitation, Aeyun knelt and sat beside him, his heels kicking up soggy dirt.

"There's a saying here in Mhedoon—" Davah paused briefly before reciting: "The day will break, and the dusk will fall; tales will be borne, both large and small; from ashes the bones of gone do sing; together we will be, when darkness rest does bring."

Davah huffed and tossed his ripped green shards to the wind. Together they watched them bounce along the breeze until they fluttered down, escaping sight.

"It's morbid maybe, but we Mhedoonians understand the fleeting quality of life. We also understand that life isn't really fair. Things happen, we despair, and we grow. Keep striving for a better tomorrow, whatever that might look like, even if it's unachievable." He sighed, seating himself fully on the ground with one heavy roll from his haunches. "What I'm saying is: it's okay to admit that it's all a bit shite. That there are things you wish didn't happen. Maybe some of these things you couldn't even stop if you wanted to. It's okay to admit that you're not . . . not really over it. But, like, tomorrow brings another sunrise, right? The morning will rise with you. But it's okay to be angry with the realms for what they stole from you."

Aeyun scrunched his nose and swallowed. He really did want to blame the endless horizon for stealing Jourae from him. For stealing Jourae and everything else, leaving it with him to just figure out. He wanted to throw that on someone else's shoulders. He didn't want to contend with the notion that he brought his father's demise. That he caused Raeyu and Uruji to be on the run. That he helped to cultivate what Seraeyu had become. That, in what felt like a different lifetime, he had been the one to unwittingly lead those zealots back to his family's home. That he had abandoned his sister, leaving her there to rot. That those around him withered.

Because it wasn't fair. It wasn't, was it? Why was he pelted with misfortune? Why was he addled with death around every corner? Was it him and his mistakes, or was it luck gone awry? Were there better choices he could have made? More that he could have done?

Aeyun collapsed, his own weight becoming a burden, and his fingers dug into soil as his body shook.

Why did he constantly feel like such a fool? Why couldn't he just *figure it out*? What would it take for him to do it right; to end this awful cycle of suffering that plagued those around him? Was there something he could find, something he could understand, that would make it clear? Nothing would truly revive the dead, but surely there was a path for the living.

A warm hand rested on his shoulder, but the two said nothing. Instead, Aeyun watched the sky darken, letting go of its clutch on daylight and instead embracing the serenade of chittering nocturnal bugs crooning among the brush.

When Aeyun did stand up again, wiping at his face, Davah indicated for him to follow towards the lighthouse. Aeyun did so mechanically. He vaguely registered that the stars shined brightly in the sky that night, a glow blanketing the oceans, making it almost ethereal. As they entered the musty, round interior, Davah walked towards a chest to the right – one of the very few pieces of furniture below the winding stairs that wasn't an antique-looking couch, or a cupboard awkwardly snugged against the wall. At least there was a hearth hugged between soot-stained stone, promising some warmth in the evening's chill.

"Here," Davah said, producing what looked like two loosely tied sacks. He laid them both on the ground and pulled the bindings free, revealing sheets of tightly woven, fibrous material in one and a stash of glowing ore in the other, the pile of which was dim from being kept in the dark so long. "You said three, didn't you?" He began to parse out sheets and alicant to match the number. "We'll go with four, to account for collateral."

"Davah," said Aeyun. He wasn't sure where to go from there.

"You can tie the ore to it like this, right?" Davah showed an example. "And then you can loop the fabric like this. It's not the most attractive lantern, but it does the job."

"Thank you."

Davah looked up from his ministrations on the makeshift lantern. His expression conveyed that it was one of too many he'd crafted in his time.

"Yeah," Davah said in response.

They finished the lanterns in the light that streamed in through the open door, quiet all the while. Once all four were bound and completed, they strode back out to the grassy outcropping, something unspoken lingering between them; something grim.

"You any good at attuning to air-based things? We can have you set them afloat, or I can do it, no bother," said Davah.

Aeyun bit his lip in shame. "No, I'm not."

"No worries, friend. That's what I'm here for."

Davah rooted around in his satchel for the right ore and made a noise of success when he'd found it. Pulling it out, he exchanged the pearly water alicant he had set in his thin bracer, replacing it with the powdery white and red alicant instead. One by one, he gently launched the lanterns into the humid evening air, helping them catch the updraft with a guiding swoop of his arm and setting them aloft above the sloshing ocean below. Aeyun watched each of the four lanterns drift up and further from them, their dim ore getting brighter under the twinkling night sky.

"*Cah eh'ju, a'garu ca'ju,*" Aeyun said softly. "*A'pan o. A'garu ca'ju.*"

Davah watched him inscrutably, and then, in ancient Mhedoonian tongue, he said, "*Ka'gh a'ga'ru, Ka'ur'ogh da'ga'ru eoi'mhe.*"

Aeyun closed his eyes and basked in the night's gleam, revelling in the cracks that fissured through his carefully crafted lie.

"Let's head in. I'll light a fire and we can warm up. No need to freeze tonight, I think."

With that, Davah turned and walked into the lighthouse, giving Aeyun a moment alone. Surrounded by the sounds of crashing waves and the caresses of wisping wind, Aeyun did not wallow. Instead, he breathed out one long, mournful sigh. It wasn't long after that he followed Davah into their temporary accommodations.

Inside, Aeyun found him stoking the fire. Quietly, he dropped onto the couch and stifled a cough at the cloud of dust his actions had pushed into the air.

"We'll have a good rest now; head out tomorrow," Davah said, dusting his hands. After retrieving bedding supplies from the cupboard, he tossed a bundle of padding and blankets to Aeyun, who deftly caught it. "Here, make yourself comfortable. I won't pry. It's your business."

Aeyun hesitantly laid out a space to sleep. Far enough from the fire that he didn't have to stare at it, but close enough that he could feel its heat.

"Thanks, Davah."

As Aeyun laid down to sleep that night, he rested a hand over his chest. There, he felt the soft rhythm of his beating heart and, somewhere behind it, across the realms, he heard the answering echo. *Ba-dum, ba-dum, ba-dum,* it lulled him into a trance-like slumber.

"Hey," Davah called and Aeyun awoke with a start. Daylight was seeping through little crumbled crevices in the lighthouse walls. "Fire's out. Let's get going, yeah? Not sure what we'll do, though. I'll bet the realms are in an absolute frenzy right now. Might be best to go somewhere to lay low for a while."

Aeyun considered the sentiment, groggily offering, "Maybe back to Tenebrana, or to Quinga?"

"We could try Tenebrana, yeah. No one would want to get too deep towards the acid swamps. Quinga might be the one for the win, though. The whole feckin' realm is like a never-ending metropolis. Sometimes the best place to disappear is in plain sight." Davah paused as he was shoving their bedding back into the cupboard. "You think we can make it in time to see whatever dreadful excuse the Thasian runt came up with?"

"We can try. But if we don't make it live, I'm sure that we'll find out soon after."

Aeyun felt queasy all the sudden. A storm was brewing, he was sure of it. He could feel the beginnings of it rolling in, and he wasn't keen to find out what sort of devastation it would bring.

By the time they made it to the Great Sea Gate, the midday sun was beaming down steadily, heating up the inside of the sea-skimmer like an oven. Davah was quick to spot the sea-sentries scattered around the terminal's entrance, and the gatekeeper's lights were glaring a bright, ominous red.

"Ah, Aeyun. I think it's back to the dormitory with you," Davah said apologetically.

Aeyun scowled – he was getting sick of the dormitory – but complied anyway.

Just as he slipped the door closed, he heard Davah offer a Sentinel a cheery, "Hello, friend!"

Aeyun sat in the dark, the wobbly old excuse for a door having blocked out the day's rays, and leant his head on the wall. The muffled conversation beyond the barrier was sounding more strained than usual, but Aeyun trusted Davah's silver tongue to get them through the Great Sea Gate without too much hassle. He didn't know exactly how Davah did it, but he managed to turn most situations around with a few well-placed jokes, or some cheeky underrepresentation of his own intelligence.

Eventually, as predicted, the craft started moving again, and Aeyun closed his eyes in anticipation. Maybe he should–

But no. Hadn't he pushed it too far too recently? The temptation to *try* was ever-present, though. He could feel the atmosphere begin to shift and the air reeked of ozone, the vaporous thick of it crawling into his orifices. That liminal space was encroaching, and he could almost swear that his bones knocked in anticipation.

A moment later and he was there, suspended in that odd non-space, surrounded by pockets of bright, glimmering energy among Essence. Aeyun looked down to that unyielding tether. It remained, flowing and somehow intangible, but there. Something about it caught Aeyun's eye as he stared. Charging through the thread-like connection, little streaks of inky black slithered around the bind in ways it hadn't before. The image of it brought something to mind, an idea of something that he couldn't quite place. He brought his hand up and it stuttered through its progression as it reached his chest, as if his vision came in stilted frames.

This time, the manifestation was almost instantaneous.

Aeyun felt as though he were pulled through a vacuum, at the end of which lay Raeyu's impression. A silhouette of her being, caught up in the wild Essence, somehow dulled and dimmed.

"Rae!" Aeyun called out, but the words felt more like pulses than true language.

The vision of Raeyu awakened, eyes opening and reflecting what looked to be the starry sea itself. Her body illuminated and she reached out a hand, movements soft and fluid compared to Aeyun's unnatural choppy ones. Aeyun tried to grasp Raeyu's hand, their fingertips almost connecting.

"*Aeyun.*"

"I fecking figured," Davah's voice called out, and Aeyun jerked forward, teetering over and slamming against the sea-skimmer's floor. "Wipe your face; you look scary as all get-out."

Aeyun blinked and swiped the back of his hand against his cheeks. Red.

"Glean any new info in whatever you did between the gates?"

"I'm not really sure," Aeyun said, noting that something didn't seem . . . right. As if he were missing something, a notion that was just beyond his perception, evading him.

Davah raised an intrigued brow.

"Okay, well, you stay in here a bit longer. I'll get us past the gatekeeper and let's see if we can't swing by the capital for a night to find out what's going on in Haebal."

He didn't wait for a response. Instead, he slid the door shut behind him, leaving Aeyun in the dark once more.

Davah wasn't wrong. The realm of Quinga was like a continuous sprawl of urban expansion, connected by canals and rivers. Where the oceans and seas did exist, they were often host to a myriad of long-since constructed passageways both above and below the water, with suspended centres of planned communities between them. Hovering among them all, the hyperline – Quinga's claim to fame in the industry of fast travel – connected one city to the next. The capital Kwe was the largest, but Kwe meshed with the neighbouring Linao as much as it did the slightly further out Yeshen, and so on and so forth with those that stood next to those cities. Where the realm lacked in open space, it made up for it vertically. Climbing greenery and towering farm structures always held a district in each conglomeration, just large enough to sustain a set number of blocks before the sequence began again.

Quinga was a realm of two extreme seasons. Aeyun and Davah were unlucky enough to be there during its sweaty, rainy one rather than its dry and frigid one. Were it in winter's grasp instead, it would have been much easier to stay incognito. Instead, they'd have to bear with the overwhelming heat and sweltering, sweat-doused months.

Before they departed from their sea-skimmer at the palm-lined docks, Davah went to the magnavaid and dug out both it and the alicant that powered it; a shiny black stone that glinted in the right light. He shoved the screen panel into his shoulder-slung backpack, and the alicant found a home in his satchel. He patted the fibre-woven bag once it was closed tight.

"Look, we can lose the junky craft, but not this baby," Davah

231

said when he noticed Aeyun's questioning gaze.

Aeyun shrugged in response, pulled his hood over his head, then hoisted himself out of the rooftop hatch and into the day's light, floral-scented drizzle. A by-product of the pollen absorbed into the moist air. Davah joined him on the well-kept pier, all straight lines and scrubbed boards, then they made their way to the central reception area. Nearing the start of the jetty, they were flagged down by a Sentinel.

"State the reason for your visit and your last whereabouts," the Sentinel intoned, his face hidden behind a unique ore-crafted barrier that shrouded the wearer's features. It had an opaline quality that rippled like an oil slick. It made for an uncanny and unnerving impression, and Aeyun willed his racing heart to quiet.

"Heya, friend. We're from Mhedoon – Dathian, the both of us – a little rattled by the state of affairs, you know? Looking for some reprieve from the horror of it all here in Kwe. We're both anglerfolk and we had trouble accepting that our cousin got caught up in – well, look. We're really wanting to try and get away from all the tears, right? It's been a lot to handle, and being stuck with the bereaved family hasn't done either of us much good, and this is kind of difficult to talk about–"

"Right," the Sentinel said as he held up a hand. "Condolences."

The offer had been curt, and the pair of them were waved on as the next visitors made their way to up the wharf.

"Cheers, friend," Davah said with a nod. He pulled Aeyun along with him towards the bustling open-air shopping district beyond. "Yun, I was sweating absolute pellets there," he whispered when they were far enough away.

"It's a good thing they didn't ask me to talk," Aeyun acknowledged the gamble.

"True," Davah agreed.

After all, Aeyun sounded much more Raenaruan and not at all like someone from Mhedoon. Although, if push came to shove, he was sure he could twist his Ca'lorian brogue into something more like a Mhedoonian lilt. As had been repeatedly drilled into his head as of late, both realms seemingly shared some sort of common history, namely in their ancient tongues. And if that still wasn't a biting revelation . . .

They weren't clear on what time of day it was – the days and nights were lengthy on Quinga, just like the seasons – so Davah made it his mission to try and determine this as they traversed the packed urban narrows, filled with vibrant colours and the clamour of everyday affairs. That same floral pungency wafted through the water-speckled passageways, almost sickeningly sweet in its onslaught. Mixing with it, the din of conversation hung low between the towering buildings, filling in gaps to provide an ambient, buzzy atmosphere that seemed busied, as if the city itself were in a rush.

"You know, we haven't talked about it," said Davah.

"About?"

"All those stones are just gone. What now?"

"Yeah, that – that's not great." It really wasn't. That was a year's worth of collecting gone down the drain, and all Aeyun was left with was the one gate ore hung from his neck in a velveteen pouch. "We can either trace down the person who took them, or we can start at it again when we can move more freely."

"Do you know who took them? You don't think it was Sakaeri, right?"

Aeyun had hemmed and hawed over that question himself. Something about attributing it to her felt *off*, much like that whole situation did. He shook his head.

"No, I don't. But I think running into her would be mighty convenient about now, too." Aeyun halted his stride and pulled on Davah's shoulder, getting him to fall closer in step. "Actually, there's something I haven't mentioned yet."

"And that is?" Davah asked warily.

"I ran into Kaisa, and I may have told him something really, really stupid."

"Oh? What was that?" Silence stretched uncomfortably while people sidestepped the pair of them, prompting Aeyun to tug himself and Davah into the opening of an alleyway to keep from impeding traffic. "Something that dumb, huh?"

"Ah, yeah. It was a bad choice. I think it may have been him that looted us, but I don't think he believed me, with what I'd told him. That he thought it was just a threat, since that angry message was scrawled on the wall. He's sharper than I'd like to admit, too. He surely figured out what those stones were, if he didn't know already, and he's probably sitting in some den somewhere trying to figure out what in the starry void I wanted with them." Aeyun eyed the satchel on Davah's hip, where Sakaeri's former communication stone was stashed away. "But Sakaeri had been there at some point, given we have her comms stone."

"All a bit weird, isn't it?" Davah asked, and Aeyun agreed.

Kaisa and Sakaeri didn't seem to be on friendly terms either, so the fact that they may have had some sort of confrontation was concerning.

"Right," Davah said, then he took a fortifying inhale. "Right, okay. One thing at a time. First, let's see if we can find out what the Thasian has to say. Even if it's not live, I'm sure there will be repeat reporting on it at the holocaster, like you said."

With a destination in mind, they slipped back into the main strait and wound through the building-shadowed streets, the majority of the rain kept off them with the numerous tarps and awnings attached from one side to the other. As they walked, tension tied around Aeyun, tighter and tighter; a coiling snake, squeezing until suffocating.

They were speaking in hushed tones when he arrived, huddled in a dormer in the long hallway. It didn't look like a particularly happy conversation, but it also didn't look like an alarmingly escalated one. Regardless, it was a weird sight to witness.

"I said no."

It was hissed, as if the sentiment was venom itself, and he scowled at the insistence of it. There was an empty pull in his gut, like something should be swirling in derision, but it wasn't there to stir. Instead, there was a forlorn absence that sang a song of discomfort, and it made him glower deeper.

"What crawled up your arse?" The question was directed at him this time, his presence having been noticed, and he poised himself to counterstrike. It was a useless endeavour, however, because she just turned back to her previous conversation partner. "It's just an offer."

"And I said no."

There was a sense of finality to it as feet fell heavier than normal upon the floor, echoing off the walls. For the briefest moment, he felt transparent.

CHAPTER TWENTY-FOUR

It was maybe an hour and a half into the announcer's continued harping about the anticipation of Seraeyu's statement that the feed finally changed to an Eye on the ground. When it did, the knot in Aeyun's stomach lurched, and he could immediately tell that the setting was staged.

Seraeyu was dressed in ceremonial garb that included gemstone-laden adornments strung across his horns and a traditional robe, intricately patterned with Haebal's national deep rouge – greyed in the holocaster's reflection, as was everything else. He sat amid the destruction of Oagyu's office. The back wall, where the once-extravagant window-framed view of Haebal used to be, was completely blown out, and there were dark blood stains on the luxurious rug that Oagyu had ordered specially from the finest weavers on Orin. The desk had either been exploded to bits, or it had been removed. Centred in the Eye's vision was Seraeyu himself, sat upon a nondescript chair that had been pulled into what remained of the seat of power. Behind him, Aeyun almost expected to see a wall of blackened Essence, but instead it was just a view of Haebal, looking dreary and lifeless.

"My fellow realmers," Seraeyu began, looking much more collected than Aeyun felt he should be, his features clean and his previously manic locks brushed back. There was something off-putting about his whole ensemble, the matching gaze unsettling. "As you all know, the great capital of Haebal, Raenaru's centre of life, was viciously attacked nigh but a month ago. During this attack, powerful pyre alicant were set throughout the Thasian Tower, and it caused devastation that resulted in the death of not only my father, Oagyu Thasian, but the dismemberment of my sister, Raeyu Thasian."

Dismemberment? Aeyun's throat tightened.

"Our search efforts have not waned."

While to other viewers it may have sounded as though Seraeyu held a futile hope, Aeyun read it as a threat. It made his hair stand on end as gooseflesh erupted on the back of his neck.

"We have received intelligence that Tenebranan official Jjenab Betio disappeared under what are allegedly perverse circumstances, and with the recent development of the bombing at Caiggagh, we have come to fear that this is not the end."

Seraeyu had barely blinked throughout the duration of the

broadcast, and Aeyun felt as if the newly minted Praetor were staring directly at him.

"Haebal will remain in isolation while the unrest continues, as our citizens and their safety are paramount to Haebal's continued prosperity. Raenaru will also continue to enforce a policy of closed borders, with special exceptions in place, provided prior agreement is arranged. Trade will resume on a vetted basis; all gatekeepers will be made aware of the established quarantine periods and procedures. Of course, as the head of the Thasian Legacy and current Praetor and representative of the Raenaruan Council, I am happy to extend insight where I can for my fellow leaders across the realms, should they reach out."

Aeyun couldn't breathe.

"The chains that bound my tuning have been broken during this traumatic event, a testament to the innate power of the Thasian bloodsong, and I have now fully recovered and regained my strength after a period of rest." Seraeyu leant forward, fingers woven together under his chin. "I fully intend to seek retribution for the wrongdoings of the past," Seraeyu said, and Aeyun saw a glimpse of *something* that didn't belong. Like an unseen layer, just below the surface. "Those who will work with me will be welcomed. Those who stand in my way–" Seraeyu stood and Aeyun saw it again, the double vision of something not meant to be there; a duality that overlapped. "They will face a wrath the likes of which has never before been witnessed." There was a long moment where Seraeyu stared dead-eyed at the screen. "When I find the culprit of these heinous, brutal acts–"

Aeyun *couldn't breathe.*

"–they will suffer a most terrible fate."

Seraeyu then turned sharply and walked out of the Eye's view, and the broadcast was cut back to the announcer.

It was a threat, a directed one, aimed at the Essence tuner who'd caused the disarray in Caiggagh. Aeyun couldn't tell whether Seraeyu thought that it had been the work of Uruji, having witnessed him create a rift before his very eyes, or perhaps

237

the work of Raeyu, who'd managed to call upon Essence after spending a lifetime drawing it from the ore in her arm.

Could he have suspected that it was Jourae's bastard son? Or did he know that Sakaeri was actually Jourae's bastard daughter? Aeyun didn't think he knew that much, but maybe . . .

Seraeyu did know that Aeyun was Jourae's kin. If he questioned Aeyun's ability to perform ritual rites, which Aeyun now assumed Seraeyu had figured out existed as an excuse for Essence tuning, then that would immediately make Aeyun a target.

In their youth, Seraeyu had never paid much attention to Aeyun, always ignoring his presence for Uruji, his allocated tuning implement in place of his own abilities. Aeyun was fairly certain that Seraeyu had never figured out that Aeyun was Raeyu's favoured bodyguard, his face having been hidden behind the Hana mask, and *Hana*'s wielding skills were something Aeyun never showcased publicly.

Raeyu and Seraeyu were never particularly close, despite Raeyu's constant fussing over him, largely due to Seraeyu's lasting resentment over Raeyu's placement in the Thasian hierarchy. There were plenty of gaps in Seraeyu's deeper knowledge of Raeyu's daily ongoings.

Even still, this kind of disconnect, the condemnation and cruelty–

"Was the Thasian always like that?" Davah whispered.

That drew Aeyun back to the present and the excited chatter around the holocaster. The structure of it stood in an art-decorated, manicured park in the centre of Kwe, the bulk of it erected in a sunken amphitheatre that allowed for plenty of seating. It was all very public. Too public for this conversation.

"Like what?"

"So cold and calculated?"

Aeyun thought about it. "No." It was part of what was off, dissident from the bratty younger sibling Raeyu was always trying to protect. "Cold, maybe. Calculated, no. That's new."

Davah hummed. "Any thoughts on that?"

"I'm still working it out," said Aeyun. "I will say that I don't want to give him reason to remember that I exist, if he doesn't already. If I'm not a prime suspect, I'd guess that as soon as he connects two dots, the rest will follow very quickly."

"You don't think he remembers you?" Davah asked, surprised.

Aeyun couldn't blame him. From the outside, the Thasian looked to have been tightknit. Like the well-oiled, secretive conglomerate they were. They also had notably good relations with the Thasian-nee, and Uruji had, of course, been seen acting as a conduit for Seraeyu's alicant-based whims time and time again.

"Seraeyu Thasian never paid much mind to things that didn't affect him, " said Aeyun. "I was only ever a passing ghost to him."

"I'd say he was wrong about that bit, considering."

"Yeah, well. Let's hope *he* doesn't come to see it the same way." If Seraeyu Thasian targeted Aeyun, he would be out to kill him. And if Seraeyu killed Aeyun, he'd also kill Raeyu. Aeyun couldn't let that happen. "I think it's time I admit to myself that I might need a few more weapons on me. I feel like the realms are this close–" Aeyun pinched his forefinger and thumb together with very little space between them "–to disaster, and I need to have a way to defend myself without relying on non-traditional attunement."

"So, use regular auld ore tuning instead?" Davah suggested, but even as he turned to face Aeyun, a look of realisation flashed across his features. "You *can't*. Oh, Yun of the stars! You can't! That makes so much sense now!"

"I *can*," Aeyun corrected. Then, quieter, he added, "Just not well. Pretty awfully, if I'm honest."

Aeyun was reluctant to admit that he was *embarrassed* by this. For the life of him, he couldn't figure out why. He'd never once considered that he had issue with the fact that he just didn't commune with the imprisoned nature of ore alicant. That he was bereft of its control.

"Ah, friend," Davah said pityingly, then he straightened up. "No, why am I empathising with you? You're capable of wild things – feck off."

"I didn't say anything!"

"Sure."

"Look," Aeyun said, exasperated. He needed their conversation back on track. "I think it's time that 'Aeyun' disappeared for a while. We can maybe try a few smithies around the city. I'd rather forge my own supplies, but while fear and mistrust are rampant, it's best if I take a step away from crafting gear for now."

Davah's neck craned, the image of it reminding Aeyun of the mutts that lounged around Haebal's less affluent corridors. "You're a weaponsmith, too?"

Aeyun nodded morosely. "It was a hobby more than a trade. I used to – look, it's complicated, and now's not the best time to get into it while we're standing in the middle of the park. I should probably look for a mask as well."

At that mention, Davah froze up, eyes widening a fraction before he blinked the reaction away.

"A mask, huh?" he asked, strangely cynical.

"Davah?"

"It's nothing. Yeah, let's see what we can find, then we'd best find some accommodations for the evening."

Aeyun twisted the mask he'd purchased in his hands. They'd scouted a few smithies and weapons dealers that they could stop by in the coming days, but Aeyun wanted to prioritise hiding his identity. The mask itself was carved of wood, the majority of it a blank canvas. Only a stroke of iridescent powder-ore paint was trailed down its side, adding some artistic treatment.

It wasn't an uncommon mask, and there were plenty of folks who adorned a mask similar to it for various reasons; usually some sort of disfigurement from an alicant accident or a lost battle held while traversing the realms.

Not everyone got on well between the realms, and spars weren't particularly unusual. Of course, there was also the underworld of ore trade to deal with, as well as pirates and thieves and simple muggers. That said, those caught fighting dealt with legal ramifications for disruption of the peace, technically breaking a law scrawled in some ages-old treaty drawn up between the realms. The actual punishment had more to do with who you knew and what your social status was, but the threat of imprisonment remained.

In any case, Aeyun figured he could wear it without drawing too much attention. There were a few variations on the market, and the mask that Aeyun had selected at random had widened incisors on its top row of teeth, elongated down. Connected just before where his earlobe would meet the side of the mask, a succession of blue and ivory beads dangled, the ends of each side knotted in a creative weave. Davah had picked one up as well, but he had put it in the bag slung onto his back so quickly that Aeyun hadn't got a chance to look at it.

Aeyun stood from the edge of the bed he was sat upon – a budget hotel in the less posh half of Kwe's centre – and walked to the corner-cracked mirror on the far side of the room. There, he held the mask up to his face and pondered it. It did the job, certainly, as the majority of his facial structure was hidden behind its stylised shaping. One of the beaded adornments tapped at his neck, something he supposed he'd have to get used to, unless he cut them away. As he was pulling at it, he saw Davah staring at Aeyun's likeness over his shoulder, his expression spooked. Slowly, so as not to startle him, Aeyun lowered the mask and put it on the table instead.

"Sorry," Davah said before Aeyun had the chance to turn around. "Ah, sorry. Just a bit of – don't worry about it. All's well, friend."

Aeyun eyed him. "Will you actually be okay with me wearing

that and all?"

Davah nodded.

"Only if you're sure," Aeyun murmured.

He watched as Davah took long steps towards the window and leant on the sill, taking a deep breath in of the rainy musk outside.

"It just reminds me of something," Davah groused. "I'll get over it."

"Only if you're sure," Aeyun repeated.

Leaving Davah to have his peace by the window, he considered the mask again. He supposed it would be his public face for the foreseeable future.

"It makes sense for me to wear one as well," Davah called over, not turning around. "Once the chatter starts, it tends to go far. Someone might connect the Aeyun with the Doons to the Aeyun from Raenaru, and . . . we're trying to fall off the map, right?"

"Right," Aeyun answered quietly.

"Lots of people would know my face through the ore trade. Maybe it's best for 'Davah' to disappear as well."

Aeyun wanted to apologise, but he was unsure how to start.

A moment longer and Davah continued, "I'm glad Saoiri's home in Kilrona. I don't think she'd be ready for it. Not yet."

"Ready for...?" Aeyun dared to ask.

Davah finally twisted around, leaning upon the wall with his head tiredly supported on the window's frame. "Don't be coy, friend. You know that Essence itself is coming for us. It's only a matter of time."

"You sure you want to be a part of this, Davah?"

"I already am, Aeyun. And, for what it's worth, I feel like I'm exactly where I need to be."

Aeyun smirked with a small *tsk*.

"Don't be precious," Davah added, waving a lethargic hand. "As much as I'd love to say I'm in this for the noble goal of keeping you safe, friend, I'd be lying. I'm curious as a cat in a rat's nest, and I just want to see this to the end. Something in me tells me it matters, and I'm just tagging along to see why."

"That's fine," Aeyun said with a shrug. "Everyone's entitled to their own motivations."

Davah fell asleep first, snoring softly on his too-stiff bed. Aeyun couldn't succumb as easily, and instead stood before the mirror once more, lifting his mask to his face. Between the coverage it provided and the shadows creeping in from the night-time glow of the city, Aeyun looked like a daemon. Something straight out of the tales told to children so that they wouldn't go wandering at night. He adjusted the angle of his head slightly and kept his eyes on his reflection. It really was alarming, the whole ensemble of it in the dark.

Putting the mask down, he retrieved the seed from his satchel and rolled it in his hand. Aeyun hadn't yet composed his purchased gauntlet and he wondered if it was a good time to do so. His type of tuning, Vitality attunement in the manner he sought, looked nothing like Essence. Done the right way, he could likely still make use of it. Deciding as much, he set the seed on the table beside him and settled into the chair there. He pulled the half-leather, half-metal gauntlet from his bag and brushed his hand across its surface.

He had to decide how he wanted to carve it. There was a setting for an alicant between the wrist and knuckles of it, and just enough space to trace a pattern or a symbol, if he chose to. He'd have to consider its functionality. The seed was an exchanger. And a compiler. It drew on the tuner's force, and then it could expel the energy that it gathered from both the tuner and whatever else it encountered. It filtered it through its thorny vines, recycling what it drew from contact, both with itself and the tuner. This allowed for more concentrated and powerful implementations of its own strength, or the strength of what it was connected to. A storing conduit, of sorts.

A suitable match for the energies of Vitality.

After all, Vitality was very much about exchange and flow,

leaning into the natural inclination of things, rather than tearing against them like feral Essence did. He wondered if he could utilise the seed to draw upon the tamed energies within another alicant – a thought for another day, perhaps.

He wanted his attunement lines to work in tandem with the Vitality-driven flow of energy. To achieve this, he thought about how the manifestation might occur, and he slipped his – inferior but still effective, he guessed – dagger out of its holder.

It would culminate and extend down to each finger, as well as up his arm, surely. But it wouldn't be a straight shot. Energy would collect around the embedment, so he first carved a ring there, driving little channels towards the setting. From there, it would network to his thumb – a meandering crevice was sheered into the metal – and then to each finger. Heading to his arm, it would likely bow, so he etched a branching path to the top of the gauntlet, and then he looked at his work.

It wasn't pristine, below his practised standards, but he wasn't disappointed. Aeyun pushed the seed into the setting on the gauntlet and slipped it on, feeling the pulse of Vitality ebb through the materials. Testing it, he extended his arm and silently asked the seed to expel its vines, only just. Attuned to his whims, the spiky black plant material erupted from the seed. It curled out past his fingers, still twisting of its own accord, but it followed his directive with a pleasant hum. Aeyun nodded and called it back to the seed. That would do for now.

"Well, won't you be a terror?" Davah's question made Aeyun jump, his eyes darting over to meet his companion's intrigued gaze. "More interesting by the minute."

"I didn't mean to wake you."

Davah rolled onto his other side, facing away from him. "Your *shink, shink, shink* of metalwork says otherwise."

"Sorry," Aeyun offered as he replaced his dagger to its rightful place.

"Mm. Rest will do you good. Stay your mind for the night, will you?"

"Yeah." Davah wasn't wrong. "I'll try."

"I win," she stated, as if it was always meant to happen. It wasn't received with celebration.

"You always win!" The exclamation wasn't so much an objection as it was an admission, and it prompted a pesky, unstoppable grin. "But you're too smart, so of course you do."

It was embarrassing how much praise endeared her to this girl. But it did, and it worked.

"I can teach you some strategies next game," she proposed, ignoring the hopeful swing in her voice. The offer was met with a sunny smile, and suddenly her opponent looked years younger in her ostentatious dignitary attire.

"I'd love that."

She couldn't bring herself to mirror the statement, but she hoped her action of resetting the board communicated it well enough.

CHAPTER TWENTY-FIVE

Sakaeri groaned with a curse as she dabbed ointment on a fresh wound. It was just one thing after another, wasn't it?

One would think that living a life of blades and espionage would have perhaps one *millisecond* of downtime, but no. Not for Sakaeri. She lived for excitement, sure, but the price of a bounty on her head or a knife in her back did become cumbersome at best and a kiss of demise at worst. Her marriage to a mercenary's ragged, precarious dance was in one of its deeper pitfalls.

Damned Kaisa, damned alicant, and damned Aeyun for being

such a secretive brat.

All she wanted was a break, a small reprieve from his annoying attitude. But *no*, instead she got to run into his stalker and the monster from her nightmares, the one and only Kaisa. And now all his little goons were out chasing her.

She wasn't keen to go sightseeing, so she figured she'd stay in the sea-skimmer and bide her time, enjoying tea and pretending that she was civilised. Apparently, the Yun were not on her side. Lo and behold, none other than Pitmaster Kaisa came barging in, frustratingly finding a hatch that Sakaeri didn't even know existed, full of tiny little bags of alicant – she guessed it was the stash of what they'd already collected. Knowing what she knew now, it was a pretty impressive amount, considering Aeyun must have gathered it in under a year.

To make matters worse, while she was fleeing, that forsaken communication stone tumbled out of her grasp. She felt its loss deeply. Beyond its inherent value in terms of rarity, it was from *there*. Her not-home home. But that was her own foolishness manifesting, having given away its partner in the first place.

To make her escape, she'd stolen another sea-skimmer – someone dumb enough to leave the latch unlocked – and booked it to the Great Sea Gate. As much as Kaisa was fascinated with Aeyun and Sakaeri wanted him to *not* be, she also understood that being in his grasp would mean nothing good for her.

She'd failed at killing him once, and he only seemed to try and goad her into trying it again. And again. And again.

She wished the man would just croak on his own, preferably choking on his own tongue. Kaisa was truly a vile being, and the realms would be better without him. That's what she thought, anyway. And she imagined most would agree, assuming they weren't the ones who revelled in his little *games* and *shows*, as he called them.

So, this was how she found herself back in Tenebrana, sitting in the corner of a stim-caf, feeling like Eyes were constantly watching her. She hoped they weren't. They probably were.

Sneaky little fuckers, those Eyes. Sure, she'd experimented with her own vision, but that was *different*. That enhancement allowed her greater vision in dark corners and insight into auras; lie to her and she would know. It wasn't a weird, live feed for someone else. Sakaeri was still her own person.

At least, that's what she told herself.

The Sirin had made it pretty clear that it was a no-going-back kind of deal.

Still, it didn't bother her. She got to travel and learn skills she never would have otherwise. Now, she could defend herself, better than she ever would have been able to if she had stayed a housemaid at the Tower, and she understood more. And starry sea, did she love when she had the opportunity to learn.

She never was granted the chance to go to school like most children, her younger years spent stealing like a miscreant. Sakaeri never mourned the social graces those institutions were meant to bring, but she did lament the lost knowledge. When she was able to pick up bits and pieces from files and manuscripts left in offices of those far more studied than herself, she always took the chance. Soon, she knew more about theories and scientific quandaries than an average student of academia would, she was sure. What was better, she knew that they had to mean something, seeing as those who deliberated and disseminated them were seen as a threat.

It was a shame they had to die. Truly, she would have loved to debate with them.

Over time, she'd been able to build her own library of sorts, filled with stolen tomes and blueprints and journals. If only there was ever time to read it all. But alas, duty always called, and she was never at rest. A lazy day was so far beyond her comprehension it was laughable.

And now, she couldn't go back. Not to her not-home home. Kaisa would surely find her, and she couldn't have that. It was only by luck that Oagyu had summoned her that fateful day. Pure dumb luck. And it bound her to him. For years. A lost canary without its flock, searching for a new, shiny cage to call home.

She hadn't told Aeyun what Oagyu had requested in his most recent summons. It didn't matter anyway, because there was no way that Sakaeri could have gone through with it. Not with Raeyu's life on the line as well. When he'd called her into his office and said to find and hunt Aeyun, she'd wanted to ask why.

What had he done? What finally pushed Oagyu over the edge?

But she couldn't. It wasn't her place, and it wasn't her job to pry. She was expected to just carry out the requests handed to her.

While she'd been formulating a plan on how to navigate the task without killing Aeyun, Seraeyu stalked past her and . . .

Well, now she sat in a dingy stim-caf drinking rotten-tasting tea with paranoia clinging to her every thought. It wasn't nice, but Sakaeri was unfortunately used to that.

Could she have known? She asked herself that question a thousand times.

Could she have had any idea that Seraeyu was about to commit patricide, of all things? Was there any sort of giveaway that she could have noticed? Something greater than the frown that shadowed his face?

It was an odd thing to think back to. A distinctly unwelcomed memory to divine. And something about it felt all kinds of absurd.

Seraeyu was an imp. He was reckless, self-serving, and indulgent. But he wasn't *heartless*. At least, she hadn't thought him to be. She'd seen him be kind and giving; downright nurturing in the right circumstance. It didn't add up.

Her mind kept drawing her back to that alleyway. Back when her eyes didn't glow, back to when her muscles weren't developed. Back when she'd been on the wrong side of Haebal, a stupid foray to seek a tuning enhancement draught that likely never existed, and when Seraeyu had strayed too far from the safe Tower grounds.

He'd taken a literal punch for her that day, Untuned as he was, and – in a sick twist of irony – it was the one instance that made her believe Seraeyu was capable of ripping someone's arm off. Not that he had back then, but she'd never before witnessed a Yu-ta of his status quite literally shred into another man's face. She was sure the unlucky bastard still had a rake of scars where Seraeyu had dug into his cheek.

It didn't shake her to find out he'd frequented the training pen more after that.

It was the look he'd given her when he'd turned around – an odd mix of fear, anxiety, and adrenaline – that told her he wasn't like her. He couldn't shut it all off. Cut the circuit that pumped empathy into his veins. Seraeyu was many things, but *un*feeling was not one.

It only proved her point more when he'd struggled through his own sobs to ask if she was alright; meanwhile his hands were shaking so badly that she could have sworn he had tremors. Of all things, he told *her* that *he* was sorry.

She still wasn't sure what for, but if her suspicious were correct, it was probably because he hadn't tuned. *Couldn't* tune.

What in the frigid void did that matter, anyway? She should have told him that.

They'd returned to the Thasian Tower in silence, but their clasped hands said enough, his still trembling, hers an anchor. Despite it all, they knew better than to bond over it. They parted ways at the entrance, her gaze lingering on his retreating back.

Seraeyu Thasian was no daemon, so what happened?

Unfortunately, the same could not be said for his ill-fated father. Praetor Oagyu, the iron fist of the Raenaruan realm. She often questioned if the Council even bothered to protest his whims. Likely not. The Thasian loyalty was far too valuable, and much too precious a commodity to lose.

Upon the provision of her assignment, she'd wondered if Oagyu wouldn't have called for Aeyun's death had he stayed. Now, though, she figured he still would have. Perhaps even sooner. Maybe Aeyun's intuition wasn't all that bad after all, and maybe death did loom for him in Haebal, if he had lingered.

Maybe Oagyu figured it out.

Sakaeri figured it out.

It made sense now. The puzzle finally fit, and it was a relief.

Aeyun was not her brother. Not by name, not by blood. Nor was he Jourae's son.

As soon as he'd spoken of a realm beyond, one that he knew existed. One that matched the odd *seed* that only he could touch. She knew he was from wherever it was. It was the only thing that made sense, considering her mother had long passed when Aeyun was born. He'd messed up his age more than once in her presence, the absolute dolt.

Why Jourae would claim him and not her, though, that still grated at her. But then again, Oagyu had asked Jourae's actual daughter – not that he knew that – to kill his fake son. It was almost poetic, like one of those lame old dramatic tales she'd found on a dusty shelf in Paladi, that meltingly volcanic city on Orin.

Who would ever want to live there, honestly? It was boiling; quite literally.

Maybe Aeyun could always do strange things. Maybe he was a target from the start. Maybe, if he'd told her that, she would have actually tried to help him. She loved an underdog, after all.

Something about Aeyun still annoyed her though. It probably always would. He was too . . . *him.*

Too righteous, too cautious, too focused on a penance that didn't make sense. Perhaps one day, when she had the full story, it would. In her eyes, he always seemed as though he were reining himself in, unwilling to be whoever it was he could be, if he didn't live a life that wasn't his own.

She'd learnt to let go – mostly – so why couldn't he? He'd left, hadn't he?

Maybe he didn't know who to be. Maybe Sakaeri thought that was kind of sad.

She scoffed. Perhaps she did consider him like a stupid little brother after all. And, perhaps, she shouldn't have tried to kill him in the first place. Perhaps she would have regretted it. Perhaps she knew that the second she had almost succeeded.

She only hoped that his own stubbornness didn't finish her job for her in the end. Sometimes, she mused, Aeyun needed to be saved from himself.

The feeling of being watched increased tenfold and Sakaeri looked up towards the stim-caf door. There, a woman with a scarred face and a leering smile greeted her, pupils set in a cross upon her irises.

"Tell him I'm not interested," said Sakaeri.

The Kaisan's grin grew wider.

"They attacked you!"

A snarky reply threatened its release, but he bit it down. She hadn't meant anything by it, and it would decidedly just be him being an arse, so he grunted his discontent instead.

"I'm so sorry! And you're bleeding . . ."

The fussing tapered off in a whisper, and he removed his hand from where it had been applying pressure. A wound, fresh on his arm, too deep into the muscle. A warning, a task failed by an assailant, a botched effort to finish off the Legacy's only bloodsong user. The hired sword hadn't intended to leave Aeyun's limb attached as surely as they'd fully intended on dispatching the famed Thasian heir.

It had been a stupid idea for them to go out so late.

There were no flowers around, winter's frost having claimed their petals, but there was a silkspider ogling him from a dewy web. He hadn't . . . done that. Was that acceptable? Forgivable?

But he couldn't lose function of his arm. He needed to fight. To protect. So, he snatched the arachnid and its sticky threads woven of struggling insects. Muttered words drifted off his tongue, practised since childhood. They offered a silent apology behind them, a stale hope that the creature would understand.

CHAPTER TWENTY-SIX

"Here's that one we saw a few days ago."

Davah's whisper was nearly drowned out, his voice barely audible above the dull roar of rain. His and Aeyun's steps were similarly muffled in the onslaught of pelting drops, something they'd become begrudgingly used to in the past days.

They were both masked, just as they had been for the last week. Aeyun discovered the day after purchase that Davah's alter ego was also that of typical wooden construction, but his supported the stylised effect of a smiling expression. Like Aeyun's, it also sported a beaded trail attached to each side, its sequence consisting of ivory and orange.

They'd taken to murmuring among the public, careful to not give away their regional accents or dialects. For their purposes, the aim was to remain forgotten shadows in the crowd, passing by without much in the way of distinction. To do this, they had to be . . . cautious.

"Maybe we'll have better luck here," Aeyun mumbled back.

He appraised the storefront shoved between its towering neighbour and its less-than-legal-looking medicinal counterpart on the opposite side. So far, each weapon shop or smithy they'd tried was either too pricy, a rip-off for the gear being sold, or simply lacking in useful stock. This one, though, in all its faded-awning glory, looked exactly the type of place where some hidden gem could be found.

A bell chimed as they entered, announcing the next ambling purse to ensnare. The first thing that struck Aeyun was the brightly coloured bird, its fat feathery body sat upon a perch by the window. It squawked at him and Davah, flapping its wings, then it appeared to almost yawn in boredom. Aeyun gawked for only a moment, eyeing its fountaining plume.

"Fellas!" a woman covered in vibrant tattoos called from behind the counter.

Aeyun glanced over at her and immediately recognised the muscle tone that came with weapon-smithing and weapon-wielding. It rippled from her shoulders and down her arms, telling its own story. She also had little nicks and discoloured burns lashing around her forearms. Perhaps she not only sold weapons, then, but improved upon them.

Perfect.

The shopkeeper looked like she was waiting for either of them to respond. When neither did, she scowled and fanned a hand out, gesturing to the numerous wares.

"Have a look. You both seem like the type who might enjoy what you find."

Aeyun wondered what that implied about their impression – did they look dodgy? – but he nodded at her and got to searching.

Some of what he found was unwieldy, too large or too showy, but there were pieces here and there that showed promise. A thin, balanced sword, or a telescoping spear-like harpoon. Davah had his eye on that one. Idly perusing, Aeyun found a peculiar item that stood out. Too hefty and garish for his tastes, but its make had him keen to touch it.

Hung on the wall, the large, curved relic of a weapon was held up by two hooks. Its body looked to be finely carved from bone – it must have been a very large creature, judging by its sheer mass – and it was etched with carefully configured lines to optimise the flow of energy that might be attuned to its alicant nodule, sat at the pinnacle of its curve. On its edge, the bone was sawed down to a fine, sharp crease, and there were leatherbound handgrips on either side of the dual aerofoil.

"That's a traditional weapon of the early Kllun Tribe from Tenebrana. From one of their acid whales. Old as the mountains of Orin and the seas of Mhedoon." The shopkeeper paused. "You like it?"

Aeyun didn't turn to her. Instead, he rested his palm on the bony structure. When he did, a rush of unnamed familiarity hit him, and he could feel the slide of murky water against his serpentine skin, the joy of leaping out of the leagues-long swamp, trying to get higher with every attempt, and then the shredding pain that pierced into his gills, followed by a struggle as he was pulled towards the hunters he'd learnt to avoid.

An elbow rammed into the space under his ribcage and Aeyun blinked, coming back to himself as he took his fingers off the strange tool. He looked at Davah, whose eyes screamed wonder behind his mask, then nodded indistinctly at the shopkeeper.

"You have odd tastes, buddy. We used to have another bone-made weapon. Just a blade. It was crafted from the tooth of a Raenaruan sabre-maw, supposedly. Shame you missed it; was snatched up maybe a week ago." The shopkeeper smiled, her charcoal-lined eyes glinting mischievously. "Very pointy and perfect for stabbing."

Aeyun frowned behind his mask as he turned fully to the shopkeeper. The sabre-maw was endangered, slain for the very reason that their fangs were known to be nearly unbreakable. He jabbed a thumb at the hanging aerofoil instrument – it was far too large, but he felt like he needed to save it from the grimy shop – then pointed a finger at the telescoping harpoon that Davah had yet to let go of.

"Quiet one, huh?" The shopkeeper snorted and punched a few keys on her register. "You owe me this."

The holo-display lit up above the register, and the shopkeeper tilted her chin at it, nonplussed. Aeyun nodded, dug in his pocket for his share, then held out his hand expectantly for Davah's. Davah groaned and retrieved his due, unceremoniously dumping it in Aeyun's outstretched palm.

The shopkeeper flitted her gaze between the two of them as they paid, pursed her lips, then held up a finger.

"Hold on." She came around the counter and snatched a harness from the wall, complete with adjustable buckles and two large securing clasps on its body. "It's made to hold all variety of large weaponry on your back. Take it. Not sure how else you plan to carry that awkward monstrosity there."

Aeyun's eyes followed her indication towards the curved bone on the wall. The woman gave him a bemused look, a snort ready as he hesitated.

After fastening the harness on himself, Aeyun nodded at her once. On his way towards the door, he grabbed the aerofoil off the wall. At first, its weight fell heavily in his arms, as was expected, but once in his hands, it became light and accommodating.

Interesting. Aeyun latched it upon his back.

As he left the shop, he heard the keeper utter, "Stars, you must be stronger than you look."

Once outside, Davah's fingers dug into Aeyun's shoulder. "Your eyes went like porcelain. Not black and starry, but *white*. What in the frigid void, friend?"

Aeyun smiled wryly. "My type of Essence," he murmured back. Davah didn't back off, so Aeyun continued, "I'll tell you, probably sooner than later."

Davah seemed to accept this, retracting his vice grip. Temporarily placated and shaking off his apparent shock, he rolled back on his heels, condensing his new harpoon into something more manageable before attaching it to his belt.

"Not what I thought you'd go for. You've been looking at flat blades and those chained flail things elsewhere," Davah said lowly as they passed a gaggle of gossiping elderly, all of whom hobbled in staggered paces down the street.

Aeyun nodded sagely. "Right, the chain-flail is useful when you have several opponents and you're aiming to wreak as much havoc as possible – not exactly what I'm trying to do. I was remembering that it was a particular favourite of our one and only recently risen to power nuisance. That, and that damn double-sided lance."

Aeyun could distinctly remember Raeyu having come around with dual-slashed wounds after an *accident* in a *simple sibling sparring match*. Right.

"The flat blade would have been more practical, but I'd want that plus a shield of some sort, and we were priced out for what was honestly *awful* quality–"

"Gear snob."

"–so, those were a no. I was hoping to get something ranged as well, and this isn't exactly subtle, but it'll do the job." Aeyun patted the aerofoil strapped to his back. "Hadn't considered it before, but it'll do nicely as a shield in a pinch. And if someone is close enough to me, I have that dagger I picked up. Hopefully this thing will keep most encounters less lethal and more of a knock-out contest."

"Else I can pick up the slack with this handy extending harpoon – how's that engineered, anyway?"

"A series of interlocking mechanisms that–"

"Hey, uh – hey," Davah said, patting the shoulder he had so recently abused. "I wasn't actually asking. I guess that's how you feel when I talk about ore."

Aeyun willed back his urge to explain the rest of the weaponry's inner workings. It had been too long since he'd had the chance to indulge.

"Right," he said.

It was halfway into their evening feast – a meal taken in their shabby accommodations – that Davah nearly missed his own mouth.

With a clipped exclamation, Davah shoved his hand into his satchel and pulled out a communication stone. He gave it an endeared smile, then proceeded to etch a message back to – Aeyun presumed – Saoiri.

"She's doing okay," Davah said after a moment. "She's wondering how all is for us."

"For you, or for us?"

"Eh." Davah waved a hand in the air. "It's ambiguous. I'll say we're safe."

A long pause followed, during which Aeyun scarfed down some more dinner. He found his mind wandering. Was Saoiri okay? Had she considered the circumstances since they'd separated outside Kilrona? Was she angry at Aeyun for luring Davah away?

Aeyun stole a glance at the way Davah caressed the stone, focus trained on its smoothed surface as he waited for a response. It had Aeyun's attention darting to the floor, a whirlpool of something sombre tugging on his soulsong, a shame flushing through him.

"She said that Beldur was once a big city of commerce? Seemed small for that, but sure. A centre of trade, or something. And she's found references to something – just once or twice – that she doesn't understand? The – wait, she's spelling it – A L K O N O S?" Davah frowned and looked up at Aeyun. "Any clue what that is?"

"Nope," said Aeyun.

It did pull a thread of recognition somewhere in his brain, however, in the far recesses. So perhaps he'd heard it, or something similar, elsewhere.

"Maybe," he corrected. "But I don't really know."

"Great help you are." Davah snorted and focused back on the stone. "Context: the text seems pretty hazy on it as well, apparently."

"Tell her thank you, please," Aeyun asked and Davah nodded.

After a few more messages, Davah put the stone away and hummed contentedly. His muscles even seemed to have relaxed, the tightness that drew his brow loosening to a soft ease. Where his gaze had landed, somewhere distant beyond the smeared windowpane, it watched something only he could see, his lips wavering, not quite a sulk.

Aeyun couldn't help himself. "Do you miss her?"

"Hm? Sure, I do. We'll reunite someday. She's the one who helped me get my feet back on solid ground – did I ever tell you that?" Davah laughed as if he'd spouted an inside joke. He looked at Aeyun, a sad smile stretching across his freckled face. "She saved me, you know?"

"I can understand that all too well," Aeyun muttered, taking up refuge by the windowsill, staring out at the darkened city. "I have a story like that, too."

"Is that why you're so determined on this?"

It took a moment for Aeyun to comprehend what Davah was *actually* asking. "Partly."

"Does that story have to do with your enigmaticness?"

Aeyun could tell that Davah was trying, and failing, to rein in his curiosity.

"That's enough questions," he said.

On the other side of the room, Davah harumphed and kicked his feet up on the table. Aeyun gazed out and up, trying to see what the night's veil hid, and what the buildings kept obscured. He couldn't manage to see past the next block over.

"I'm going out for a while," he told Davah.

On his way through the door, he snatched his mask and secured it in place, then fastened the aerofoil on his back as well. Just for good measure.

Aeyun took the hotel's stairwell up and up and up. The tall structures in Kwe felt endless, even to those in the best shape, and he wasn't ashamed to be huffing as he climbed the final few flights. When he reached the rooftop terrace, he was pleased to find it abandoned, only home to some plants and a few stray birds. There, he sat under the graciously rainless sky, and he stared up at the painted lunar landscape. Thoughtless in his action, he placed a hand over his heart and the scar that rested above it.

As he sat, he had the faintest notion that something warm rested beside him.

With a sigh, he swung the aerofoil from his back and laid it out on the roof's slabs.

"What's your story?" Aeyun asked aloud.

He ran the hand that wasn't covered by a gauntlet over the ivory. Uncanny impressions of practised techniques filled his mind as he brushed across the intricate carvings; the image of calloused hands working against a once-brighter canvas. He traced the surface, following natural striations, and he was immersed in wider seas, finally beyond the acid marshes, only marginally familiar with the underwater topography there.

Gentler, Aeyun asked, "Who were you?"

He splayed his fingers across the hefty bone. Pushing to the surface, his mind became awash with a phantasm, an existence where he was once young, curious and playful, enjoying the dance of a strange and charming ecosystem. Friends like himself grew and aged, and eventually came time for the coming-of-age migration. A reference, indecipherable, whispered to him. The second migration came and went, and it was the third – *Azura* – it was the third – *Azura!* – when the hunters arrived.

"Thank you, Azura." Aeyun pet a hand down the ivory. "I'm glad you trust me."

"*Wow*," a voice whispered in his ear, disembodied. Aeyun startled straight and turned, but he found no one. "*I wondered why you cried so much when we found that fencat.*"

"Rae?" Aeyun called softly, reaching towards where he thought the presence was, but it was hard to determine. Raeyu's presence felt as though it were everywhere at once.

"*I didn't realise it was like this,*" Raeyu said, and it reverberated around Aeyun's head.

"How are you–"

"*Close your eyes.*"

Aeyun did as asked, then felt the disembodied tickle of fingers in his hair and the heel of a palm on his right temple. "*Now open.*"

Aeyun listened once more and the realm was hazy around him, some colours too muted and others too bright. That wasn't what held his attention, though. Instead, he focused on the ghostly visage of Raeyu, who stared at him with star-dotted eyes, more brilliant than shadowed.

She smiled. "Hi."

"Rae." Aeyun was too stunned to move.

Hesitantly, as if the realm would crash down with the slightest provocation, he lifted his gauntlet-covered hand to rest on Raeyu's. Distressingly, Aeyun noticed that their touch wouldn't catch. What his fingers did catch on was the edge of his mask, and he made to flip it up to remove the unwelcomed barrier.

"Don't," Raeyu said quickly, and Aeyun felt the phantom sensation of her claw-like nails accidentally scraping his scalp. "You probably have that on for a reason. I can't do this long."

"What is this? How are you doing it?" Aeyun asked. It wasn't the first time Raeyu had managed to connect with him across realms, though his experiences were confined to the in-between, and he couldn't wrap his head around this. This moment. "Your eyes are–" *like the starry sea, inversed.*

"I must be attuned," Raeyu said with another smile and a light laugh, something airy despite their circumstances.

"To Essence? To Vitality?"

Raeyu is in front of me, talking to me.

Aeyun acknowledged Raeyu's apparition, really taking in her lack of a right arm for the first time. It stabbed at his heart like a splintering tear, wedging into the twisted muscle. She looked unwell; exhausted. And she had on a patchwork cloak that Aeyun found vaguely familiar.

Raeyu's fingers pulled at a lock of Aeyun's hair, but it didn't quite fit in her pinched grasp. "To you."

"What?"

Raeyu indicated with a subtle nod to where Aeyun's hand had subconsciously come to rest over his heart again. "I'm attuned to you. You called me," she said. Raeyu smiled once more, but it held something behind it. A hidden twinge of pain. "I can't stay here."

"I called–"

Each time that Aeyun had encountered the spectre-like image of Raeyu played in snippets across his mind. Each time, he'd called to that tether. Each time, Raeyu had opened herself to it.

"I called you," Aeyun said with realisation.

Raeyu chuckled softly, and Aeyun felt a prickle of nostalgia. Memories of kinder moments, more forgiving. Less desolate.

"I can't stay," she repeated. "Your sister is well. Uruji is recovering."

"Wait."

"I have to go," Raeyu said, and this time her smile fell in favour of a grimace.

Aeyun's heart lurched. He couldn't distinguish the origin of the painful sensation, only that his field of focus was narrowing, and the rim of his vision was darkening.

"What's wrong?" Aeyun asked, reaching out to try and touch Raeyu once again, but she flinched away. Aeyun's eyebrows knit behind his mask. "Rae?"

"Sorry, Aeyun. I really am. I have to leave."

As abruptly as her whisper had arrived, Raeyu clipped out of existence and the realm faltered, becoming an inversion of reality before it fell back into itself and made sense again. Aeyun blinked and dropped his hand from where it hung in the air. His breath – had he been holding it? – came back in full force and his body crumpled forward, a deep-seated exhaustion overtaking him as his palms caught the rough slabs of the roof.

"What even – what happened?" He watched the empty space on the rooftop through a long inhale. Finally, he sat back and caressed his hand across the aerofoil again. "You saw that, right, Azura? That wasn't in my head?"

In that unusual, turned-around plane, the bony structure had an energy abuzz, flowing around it excitedly. With a sigh, Aeyun grabbed the ancient weapon and secured it on his back as he stood, wobbly. He gazed up, trying to see deep within the distant reaches of the starry sea.

"I'll get there soon."

"Not everyone loves her like we do, you know."

It was an odd experience to be sharing any sentimentality with someone who'd lodged a blade in his gut, but he figured he'd already suffered stranger things in his life, so he responded, "I know."

"You say that–" Attention was turned to him, and he cursed himself for wanting to wither under the intensity of it. "–but I'm not sure you do."

"Is that what all your murdering has taught you?" As the words left his mouth, warped and loathing, a shadow of the same feeling crept up on himself.

He tried to stamp it out, like he always did. But it lingered.

"Yeah," she responded, uncharacteristically sombre. "That's what all my murdering has taught me."

CHAPTER TWENTY-SEVEN

"You want to go to a Kaisan Pit?" Davah asked, each syllable dripping with disbelief.

"It'd be the best way to find him and see if we can get those gate ore back," Aeyun reasoned, as if it weren't a stupid idea.

Davah floundered, a croaking noise escaping his throat. "Aeyun, friend. I admire you fiercely, and your tenacity is truly astounding, but this is not a plan."

"It's something that we don't have right now, so there's that."

"And what's *that*?"

"A direction to follow."

Aeyun was getting antsy. They'd been in Kwe for a month total, biding their time, and there'd been no word from Seraeyu, no word from Saoiri, and no word from Sakaeri. No word from Raeyu, either. And nothing was as disquieting as silence.

He'd tried to establish that connection again, but it felt blocked. As if it were cordoned off by something. The whole of it made Aeyun's nerves sizzle.

"Where do you propose we go? There's only one Pit location I'm sure exists, and it's that spot on Lu-Ghan that Kjar mentioned." Davah made a face at Aeyun's insistent eyebrow raise. "Right. You plan to return to Lu-Ghan, then." He sighed. "Dammit, Aeyun." Then he let loose a mighty groan. "We probably have to buy a new craft. *Again.*"

Aeyun nodded, his own disgruntlement pawing at his mind. They couldn't take a run-down sea-skimmer from Mhedoon back to Lu-Ghan, and especially not one that could theoretically be cited as fleeing the devastating scene at Caiggagh. They needed to separate themselves as far from there as possible and, if he was to achieve the insurgency into the Kaisan Pit that he desired, they had to remain anonymous. Elusive, like the shadows they ought to be. And they were running low on money.

"We have no money," Davah said, and Aeyun was suddenly struck with the thought that he and Davah were spending way too much time together. "We should have been taking more jobs while here. Well, we can start now." He paced back and forth across the hotel room, carving out an imaginary map with his finger as he went. "We can work our way through Linao to Yeshen, then to Pan and on to Gebao. Frequent all the for-hire haunts as we go."

"How long will it take until we're liquid?"

"However long it takes, friend," Davah said with a frown. "We're nearly starting from scratch here. We only have enough for another two weeks' stay and some stingy meals."

"Great."

"Isn't it?" Davah asked, sarcasm thick. "Right then, are you and *Azura* ready to explore?"

Davah heard Aeyun call his bone-carved aerofoil that a few times, and he had subsequently made fun of him for doing so. *Am I being replaced?* he'd tease. *Is Azura a better conversationalist than me?* he'd jest. Shortly after, though, Davah fell into the habit of calling it that himself, albeit with a playful drawl.

Aeyun had yet to tell him that it was the creature's name when it had been living.

The idea of taking any longer than necessary didn't appeal to Aeyun, but they didn't have much choice if they were on the brink of being broke. Compounding that, the rooftop terrace was running out of plants for Aeyun to snatch up and stitch a tune with, his quick fixes becoming a more frequent necessity.

Between the weapons, their temporary accommodations, and their new attire – they couldn't very well be dressed in anything distinctly regional – their coffers were nearly empty. Now, equipped with masks and all-black, hooded garb, they looked as though they could be in ranks with the Sirin, if anyone lived through seeing one of the feared mercenaries to ascertain as much.

"We always were," Aeyun said, answering Davah's query, considering a strange fondness for the ivory on his back. "Let's go."

It was on the transition from Kwe into Linao that they dropped into their first for-hire haunt that Davah had so casually mentioned. There, a mismatched collection of brutes, scavengers, and career bounty-seekers collected in a stim-caf. It was one of the finer ones that Aeyun had ever set foot in. Its interior was crisp and clean, and the back wall was all clear panels, offering a magnificent view of the watery horizon that merged with the bridged route to Linao.

If Aeyun didn't know better, he would have said that he was in a seaside pub that looked over the marina in Keou, the portside town that took locals and travellers alike to the urban centre of Haebal City. The journey was via hyperline, a high-speed transport wire copied from Quinga. The comparison made Aeyun wonder which image influenced the impression of which in his mind.

Davah nudged Aeyun, gesturing for him to follow towards a wall with posters. Some of the papers there had big crosses drawn over them, an indication for whomever the owner of the stim-caf was to take it down at the end of that day, and others were hidden under layers of other random requests. Davah began to leaf through the sheets, looking for a suitable contender that Aeyun and himself could take on. With a delighted noise, he yanked one from the underbelly of a stack and shoved it in Aeyun's face.

In need of new alicant accessories, jewellery, or gear, it said.

Aeyun took half a step back and marked a large X with his arms. Davah clasped his hands together, awkward with the post between his palms, and silently begged. Aeyun indicated an X with his arms again, more forcefully. Davah grunted, annoyed. The sheet was tacked back onto the board with what Aeyun assumed was a nasty look from Davah – it was hard to tell with the mask – and then another ratty parchment was snatched up.

Aeyun considered it, then he jerked one fist forward in the air, indicating approval.

It was a request for water-based alicant, *by any means necessary*. With their ore stash long gone, they'd have to seek out a new one and return to the location indicated, at the time the post demarcated. Aeyun was confident that they would be able to find some. They knew the tells of where it might be hidden, so if they kept a sharp eye, they'd surely find some by the day's end. As it stood, they had a deadline of dusk.

Aeyun followed Davah out of the stim-caf and they walked to the start of the trans-city bridge. Looking over the edge, he could see a long set of stairs that led to the distant shoreline. Beyond their landing, sparsely stationed anglers dotted the rocky beach.

"Well, no better place to start, right?" Davah whispered, already sounding as though he were ready for the ordeal to be done. "Look for barnacle collectives; we know they like to feed around ore veins. If we can't find alicant there, we can head towards the water and search the bed of the ocean itself. Worst comes to worst, there are a few fish species around here that like to eat kelp-ore – you know, that slimy green one that's found with seagrass?"

It really never did lose its gooey surface, and Aeyun couldn't get over how gross that was.

Aeyun let Davah lead him to the gate. They hopped over with little hassle, continuing down the stairs to the pebbly beach. As they walked, the crunch of their boots on the rocky shore drew a few glances from the anglers they passed, but most paid them no mind. Too many people around Quinga to worry about each passing pair.

From their new vantage, Aeyun could see that much of Kwe was actually on stilts, rising high above the natural topography of the realm. Camps sprawled along its underside, congregated into small communities.

While their crew had frequented Quinga, their traversals had involved slipping into estate auctions of too-lavish apartments that towered over the streets far below. It had been a one-two-three type of job: one of them distracting the auctioneer, one of them keeping watch, and the last of them swiping the goods. Aeyun was always astonished how easy it had been. After a while, he'd begun to suspect that the auctioneers didn't actually care.

Davah led them further down the coastline, on the lookout for any tells. Finally, with the majority of the anglers behind them, he paused. In that more secluded expanse, Davah turned on his heel.

"Where are the fecking barnacles? They have an aversion to Kwe, or something?"

"This is a densely populated area. It's likely that a lot has been picked over by those willing to tread further than their doorstep."

"I miss the wilds," Davah whined.

Aeyun knew that wasn't entirely true. Davah definitely enjoyed an urban habitat; he was always overjoyed to spend a night in one of the soaring cityscapes across the realms.

Aeyun faced the water. He'd been dreading this.

"Uh, about going under . . ."

"Right," Davah said with a sigh. "How'd you do it last time?"

As much as Aeyun didn't want to admit it, he answered, "Sakaeri."

"Class. Right, okay."

Davah flexed his wrist. His bracer was already set with a pearly water alicant, similar to the one that Saoiri wore around her neck. It was an alicant native to Mhedoon, a fact that Aeyun had learnt when he'd first thought to ask.

Davah looked over at Aeyun, expression shrouded but mask smiling. "So, she knows?"

"Not everything," Aeyun supplied. Was it really the time?

"Right, okay," Davah said again. He first looked to the left, then to the right.

Many people tuned with alicant across the realms, but the laws were different realm to realm. It was generally frowned upon to flagrantly exercise tuning without purpose. Children and the general youth did, of course, as they often tested their boundaries. But alternative to this tuning, it was mostly seen beyond town borders, or for industry and martial purposes. Otherwise, it held a place on the more disreputable side of life that included dubious dealings and illegal fighting practices. Such as the Kaisan Pits, Kaisa's own personal empire.

Despite the somewhat fluid regulations around alicant practices, it wasn't uncommon for mercenaries and ruffians to be running about, as *someone* had to carry out the deeds that the average citizen didn't want part in. Weapons in and of themselves weren't outlawed: only if you were caught making a scene did it cause trouble. And alicant accessories were typically a part of someone's ensemble if they could afford it. They could present through the subtleties of jewellery or the brazenness of war-gear, like Aeyun's gauntlet. Dignitaries, like those of the Thasian Legacy, were often dripping in finely constructed rings and earrings and bracelets of all kinds, each with expertly faceted ore or gem alicant – gem alicant were true, potent treasures.

Based on the material it was set in, the quality of an accessory's construction, and the skill of the alicantologist – a career alicant craftsman who turned raw materials into cleaner, more compliant conduits – the results could be anywhere from shoddy to astounding. To achieve the best outcome one typically needed money, and lots of it. Unless, of course, your own talents were up to the task.

Like Jourae Thasian-nee's had been.

Aeyun was a skilled smith. He knew his way around metallurgy and how to best construct something with attunement in mind. From battle gear to smaller, more delicate items, he could construct beautiful masterpieces, having learnt from the very best. Uruji, on the other hand, was a truly exceptional alicantologist. He had a talent for understanding the way alicant would mesh with its setting as well as its alicantist, the material's compressed energy acting as his guide when he carefully faceted a piece. He was also insatiably curious about the *whys* and the *hows*, questions that contributed to results that outshined most other competitors on the market.

Together, Aeyun and Uruji challenged even the work of their father, and maybe outmatched him.

"Looks okay," Davah said, drawing Aeyun's attention. "Let's go, then."

He looped an arm into Aeyun's and walked them towards the lapping waves, holding his free hand out beside his hipbone, fingers splayed to the air. As they stepped into the shallows, the water began to part, and soon they were submerged below the surface.

Without the four of them in a group, Davah's tune was different, encasing the pair of them with what felt like a thin film of airy separation between their skin and the water. It left them to float under the ebb and flow of the ocean, pulled gently with the wane of the tide. This time their feet didn't seek solid ground, and they remained suspended, able to swim. It was a slightly awkward tug-of-war, due to the compulsion of Davah holding onto Aeyun's arm to extend his alicant attunement to him.

"Pretend I'm an alicant on the shores of Kwe; where would I be?" Davah asked.

"No coral here, too dense and industrialised," Aeyun reasoned as they swam downwards.

"Right, right. I don't think there are any sea vents around here either."

"Right." A lull followed, only the slosh of water echoing around them. Oddly, Aeyun was reminded of foreign memories of acidic marshlands. "Surely these people get water alicant from somewhere by the shoreline?"

"I mean, it was a request in a for-hire haunt, so . . ." Davah let his sentence trail.

Aeyun fought back a grumble.

"Okay, so sometimes ore veins develop in unexpected places, right? So, it could be hiding under a giant rock–" he pointed away from them to a very heavy-looking mass. "Like there!"

"And you propose we move that how?"

"With Azura's help," Aeyun said simply.

Davah muttered something that sounded awfully close to a curse, then he directed them down and towards Aeyun's discovery. Once there, Aeyun removed Azura from his back and lodged one end under the boulder like a fulcrum.

"Help me out, please," Aeyun murmured to the aerofoil, and Davah's head tilted in what Aeyun assumed was a *look*.

Aeyun positioned himself on the opposite end of the bony weapon. Grasping it, a silken flow coursed through him. Iridescent streams of energy filtered down from his hands, crossing through the carvings in the ivory. With a sudden burst of propulsion, Aeyun was able to push down far too easily, and the rocky mass went shooting through the water with unnatural force.

"Fecking *Yun of the stars*!" Davah cried out beside him.

Aeyun stared from where he'd landed on the sandy seabed, having half-pulled Davah down with him during his plummet. He could swear that Azura was vibrating, almost joyously. He petted his left hand down it once, then gave it a pat for a job well done.

"Wow," Aeyun said, slowly righting himself from the grit below.

"You don't even have an ore in that to attune with!" Davah half-yelled, and Aeyun chuckled awkwardly. "I – you know what? Whatever. Look, there's nothing here, so let's go dislodge and fling a few more across the shelf while we're at it, huh?"

Davah, distressed, dragged Aeyun to the next hefty rock.

By the seventh boulder and a swim away from the coastline, they had some luck. While the heavy rock tore through the water, soaring away from them, they spotted a turquoise-coloured crystalline deposit under where said rock had been. Victoriously, they pried up all the shards they could manage to break off, then they headed back to the pebbly beach. As they broke the watery meniscus, they were introduced to a drizzle of rain, a prelude to the later torrent to come.

"We're keeping some of that as collateral," Davah announced quietly, only after they'd stalked away from the angler they'd managed to scare upon their re-entry into the open air.

"That's fine," Aeyun told him. He thought that Azura deserved a gift after all the work it had done, too. Perhaps of the alicant variety. "It's nearly dusk," Aeyun noted. "Will we head to the bridge?"

The post had requested that they meet the client in the middle of the Kwe–Linao trans-city bypass, on the pedestrian route. It wasn't much of a trek, but Aeyun didn't want to miss the drop-off window.

Reaching agreement, the pair of them backtracked along the beach and up the stairs. Aeyun glanced back at the undercity with a frown. It had a distinctly forlorn energy, left to rot away on its own under the high-rises above.

They made it to the bridge and traipsed along its footpath, reaching the middlemost point just as the drops falling from the dreary sky got thicker and more frequent.

There, leaning on the rail, was a petite hooded figure. Their head was angled down to avoid the onslaught from above, and they didn't seem to hear Aeyun and Davah as they approached. Davah gave the person a light tap on the shoulder.

A young woman, perhaps in her late adolescence, jumped and skittered back, her eyes darting between their masks. Davah pulled out the request sheet and pointed to it, then elbowed Aeyun. In response, Aeyun dug out a portion of their collected crystalline ore, presenting it to the girl.

"This is – you answered it?" she asked, hesitantly reaching for the sharded pieces. "I've been asking every day, but . . ."

Aeyun noticed that she looked dirty, muddy impressions left on her pants, and her hooded jacket was torn and tattered. He'd gamble. Just this once, because if he was right, he wouldn't be asking her for payment. In preparation, he cleared his throat. It was an accent that he had trained out of his speech a long, long time ago.

"Are you from down below?" Aeyun asked, his Ca'lorian brogue perhaps too thick.

She looked taken aback. Beside him, Davah twitched, but otherwise remained aloof.

"Is it that obvious?"

"Take it," Aeyun continued. "It's yours."

The girl's eyes shifted down to the ore in her palm, then to Aeyun's masked face again. There was a spark behind her gaze, quick and furious, and Aeyun could swear that the direction of the rain shifted, if only for a moment.

"I won't have your charity." She plunged a hand into the purse hung across her body, then tossed a collection of coins at Aeyun. They landed with a wet clatter at his feet.

"Thank you, and may the alica find you favourable," she said in parting before shoving past them.

It wasn't often that people spoke of alica, that seemingly elemental energy inhabiting alicant, with its own agency. Even less common that they preferred it over referencing the godly Yun. Aeyun's thoughts warped in an unceremonious churn as he watched her disappear.

The rain pelted on as Davah lent down and picked up their payment.

"You've really got to think before you do something like that, you know. Not everyone wants a saviour. The likes of her? She probably thought you were looking down on her. Probably wanted this for a long time, and you managed to steal that gratification from her." Davah stood with a sigh after grabbing the last coin. It was a third of what they could have sold it for on the market. "And, I'm sorry, *what* was that voice you did?"

"It's like nothing you've heard, right?" Aeyun asked.

Davah nodded, and Aeyun could imagine the suspicious expression that was likely hidden behind that wooden mask.

"I hadn't thought I'd offend her. I was just trying to help."

"Some people want it, others don't. Sometimes even the ones who need it most. Best way to help everyone is to change the flaws behind why they need help in the first place, but with the realms how they are, well – we all know some things are so broken it'd take the Great Starry Sea itself razing them to fix it all." Davah shrugged. "Nothing's wrong if nothing's there, right?"

"That's a little extreme, isn't it?" Aeyun muttered.

A discomfort scratched under his skin, and he leant upon the railing, his gaze drawn to the darkened shadows below the city's stilts. Little pockets of light crackled in haphazard spacing, drawing indiscernible figures to their warmth in the seemingly endless blackness. He blinked and had to double check that his feet still had solid matter beneath them.

"Dunno, is it?" Davah pushed back his hood and pressed his back upon the metal barrier, his elbows latched lazily to its surface and his masked face angled up towards the crying sky. "Well, job done." He heeled a soggy boot into a puddle. "We're halfway to Linao. Let's use what we earned for a stay somewhere and then work up twice as much tomorrow. We've got it in us, I'm sure."

Aeyun rubbed a spot on his chest, just under his collarbone. "Sure, Davah."

He hadn't expected to encounter anyone awake when he returned, but there they both sat, dressed in soft cotton and drinking tea, of all things. They looked for all the realm the high-society regents that, he supposed, they actually kind of were. He did his best to ignore their stares, both a little sad and a little disappointed, as he stripped off his protective gear and set his mask down on top of it.

"You don't always need to play the hero."

And if it wasn't a stab in the heart to hear someone younger but so much wiser tell him so.

"You're doing enough as is, kid. And I'd like you to stay alive to keep doing it."

The mirror at the door mocked him with bruises under his eyes and the reflection of two concerned expressions. "I'm alive. And I'm definitely not a hero."

He didn't look back as he trudged up the stairs.

CHAPTER TWENTY-EIGHT

The realm spun into place and Aeyun was back in that sprawl of gardens, the one that acted as a barrier between one of the working-class districts of Haebal – Danu, a place of familiarity, gained in his earliest days on Raenaru – and the forest beyond. Aeyun knew the scene: it started with Raeyu and himself exiting the forest, where they'd often scamper off to, given the opportunity. After all, there weren't many places that Raeyu could go in Haebal without being noticed, and something about their fateful meeting place called them back time and time again. Surrendering to that pull, their free days often saw them treading those same paths, all the way to the belly of fragrant prickles and blooming ashenwoods.

Aeyun knew, once they emerged from the brush and foliage, they'd have a few fleeting moments in the twilight hours where Raeyu would admire the season's blossoms, commenting on the lunarius, a radiant flower that only unfurled at night. As Raeyu waxed on about the intricacies of the species – many facts learnt from Aeyun's own studies, relayed to Raeyu years prior – Aeyun would feel the watchful gaze of another.

It was the same. Always the same.

Sakaeri's prowling, cat-like eyes, seen for the first time, would appear in the distance, under the shadow of a weeping tree. Then she would spring at Aeyun. His heart racing, Aeyun would dodge, and then he'd be forced to dodge again, but Sakaeri's dagger would shatter his Hana mask, a nicked fissure spanning from its grazed edge. Raeyu would protest her assault, readying herself to tune with one of her many jewelled adornments, but Sakaeri would bind her with terrifying skill, broken apologies on her tongue.

It always ended the same, too. Sakaeri would manage to avoid the sharp edge of Aeyun's sword swing, then she would use the opening to drive a dagger into his gut. Were it anyone else, the gash would be fatal, but Aeyun, attuned to Vitality, could stitch the wound shut, as he always would. Before fixing himself, though, he would deftly tend to Raeyu, who would suddenly find herself bleeding out as the dagger dug into Aeyun's innards.

It had been a gnarly way for Sakaeri to discover their bound nature, and her grudge against Aeyun – her desperate need for vengeance against his stolen life he'd lived so blissfully in her eyes – was smothered, doused due to her dedication towards Raeyu. As she watched Aeyun descant, mumbling foreign words as a milky glow emerged upon his and Raeyu's skin, leaving barely-there scars in its wake, she'd break down, distraught. Confused and deeply wounded herself when Raeyu solemnly admitted that she didn't think Sakaeri would ever actually go through with killing Aeyun.

The fact remained that, at one point in time, Sakaeri brandished her weapons, intent to drive Aeyun into an early grave.

It was always the same, each time Aeyun's subconscious drew it to the surface, but as his foot stepped into a water-coloured garden, a feeling of *wrongness* permeated him to his very bones. Another step and Raeyu was already by the lunarius. Her movement was too quick.

Another step and the once-vibrant hues faded, melting down the garden's edges. One more, and that familiar stab pierced into his stomach. When he looked down, it wasn't through the eyes of a mask. His bare face met Sakaeri's broken expression, something tired and dull.

"I don't want to do this anymore," she whispered, blood coating her scarred hands, garish splashes of it somehow splattered across her pallid cheeks.

"What?" Aeyun asked, befuddlement twisting his thoughts. This wasn't what happened; this wasn't right.

"I'm tired. I don't want to do this," Sakaeri said, and her form shifted back. Aeyun looked down and the dagger was gone, dissipated, as was the ground. Instead, an inky blackness engulfed them, pockets of energy building and flowing in the distance.

When he looked back up, Sakaeri was still there, but she was huddled in a ball, her hands over her head, her miasmic impression dim and translucent. A hand reached out beside him, and Aeyun watched as claw-nailed fingers stretched. Instinctively he responded in kind to the offered comfort. When his gaze trailed up, he expected to find Raeyu looking back, but instead it was another hauntingly familiar pair of amber eyes.

Meeting his companion's gaze, Aeyun observed that this wasn't Seraeyu of the holocaster, the one who was cruel and rigid, adorned with the lavish riches of a diplomat. Instead, it was a much-wearied version, stained with long-held worriment glued to the gentle features he shared with Raeyu, courtesy of their mother. This was much more the Seraeyu that Aeyun knew, but rarely saw. It was the version that only existed when Seraeyu thought he was alone, with enough privacy to finally drop his pompous exterior.

Seraeyu stilled, gaze both penetrating and curious, brow drawn down. He dared to take a step closer. With a fretful hesitance, he plucked at Aeyun's fingers. In turn, Aeyun remained in place, his body as good as petrified.

Seraeyu's eyes coursed up, his glance a questioning observance, then he pressed their palms flat against each other and lifted their hands into the air. A simple test to answer a simple thesis. Aeyun, however, wasn't sure what the query was in the first place. He provided just enough pressure to keep the connection aloft, his wonderment getting the best of him, and then Seraeyu's fingers cautiously thread into his own. The two of them gazed at their intertwined grasp, Aeyun's mind lost in a fog of confusion. Why was Seraeyu here? What did Seraeyu want?

Behind their hands, Seraeyu's head lulled to the side, a reflection of his own bafflement. His focus shifted up towards Aeyun's eyes once more, searching. Even so, he said nothing, and neither did Aeyun. There was a serenity to the silence, though. Like the gentle inhale and exhale of breath, the very space around them awash with balance; a push meeting a pull.

It wasn't until a long, immeasurable moment passed that Seraeyu finally seemed to take notice Sakaeri's crumpled impression. Aeyun marvelled at the revelation that showed so clearly on his face, his expression swiftly shadowed with conflict. As if by sheer instinct, Seraeyu's other hand lifted towards her, reaching, a sad, forlorn quality to his movement.

Aeyun, without hesitation, found himself mirroring the action. Together, they tried to breach the vast dark and bridge the distance.

Aeyun awoke with a gasp, waist folding sharply as he startled, his ratty blanket falling to the side. His heart thudded against his ribcage, leaving echoes of bewilderment reverberating throughout his body.

"Yun, friend! What? What?" Davah grumbled next to him, half asleep and annoyed.

The bed they shared was too short for their legs, and one of Davah's was cascaded over the opposite edge of the mattress. He'd woken at Aeyun's jerky movement, and he didn't seem happy about it.

"Sorry," Aeyun mumbled back, willing his brain to catch up with reality.

He glared at the wall, attempting to gain his bearings, then swung his legs down, feet hitting the floor. As an afterthought, he retrieved the worn blanket from the floor and tossed it over Davah, who seemed to have lost his own during the course of the night. It didn't help with the dewy mugginess of the evening hours, but it did deter the biting gnats that always managed to find their way indoors.

Aeyun decided to instruct a dazed, "Go back to sleep."

Davah offered what was probably meant to be a comforting pat, but it ended up more like a lazy smack on Aeyun's back, then he turned and faced the opposite direction.

Aeyun looked at him, brows furrowed, not really seeing past his own foggy brain. He tried to put the pieces of his life together, all jumbled in his grogginess. When he finally remembered that yes, this was the present, and his most recent memory was going to bed in this rundown Yeshen hotel room after a long day of for-hire work, he sighed.

It was hot and humid in Quinga, and it spread across the realm like a fever. The half-broken fan in the corner of the room did little to quell the heat, and Aeyun was sweating through his thin excuse for a shirt. His eyes travelled down to his right arm, illuminated in the lowlight that crawled through the window, swapping from green to pink in timed intervals. He observed the twisting scar there. It had spread considerably, but he'd expected that after months of tuning stitches on an otherwise dead limb. The raw Essence that had a chokehold on the tether he and Raeyu shared ensured that every descant left a record, winding and hooking into his flesh.

It had been far too long since progress was made.

Aeyun and Davah had been taking gigs for almost a quarter of a year, and Aeyun only had brief connections with Raeyu in that time. They were more like pulses than anything else. Simple reminders that they were tied, and that Raeyu was still out there, somewhere.

But that dream had felt tangible in a way it shouldn't have.

He wasn't a stranger to nightmares; never had been. He often had them when he was younger, reliving twisted memories that he'd rather have forgotten. After the incident on Caiggagh, they'd returned twofold. His mind was too frequently taken on a journey that was filled with strife and then anguish at its bitter end. Those moments of suffering made sense to him, though. A way for his mind to furnish thoughts of how horrible he'd been, what terrible things he'd done. It was almost more cruel when he dreamt of happier times, feelings of love and warmth and camaraderie. A day on the sea, celebrating his spoils with a few good mates. Coming home to a delighted grin, one that proudly displayed a missing tooth, and the endeared smile that reflected the same joy, given to him by a kind face with adoring eyes.

Those had him waking feeling sick to his stomach, something roiling in his gut.

This dream was different, though. Was that Raeyu reaching out to him, or was that Aeyun's own manifestation? And what was going on with Seraeyu? With Sakaeri?

He still hadn't heard anything from her – not a word – and a sick spiralling feeling accompanied that thought. It wasn't right. Sakaeri was too stubborn to leave things to chance, and sticking with Aeyun was her best bet if her aim was to ensure Raeyu's safety. That had to mean that *something* had happened, and he suspected that *something* was a big deal.

Aeyun convinced himself to stand and he found his knees stiff and creaky. He and Davah had been working themselves ragged. The money wasn't what they needed it to be, but they were getting closer to their goal. Enough for a sea-skimmer, and enough to make it a while in a new realm. It was likely well past time to switch districts. He suspected they were starting to encroach on someone else's turf and someone else's profits.

He rubbed the heel of his palm into his eye. He was tired.

Saoiri had been chatting with Davah semi-regularly in the first two months or so, and then there was only silence after a message that said one word: *pause*. It seemed to have affected Davah more than he let on, and Aeyun noticed his anxious fidgets worsening in times of stillness, as if he couldn't take the pressure of his own mind and imagination.

That being the case, Davah had been incessant in his push to fill every waking moment with some sort of activity, be it for-hire work, chatting about meaningless nonsense, or working out or training with their now not-so-new gear. The constant workshopping had allowed Aeyun to refamiliarise himself with combat techniques. It turned out he was more disciplined in his practice than he'd assumed, judging by Davah's first reaction at watching him.

It was Davah who had offered the real stunner, though.

When Aeyun watched Davah wield his telescoping harpoon, and it was clear that it was not his first time handling that type of weapon. Davah had moved fluidly around the small beachside alcove they'd found, his footfalls sliding on and shifting the sandy surface. While the harpoon was at full length, he'd use the implement with deadly force and accuracy, carving through the air with swift strikes that would surely sever muscle. Other times, he'd twisted it like a staff, combining its spin with a wind-based tune, causing a small cyclone to project on each forceful push.

Then there were times he used it as an actual projectile.

The harpoon now sported a winding coil around its shaft, the blunt end of it curled in a loop. Davah had tethered a generously long, thin chain to the weapon's body, turning the tool into something that could be pulled back to him with a simple tug and recoil. To Aeyun's amazement, Davah seemed to have keen enough aim to hit his target nearly every time.

Aeyun didn't comment on it. He did, however, greatly appreciate Davah's precision when he'd spear them a few fish for dinner.

Conversely, Davah did comment on Aeyun's skill.

One time, he watched Aeyun toss Azura out across the ocean, jump and twist in the air, then swing out a slice and punch a few jabs with his dagger, held in a reverse grip so that he could force the pommel with his opposite palm. He'd accomplished a handful of stabs to the air as he waited for the dual-sided aerofoil to return. In the midst of it, Aeyun turned his body languidly, distantly reminding himself of the way Raeyu fought as though she were dancing. He then sheathed his dagger, caught Azura, and spun it in an arc around himself, releasing it and letting momentum lodge it into a rocky wall, making a platform that Aeyun could jump up and land on. Davah had chuckled, telling Aeyun that he must've trained for years. Aeyun responded that he had, but not with something like Azura.

They did practise together occasionally, but it was always hand-to-hand combat. Aeyun could tell that each went easy on the other, though. Either due to not wanting to cause harm, or because of a hesitance to show their true extent. Like a final barrier before their daemonish shadows showed their true forms, indicating a nature they'd rather keep hidden.

In the hotel room, Aeyun stretched his arms above his head, elongating a few sore kinks. He walked to the scratch-ridden dresser and plucked his mask from it, securing it on his face as he considered Azura where it leant against the wall. Deciding against lugging it with him this time, he snatched his dagger and his alicant pouch, fastening them loosely on his waist – he noticed his belt needed to be a couple of notches tighter. He left the room with a twist of the key, ensuring Davah still had a safe barricade against the outside realm.

The hotel they stayed in was by the ocean, its façade peeling from poor upkeep. It was the type of joint that Aeyun and Davah quickly became accustomed to, their days of luxury long behind them. The mist from the water floated across Aeyun's skin as he made his way up the external stairwell. Night-time hours by the coast always held a peculiar liminal quality, half caught between the nefarious grime of the obscured, often piss-soaked, alleyways and the crisp, wispy gusts that wafted from the water far below.

Aeyun planted himself on the roof, as he often did when he couldn't sleep. The sky was overcast that evening, obscuring the Great Starry Sea beyond, and the ocean sloshed in rhythmic waves, black in the darkened atmosphere. Something about it reminded him of when Sakaeri had brought him a pastry that morning in Kilrona.

Sakaeri's absence was eating at him. The ambiguity around it was discomforting. As much as he and Sakaeri had a troubled past, she reminded him of his youth and his home on Raenaru. She was present for much of his adolescence, both of them just on the periphery of the Haebal legates and their lives, slipping around the grey space between inside the circle and outside the circle.

Sakaeri was first introduced to him as a housemaid of the Tower. Aeyun was delivering wares that Jourae was too busy to courier himself, instead bestowing a young Aeyun with the task. At the time, he'd nervously made his way from Jourae's smithy in Cheyun to the Thasian Tower gate. After being granted access, he'd walked through the courtyard and entered the main lobby, where he'd promptly lost his sense of direction and ended up in a long corridor on some upper floor that he'd never been to before. As much as Raeyu had shown him her world, Aeyun wasn't often in the Tower at that age.

It was there that he'd run into Sakaeri, a meek girl with a sallow complexion and bright blue eyes. Her head was covered with a ridiculous tall hat and an ivory shroud then, not uncommon for Tower staff, and her hands were hidden in gloves.

It hadn't been an interaction to marvel at. She'd asked him if he was lost, to which he responded yes, and then she'd led him to where he needed to be. He didn't see her again until she had accompanied Raeyu on an outing in Haebal. Maybe a year after that, Sakaeri seemed to have uncovered broken testaments to her past, and her building disdain for Aeyun grew and festered after she'd heard gossip about his rumoured father and mother.

It took Aeyun longer than he'd like to admit to realise her ferocity spawned from his theft of her true heritage. Still, the majority of their relationship was a strained stalemate. A stand-off testing who would break the unspoken treaty first. It had eventually been Sakaeri, of course, the same night her eyes adopted a haunting glow and slitted pupils. But after his and Raeyu's admission about their bound nature, seated in Essence, their stalemate started anew.

There were years after that when Sakaeri had disappeared for large chunks of time. Aeyun learnt that she'd left the Tower's employment only to become a Sirin. A part of him wondered if it had happened around that time, when her eyes had changed. If it was some kind of deal. He'd never asked. It wasn't too long before her appearances around the Tower became frequent again, seemingly under Oagyu's employment once more, though in a very different capacity. Where she had once been viperous and rash, she'd become prowling and steely, as if her sharp edges were refined.

While Sakaeri had been an unwelcomed presence, she had been there all the same.

Aeyun's dream – he was still figuring out if it *was* a dream – bothered him.

He'd seen Sakaeri break down, and he'd seen her in a fit. What he'd not seen was her look as though she'd given up. Not once. Disturbingly, in that void-like space, that's exactly how she appeared. And, for whatever reason, Seraeyu had been beside him. He'd also reached out to Sakaeri, looking for all the realms as if he was drowning in distress. Next to him, without hesitancy, Aeyun had mirrored his action.

What struck him as the most odd, however, was that it didn't feel like an active decision. In that moment, in the vacuous void, it felt as if everything was culminating at once. As if it had been written in the stars they were surrounded by, an inevitability demonstrated a thousand times over. As if something was slotting into place, as it always should have done.

To Aeyun, that notion was the most baffling and terrifying yet.

He was often a keen observer, picking up on little things that seemed inconsequential, but later turned out to be useful. He'd noticed that these nuggets of knowledge would pay off, so he made a point to keep his eyes and ears open, just in case something happened that he needed to pay attention to.

Sometimes, he wished he didn't. He already knew the tells of when his mother would re-live some nightmarish memory, and it always turned out to manifest. He'd wake up to screaming in the other room, and then it would get eerily quiet. The next morning, his mother always seemed fine, in better spirits than the day before, but his father would look haggard.

When she'd broken down by the doorway one evening, he watched in terrified awe as his father stroked her hair, thumbs at her temples. He whispered foreign words and his mother fell silent, as if sedated.

He was told to forget, but he didn't think he ever would.

CHAPTER TWENTY-NINE

Davah shouted something unintelligible as he and Aeyun were thrown out on a seedier backstreet of Yeshen. The commotion drew a few probing gazes, but they were fleeting in the late-day downpour. Davah leant toward Aeyun, who groaned in discomfort at the way Azura had slammed into his back, caught between himself and the cobbled ground.

"We were just asking for what we're owed," Davah whispered to him irately.

"They're assholes," Aeyun growled back, tone low so that it wouldn't carry. He shifted his weight so he could sit, ignoring the uncomfortable damp of the street. "But we won't be doing ourselves any favours by causing a scene."

Beside him, Davah made a rude gesture towards the door that had been slammed in their faces. "They gave us half our share, with the pitiful excuse that it *took too long*."

Davah scoffed, folding his arms when he got up, sending what was most certainly a glare behind his mask at the egress. Aeyun stayed on the ground, seated with his arms pushed out behind him to support his weight. Davah didn't move for a moment, then he seemed to hesitate, and finally he leant down to whisper to Aeyun once more.

"What are you doing?"

"I'm sitting," Aeyun answered simply.

"Mhm. And why's that?"

"I didn't sleep last night. I'm tired."

It was true. Aeyun's sleep was seldom uninterrupted in recent days, always subject to a dreadful memory-gone-wrong. It was Raeyu's death, Sakaeri's assault, or some manifestation of Jourae's demise and Uruji's rift-opening descant that he'd not even witnessed himself. Then, there were the hazy recalls of his parents' slaughter, compounded by the terror of a then-twelve-year-old Aeyun. Or visions he couldn't begin to parse because he wasn't even sure where their phantasms manifested from. His nights were far from restful.

"Yeah," Davah said softly, sounding contemplative.

Out of the corner of his eye, beyond the lashing rain, Aeyun spotted movement near the opening of an alleyway. He snapped his head in that direction and caught sight of wide, inquisitive eyes, belonging to a small child who wrapped himself around the corner of a building. A child with two blunted horns on the top of his head, nearly shrouded by his mop of messy, matted locks.

"Hey, are you alright there?" Aeyun called out instinctively, voice muffled in the damp atmosphere, but loud enough to be heard.

He'd allowed his distinctive Haebalian inflection to slip through on a hunch. The boy, who seemed to pick up on the accent, perked up, but didn't move.

What, Aeyun thought, *is a Yu-ta kid doing in Yeshen?*

"What are you doing?" Davah chided, gripping Aeyun's shoulder too tightly.

Aeyun was getting tired of that being Davah's go-to move. One day, he was sure he'd find permanent bruises where his fingers had clamped down too hard.

After what looked like a short internal debate, the boy glanced up at the sky, then watchfully stepped into the street. As he neared the two of them, Aeyun could feel Davah's hesitation.

"Hello," the boy said, shy and cautious, gaze shifting from one mask to the other.

"We won't hurt you," Aeyun assured the child.

He felt weird speaking so normally behind the daily barrier he'd adopted. It seemed to coax the calm he'd intended, however. The boy stopped just beyond an arm's reach of them, something in his expression brightening upon hearing even more of Aeyun's speech patterns.

"Are you from Raenaru?" the child asked, voice small but disposition more open.

Davah's grip tightened painfully, but Aeyun nodded affirmatively.

"Can you help me?" The boy looked on the verge of tears, his watery gaze a darker shade of emerald in the overcast of rainclouds.

For the briefest moment, Aeyun could swear that it was a young Uruji in front of him, and his heart lurched. Perhaps that's why he was compelled to respond, "What do you need help with?"

The boy's mouth scrunched as he held back a sob, stuttering out, "I'm lo–lost!"

As the child's head bowed in shame, he slammed his hands

harshly against his face, connecting with a sharp clap that shouldn't have been comical. The pressure of Davah's digging fingers lessened. Aeyun could swear he heard an aborted laugh from the man, probably an unintentional reaction to the dramatics.

"Okay, it's okay," Aeyun tried to console the child, switching his stance so that he was on his knees. "Let's get you out of the rain and see if we can find your home."

The boy nodded, but he didn't remove his hands from his face. He also didn't move. At all.

After long moments without progress, Aeyun sighed. "Hey, where are you from?"

"Penthyun," the boy managed to say between his fingers.

It was a parish beside Cheyun in Haebal, and a name Aeyun had not expected to hear. He distractedly batted Davah's insistent grip off his shoulder.

"You're from Haebal?"

The boy nodded.

"I'm from Haebal, too," Aeyun told him, and the child finally peeked an eye between two digits.

"You are?"

"Yep."

"My *nayu* said not to trust people from Haebal," the boy told him with a sniffle, and Aeyun marvelled at how long it had been since he'd heard someone say *nayu*, a term colloquially used for one's mother across Raenaru. "*Nayu* said it could be dangerous if they knew where we were."

The child, becoming more skittish, stumbled back a step. Aeyun, now curious who this *nayu* was, reached out a hand, trying to indicate for the boy to stop.

"Your *nayu* sounds very smart. I don't want people from Haebal to know where I am, either."

As soon as the words left Aeyun's mouth, Davah's hand was smacking the back of his head. Aeyun ignored it.

"Hey!" Davah called out in warning.

"You won't hurt me and *nayu?*" the boy asked, and Aeyun shook his head. The child seemed to contemplate the answer, then frowned. "Your mask is scary, though. And I–" Aeyun could see it coming before the dam let loose. "I lost my cap!"

The boy's sobs returned, as did his hands on his face.

"Okay," Aeyun said, standing to his full height. "Alright. Okay, it's okay."

He fumbled around for something to offer the child, and then the wailed admission started to sit oddly with him. A cap for his head, so . . . was the boy trying to hide his shaved-down horns? Or was his mother? They didn't want him seen as a Yu-ta child? The thought made him search with greater earnest.

Aeyun was at a loss, and he could feel Davah's judging gaze upon him. Aeyun cursed his own soft heart. Really, he knew this was what would happen. He knew that he would inevitably shepherd the lost child to his home, and infallible anonymity would likely not remain. He bent down again, trying to get to eye level with the boy.

"Hey," Aeyun called, and the child removed a hand to wipe his snotty nose. "You want to know a secret?"

"Don't do it." Davah's sharp warning washed over pointlessly.

The child looked absorbed, and Aeyun leant closer, lifting his mask just enough that the boy could peer under it.

"I'm Aeyun of Krunan."

Aeyun could see the recognition as it seeped into the child's features, raw and embracing, awe replacing the despair.

"*Nayu* talks about you!" the boy said excitedly, and Aeyun's nerves buzzed, an uncomfortable twitch needling at his temple.

She does, huh?

"She says how you're lucky, and how maybe you're with them!"

"With them?" Aeyun asked, then thought of a more pressing question. "Who's your *nayu?*"

"My *nayu's* name is Loua. She worked at the Tower."

The boy's words sunk in, pulling Aeyun down like a whirlpool.

291

After he replaced his mask, he chanced a glance back at Davah. He hoped that the wordless exchange was enough to convey his sudden urgency to find this child's caretaker.

"Let's find your *nayu*," Aeyun said with more conviction.

Davah didn't argue, so Aeyun offered the child his hand as he stood. When the clumsy clasp was solidified, Aeyun held on tight and steady.

It was nearing night by the time the boy finally seemed to get his bearings about where they might need to go. The rain hadn't let up, so Aeyun felt much like a drenched rat. Compounding that discomfort, Davah hadn't spoken a word since the boy had joined them.

"Oh!" the child exclaimed; Naeyuji, as Aeyun had come to learn.

Naeyuji pointed to a slim row home, squished between similarly modest neighbours. The humble, nondescript estate was on the outskirts of the Yeshen, dreary and tacked onto the edge of one of its border districts.

"Here, it's there!"

The three of them walked up to the door Naeyuji pointed out. Once they reached it, Aeyun gave a hesitant knock. It took a minute, but the door cracked open a sliver, obviously still latched on its chain. The piercing gaze of a woman met Aeyun's eyes through his mask.

"Who are you? What do you want?" she asked.

"*Nayu!*" Naeyuji called and pushed himself off from Aeyun, where he'd previously had a death-grip on his hand.

"Naeyuji!" Loua cried, shutting the door quickly to slide off the chain and open it once more, wide enough for Naeyuji to jump in and embrace her. "Thank you for bringing him home. Are you mercenaries? Should I – do I owe you payment?"

Her words became less sure as she looked the two of them up

and down.

Aeyun recognised her. She was a housemaid from the Tower, one with whom he'd exchanged plenty of pleasantries over the years, and one he was sure had been acquainted with Sakaeri when she herself was a housemaid. The encounter was making his head spin, and his lips felt frozen.

When the silence dragged on, Davah finally spoke up behind him and said, "Sorry to be a bother, ma'am, but can we come in from the rain? We've been pelted for a while now, and the dry would do us some good. I have a feeling you'll be wanting to talk to my colleague here as well."

"You're not from Raenaru," Naeyuji stated upon hearing Davah speak, sounding almost disappointed.

"Nope, I'm not," Davah said grumpily.

"You're not from Raenaru," Loua repeated, looking at Davah with a strange expression, then she shifted her gaze to Aeyun. "But you . . . ?"

"*Nayu!*" Naeyuji tugged at her arm impatiently until she awkwardly bent to the side. Once she did, he whispered in her ear and her eyes got wide.

"In! In, in!"

Loua ushered them with haste, slamming the door shut after all but shoving them into the foyer. She guided them to her sparsely furnished living room, then knelt down to Naeyuji.

"We will be having a long talk about you wandering off later – I was beside myself with worry – but right now I want you to go upstairs, wash, then settle down for sleep. You had a long day, didn't you?" she asked, and what started as authoritative ended on a note of endeared resignation, her palm cupping his cheek.

Naeyuji nodded with a quivering lip, then he hugged his mother and offered a wave over her shoulder. Aeyun offered his own in response.

"Goodnight, mister Aeyun! Goodnight, mister masked man!"

Davah snickered quietly at the reference to himself as the boy pattered upstairs.

Loua turned around and considered Aeyun with a tight gaze. "Is it true? Are you him?"

Aeyun slowly untied his mask, pulling it away.

"Yun! Oh, *Yun*! It really is you, Aeyun!" Loua's hands came up to cover her mouth and she shook her head a few times in disbelief. "Oh, Aeyun, love, I'm so sorry. I'm so sorry about Jourae."

Aeyun's stomach flipped. "You knew?" he asked, feeling naked.

"I was only young then, but it was easy to tell that Ube and Jourae weren't *just friends*. And when she fell pregnant and then passed . . . The story that you were the lost child of his late friend, taken under his wing as an apprentice? The puzzle just fit."

"Your mother's name was Ube? That's not a very Mhedoon-like name," Davah commented, and it made Aeyun wonder if Sakaeri had told him that her mother was from Mhedoon at some point, because Aeyun certainly hadn't.

"Ube's mother was from Mhedoon. Sinagh Babh, I think was her name?" Loua looked at Aeyun as though he could confirm that. He found himself feeling guilty that he couldn't. One more tick of the clock saw Loua turning to Davah. "I assumed you might have been from Ube's family, given your accent, but I suppose I'm wrong?"

"No," Davah said after a long moment, something in his voice sounding off in Aeyun's ears. "I'm not from that family."

"Ah," Loua said, nodding to fill the lull in conversation.

"Loua, I have many questions," Aeyun told her, drawing the focus back on himself. "I'm sure you do as well. I have to know, though, have you heard from Sakaeri?"

"From Sakaeri? Not for months. She stopped by the day that it happened – and thank Yun I wasn't working that day – and she told me that Naeyuji and I should leave Raenaru. I hadn't listened right away, and I curse myself for my lack of action. If I had, we wouldn't have gone through such hardship. As it is, we finally made it to Quinga. Sakaeri had warned me then that

Naeyuji might need his horns blunted. I thought she was daft at the time, but it made sense, in the end, even if I wish it hadn't."

Loua looked distant then, haunted by events long passed.

Aeyun considered his words carefully as he asked, "Naeyuji . . . he's Yu-ta?"

"Half Yu-ta," Loua corrected, morose. "His father was Yu-ta, long removed from the mainlines."

"I'm sorry," Aeyun said, realising the implication of her tense.

Loua shook her head. "I'm sorry, love. You lost so much that day, and here I am thinking you were lucky to have been gone. I thought that you might even be with them, or with Sakaeri."

"No." Aeyun looked away. "I'm not."

"You look thin, Aeyun," Loua said. "And pardon me for saying so, but you seem different, too. You appear quite . . ."

Aeyun nodded. "Yeah, I know. *Aeyun* had to disappear for a while. What you see is what I am for now."

An awkwardness passed, the room blanketed in silence and eye contact seeming impossible. The wind changing direction broke it, rain smattering loudly against windowpanes.

"So, the baby Thasian has gone mad, right?" Davah asked, and Aeyun had half a mind to smack him.

Loua's response stopped him.

"Yes. Entirely."

"What . . . what happened in those days, Loua?" Aeyun dared to ask, and Loua sucked in a breath.

"So much, and nothing at all. It was like Haebal was stuck in a constant nightmare. Rubble and flames everywhere. And then Seraeyu started the interrogations. Many were confused, but I knew. Sakaeri told me that Raeyu and Uruji-nee were alive, so I knew it must have been about that. That's when I knew we needed to leave, and that Naeyuji's Yu-ta heritage would become a threat to his wellbeing. Seraeyu first targeted Yu-ta folk, and some of them never returned from the Tower, blazing in that wild black energy as it was.

"When Seraeyu was seen, there was something odd about him

too. Unhinged and – how do I put this? He would sometimes get lost, it seemed. Like his mind was fractured. Sometimes, he didn't seem like he was there at all, and other times his presence would be oppressive, like it was too much. It was all very strange, and very terrifying. Something happened to that boy, I'm sure of it. He was always – Yun, forgive me – a bit of a brat, but to go this far . . ." Loua shook her head, as if the action would rid her of the trauma.

Aeyun remembered how Kaisa had described his Eye's rendition of events. It seemed to match up with what Loua told them.

"Loua," he said. "Did Seraeyu seem accompanied at all?"

"Accompanied?" Loua blinked at him. "What do you mean?"

Aeyun stared at her for a moment. "Never mind."

"I'm sorry, Aeyun. I really am. I wish I was more help. All I can say is that it was like the realm fell apart that day. Naeyuji and I were lucky to smuggle ourselves out on a vessel leaving Keou – I know an angler there who has a trader friend – and I imagine things haven't got much better if Seraeyu hasn't lifted the blockade and embargo. I don't know what caused it all, but Seraeyu, despite the narrative he weaves on his holocaster transmissions, seems like he has a vendetta against the Yu-ta, and any who associate with them."

"So, it's about the Yu-ta?" Aeyun asked.

It hadn't crossed his mind before, that Seraeyu didn't just have it out for Raeyu and Uruji, but for all the Yu-ta. That seemed . . . strange. And sudden.

"I don't know. I really don't. But it did come across that way, at least to me," Loua said and Aeyun nodded. "Would you two like some food? It's the least I can do, after you got my sweet Naeyuji home safely."

"That offer I will gladly accept," Davah said, finally removing his mask.

Loua visibly relaxed after seeing his face, and Aeyun wondered what she might have thought he was hiding under there. Rather than a scary maw, it was freckles and smile-lines exposed, and Loua seemed to welcome it.

"Loua," Aeyun called to her as she padded to the room's entrance. "After tonight, let's both pretend we never ran into one another. I know nothing of you here, and you know nothing of Aeyun, or of the two mercenaries with masks."

A dismal feeling sunk in upon his statement, but he knew it was how it had to be. She stopped, perhaps dismayed, then offered a sullen nod and disappeared beyond the doorjamb.

"You don't hear that?" she whispered, annoyed.

There was a constant buzz in her head, like chatter that she couldn't mute, but it was still somehow overshadowed by the midnight rustle of mountains' leaves and the cyclical chirps of nocturnal insects. Beside her, a groggy groan rose in the air.

"Go to sleep. Your mind is messing with you. It's been a long day."

It had been, she couldn't argue that. But she knew it couldn't just be her mind in a frenzy. It continued, as if trying to claw through her brain, and she resigned herself to it, hoping that eventually she could tune it out. That, eventually, it wouldn't drive her into madness.

CHAPTER THIRTY

"It's not fun, is it?" the Kaisan beyond the bars cooed at her.

Sakaeri spat at him in response. Jjenka, bony like the very image of a crypt keeper, was a special kind of snake who deserved nothing more than a good right hook. Or five.

He twirled the keyring around his finger and whistled, his eyes raking down the wounds on her leg, tilted grin quirking high on his left cheek. It made her skin crawl and her thumbs ache to gouge into his sockets.

"Ugh. That last fight got you, huh? Pretty nasty, that. Think it will scar?"

"Give it a rest, Jjenka," the other Kaisan said.

Wen, all slim lines and angular edges, was kinder than Jjenka.

Just *Wen*. No lineage to speak of, so no double-barrelled names of her parents to connect on a family tree. No surname to accompany lonely Wen. It was as good as being dead on Lu-Ghan. She probably didn't even have a valid signatory stamp, no form of true identity. It was a harsh existence, in Sakaeri's opinion.

Still a Kaisan, though.

"Look, just give her the salve. She's not supposed to die from an infection."

Jjenka scowled at Wen, flippantly swiping at her dark, rough-cut tresses as he paced around her. He turned his lip in a childish pout, and Sakaeri furled her own in distaste.

"You seriously ruin all the fun. Did you know that?" Jjenka pointed at his colleague. "You are a fun-ruiner."

"And you are a child," she countered, snatching at the jar in Jjenka's other hand. "Give me that!"

"I'll do it, I'll do it," he coaxed, then turned his attention back to Sakaeri. "You won't rip my throat out like that guy in the arena, right?"

It wasn't funny, and Sakaeri didn't laugh. To her credit, neither did Wen.

"Jjenka," Wen warned.

With a loud complaint, Jjenka shoved the salve jar through the bars and Sakaeri stared at it as though it were a bomb. Maybe it was; how was she supposed to know?

"Aren't you going to open it?"

"No," she snapped.

If she turned away from them, would they disappear? She hoped so.

"And why's that?"

Sakaeri snarled, "Why should I? Maybe I'd like to get infected and die. Maybe I'll have some gross disease that kills the rest of you. Wouldn't that be a dream come true?"

She faced away from the pair of them, training her eyes on a stony wall.

Yun, she hated the situation she was in. What she hated more was that she hoped Aeyun would use his head for once and come find her. Come help her break out of this literal prison – just like the damned Orinian white knight from tales of old. Oh, wouldn't he be pleased? Sakaeri would *hate* it. She wasn't the type who needed saving. People needed to be saved *from* her, not the other way around.

She'd managed, for a while, but Kaisa, as it turned out, was just a different type of threat. His bloodhounds had her scent and her trail. If only she hadn't run into him in Bhu-Nan. If only she hadn't crossed him *again* in Caiggagh. If only she hadn't got the damned assignment in the first place.

Sakaeri cursed the day she'd been tasked with his death, and she double cursed the day that she'd failed.

"You're pathetic," said Jjenka. His jeering tone did nothing for Sakaeri's patience. "I hope you lose yourself slower than the rest of them. I'd love to see you wither."

"Jjenka, that's enough," said Wen.

Sakaeri didn't respond. She didn't watch them go, and she didn't turn around until their footsteps had long faded. When her body finally did spin towards the bars, she found herself looking at the jar of salve, contemplating it.

"Dammit," she muttered, reaching for the medicine.

After unscrewing the cap, she smoothed the jelly across her torn skin and sucked in a strained breath. It *stung*; it probably would have become infected if left untreated.

And what if she had left it? Would that have been the better choice? The more honourable choice, to not allow herself to be a pawn in Kaisa's sick game? *Games*, rather.

It had been a bad call on her part to head back to Bhu-Nan. She thought Madame Reaper would have been more accommodating, given the pilfered bracers she'd lifted from the most recent Kaisan who dared confront her. But no, apparently not. Madame Reaper proved that she had very tightly held alliances, one of which was with the bastard Kaisa himself.

When Sakaeri was offered tea, she had been rightfully wary. When the Madame took a sip, aiming to placate her worries, Sakaeri foolishly complied, trying to keep up good relations. She'd watched in belated horror as Madame Reaper spewed out her drink like a fountain, cackling when Sakaeri's body slumped upon the velveteen sofa. As it turned out, Sakaeri was not privy to all the ways one could avoid swallowing poison, and she was still trying to wrap her head around *whatever* Madame Reaper had done to deceive her.

When Kaisa had sauntered in, infuriatingly smug, Sakaeri cursed the starry sea. All she needed was some better weaponry, the bulk of hers lost when she had to jump into the acidic waters at the Pllametia docklands. She still had recovering burns from that escapade, in addition to her newest gashes.

She'd never forget the predatory look in Kaisa's eyes as he stared at her that day, in all her poison-induced, hyperventilating glory. It was too similar to how he'd gazed at her the day she'd failed. Mocking. Pleased.

He was keen to get his dues, and his widening grin promised a grim future. It was the last thing she saw before her vision failed her. The next was the same forsaken bars she sat in front of now.

Alone in the cell, treating herself with a tincture provided by her captures, Sakaeri found herself agreeing with smarmy-faced Jjenka: she was pathetic.

"Ah, now," Kaisa's voice crooned and Sakaeri could barely keep herself conscious. "Can't have you dying yet, my dear. You're far too entertaining. While I'd be delighted to watch you go down, you are too profitable for that. People love your brutality."

Sakaeri tried to focus on something – anything – to steady her thoughts.

"Where–?" *Where am I? What's going on?*

"Oh, my little Sirin. You've really lost your wits, haven't you?

Don't you worry. You'll be fixed up in no time."

Kaisa's words did little to comfort her, namely because they were *Kaisa's words*, and she attempted to swing out an arm. That just prompted a burst of laughter from the man, and the unsettling feeling that crowded her already anxious mind compounded.

"What a lovely little monster I've created. Ah, dear, I've really broken you."

Time ceased to make sense until she felt her elbows make contact with the dirt of her cell's floor. With a groan, she rolled over and blinked at the cobweb in the corner. A wicked critter kept up its ritual of wrapping its prey, and Sakaeri watched, entranced.

She could barely remember. It was snippets of screams and blood and gore. Blades and limbs and cheers. Without warning, her stomach coiled, and she threw her head to the side to retch. And Yun, did it hurt. The act felt like it was ripping her in two.

With a shaky hand, she wiped at her mouth and struggled to look down at her abdomen.

It shouldn't be that red. And the crimson pool where her back had rested wasn't right, either. It shouldn't . . . that wasn't normal. Concern finally blossomed in her foggy mind and Sakaeri fought back a pained cry as she forced herself up.

"Shit," she breathed. Or at least she tried to.

Her vision waned, and the cold metal of prison bars on her forehead brought her wits back. When had she moved? A darted glance back informed her that she had either been dragged or had dragged herself across the floor, given the line of bloodied dirt that appeared there. Since no one seemed to be in the vicinity, she guessed she had crawled her own way there.

Scratch that, she thought, *someone's around now.*

Her suspicions proved true as muffled shouting continued and the heavy cast-iron door down the hall opened. Another poor soulsong a few cells down poked their hands out, the only thing Sakaeri could see from her vantage.

Were they a new addition? She thought she was the only one

in this block.

"No, Jjenka, not this time!" Wen shouted behind her and slammed the door shut with a huff.

Sakaeri found herself deliriously wishing she could see the look on Jjenka's stupid face when the metal egress latched shut, hopefully stubbing his toe. A giggle startled her, and she belatedly realised it was her own.

That's not a good sign.

Wen ignored the anonymous cellmate when she passed them, tripping to a halt in front of Sakaeri's cell.

"Hey," Wen called out, as if she were approaching a rabid sabre-maw.

Sakaeri spit since her mouth tasted bitter. More red, of course.

"Hey, are you back yet?" Wen asked, cautious, hands raised.

Sakaeri trailed her eyes back up, but they were *heavy*. Back from what?

"Oh," Wen said, as if she'd gleaned the answer. "Okay, um. Okay, you're really hurt. We need to get you patched up."

"I'm bleeding," Sakaeri stated.

Wen stared back at her, nodding hesitantly. "I'm going to help you not bleed."

Something about that offer was funny for a reason Sakaeri couldn't remember, but it didn't stop the laugh from erupting out of her diaphragm anyway. It was a mistake, though, and she coughed through a wave of stabbing achiness.

"I'm coming in, okay?" Wen told her.

Whatever protest Sakaeri may have offered didn't matter anyway. She slipped and once again found herself staring at that creepy critter in the corner.

Its prey was gone, but somehow that seemed like a dreadful, terrible thing.

The realm was red. It was always crimson and foul, and the taste of copper clung in the air.

I don't want to do this. It was the thought most often on her mind.

"Hey."

The call startled Sakaeri into awareness, her first encounter being the white of her own knuckles wrapped around cell bars. Tentatively, she pried her fingers up, stretching them to release the tension there. How long had she been holding on?

"Hey," a voice called again, deep and scratchy.

"Hey?" she said back, hesitant. The realm hadn't fallen into place yet, and she found herself befuddled.

"You okay there?"

Sakaeri took a moment to contemplate the ask. She was sore, maybe recovering. The mobility of her right hip seemed stilted, but workable. Her skin looked torn up, but nothing that would fester. One of her nails was broken – and how in the frigid void had *that* happened, because breaking one of those was near impossible – and she mused that her mind was similarly shattered.

Instead of answering, she asked, "Who are you?"

Sakaeri couldn't angle her head in the right way to catch a glimpse of him. All she saw were arms with fading tattoos. Once vibrant, now muted and indistinct. Otherwise, the only thing her eyes caught were bars, stone, and dirt, all shadowed ominously in the slivers of light that filtered through the thin windows far above.

"I'm pretty sure I told you last time."

Last time?

"Ah, fuck. Maybe I didn't. Starry sea only knows what's real at this point." There was a pause. "Goeth. That's me, I'm Goeth."

"Hi, Goeth."

"Hi, Sakaeri."

Hearing her own name put her on edge. Her shoulders hunched inwards, an instinctive motion.

As if he could sense her reaction, Goeth continued, "To be fair, you never told me your name. I just overheard fuckface mention it when he was goading you. You know, the one with the greasy hair and the greasier leer?"

"Jjenka?" Sakaeri guessed. She relaxed more against the bars at Goeth's affirmative grunt.

"Yeah, that shitstain."

Sakaeri snorted. "Hm. Okay, Goeth. We agree there."

"Glad to hear it," he said. "Now, back to my original question: you alright over there?"

"Why do you want to know?"

"Ah, who can really say. I'm bored and the furry, squeaky thing across the way – I've been calling it Beryl – seems like it finally up and died. Shame: it was the best entertainment this side of the neighbourhood."

Sakaeri frowned. Goeth seemed harmless, and his question appeared to be in good faith, but . . .

"I could tell you about Oruyu," she suggested.

Sakaeri lulled her gaze up to that cobweb she remembered in the corner. There the grotesque critter was, twisting its spindly legs and wrapping something in a silken sack.

"Who's Oruyu?"

"The foul thing in residence on the ceiling of my cell."

"Ah," Goeth said, followed by a noise between a scoff and a laugh. "Go on, then."

"It's vile," Sakaeri started. "And hairy. And always hungry, apparently. Forms a gross net of stringy threads to catch prey." She paused. "You know what, maybe I should have named it Kaisa."

"Sounds fitting; he's pretty vile."

"Agreed."

After a long stretch, Goeth cleared his throat and again asked, "You okay, Sakaeri?"

"Will you stop asking if I say yes?"

"Nah. I probably won't believe you."

At least the man was honest; Sakaeri couldn't fault him there.

"How about we leave it at *I'll manage* for now?"

"Yeah, okay."

There was only stillness until Sakaeri ventured to ask, "How about you, Goeth?"

A bitter laugh rang out and Sakaeri felt something in her chest sink, a curling pessimism slinking down her insides. She looked away from Oruyu and peered past the bars once more. Goeth's arms had retreated back into his cell. If she didn't already know he was there, she would have thought she was alone.

"Don't worry about me."

Sakaeri scowled at nothing, couldn't think of a good response, and instead said, "Yeah, alright."

When she looked back at Oruyu, she could swear it watched her as it devoured its next meal.

"I knew it!"

Those three words encouraged a startled curse to rip from his throat as he turned to look at one far-too-enamoured miniature of his adoptive father. He'd been caught red-handed – or green-handed, if one were to look at the smattering of half-disintegrated leaves in his palm – and he knew that he wasn't going to be able to battle a mind that he truly thought was three degrees sharper than his own.

"Please," he muttered, more annoyed with himself than anything else. He should've been scared, but the shine of delight and curiosity reflected in front of him calmed him. "Proceed, then. Tell me what you knew."

"You're special–" Those words shouldn't have hit as hard as they did, yet he sucked in a breath anyway. "–and I always suspected you could do something amazing." There was an indication towards his mostly healed cut, made from the careless rearrangement of weapons in the shop. "And that's pretty damn amazing."

He scoffed, but a joy welled up behind it. "I'll show you, if you agree to keep it between us."

CHAPTER THIRTY-ONE

It was odd to awaken somewhere other than a rundown hotel. Aeyun turned towards the sliver of light seeping through the crack in the curtains. The stiffness in his arm made itself known, and he groaned inwardly at the thought of the day ahead.

A little way over, Davah was still sprawled out on his bedroll, snoring, with one hand curled around his blanket. Aeyun sat up and cracked his neck, stretching it from one side to the other, then stood and went about packing up his own bedroll, stowing it in the corner of the living room. He checked back on Davah when he finished, but the man was still fast asleep. Aeyun huffed softly, amused.

As he was checking his now nearly dry garb – hung on a clotheshorse, a kind gesture from Loua – Aeyun heard a noise from the hall.

"Hi, mister Aeyun," Naeyuji said, whispering as he noticed Davah's resting form.

Aeyun turned and offered the boy the best smile he could muster, but he was sure it still looked tired. He was glad he'd purchased a sleeve to hide his tattoo-scarred arm under, else it would have been on full display now, adorned as he was in a thin undershirt and trousers. His boots, gauntlet, and other wares were huddled beside his hanging cloak. Even with the sleeve, however, the hint of woven inky markings could be seen above its uppermost hem, a side effect of Raeyu's arm having been torn at the bicep.

"Morning," Aeyun whispered back.

"*Nayu* is making food for you and your friend," Naeyuji said, considering Davah. "He's not so scary with his mask off."

Aeyun couldn't help the twitch of a smirk that pulled across his face.

"Nah, he's actually just a big goof when you get to know him," Aeyun said, moving back towards his belongings to start gathering them. "Although," he paused, "he's pretty serious sometimes, too. But he's a nice guy."

"You're a nice guy, too!" Naeyuji said, as if he were defending Aeyun.

Aeyun tossed a look over his shoulder, bemused, and gave his thanks.

"Naeyuji!" Loua's reprimanding voice reached them first,

then she appeared in the doorway, flustered. "Did you wake them up?"

"No," Naeyuji responded defiantly, volume still dimmed. "But you'll wake *him* up!"

Loua's cheeks flushed when she followed Naeyuji's purposeful point towards the snoring Davah.

In a much lower tone, she said, "Sorry."

Turning to Aeyun, she caught him in the middle of lacing up his boots – struggling one-handed – and he was instantly aware of her gaze on his limp arm. It made him think he should have pulled on his shirt first, even if it was clammy from drying overnight. Tearing his focus from his shoes, Aeyun dared to look up towards Loua. Her expression was torn between baffled and curious. There must have been something held in his own stare, since her eyes diverted from his as soon as they connected.

"I never knew you that well, Aeyun. But I imagine these months have been tough on you."

Aeyun didn't answer, instead solely focusing on lacing his boots. Once he'd managed that, he moved on to awkwardly slide his top over his undershirt, covering the rest of his exposed body to his neck. In that time, Loua must have urged Naeyuji elsewhere, if the patter of feet was any indication.

"Raeyu was always so kind," she said suddenly. Aeyun couldn't quite find it in himself to turn back to her. "Both she and Uruji-nee were so pleasant to us. And Raeyu was always fighting in our corner. It was thanks to her that many of us found our place there, saved from horrible circumstances, like she did for Sakaeri."

Aeyun never knew the whole story, but he knew that Sakaeri hadn't come from a pretty place.

"Uruji-nee was always a voice of reason standing next to Seraeyu, and Raeyu would have changed things, I just know it. She would have taken the Legacy and built upon it, something good, I'm sure of–"

"Please stop," Aeyun muttered, head still dipped. "Stop

talking about them like they're dead."

"I didn't mean–"

"I know," Aeyun said, finally meeting her head-on. "I know, but please don't."

Loua looked on the brink of tears, and her fingers gripped the doorjamb so hard they lost their colour. Aeyun's expression thinned, and he sighed. He didn't have the mental fortitude to tackle his own nihilistic thoughts, so he sure as all the frozen void couldn't take hers on. He felt for the fear she must hold, but he had his own concerns. Like re-establishing a broken connection between realms – that was a pretty large one.

"How do you know they aren't? Wouldn't she have come back to help us?"

"You place too much burden on her shoulders," Aeyun murmured, tugging his gauntlet over his numbed hand.

"Perhaps you don't place enough?" Loua countered, and Aeyun pulled too harshly on the gauntlet's last latch. "We are her people. We are her responsibility–"

"You are a people," Aeyun corrected, trying to keep his tone even. "She is not your king. The divined Raenaruan kings of the past have all fallen, and the Thasian are just a family."

"At the seat of power because Raenaru demanded it," Davah interrupted sleepily, having woken up at some point during Aeyun's commentary. "And the Thasian vied for it time and time again, building their Tower and their empire on corruption, manipulation, and money."

Aeyun knew he should stop Davah, but he didn't, and Loua just stared.

Davah asked, "What would Raenaru do without its blessed Thasian and their Legacy? Where would Raenaru stand without that poisoned power?"

Aeyun glanced over at him, shame colouring his features. He should really stop him.

Davah grimaced. "Someone needed to be blunt about it."

"Davah . . . " Aeyun groaned under his breath.

"So, you think it's best that she leaves Haebal and the entire realm to suffer at the hands of her brother?" Loua asked boldly, but her body language was clammed up.

Aeyun disliked the feeling of knowing it was them who caused her to recoil. He cleared his throat, dislodging the gravel that had thickened there during Davah's lecture.

"I think that if Raeyu *could* be there, if she could do anything to help, she would." Softly, and with a little annoyance, Aeyun added, "She's very bad at self-preservation." He stood and snatched up his cloak before tossing it over his shoulder. "What I think doesn't matter anyway."

"It does, though, Aeyun!" Loua protested. Despite himself, Aeyun's actions halted. "Raeyu has her bloodsong, and she is the most powerful defence that Haebal and Raenaru have. Uruji-nee is a talent unmatched, an amazing alicantist; he is able to achieve some of the most precise attunement I've ever witnessed. He is also a lasting survivor of the mainline Thasian-nee, as are you. I know that Jourae-nee must have mentored you more than was let on, and that some of his wares must have been yours. Beyond the implications of all that knowledge and power, they both adore you! You could whisper almost anything in their ears, and I'd be willing to bet they'd do it. That means that your thoughts most certainly matter, Aeyun."

Aeyun stared unblinkingly, then asked, "You hope for my manipulation of them to save you?"

She didn't respond, tense in her own conflict.

"*My* thoughts are this," Davah chimed in again, lifting himself off the floor. "Why are you Raenaruans watching and waiting for a saviour? Raeyu Thasian is one woman. Uruji Thasian-nee is still only young. There is an entire realm waiting with bated breath for what terror the mad Thasian might bring upon them. Why?"

"His bloodsong is stronger than Raeyu's–"

"And you're all fools if you allow one man, only in the infancy of his third decade, to singlehandedly overpower a nation.

Seraeyu is no god, just as Raeyu is no king, like my friend here so astutely pointed out," Davah jeered, his patience clearly waning.

"We would perish," Loua said, voice shaking.

Aeyun couldn't help it when he asked, "So you would rather Raeyu perish for you?"

"She gladly would, from the sounds of it. And everyone would sleep easy at night, knowing their martyr did it all for them, or that at least she tried. It's easier that way, isn't it?" Davah said, collecting his things with a scoff.

Aeyun took a breath to collect himself, then he offered the Raenaruan sign of thanks, a hand placed perpendicular to his chest, over his heart. He intended to give his gratitude and gain some distance from the situation. Instead, he felt it immediately, his thoughts so focused on Raeyu. There was a distant pull and then the realm was marred with an otherworldly haze, colours distorting and becoming a mix of too bright and too dull.

Loua's shriek sounded echoey and far away, but Raeyu's presence felt near and warm and thrumming. Her phantom visage manifested in front of Aeyun, a sort of caught-out expression on her face, her arm curled to hold a pile of books.

"You broke it," Raeyu stated, owlishly blinking starry eyes.

"I . . . How?" Aeyun asked, suddenly having lost his wherewithal at the interruption.

Raeyu seemed to collect herself, shook her head, then placed the books on a table where they fell out of Aeyun's sight. Aeyun tilted his head curiously at the development.

"You shouldn't be doing this. Have you been working too hard? You look like you've not been taking care of yourself," Raeyu said, frowning.

She stepped forward to reach out and touch Aeyun, then she hesitated and kept her distance. Raeyu's eyes flitted down to Aeyun's gesture over his heart, and she paused.

"Are you with others right now?"

Another voice drifted through the void, saying, "What are you doing?"

Aeyun's pulse jumped. That was . . . That was–

"How?" Aeyun found himself asking again, breathless.

There was no mistaking it. That had definitely been Uruji's call. Uruji, alive and talking, inquisitive like he always was. Somewhere in the starry sea, safe with Raeyu, together.

Raeyu looked off to the side, seemingly startled, then in that same direction she held her hand up in a disarming gesture. "No, wait, it wasn't me, I promise. It was him." Raeyu laughed awkwardly. "He broke it."

Aeyun bit back a stunned chortle at Raeyu's childish redirect.

"Of course he did," Uruji commented, his voice still bouncing from invisible walls, disembodied. "Aeyun!" His shout made both Aeyun and Raeyu jump. "Stop messing with things you don't understand! You're only going to make it worse!"

"Well, you–" Aeyun started, but Davah interrupted him.

"Seeing shite again, are you?" Davah's voice drifted over Aeyun's shoulder, and it had Raeyu's head snapping back, fruitlessly trying to peer behind Aeyun. "Snap out of it, friend. Your Tower woman is about to have a breakdown."

"Shit," Aeyun said, willing himself to react. "Sorry, sorry! I'm sorry!"

Aeyun forcefully pushed away the connection and it dissipated, carried away like fog in the wind. Just like before, it was as if the realm inverted for a moment, and everything was out of place, then the realm righted itself and he was surrounded by the living room as it was before.

"Well then, we've gone and made a mess of things," Davah commented.

Aeyun was met with the frightened image of Loua, her hand covering her mouth in a long-held silent gasp. The terror in her gaze was the first thing he noticed. The second was her defensive step backwards.

There were some days that were worse than others. The ones where he just couldn't get out of his own head. Sometimes, he wondered if that was the problem. Was any of it real, his past?

There were signs, weren't there? If it was real, what did that say about him? His place? His value? His ability to do anything he was meant to do?

Those days, he didn't stray from the forge much. The monotony of molten metal soothed him, and he allowed himself to mindlessly drift away, crafting things in a realm that felt real and false. Living a life that felt real and false.

Existing in a very tangible way but delivering everything with an unwavering falsity.

CHAPTER THIRTY-TWO

"Okay," Aeyun said, massaging his deadened wrist. "I know that was–"

"I was weirded out when I saw it too," Davah offered offhandedly, ignoring the discomfort hanging between them.

"I don't understand. Your eyes were of the legends!"

At her comment, Aeyun glanced at Davah dejectedly. "Am I the only one who didn't pay attention to that bit of lore?"

Davah shrugged.

Aeyun held a hand up to try and calm Loua, who seemed at the fraying ends of her wits, knuckles gone white around the doorjamb again. "What you saw was–"

"This is why we wear masks, Aeyun," Davah interrupted him,

and Aeyun scowled in his direction. "I knew this would be a mess as soon as you said, *hey*, like a prick."

"Let me speak!"

"Aeyun is–"

"For the love of – Davah, please shut up." Aeyun groaned, trying to wrangle the conversation.

Loua's attention was pinging between the two of them, but her fingers were pried looser, if only slightly. While she'd stopped her retreat, she looked ready to bolt at the slightest provocation.

Aeyun sighed. "Loua, that was just tuning. I was just attuned to something. It's nothing fantastical; I was just tuning."

"Just tuning?" Loua asked, disbelieving. "Your eyes were black and glittery–"

"That's a new one. I'll tell the Sirin that your eyes glitter when we see her next."

"Davah, honestly!"

"Your eyes looked like how those of the Yun are described!" Loua said, and a pregnant pause followed.

Aeyun inhaled, hoping for wisdom. "Loua, it has nothing to do with the Yun. I was just attuned to something. It was just tuning."

He racked his mind to make sense of the situation. Everything kept leading to one solution. It was one that he'd only ever seen done second-hand, and not since he was a child. It wasn't ideal, and it wasn't something he'd wanted to enact, but . . .

"Loua," Aeyun said, taking a step forward. "I was just tuning. It was a simple tune. Everything's okay."

Another step and Loua regarded him warily.

"Friend?" Davah called questioningly, recognising the odd change in Aeyun's behaviour.

Aeyun blinked a few times, and he could feel the shift in his being. His Vitality seeped through, permeating the space around him. Loua began to look dazed, her eyes taking on a milky sheen. Silently, Aeyun reached up and pressed his working thumb to her temple.

"*Cah da'gum, da'ju cah, a'gam po.*" Aeyun bit back his discomfort. "*A'pan o.* I just tuned. Something simple, to dry my gear. We can't stay for breakfast." He hung his head, overwhelmed in his disgrace, his descant fading. "Thank you for your hospitality. I hope we meet again under more favourable circumstances. Until then, please forget we were here, and who we are."

Aeyun swiped his thumb off her face. He couldn't bear to look up. Without indication for Davah to follow, he strode towards the door. Davah wouldn't be far behind, he was sure.

"Bye, kid!" Davah hollered to the house as they left.

As soon as they got back out into the humid morning air, Aeyun darted over to a small smattering of trees and gagged. Behind him, Davah made a disgusted noise and haphazardly patted Aeyun's back.

"Ugh, I hate this," Aeyun grunted between a spit.

"You done?" Davah asked, and Aeyun nodded morosely. "Good. Here. Put this on," he said, shoving Aeyun's mask in front of his face. "So? You gonna mention anything about whatever the fuck that was?"

Aeyun did as he was told and shakily stood up. He really, really didn't want to talk about it. At all.

"It was something I'd seen done before, when I was a child. My father had done it to calm my mother's nightmares. To – I don't know, move her memory? I'd never done it myself."

At Aeyun's admission, Davah's posture went rigid. "You can take away memories? To what extent does that go? How do you even go about that?"

"I don't really – I'm not sure. I don't think it takes them away, just softens them into something less alarming," Aeyun admitted, feeling sick again.

"Wow," Davah admonished, laughing at the absurdity. "Did you just jumble up that woman's thoughts without even knowing what you were at?"

"Davah, I can't think about it right now," said Aeyun.

He turned to leave the estate, a bubbling pit of acid forming inside him. His heart pumped in his chest, and his nerves trembled, as if they'd been hit with Raeyu's lightning. It was so visceral that he shivered.

"I think you should, friend. You just jumbled up the mind of a single mother, on the run from a rampaging lunatic throttling an entire realm, and you left her in some unknown state. Your actions have consequences. You have to start thinking things through."

Aeyun's breath was coming in shorter spurts, his chest compressing. "I know, Davah. I know."

Aeyun wheezed behind his mask, his feet tripping over themselves.

"Friend–"

"I know, Davah!" Aeyun choked out, turning a corner, nearly slamming into a lamppost.

"No, Aeyun."

Davah had jogged up to him, pulling him by the arm into an alleyway. When had Aeyun got so far ahead? When had he strayed so far from the neighbourhood?

"I don't think you're okay. I think you need to sit for a moment."

Aeyun leant against a wall, Azura digging into his back – had Davah grabbed his gear, too? – and he focused on the feeling of his fingers across the uneven surface behind him.

"You with me?" Davah asked, and Aeyun nodded mechanically. "Okay, good."

"Sorry." Aeyun wasn't sure which part he was apologising for.

"Look, we should have a chat about, uh, procedure, or something. But we don't need to have it right now. Let's get you functional, alright?"

Davah sent a glance to his left to peer out the mouth of the alleyway entrance. The morning was young; not many pedestrians were milling about yet. But the risk still remained. Davah knew that. Aeyun knew that.

Aeyun breathed. His fingers tapped against the porous wall; his sluggish mind counted the beads hanging down the side of Davah's mask. Davah, for his part, stayed in place, asking him simple questions, like what did he smell, *ocean musk*, what did he hear, *the dinging of the morning market bell.*

"Sorry," Aeyun offered again, when the realm felt less like it was sucking the air out of his lungs, and more like the routine cityscape it was.

Davah shook his head. "I've been there. It's fine. You all good now, friend?"

Aeyun nodded and kicked off the wall, which he only now realised he was half-slumped against. He needed to stitch a mend on his useless right arm, but he couldn't stand the thought of tuning right then, nor did he think he had the energy in him to do so, so he resolved to deal with the deadened weight for a while longer. In the back of his mind, he wondered if prolonged disuse would cause lasting damage, but it didn't dissuade him from his decision.

"Maybe we plan on heading to Pan today?" Davah asked.

Aeyun was quick to agree. The more distance, the better.

The receptionist slid over two keys and Davah gave them a nod in return, dropping the appropriate amount of coin on the counter. He prodded Aeyun's deadened arm, which Aeyun only realised since it caused his balance to falter, then they made their way to their rented accommodation.

Once inside the safety of the hotel room, Aeyun tore off his mask – gulping in unhindered air, the mask's barrier having felt suffocating on the way over. He dropped unceremoniously on one of the creaky beds.

Davah dislodged his mask as well, giving Aeyun a pitying look as he did.

"I shouldn't have just run out like that. Loua is an innocent, and she has a son to care for. I had no idea what I was doing, and I did it anyway because – because what? I'm afraid of being hunted? Shit, I don't know."

"Ah, well," Davah said, leaning on the blank space beside the door. "There's a reason you saw Raeyu Thasian the first time you tried to reach through that *whatever* between the gates, right? That's who you were talking to, right?"

Aeyun was exhausted. Mentally, physically, and everything beyond it. So, instead of answering directly, he said, "I think she heard your voice."

Davah hummed at that bit of information.

"I've really been trying, you know? To keep a respectful distance and give you the space to be honest when you wanted to be. But now you're going around doing things like today and talking to someone on a different realm as if they're in front of you. And you're not *Yun*. Like Seraeyu, you're no god."

Davah stared at him, and Aeyun was feeling more than vulnerable. It was a raw realisation, and he wanted to curl up and block out the realm just as much as he wanted to spill every last secret he desperately held onto.

"I think it's time, Aeyun. I think I need more now."

Aeyun weighed the pros and cons. He gazed back at his friend, colleague, and more recent confidant of well over a year now, and he felt the weight of the realms press down upon him. Every misdirection, every hidden truth, stacking themselves on his shoulders.

"I'm not . . . from here," Aeyun said, finding it hard to form his tongue around the sentiment.

"Well, yeah," Davah countered, as if he'd figured out that much.

Silence passed between them, and Aeyun looked away from Davah's watchful eyes to focus on the loose thread beside his own thigh.

"I was born A'vor. A'vor of Ca'lorus." That amassed weight

lessened, and Aeyun pulled at the defiant string, unravelling it further from its weave within the bedspread. He didn't dare look up. "Ca'lorus is where, um, it's where Raeyu and Uruji are now. I don't know why or how Uruji found it. But it's the realm that no one seems to know of."

After a few moments of quiet, Davah prompted him to continue with a simple: "Okay."

"I know how to do what I do because of my time on Ca'lorus," Aeyun said, feeling like it wasn't only the hole in the quilt unravelling.

"So, what you do, it's common there?"

"No, not like how – not exactly. Kind of."

"Kind of?"

Aeyun looked up, a quiet desperation building behind his chest, and he gave Davah a pleading look. He was fascinated to find a solemn interest on his friend's face, not unlike his demeanour after the Caiggagh incident.

"Kind of," Aeyun repeated, softly. "It's all based on exchange – a give and take of natural order, I guess? It's hard to explain. It's nothing like alicant tuning, in principle. It's more like resonating with something's self; its very being and soulsong. The people of Ca'lorus, we're attuned to the Vitality of things. But, no, not everyone can do what I do."

"Or someone," Davah interjected, and Aeyun found himself flustered.

"What?"

"Resonating with something, or *someone*, right?" Davah asked, having put a few pieces together in his head.

Aeyun took a moment to catch on to the reference, undoubtably about Raeyu. He was struck with the complexity that was the web of untruths in his life, constantly moving and building towards . . . something. A cold feeling manifested, lingering somewhere between his head and his heart, and he wondered what would happen if the web dissolved. What if it all just came tumbling down?

"Ah, yeah. I mean, yeah. But–" Aeyun heaved in a breath and the lingering fear that he couldn't quite let go of – the one that wanted to shield his and Raeyu's fated tether from harm – didn't relinquish its hold on his paranoia. Instead, he finished his statement with a quiet, "Yeah."

"But you didn't have those strange alabaster eyes when you spoke to her," Davah said, and it punched a few new holes in Aeyun's façade.

"Um, yeah," he responded weakly, with a disheartened chuckle. "It's not . . . it's not just Vitality, with her. Essence is involved."

"Which you've learnt to tune with in the realms?"

"Davah," Aeyun called out tiredly. It was a lot for his already fragile state of mind.

"Aeyun, I don't think anything good is coming down the line. I can't go at this blind anymore. You need to *talk.*"

Davah's words cut at him harshly, but Aeyun couldn't argue with him. He could feel it – the unrest that would surely meet them soon. He suspected they were on a precipice, and that Seraeyu's most recent coup would likely be a catalyst for darker days. As the months progressed, he could feel the concern of the populace growing across Quinga, and he imagined it was similar on the other realms.

The calm would break. It was only a matter of time.

"Ah," Aeyun started, and it pained him to do so. "I knew it was complicated in my head; I just haven't had to talk it all out with someone at once. Even with Raeyu, it was bits at a time," he admitted, finally letting go of the frayed string to run his fingers through his hair. "Dammit."

"Aeyun." Davah crouched down, looking up at Aeyun. "Look, I'm not persecuting you. I'm behind you. But it's time I know what I'm fighting for with you." An unreadable look tainted his features, fleeting as it was, but Aeyun thought he mainly read concern. "And I do think we'll be fighting. The signs are there. The boiling under the surface. It'll happen."

Coming from a man who'd been born and reared on a realm riddled with hardship, Aeyun believed his prediction as much as he did his own intuition.

"Okay, okay." Aeyun collected his thoughts. And then they spilled over like a tipped bucket. "I was born A'vor *a'Ca'lorus,* brother to Da'garu, and son to A'ra and Ca'rud. Terms like tuning and attunement weren't in my vocabulary until I was in the realms. It was just a way of life, but most don't attempt more than simple feats. I'm of Ca'ille's line, though. We're said to be cursed, and you don't want to be considered cursed in a community that small. My family learnt to protect ourselves–"

"I'm sorry, *cursed?*" Davah asked, and Aeyun scoffed.

"Yeah, I don't know, either. It ended up getting my parents killed, by those who let fear and prejudice rule them. That's how I ended up here, and then there's Gama-of–"

"Wait, woah!" Davah resituated himself from his crouch, instead plopping down on the stained floor, resting his chin on his knees. "First, I'm sorry to hear that, friend. Second, fairly sure you skipped something there, like *how* you got to the realms."

Aeyun blinked. "Ah, right. Right. It was the night of my parents' murders."

The admission still felt cruel all these years later. Davah's mouth tugged down in a frown, but he didn't interrupt again.

"I was trying to find my sister. I didn't, by the way. Not then. I ended up in some underground aquifer or something after taking a tumble, and then I–"

His words cut off abruptly as he recalled the day. He hadn't given it true thought in a long, long while, but the vision was clear in his mind then. Aeyun had come across that isle in that cavernous space, marred with a dark, swirling pattern. He'd not known at the time, but he'd come across an–

"Essence scar," Aeyun said so low it was almost a whisper. Davah gazed on, intrigued. "I came across an Essence scar," Aeyun repeated, and the chance events felt slightly less disparate in his mind. "And it brought me to Rae."

"Oh," Davah said, contemplative. "That's random, I guess?"

Aeyun was too caught up in his own head to answer.

"It brought me to Raeyu," Aeyun said again, mulling over the revelation in context.

"Could it have something to do with her bloodsong, or something?" Davah asked, his own curiosity piqued, and Aeyun distantly shook his head.

"No, that's not–"

He was nearly going to finish with *possible, because it's a farce*, but then he remembered just what allowed that lie to manifest and he blanched, jaw unhinging. An alicant with harmonised potential stored in it, capable of recreating a tune that should only be possible if one were well attuned to both Vitality and Essence. And it certainly hadn't been Raeyu who had imprinted the ground with that etched marker of power.

If not her . . . who? A previous Thasian who harnessed the forces it channelled? It only made sense that Aeyun was pulled to the one thing connected to that scar, which would be its source. Perhaps even the alicant that played conduit. So, had the Thasian once been on Ca'lorus?

"Aeyun?"

And now Seraeyu had something connected to Ca'lorus, if Aeyun's assumptions were correct.

"Aeyun?"

Seraeyu Thasian, who tore his own father apart. Who hunted his own sister, as well as Aeyun's brother. Who could decimate a people unfamiliar with realms that regularly tuned and toiled. Who had gone mad, seeking some unknown end.

"Oh, no," Aeyun breathed out.

It was all adrenaline, sweat, and rapid breaths when he came to, his fists clenched. The whites of his knuckles shown not for a sense of determination and bravado, but for fear and cowardice.

In his nightmare, he had been shrunken into one of the craggy outcroppings by his ravaged home, hauntingly familiar corpses staring at him asking why? Why did you run? Why did you leave us? How could you have left us?

And then there were the snarls from monsters in the shape of people, ready to run him through, just like they had his parents. Terror had woken him and remained unfaded, even with his eyes open. In the shadows of the room, he saw sightless eyes staring and bloodied mouths mocking, their voices a serenade of pragmatic trickery and deception.

CHAPTER THIRTY-THREE

That odd feeling that he was blockaded from connecting with Raeyu was back again.

He'd tried, after his revelation that Seraeyu may have a yet undiscovered access to a realm he could devastate with a few simple swipes of his hand, but his energy – *and* Essence *and* Vitality – were spent from his earlier deeds. Hand over his heart, the constant thrum of lifeforce that tugged there sputtered and deflated, like a needled balloon.

Aeyun had spent the rest of the morning in a fit, avoiding Davah's probing left and right while he tried to work out solutions in his head. For all his effort, he came up short.

Eventually, Davah relented and excused himself, leaving Aeyun to pace. Later, Aeyun discovered his departure had been to get some much-needed food to put in their bellies. Upon his return, Davah parsed out the boxes of takeaway goodies, handing Aeyun a utensil with an expectant look as they settled on the floor.

"Sorry," Aeyun muttered, constantly unsure as to what exactly he was apologising for.

Davah stabbed a piece of breaded meat and shoved it in his mouth, giving it a chew before asking, "Wanna talk about it?"

Aeyun shrugged defeatedly. "I don't know. Not really. Not right now."

"Wanna pick up at a different point, then?"

The question was asked in a light tone, but expectation was clear beneath it. Aeyun's bite of food suddenly tasted bland, feeling gritty on his tongue.

"That girl we saw with Rae in the rift?" Aeyun said as if it were a question. Davah urged him on with a distracted hum as he ripped a loaf apart. "That was Da'garu. It couldn't not be."

Davah's gaze shot up in interest. There was a blink, a moment of processing.

"No way. Your lost sister?" Davah slowly went back to tearing the bread, but his attention was clearly rapt. "Ah, feck. You *did* shout that then, didn't you?" He tutted. "*Look to the heavens*, you said. Ha! We're gullible."

Aeyun swallowed and hummed. "It's been a long time since I've seen her. She was so young then. I wonder if she even remembers me."

Davah's eyes narrowed, then he raised his hands and waved them in a criss-cross in front of himself. "Wait, wait, wait. So," he began, all exaggerated gestures in true *Davah* fashion, "you have a sister, a blood sister, on this *Ca'lorus–*"

Aeyun was mildly impressed by Davah's pronunciation but, then again, he had already heard his ancient Mhedoonian tongue.

"–and then you have a brother here, and the Sirin is your sister . . . too?"

325

Aeyun wanted to groan and cover his face. Hide from the questions.

"I have a sister-in-blood on Ca'lorus, yes, who I've not seen since she was six years of age. I have a brother-in-name that I basically took part in raising since *he* was just a child. And Sakaeri's actual blood-mother is my claimed-to-be mother."

Each statement was counted on one of Aeyun's fingers while he looked up at the bubbled paint on the ceiling, as if it would help him recount each sentiment.

"Right. Makes sense," Davah said with a sardonic drawl. "So, you're not actually blood related to either of them. You're not even at all Yu-ta?"

Aeyun hadn't considered that quandary much, that he would ever be proclaimed part Yu-ta. But, with Davah spelling it out like that, of course he'd be considered part Yu-ta, if Jourae declared himself his father in certain circles. In more ways than he could recount, Jourae was a father to him, but not by blood.

"No," Aeyun affirmed. "I'm not even at all Yu-ta."

"Weird," said Davah. "But you can do what they do."

"Hm?"

"The whole Essence thing. You can do it."

Aeyun's forehead wrinkled as his expression soured. He watched as a peeled chip fluttered down from the ceiling.

"Oh," Aeyun said, as if it were an answer.

When he didn't continue, Davah rolled his wrist, a silent ask to go on.

Aeyun dug his teeth into his bottom lip, then said, "It's not all that different." He considered the nature of both tunes, one smooth and fluid and circulating, the other wild and reckless and boundless, but also living, in a way. "It's like . . . breathing. The Vitality of things is like inhaling while the Essence of it all is like exhaling. Two sides of the same function.

"But it doesn't feel like it belongs to you like ore tuning does. It's independent of you, both there whether you sing its song or not. Attuning to either is like borrowing something, moving it from one place, one state, to another, but understanding that it's not *yours*. That's the use of descanting, too. To tame the call and guide it. Give it intention."

"So, because you were familiar with one, you could tap into the other?" Davah asked, having now abandoned his feast entirely.

"I guess? I'm really not good at working with Essence, and I don't think it yields well. It's too–"

"Chaotic?"

"Well, yeah. It's like trying to turn smoke into something solid. Vitality is more like water; directable."

Aeyun silently added that ore alicant were like bombs. Quick, loud, potent, and fleeting.

Davah leant forward over his knees. "So, what's the conduit for it?"

"Me, I guess? That makes sense, right?"

"I mean, your eyes do start seeping red, so . . ." They stared at each other. Not uncomfortable, just stilted. "And when your eyes go starry? It's the two of them?"

"Yeah," Aeyun said, feeling bothered again. He couldn't quite place why. "That's like . . . becoming."

Davah blinked at him. "What?"

Aeyun struggled to find the right words, then said, "Maybe it's more like *succumbing* to the everything that is? Like, letting yourself be consumed between it, and just shifting *with* it? Almost like walking through the Ou'grobh."

"The what?"

Aeyun groaned and flopped back on the grubby carpet. He rested his working arm over his eyes. "It's too much."

Davah let loose an amused chuckle. "Yun. We really are ignorant here in the realms, huh?"

"No," Aeyun said, not moving. "There's just so much else if you look, and once you've discovered it, you find more and more threads, apparently." He paused. "Can we stick to, maybe, a few facts a day or something? My head is pounding."

"I'm holding you to it."

"Yeah, yeah."

Come a few days later, they had made enough coin to finally feel comfortable seeking a new sea-skimmer. Davah had also learnt several facts: the Ou'grobh was the forest that surrounded The Hold, which was the urban centre of Ca'lorus, and that the forest on Caiggagh's island was similar; Ca'lorus was surrounded by what was known as The Veil, a reflective barrier, beyond which – if there was a beyond – was a mystery; Aeyun's family was condemned for their ancestry, who suffered from long-held superstition, the basis of which was lost generations prior; Aeyun didn't know the extent of Vitality and what one was capable of when attuned to it, he only knew what he'd observed from his parents and his own experimentation; Da'garu was always oddly connected to animals, and Aeyun suspected that *something* was going on there in terms of tuning.

He hadn't even progressed past Ca'lorus yet, but Aeyun suspected the next bit of information was sure to intrigue. Davah, like many, did not seem to be immune to the stories spun about the great and powerful Yun.

"So, you ready for more?" Aeyun asked in a traitorous whisper as they made their way to Pan's docks.

All of Quinga's cities looked like copies of their neighbour, one metropolis blending into the next. Used to the urban landscapes by then, the two of them were able to navigate the narrow lanes with ease.

"Hit me," Davah murmured back.

"Oh, I will." A vindictive chortle spilled out unintentionally, and Aeyun imagined that Davah gave him an odd look behind his mask. "I guess it's time you learn about Gama-of-Yun."

Davah's steps faltered, leading him to stumble. "Sorry, did you just say what I think you said?"

"I did."

328

"Okay," Davah said, more so to himself. "Okay, go on."

"Gama-of-Yun is this absent-minded sage who lives in the old a'teneum in the Ou'grobh. Gama's nothing spectacular. Literally does nothing of note, just exists. The only weird thing is that no one can find the a'teneum – sorry, um, library, I guess? Maybe more like an archive. Only my family ever visited, I think."

"That's weird, friend. Really weird." Davah rolled his shoulders. Aeyun sincerely doubted the movement did anything to help him accept his newfound enlightenment. "So, you're saying that you personally know a god?"

"No," Aeyun said resolutely, pausing their progress down the path. He rested his gauntleted hand – now stitched and functional – on Davah's shoulder with purpose. "I'm saying that Gama is exceptionally ordinary. The *a'teneum* is weird."

Davah's masked face stared back at him, frozen and smiling. People wove around them, moving in a constant throng, chattering about inconsequential things.

"I don't know what to do with that," said Davah. "I'm not – I don't know what to do with that."

He started walking again, and Aeyun jogged to catch up.

"That's it? That's all you have to say?"

"Yep," Davah responded, popping the *p*. "That's it."

They made it a few more steps.

"For now."

"Okay," Aeyun replied, recognising the clammy tickle at the nape of his neck as guilt.

"Tell me something," Davah whispered as they entered the marina district. "Why did you ask if you-know-who was accompanied when you were talking to that woman?"

"Oh." Aeyun fidgeted uncomfortably. "Kaisa witnessed a feed from his Eye and said *he* looked accompanied, somehow."

"So, you had a chummy chat with Kaisa?"

"No." Aeyun scowled. "He cornered me at Caiggagh."

"Ah, it was when you told him something dumb." They could see the moored ships and sea-skimmers bobbing on the water now. "What was that dumb thing, by the way?"

Aeyun scowled deeper. It wasn't the right time or place for that conversation. "I'll tell you. Not here, though."

They arrived at a second-hand dealer, its signage a perfect representation of the hodgepodge of wares in stock. While the merchant was preoccupied drying the sweat on his shirt and shoving his face in front of a fan, Aeyun and Davah perused their options. The sea-skimmers dipped up and down in the water's wake, none looking particularly more intriguing than the next. Davah, of course, was inspecting each craft diligently, and Aeyun was thankful since these types of mechanics were not his area of expertise.

After what felt like a century of poking, prodding, and investigating, Davah found one that he liked, it seemed. But then he looked at the price and scuffed his boot into the docks. After a silent debate with himself, full of indignant posturing that Aeyun found highly amusing, Davah tugged Aeyun to follow him to the merchant. Standing in front of the shoddy fold-out table, Davah dropped a moth-eaten coin purse on the weather-worn surface. It landed with a jingling thump, gaining the attention of the man losing his mass in salty perspiration.

"Eh, what's this? What for?"

The man plucked open the small bag, counting the coins as he went. Davah didn't stick around. Instead, he walked back to the sea-skimmer and smacked his hand upon it. The merchant looked up.

"That one? No, no. It's not enough."

Davah smacked the craft harder, his other hand drifting towards the harpoon on his belt. The merchant flicked his eyes between the rocking sea-skimmer and Davah's unspoken threat.

"Um, ah. Right. Alright. Fine, yes, take it."

Davah abandoned his weapon in favour of tossing the man a thumbs up. Aeyun didn't quite manage to swallow the entertained snort that escaped him.

Satisfied with their purchase, Aeyun let Davah focus on

unknotting the rope that tied the craft to the docks while he climbed into the belly of it. Dropping in, he noted that it was oddly barren, lacking any comfortable furnishings, yet somehow that felt appropriate. Aeyun stood in the middle of the metallic shell, a morose solace folding into him, and then he noticed Davah staring at him through the dirty glass panels. Suddenly aware of his own fingers digging into his arms, Aeyun dropped his hands to his sides.

"First thing's first: let's install our own magnavaid," Davah announced when he closed the uppermost hatch behind him on entry. "Good thing we have one, too, considering this one lacks it in the first place – absolute messer, this guy. Asking what he was. Despicable." Davah continued to mutter to himself about the crimes of the greedy merchant while he set his preferred navigation contraption in place.

As Davah went about his business, Aeyun wandered more, the emptiness suddenly feeling more amiss than it did before. He started considering how the space might be filled, and what types of things could be added for the likes of Davah, or for Saoiri. He ducked his head into the dormitory and found it void of sleeping gear, gutted like the rest of the sea-skimmer, and he didn't realise he'd stepped into the cavern of it until he was stood in the middle and his fingers found his opposite elbows once more.

"My favourite enigma," Davah called in a sing-song way from the other room; a nickname that he'd taken a liking to as of late. "I think we're good to go."

Aeyun ducked back into the hull, apologising to Azura when the aerofoil caught on the doorframe. "Right. Will we leave?"

There must have been something about the way he said it, because Davah paused.

"Tomorrow," he said. "We'll go tomorrow. Let's dock this somewhere else for the evening, though. Get it cleaned up." Davah started up the craft, ready to steer it manually. "Maybe get some shite to, I don't know, make it homier in here?"

"Only if you want to," Aeyun told him, his head swirling with ideas and visions already.

"Yeah, friend," Davah said as he manoeuvred the craft out of the merchant's dock. "I'd like to."

They were lucky enough to find an open mooring spot a little way down and Davah navigated them into it. He patted Aeyun's back encouragingly when he passed him, then scuttled through the rooftop hatch and tethered their craft in its temporary resting place.

Aeyun scanned the sea-skimmer one more time, eyes roving over the rusted crevices and the scratched flooring. He pictured a table in the corner, flanked with two rickety chairs on a coiled rug, and a stack of blankets piled beside it. Especially the cosy, knitted kind that Saoiri liked. Beside that could be a small chest of drawers, maybe with a kettle for tea. Sakaeri seemed to like making use of that when she'd been around last. Aeyun knew that Uruji would love to chatter away to Davah about the mysteries and intricacies of the magnavaid, along with the unmarked blips that popped up on their particular iteration of it. And he'd bet that Saoiri would surely take a liking to Da'garu, no doubt probing for information about how Aeyun acted as a child, and then Aeyun could point out the starry skies to Raeyu from the middlemost ocean of each realm, exploring how it might connect them all as he recounted–

"Aeyun?" Davah called from above, hanging through the hatch.

Aeyun shook his head. "Sorry," he said. "Yeah, coming."

They hadn't found a table and chairs. Despite this, they did find an intricately designed rug, a few blankets to throw around the place, and a pre-loved kettle. After a thorough clean of the interior, Aeyun and Davah populated the sea-skimmer with their new wares, plus some bedrolls and food goods.

By the time they returned it was evening, and the ambient light of their sporadically placed ore glowed in the hollowed metallic hull. They sat on their respective makeshift beds, wrapped in blankets while they waited for water to boil, mugs placed before them. Aeyun stared at the bubbles behind the kettle's measurement panel, his fingers massaging his achy bicep.

"Saoiri contacted me," said Davah.

Aeyun glanced over at the unexpected announcement. Davah didn't look back.

"A month ago."

"What?" Aeyun asked because . . . *What?*

Davah still didn't turn his way.

"I didn't want to get you worked up. But we have this now." Davah gestured vaguely to the sea-skimmer. "So." He finally connected their gaze, and an intangible weight settled upon Aeyun. "Mhedoon is occupied."

Aeyun's heart dropped. "What?"

"Yeah," Davah responded, too evenly for a man who'd just relayed that his homerealm under martial rule. "It was in the works for a while, by the sounds of it. Kept quiet for the most part, but it happened. She said there's a mandatory curfew in Kilrona."

Still processing, Aeyun asked, "And this occupation is Raenaruan?"

"No," Davah said, as if the word itself was bitter. "It's Orinian."

As soon as Davah said it, Aeyun knew why he'd announced it so distastefully. Raenaru and Orin were politically close. Orin was a treasure trove for alicant, its strata bursting with natural ore veins, and Raenaruan leaders had always been happy to keep up good relations with the realm. Prosperous in large part due to the Thasian Legacy, the Raenaruan Council deferred to Haebal's decree, meaning that Seraeyu presumably had free rein over treaties and governance. If that was the case, Orin's occupation of Mhedoon was most assuredly, at least in part, of Seraeyu's design.

"You should have told me."

"It wouldn't have done any good. You were looking near death for a while there, friend," Davah said, seemingly exasperated.

The kettle stopped boiling, its switch clicking upwards, leaving only an echo of comfort behind it.

"I was?" The question had come out too soft, and Davah looked at Aeyun pityingly.

"I was considering writing a eulogy."

Aeyun dropped a teabag into his mug and poured the steaming water over it. He set the kettle back on its plate and leant back, staring but not seeing.

"We'll go to Mhedoon."

"We *won't*," Davah countered, not having made a move towards his own brew yet. "Look, we head there, we'll be carted off to whatever holding place the Orinians are keeping suspicious characters. If we go there, we're asking for a fight. Saoiri is frustrated, sure, but she's alive."

"She's not safe," Aeyun said, still staring at the mug and its foggy evaporation curling into the stale air.

"She's stronger than you think, and no one is out for her blood."

"We left her there–"

"Aeyun. Saoiri decided to stay. She wanted you to progress." Davah sighed and finally went about brewing his own tea. "She'd be very angry if you jumped backwards for her sake, and she'd likely take it out on me. So, please, for *my* sake, let's keep on, eh?"

Davah gingerly poured hot water into his cup, assisting the steep of his dried leaves with a few delicate plunges, fingers pinched upon the branded tag.

"But fuck the Orinians."

"I really don't like this," Aeyun muttered, pulling his blanket tighter. "I think we should try. I think we should–"

"My favourite enigma, why do you want to go to Lu-Ghan?"

334

The question caught Aeyun like a rock wedged in a wheel, and he floundered for a second before saying, "to find a Kaisan Pit."

"Great. Why?" Davah pushed, subtly gesturing to Aeyun's tea to remind him that it was there.

Aeyun absently latched onto the mug's handle. "To find Kaisa."

"Great. Why?"

"What? I mean, because he has what he stole–"

"Friend. You woke up one day and proclaimed we go out of the blue. Why?"

"He's where it all stopped!" Aeyun said, more forcefully than he meant to, and he cursed when a hot splash spilt over his hand. "He's where all our hard work ended up. He's where Sakaeri was last, and I feel like he's connected to it." Dread curdled Aeyun's stomach again and he put his mug back down. "She really didn't like him, and they knew one another. Sakaeri should have found us by now."

"So, you think we find Kaisa, we find our ore and our Sirin?" Davah asked.

He took a sip of his tea and looked at Aeyun expectantly over the brim. Aeyun reached for his own mug again, defeated.

"Yes."

"Cool. That's that, then."

"Right," Aeyun said, bitter.

He didn't know why, but he felt like Davah had drawn something out of him and he felt juvenilely upset by it. Aeyun peered at him as he took his own sip. Davah was considering the arrangement of glowing alicant and their reflections on the walls, paying Aeyun no mind.

"Happy?"

"Delighted!" Davah smiled. "You've seen reason. I'm so glad." He finally turned to Aeyun, his smug exterior melting into something more solemn. "You can't save everyone at once, Aeyun."

"So, we leave Saoiri, then? You're okay with that?"

"No," Davah said, tone stern. "I hate it. And I despise myself for letting it happen. And yet, here we are at a crossroads. Our actions have to take us somewhere, else they won't lead anywhere at all."

Aeyun frowned; he understood it. He really did, but that didn't mean he had to be chipper about it. He could choose to be foul if he wanted.

"I'm not happy," he declared.

Davah laughed and asked, "I'm sorry, are you ever?"

Aeyun cocked his head, trying not to be offended.

"Happy, I mean. You're so moody. Like, if you're not grouchy, you're sombre. When you're not those, you're just drowsy. On the rare occasion, you're a smidge too enthusiastic about smithing. And then you were just pissy with the Sirin."

"Sure, I've been happy," Aeyun said, trying to think of the last time he was. He realised that bliss – something real and honest – had evaded him for quite some time. Davah hummed, a clear sign of his disbelief. "It's been a while."

"And what, pray tell, made our dear Aeyun happy before?" Davah took another sip of his tea, one brow raised.

"It was . . ."

Aeyun thought about the little things. Uruji dragging him to the Festival of Hana, delighted when his big brother got the top prize at one of those gaudy stalls. Jourae grinning proudly at Aeyun's progress and his newest finely tempered creation. Raeyu snickering with him as they snuck out the Tower courtyard, hiding from the Sentinels on duty.

"All the moments in between," Aeyun decided.

Davah watched him, considering.

"You know," he said, taking a contemplative breath through his nose, "it's difficult to find joy when everything seems so grim. But light sparks in odd places. It's easy to miss it if you're only looking for darkness."

"I'll try to be happier, Davah."

"You don't need to do fuck all for me, friend," Davah clarified, shaking his head. "I'd much rather you did it for yourself."

He watched, mindful enough to not step out of his given zone, hazarding no more than two steps in any direction. It was like he was forgotten half the time, in a different room entirely. Or a different life entirely, given the non-attention he received within brushing distance.

He watched as robes with odd designs fluttered past him, followed by a quiet muttering that made little sense to his ears.

He watched as books and tomes and odd-looking artefacts were shuffled around, placed in what may have been a pattern or something equally less nonsensical, but it was difficult to tell in the clutter.

He watched as the man dropped his manuscripts, pages flying out with the momentum, and he turned, contemplative as if he had something to remember. But he never did. He just picked up the papers instead.

CHAPTER THIRTY-FOUR

Wisps of black rippled as Aeyun walked, the wake of his steps repeating in concentric resonance. Around him, a sea of ink ebbed and flowed, swirls of colour erupting in the distance before they imploded and started anew elsewhere. Aeyun took another step and his heart beat in time with nothing, knowing no rhythm or pace.

He walked for hours and seconds, his body compressed and freed in cycles, his being skipping through the bloated emptiness. The horizon stretched and fell in jagged planes, stacking one on top of the other, dipping endlessly as he glided and stumbled through the boundless aetherscape. A radiant buzz popped beside him, and he felt a wave of sizzling energy spark across his frame, siphoning through him and manifesting again far behind, amid the ambiguous black. Aeyun stared at it, suddenly found himself pulled towards it, but it was as if he'd not moved at all. He extended his arm, fingertips grazing the pulsating periphery.

"*A'vor.*"

It was everywhere – in his head, below his feet, far off in the void, beside his ear.

Multiples of himself formed eerie shadows, twisting from his heel and coming to face him. Aeyun stared at his reflection, starry-eyed and concerned. He reached out and his hand phased through his doppelganger. When he stepped again, a crushing weight carried him down. Then his eyes opened.

Around him was a room of stone, and he was sat on a rune-covered floor, his robe fanned out around him. The walls were lined with shelves full of books, and the windows were carved so that the night's glow converged where he rested. Slowly, Aeyun stood, the world feeling fluid around him. He knew this place.

He stepped and his bare feet met the floorboards, the runes igniting and evaporating where he walked. Dazedly, Aeyun kept on, making it to the door. It opened as if sheer force had compelled it to do so, and Aeyun took it as a sign to keep going. As he descended the turret, wisps of energy alighted, runic patterns glowing beckoningly. Aeyun continued, and the atrium of the derelict building came into focus, the a'teneum lit in flashes from the fire in the hearth.

Voices reached his ears and he struggled to understand them. They were loud and booming, yet quiet and fragile. Aeyun took his next step, but instead of halfway down the stairwell as he ought to be, he ended up in the middle of the a'teneum, sigils sizzling to life below him on the wood and on the walls between the shelves, shrivelling in on themselves before disappearing entirely. Three figures startled and stood from their placement on plush sofas, and Aeyun saw an aura-like impression where they rose. Lights danced around them, swirling in an obsidian shadow. One was gilded in a blinding brilliance, the other a dichotomy of both, oddly regulated, and the last was mostly dark. It was the shadowed one Aeyun was most drawn to.

"Gama-of-Yun?" The question echoed relentlessly, bouncing around his perception painfully. The voice was familiar. Why was it so familiar?

The darkest shadow came closer, hesitant. Aeyun's head hurt. His eyes ached too, and something rolled down his chin. The inky spectre lessened the gap still.

Softly, and clearly, the shadow spoke, "Aeyun."

The colourless thread burst to life and zipped across the space, impacting the being in front of him, manifesting Raeyu from her core. As Raeyu became corporeal, Aeyun felt more aware of himself.

"Aeyun, you can't–" her protest was cut short when the second ghostly form pulled Raeyu back, his own impression filling out and becoming recognisable as Uruji.

"Aeyun!" Uruji said, alarmed.

Mind in disarray, Aeyun looked back at his brother, then to the hand that held Raeyu back, then to the saddened, reluctant expression on Raeyu's face. Aeyun almost stretched his hand out, but he felt eyes boring into him, and that bright, luminescent being beside Uruji silently called his attention. Aeyun stared. And stared and stared. It was familiar.

Something in him shifted and the images of Raeyu and Uruji clouded. As they did, the third, bright presence became clearer. Soon, he was looking into alabaster eyes, and something yelled within him; a child-like cry, shouted in craggy fields. She stood before him, unmoving and cautious. Older than she had been, a version that he didn't know, but the underlying soulsong sang a tune he recognised. She must have heard it too because she voicelessly spoke his name. His birth name, from years long passed. But her mouth was silent. Why was it silent? She mouthed his name again and stepped back, perplexed and . . . and fearful.

"You have to go," Raeyu said from afar, but Aeyun couldn't break his contact with Da'garu. Why couldn't she speak? "I'm so sorry, Aeyun. Please don't come for us." Aeyun's head filled with pressure, and spreading black invaded the edges of his vision. "Please. Please, you can't. It can't happen. Please, you have to–"

A deep, humming cadence came from Uruji, and he had vocalised it so forcefully that it reverberated throughout Aeyun's reality. "You must leave and don't come back, Aeyun!"

His brother's haunting descantation picked up again, and Aeyun felt like he was on a sickening festival ride, the room spinning and flashing in and out of his perception. He could see Uruji scraping burned-up symbols back into place, using a Thasian-nee dagger Jourae had gifted him many years prior. Da'garu folded her arms around herself and Raeyu, retreated and forlorn, gazed back at him.

She put her hand on top of her heart, and everything stilled at once.

"*I'm sorry. You can't come to us. It will be the end of you. You can't.*"

Her words rang out clearly, and the next time Aeyun blinked, he saw through Raeyu's eyes. In the middle of the a'teneum, blazing with tendrils of ink-dyed fire, burning amid a daemonish radiance, stood Gama-of-Yun. He looked like a nightmare come to life, gangly with crimson seeping from his eyes. Time halted further and Aeyun could feel Gama-of-Yun's penetrating persona surround him.

"*A'vor.*"

The realm shattered and Aeyun was hurtled across a blackened expanse, colourful pockets bursting and flowing, direction meaningless as linearity became unrecognisable. Aeyun reached out for something he knew – anything at all – and when he latched on, he pulled at it.

Blood splattered across his face and cheers became a deafening roar around him. Aeyun looked down at his red-soaked hands and saw the gore caked under his claw-like nails. He stumbled back and flipped his wrist, seeing dry, cracked knuckles on feminine hands, then he looked up at the jeering crowd, his eyes catching on the luxurious box where a leering presence leant against the rail, looming.

"*Get out!*" Sakaeri's voice trilled and Aeyun ceased to exist within her.

Aeyun woke up shouting. Davah was quick to rise on the other side of the hull, where they'd laid their bedrolls for the evening in lieu of the cramped dormitory space.

"Yu – damn! You're bleeding again," Davah said in a confused rush, then he tuned with some of the surrounding ore to brighten the space. Aeyun wiped at his face, smearing blood across his hands, then held his pounding head, feeling the need to try and force it back together.

"What was that?" he cried out, something between a gasp and a whimper. A sharp, electric shock zipped from one temple to the other and Aeyun groaned. Ignoring Davah's muttered questions, Aeyun smacked his hand across his chest and yelled, "Rae!" Nothing. "Rae – fucking, dammit! Raeyu!" Aeyun stared at the clouded night sky, fingers digging into his shirt. "Uruji!" he tried. Finally, he shouted, "Gama! Gama, I will not rest! What have you done!?"

Aeyun didn't realise he'd stood until Davah was urging him to sit down again.

"Friend?" Davah asked, calmer than he should have been. It made Aeyun wonder what sort of state he looked to be in.

"I won't rest," Aeyun mumbled, feeling outside his own skin. "Why would they – why was Da'garu–" His mind wandered to the last of his experience. The carnage, the stadium, and Kaisa's self-satisfied smirk. Sakaeri's demand. "What in the frigid *void*?" It was all Aeyun could put in words, his reaction to the entire affair. "What the fuck has he done?"

"Aeyun?" Davah's question was more forceful this time.

"I was right," Aeyun said, making Davah shake his head at him, baffled. "Kaisa has Sakaeri. He's done something to her. I'm not sure what, but he's done something." Davah was giving him a look that Aeyun didn't like. "I'm not fucking playing around; I saw it."

"How?"

"I don't know, but my eyes are bleeding, right?" Aeyun swiped at his face again. "I tuned with something, right?"

Aeyun wasn't sure what.

Davah held his tongue and nodded, whether he was convinced or not.

"Okay, well." Davah appeared to consider the situation, a lazy rub of his eye indicating his lingering lethargy. "We're up now. Maybe we should just head?"

Aeyun nodded. He gathered himself from the floor, wiped his face down with a spare cloth, then went about tidying the small, sparse hull. As he did, Davah quietly calibrated the magnavaid.

While Aeyun was considering the fogged panels, Davah looked over his shoulder.

"Aeyun?"

He hummed in response to the call.

"Just, be careful, okay?"

"What do you mean?" Aeyun frowned.

Davah shook his head and went back to his task.

"Alright," he announced. "We're set. Let's see what jumping realms looks like these days."

As they predicted, security was tight around the Great Sea Gate, sea-sentries stationed in the choppy water, red ore glowing prominently at the station. Davah disengaged the magnavaid so he could manually handle the steering. With an annoyed tick of his head, he turned to face Aeyun, who'd taken up refuge on the floor beside the blankets.

"Well. Looks like this'll be fun. Who're we this time?"

"Can you copy another accent?" Aeyun asked, already pulling up his mask to secure it around his face.

Davah grimaced. "I can tamp it down, I guess." Clearing his throat, he said, "Hi there, I'm not from Mhedoon, if you were wondering."

It sounded flat and unnatural, and Aeyun made a face, though the impact of it couldn't be appreciated behind the newly placed barrier he'd just tied up.

"That's awful," Aeyun decided, and Davah chuckled.

"Will I just be mute, you think?" When Davah asked the question, Aeyun's heart jumped involuntarily. He clenched his fist over it to dispel the discomfort.

"Yeah, maybe." It only took a moment for Aeyun to realise the roll-on effect of that choice, and he voiced his distaste. "Wait, so I have to talk to them?"

"Afraid so, friend."

"Who's going to let two masked men jump realms without any questions with the current state of things?" Aeyun groaned at Davah's unhelpful shrug.

"Guess we will find out."

"And if they don't let us go?"

"Dunno. Do you?" The way Davah asked the question indicated that he clearly thought Aeyun *should*, and it had Aeyun uneasy. His suspicions were validated when he went on to ask, "You couldn't, you know, *convince them* somehow, right?"

"Davah," Aeyun intoned. "Weren't you the one who warned me against that?"

"These folk?" Davah asked, gesturing to the bobbing sea-sentries blockading the space between themselves and the gate. "Takes a certain individual to sign up for this role. I've no qualms if they get a bit mind-muddled in the process."

"That's a little much, isn't it?"

"I don't know: is it?" Davah flicked his wrist in disinterest, then turned so his back faced Aeyun. "Not sure we can afford to not pick battles anymore." He paused, then added, "The right ones."

"Maybe," Aeyun responded, unsure.

"Alright, well. I guess we'll find out. Here they come."

Behind Davah, on the other side of the glass panels, two sea-sentries were gliding across the water, towards their own beat-up sea-skimmer. Aeyun took a deep breath and stood up, switching positions with Davah. His pulse picked up in the hush that thickened upon the Sentinels' approach, and he watched them get closer and closer until they loomed before him, one flanked behind the other.

Aeyun waited for the closest sea-sentry to signal for him to open the hatch. He shouldn't have been surprised that it would be an inspection instead of a quick communication through the receivers – and Aeyun wasn't even sure their sea-skimmer's equipment worked – but dread filled him anyway. He walked on wooden legs to the hatch and dislodged it, allowing it to be flipped up. Heavy boots landed on the top of their dingy craft, thumping across it until a Sentinel dropped into the hull, one hand held upon what looked like the grip of a whip. Aeyun suspected that it was a pyre whip, given the ore that glinted on the hilt.

"Names, occupations, and destination," the Sentinel questioned with a sneer, his eyes roving over the near-empty hull, his visor lifted to stare with practised intimidation.

Aeyun swallowed his anxiety.

"Uh, hi," Aeyun said, his voice dipping into a general Tenebranan cadence. "We're from Jjankatot. Going home, that is."

The Sentinel lurked around the craft, his weighted steps tinny on the metal. He wrinkled his nose at the cocked head Davah gave him.

"Right, sure. And names and occupations?"

He poked open the dormitory door and furled his lip at the emptiness. Aeyun sensed a buzz starting from his toes. It felt as though it were choking him up to his throat. Ignoring the sweat forming in his palms, he stepped towards the Sentinel, resolve building.

"We're clockmakers. I'm Yev Hidrif, and this is Kivvra Farnja."

The Sentinel finished inspecting the hull with a dissatisfied look, his eyes landing on Aeyun's mask. "Will you remove this for me?"

"No, sorry," Aeyun said, heart pumping wildly.

The Sentinel narrowed his gaze.

"Why?"

"We had an accident in the acid swamps," Aeyun supplied, holding onto futile hope.

The Sentinel turned to Davah and asked, "That what you have to say about that as well?"

Davah patted his throat.

"He's mute," Aeyun said, then added, "sir."

"Right," the Sentinel said, his eyes flicking back to Aeyun with a twisted pull of his lips. "Think I might just have to see your ugly faces."

"Ah, okay," Aeyun said, taking a steadying breath. He allowed himself to reach into his Vitality, and when the realm reflected more radiantly around him, he knew that his eyes were glowing white behind the mask. "Okay," he repeated, more to himself.

Ensuring that his back was towards the panels, Aeyun stepped close to the Sentinel and dragged down his mask so that only his eyes showed.

"What is—"

The Sentinel's statement was quieted as his own eyes took on an ivory film, making him look dazed and lifeless. Aeyun could only hope that the other Sentinel wasn't paying much attention.

He reached up and pushed his thumb against the skull of the Sentinel before him and said, "*Cah da'gum, da'ju cah, a'gam po.*"

Aeyun steeled himself and tried to stamp down the sick churning of his stomach. "We're simple clockmakers from Tenebrana, going home."

"Tenebranan clockmakers," the Sentinel repeated. "Going home."

"Right," Aeyun said, disgusted with himself. He couldn't stare at the man's porcelain gaze anymore. "Please leave."

The Sentinel nodded mechanically and hoisted himself out the hull, stamping back to his sea-sentry. Aeyun watched him go, but the clawing nausea of nerves and self-loathing didn't abate.

"I think we should go, and quickly."

Already on his feet, Davah said, "Right with you, friend."

He took the wheel and swivelled them around the sea-sentries. Aeyun observed the second Sentinel standing from the craft, calling to his partner.

"Shit," Aeyun muttered. He could imagine that the man was like a baffled buffoon in his current state, and it would definitely raise a red flag. "How are we meant to–"

"We don't have time for the gatekeeper, do we?"

"No," Aeyun admitted.

"Can you do it?" Davah asked.

Aeyun wished he hadn't. He knew what he meant: could he call upon the Great Sea Gate to lead them to their destination? Did he have the aptitude to do that? The structure was in place, after all. All that was left for Aeyun to do was to commune with it, ask it for entrance to its sister in Lu-Ghan.

"I don't know," said Aeyun.

"Figure it out fast." Davah's demand was complemented by the sound of sea-sentries revving up behind them. Aeyun assumed it must be the Sentinels rearing to chase them up.

Aeyun shook his head to centre himself, then turned to focus to the Great Sea Gate that they were fast approaching. He scanned its stony surface, tracing the runic symbols and interspersed ore. Calling forth Essence to balance his Vitality, Aeyun tried to find the tune that needed to be sung. His vision became tipped with zaps of black and pops of vibrancy that didn't belong, and Aeyun watched as vague reflections of destinations poured into his mind. Beyond these abstruse manifestations, Aeyun could see the Great Sea Gate crackling to life, water floating upwards in unnatural rivulets. Aeyun tried to focus on Lu-Ghan.

On Lu-Ghan, Lu-Ghan, *Lu-Ghan*!

Energy imploded around them in the terminal surrounding the gate, and Aeyun's mask started burning up, the smell of charred wood filling his nostrils. He ripped it off and tossed it on the floor as sheer force of power ripped into his body, siphoned through it, redirected towards the Great Sea Gate. Unable to help it, he shouted out to dispel some of the agony that came with the feeling.

Then it struck.

They were in that familiar in-between, and he embraced the stretching abyss. Still holding onto his tune, he felt pressured, as if the vast starry sea itself was trying to crush him. There, in that place all his own, he let himself whimper in the anguish of it all – everything that he'd endured. His knees buckled and he collapsed amid the nothingness, his body falling between the black. The plane dimmed, fractured, and the flowing pockets of energy around him faded out. Soon all that was left was a quiet glow.

A searing feeling ate into his chest, and he cringed but couldn't move. It felt as though his bones would disintegrate to dust if he tried. There was a distinct impression of something flipping, an odd inversion as much as it was an invasion, then suddenly he wasn't alone. Aeyun looked up, and there crouched a familiar entity, his smile sardonic, an ethereal aura making his impression seem otherworldly.

"You're relentless, aren't you?"

"How–?"

His question dropped out like shattered glass, and a soothing stillness washed over him. Some of the aching pressure in his mind released as he subsided, weightless.

It was her preferred perch, the one she always returned to. Just enough in the shadows, the flickering lights licking at her heels, but never reaching her. Not entirely.

She watched as the door to the smithy opened, revealing a wide grin on a scarred face, a broad hand clapping a back. Her scanning eyes latched onto the little things, like the shift of weight to a more dominant foot while idle. She also did that. Or how lips quirked a little higher on one side, creasing a dimple that only appeared on rare occasions. She shared that trait.

When his conversation partner was ushered in, she saw the brightness fade, leaving a wearied expression. A once livewire spark that had laid witness to too many atrocities. She found familiarity in that, too.

CHAPTER THIRTY-FIVE

"Sakaeri!"

Raeyu's call prompted a delighted bubble of giddiness in her stomach, and Sakaeri stifled a giggle where she hid under the skirt of a table. The sound of footsteps getting further rebounded off the walls and Sakaeri felt a certain sense of accomplishment at besting her friend. Sakaeri was good at hide-and-seek – no, she was *great* at hide-and-seek!

"What are you doing?" Seraeyu whispered and Sakaeri spun to meet his gaze, where he'd pulled up the table's draped cloth to stare at her curiously.

Sakaeri glowered – Seraeyu was *not* going to mess up her

349

winning streak! – and she placed a finger over her lips, indicating for him to keep quiet. To her dismay, Seraeyu crawled under the table to join her, eyes studying the bottom of the wood.

"Are we hiding?"

"Yes!" Sakaeri hissed, pointedly ramming her shushing finger too hard against her face, nearly poking it up her nose.

Seraeyu swallowed a giggle and nodded, pulling his knees up to rest his chin upon them. Sakaeri glanced over at him and scowled.

Whatever, she thought. *If he's quiet, it's fine.*

"Sakaeri!" Raeyu's call, sounding much closer than expected, made them both jump. Subconsciously, they scooted closer together, as if it would keep them from revealing themselves under the table. "This isn't fair," Raeyu whined, and Sakaeri could spot her little feet stomping beyond the fluttering fabric. "You're too good at this!"

"Uh, hey."

The voice made Sakaeri's eyes roll. It was *him*, that brat from town. The one who kept stealing Raeyu's attention away from *her*, where it should be.

"What are you doing?"

"Looking for Sakaeri," Raeyu said, as if it were plain as day. "We're playing a game, but she's too good at it!"

"Oh," Aeyun said, sounding like a dunce to Sakaeri's ears. "That's a shame."

Why did his voice have that odd accent anyway? Was he from Mhedoon? Some weird, remote part of it, or something? She'd never asked.

After a laugh, Raeyu responded, "No, it's not. It makes it a challenge!"

"Oh, really?" Aeyun asked.

Yun, he's an absolute dolt, Sakaeri thought.

"Let's split up and look for her! Two heads are better than one, right?" Raeyu asked.

Sakaeri frowned. She didn't want Aeyun to join the game.

This was her and Raeyu's game, not Aeyun's. Her gaze darted to the side. Or Seraeyu's.

"Sure," Aeyun said, and Sakaeri fought a sigh.

Nothing ever worked out in her favour, did it? Raeyu's feet skipped up and down and soon she was scampering off in the other direction. They'd set up boundaries, so Sakaeri knew she wouldn't go far. Still, she was disappointed that Raeyu had run the other way, but Aeyun had stayed here.

Her disappointment grew when he lifted the table skirt.

"Hey," he said, then his focus drifted to Seraeyu, who was pouting at him where he sat beside Sakaeri. "Hey?" It came out like a question, and Sakaeri couldn't blame him for it. She couldn't remember when she and Seraeyu had been in one place together, much less played together.

"Are you gonna give us up? That's no fun," Seraeyu whinged, voice pitchy and annoying.

Sakaeri rolled her eyes, readying herself to stand.

"No," Aeyun said, and Sakaeri's rump found the floor once more. "I guess that wouldn't be fun, right?"

"Aeyun!" Raeyu called from down the hall and Aeyun slid himself under the table, dropping down the linen after him. "Aeyun, where are you?"

Both Sakaeri and Seraeyu watched him scuttle in with wide eyes as he tucked his legs under himself – he was the tallest of all of them, so certainly the biggest danger to them being found if a stray foot were to give them away. Sakaeri cupped a hand over her mouth to keep from laughing aloud when Aeyun almost smacked his head on the bottom of the table. Seraeyu, oddly enough, took her other hand and smacked it over his mouth, she guessed to keep him silent as well? She gave the youngest of them an odd look before forcibly halting an amused snort.

"Ae – oh! Uruji-nee. Have you seen Aeyun? He's supposed to be helping me look for Sakaeri."

"No, I was looking for him because he's supposed to take me home."

"Oh," said Raeyu.

Was she disappointed that Aeyun would be leaving? Sakaeri's gaze floated back to the boy in question, his round face looking conflicted as to what action he should take next.

"Well, we can look for both of them? I'm going to head that way next."

Uruji must have nodded, since Raeyu darted off down the hall, opposite to where she'd come from. After her footsteps faded, Aeyun reached out under the fabric and grabbed Uruji's ankle.

Realistically, he should have known it would end in disaster. Uruji yelped loudly and kicked at Aeyun's hand, earning himself a noise of complaint, and then Aeyun lifted the skirt enough for Uruji to spot the three of them huddled there.

"You're playing hide-and-seek?" he asked, and Sakaeri appreciated his shrewdness.

"He's smarter than you," she informed Aeyun, who stuck his tongue out at her, and then she beckoned Uruji into the small space.

Why not? They were bound to be found soon, anyway.

Uruji looked hesitant, but he soon crawled under when Raeyu's footfalls sounded like they were on the way back.

Uruji sat himself next to Seraeyu, who gave him a small nod of greeting. The other nodded back, and Sakaeri couldn't help her eyebrow raising. They looked like strangers, for all the time they spent at each other's side. Raeyu paced in front of the table a few times, probably thinking, and Sakaeri felt Seraeyu's fingers wrap around her wrist. When she looked down at him, he didn't even seem to realise that he'd done it, his gaze trained on his sister's weaving walking pattern.

"You all disappeared . . ." The cloth was yanked up, revealing Raeyu's smiling, victorious face. "Here!" She blinked a few times, looking between four faces. "Oh, wow, everyone's together!"

With a delighted laugh, she launched herself under the table with the group of them, wrapping her arms across them all as best as she could, despite the groans of protest when they were dragged down by her weight.

In that moment, enveloped in mirth, Sakaeri's soulsong felt as light as a feather.

Tap, tap, tap.

Tap, tap, tap.

"Hey!"

The call jolted Sakaeri to consciousness, her body going rigid with the constant ache in her muscles and the ill-recovered injuries littering her innards.

"Get up, daemon. You have a battle in two."

The Kaisan stalked away, and Sakaeri pawed at the discomfort searing into the bottom of her neck.

"Dammit," she said. Then, softer, "Dammit . . ."

"You okay over there, Sakaeri?"

"Sure," she answered Goeth blithely, beating down the urge to bang her head against the cell's bars.

"Doesn't sound like it, if I'm honest."

Sakaeri scowled. "Well, good thing no one asked you, you nosy old goat."

That apparently earned her a chortle. She grimaced as she forced herself up, limping on a knee that clicked in a way she wasn't comfortable with. Or maybe it was still her hip. She couldn't really tell anymore.

"How'd you know I'm old?"

"You just sound like it," she barked, but it lacked any bite.

Goeth was something of a respite. Having him there, another person who shared in her trauma, was comforting. It kept her from spiralling. Doing something mad like claiming that damned furry-legged menace on the ceiling was her child, or something equally bizarre.

Truly, if Goeth weren't there, she would have lost it ages ago.

"Your manners are lacking, girl."

353

"You also talk to me like I'm a child. And I'm not. Ergo, you're older than me."

"No manners, but plenty of pluck, I see."

Sakaeri would have continued their banter, perhaps, if it didn't feel like she was about to teeter over if she so much as turned her head to the side. Yun, how was her body even holding up anymore? She was refusing more medicine these days, despite Wen's continued protests, and the broken memories she did recall had her flung around the arena like a ragdoll.

And still she won. Every time. Gruesomely.

"Hey," Goeth called, and it felt as though the atmosphere shifted. "Be careful out there if you can. There's something . . . something off. Whatever it is, I don't like it."

The statement gave her pause, and she leant heavily against a stony wall as she asked, "What do you mean?"

There was a long, contemplative lag, then finally, "I don't know. Something just feels wrong. I just . . . it's a silly premonition. But maybe you ought to listen to it."

It wasn't a situation where one would easily jest about these kinds of things. Anyway, Sakaeri had long since learnt that Goeth wasn't the type to throw around faulty warnings. In their shared time among the rot and ruin, he'd voiced his own steadfast disdain for Kaisa and his followers, and his advice only ever helped Sakaeri stay alive and as in tune with reality as she could be.

"Yeah. Okay, Goeth," she said, softly resigned.

It was when she was forced to walk out on scarlet-dyed dirt, under the intense scrutiny of spectating crowds, her mind semi-lucid in failing autonomy, that she thought she spotted recognisable and regally adorned horns in the sea of forgettable faces. It was then that Goeth's warning felt heavier, and a new fear crawled into her chest.

When calculating eyes zeroed in on her, and a once-familiar face twisted into a daemonish impression of the one she thought she knew, Sakaeri's blood ran cold.

"Are you . . . are you sure you want to try this?"

It felt like mockery, asking her of her certainty when it was him quivering.

"Yes." It was delivered with such unwavering force that he felt his own back straighten in response.

"I don't know if it can be undone, and I don't even know if I can." His reasonings were moot. He knew this, that it wouldn't change the outcome. It was decided.

"Yes, I want to protect him. From this. From all this." She wasn't smiling now, and everything felt so wrong. So serious and morbid, as if the realm itself depended on his actions.

To protect him?

He looked at the slumbering child on the chair, a draught having been delivered by his sister's hands during his last meal. He looked so small like that, crumpled against the wing. He looked so unassuming. Harmless, and perhaps helpless.

To protect him? Was this . . . Was this protection?

He reached out, an unsure placement of his thumb on a temple. Was this protection?

CHAPTER THIRTY-SIX

"Oh good," came Davah's drawl as Aeyun struggled to return to awareness. "You're awake."

"Hmm?" Aeyun voiced, groggy.

Things didn't quite make sense yet. His bones felt stiff and his head heavy. Making to right himself, he realised that he was sprawled across the sea-skimmer floor, its coldness unwelcome against his skin. Davah was looking a little green himself, pressed up against the wall on the opposite end of the hull, wooziness colouring his features.

"Not sure where you took us, friend."

"Took us?" Aeyun asked, pushing himself off the floor.

He wiped at his face – something he was getting too used to doing, and the crimson smear that scrubbed away with his fingers' brush becoming too common an occurrence – and squinted through the dirty glass panels of the sea-skimmer. His head was pounding.

They weren't on water. They weren't on water, and that didn't seem right.

"I don't get it. Where are we?" Aeyun murmured, trying to ignore the ache that permeated his being. He felt like he'd been awake for days, maybe weeks.

Davah moved slowly, groaning as he prodded a blooming bruise on his shoulder. "Well, I was hoping you had a clue. Because I fecking don't."

Aeyun rubbed at his eyes again and really tried to peer into the realm beyond.

A familiar feeling engulfed him, but something distorted and unknown at the same time. The picture framed outside the glass was a grassy flatbed on a rocky shore, where their craft was settled on the overgrown, stony surface. The shore was greeted by a stormy ocean and flanked by the towering presence of mountains, a weedy stairwell curving around and disappearing into one of the valleys. Aeyun couldn't shake the jolt of connection that pulled at him. His heart pounded and he found himself scrambling to hoist his body out of the rooftop hatch.

"Hey! What? What are you doing?" Davah shouted from below, but Aeyun continued on.

He could feel it, hanging there in the air, carried among the salt and spray. The realm sang a tune that he hadn't heard in so long – *too* long – and he'd been fearful that if he were to return to it, he'd go back again and never leave.

Well, now he was back. And Raenaru greeted him like a long-lost friend, embracing him in its call, singing a lullaby that felt like breath filling his lungs.

"Shit," Aeyun said, stumbling forward as he slid down the sea-skimmer's side.

The rocky outcropping they were perched upon was blanketed with grass and thistle and weeds, obscuring its grey form. On a whim, he tugged at some dewy green blades, ripping them away from their roots, and he kept at it until he found what instinct screamed at him would manifest.

"Aeyun!" Davah called, hanging halfway out the hatch. "What is it?"

Beneath Aeyun's shaking fingers, a scrawled, weathered rune was seared into a half-buried piece of rubble, looking as if embers had only recently turned to ashes in its grooves. Knees weak, he followed on in a curved line, finding another broken fragment, a rune carved there with a divot where an alicant had surely once sat embedded, and a breathy curse escaped him.

"Aeyun!"

"It's a gate!" Aeyun called back, unable to keep the excitement from his voice. Davah watched his impromptu weeding, curious. "There used to be a gate here. But it's not like the Great Sea Gates – it's like the one on Beldur. This is amazing!"

"Aeyun," Davah said, drawing out the last syllable.

"Hm?"

"Where are we?"

"Oh," Aeyun said, standing up from where he was crouched. "We're on–"

The reaction came on suddenly and Aeyun heaved, coughing up a splash of red, colouring the greenery below. Davah was quick to hop through the hatch and skitter to Aeyun's side, leaning down in concern. Aeyun held a hand up and sputtered more before he wiped his wrist across his now copper-tasting lips.

"I'm fine," Aeyun said, lightheaded.

"Sure you are," Davah responded.

"We're on Raenaru," Aeyun finished his earlier statement, and he shoved his palms on his knees, taking a long look at the horizon as he regained his composure. "Somewhere," he concluded.

"How?" Davah stood up fully once he was convinced that Aeyun wasn't about to keel over. "That wasn't anywhere close to what we were aiming for."

"No, it really wasn't," Aeyun agreed, baffled himself. Thunder rattled through the sky, and he glanced across the ocean before turning to the mountains. "Wanna climb?"

"Not really, but we're going to anyway, aren't we?"

Aeyun grinned at Davah, which probably looked quite terrifying with his red-stained teeth.

"Yep."

"Can you even do that right now? I mean, you seem–"

"I'm fine," Aeyun said stubbornly.

He took a step, steadied himself, then clambered back into the stranded sea-skimmer to retrieve Azura. His mask, however, was a lost cause. It didn't look as though this corner of Raenaru was well populated, so his bare face likely wouldn't be an issue.

A few minutes later, Aeyun and Davah breached the threshold between the flattened coast and the shadowed foothills. Nearing the neglected, battered stairwell, Aeyun trailed his gaze up the length of it, but he couldn't see past the next peak, or the one beyond that. Beside him, Davah observed the distance, adjusting the bag on his shoulders. He'd taken the blankets with him, just in case.

They started their ascent, the wind picking up and biting at their ears, each step feeling more dooming than the last. Aeyun couldn't shake the unease that clung to him, the soft ballad of the shore left behind, overpowered by the chorus of the whistling wind and the jagged, forested pinnacles above them. He shivered and tried to ignore it, along with the odd look Davah gave him.

Around the next turn, the whispers started. The incessant murmurings of *something*, careening around boulders and bouncing beside his head. Aeyun's brows knit, but he kept his head up, looking straight forward.

"Aeyun," Davah said, sounding unnatural, and the whispers became clawing screeches for the duration of it.

Aeyun whipped his head to side and placed a finger very clearly over his lips, indicating silence. Davah opened his mouth in a gape, seeming puzzled, then closed his jaw and nodded.

The clouds hung heavy with the threat of rain above, and Aeyun could only hope that they were close to their destination now, wherever that might be. Just as the sky began to sob, heavy droplets pattering down on his shoulders, Aeyun saw a break in the mountains. Taking the last step to overtake the precipice, he gazed at what looked like a monastery cradled in the highland, beyond a looming pass, ancient and neglected, left to wither in the elements. He hadn't realised the whispers had abated until Davah spoke beside him.

"Wow," he said in awe.

Aeyun couldn't disagree. He decided to leave mentioning the ghostly voices for a different time.

They lessened the distance between themselves and the ruined depictions of figures chiselled into the mountain's narrow pass, Aeyun's eyes raking over every detail.

The faces of those forever resting among the rocky walls were faded, worn from wind and rain. As the passage opened up, several structures were scattered among the hilly expanse, all dilapidated, half crumbling, and some home to nests of birds, a few of which flapped between the ruins and the trees that dotted the grounds. It all culminated at a shrine on the highest elevation, the bow of which reflected symbolism that looked celestial.

Staggered, Aeyun blinked at it, frowning. Then he walked forward, always forward.

The shrine itself wasn't small or humble, and it looked as though it continued beyond its preface, dropping down the exterior of the mountain. When they finally entered that central building, the last one intact, Aeyun's vision was drawn to the runic markings on the black marble floor. For the briefest moment, his eyes caught on Davah's, then Davah's gaze was drawn elsewhere.

"*Yun of the stars,*" Davah breathed out, and Aeyun snapped his attention to where he was looking.

Decomposing on the floor were corpses, dozens of them, strewn haphazardly among the beautiful markings adorning the inner sanctum. Aeyun tensed, instantly alert for danger, but all he felt was a morose echo of the horrors that had occurred mere paces from where he and Davah stood.

"What even happened here?" Davah asked aloud, scrutinising the scene, but not daring to continue on.

Aeyun felt something; an unnamed inclination. A pull towards the tragic victims in this temple that called to him, crying out endlessly. He didn't know he took a step until the drop of his boot resounded through the ornate interior, the twisted beams and colourfully painted symbols bearing down on him as if to signal his welcome.

A bell chimed somewhere in the distance, followed by another chime and another, and Aeyun felt Vitality seeping from him, curling out and reaching beyond his fingertips. His vision grew radiant, and cries rung out, distant and far away. As if they were in the valley. Aeyun turned, breezing over Davah's strange expression.

"*Cah, ou'uo'ca,*" Aeyun said, drawing forth a tune despite the sparking protest in his chest, calling those banshee whispers towards him. They cried louder, and louder and louder and louder. Aeyun concentrated, reaching out his right hand. "*Ca'ne!*"

Something intangible shattered in the distance, and Aeyun felt a rush of energy encroach upon the shrine, panicked brightness collecting just beyond the entryway, the ancient runes alighting on the ground there. Aeyun glared down at them.

"*Ca'ne!*" The markings sizzled to nonexistence, only a trace impression of what once sat there prominently, and the whispering spirits flooded in, zipping into corpses. The instinct to mourn dripped into every desolate fibre of Aeyun's soulsong.

He whispered, "*Cah eh'ju, a'garu ca'ju.*"

Whatever spell Davah was under, his resolve seemed to have broken it. He came to stand beside Aeyun, reaching a hand out to his arm, gripping. Aeyun startled when Davah's eyes faded into a milky reflection, Davah mirroring the reaction.

He looked around, gaze distinctly drawn to each body, where little dim lights refused to evaporate, then he turned back to Aeyun, glowing ivory eyes wide. Aeyun stared back for a moment, then turned back to the scene of the temple, repeating his last mantra.

On Aeyun's third iteration, Davah joined in, saying "*Ka'gh a'ga'ru, ka'ur'ogh da'ga'ru eoi'mhe.*"

With his added cadence, the brilliant vestiges clawing at the corpses began to cool, the once hectic energy becoming calmer, more docile. Between the two of their descants, the floating cores glittered ethereally before becoming soft particles, dissipating.

At least there was peace for those traces now, urged to return and be one with the aether, relinquishing their desperate hold upon what remained of life. Unsatisfied soulsongs that lingered outside the memory of their bones existed in torment, propelled by instinct alone, forever seeking to satisfy their last whim. A lesson once learnt from his mother. He wouldn't wish that fate for anyone.

In the silence left behind, Davah withdrew, and the clouded white film over his eyes fell away with his retreat.

"That's something else," Davah said in a whisper, as if anything even a decibel higher would be too much.

Aeyun nodded, chancing a glance at Davah's pensive expression before he looked away. It wasn't odd that Aeyun could reach Davah with a tune – that would happen with those whose memories he influenced – but it was odd that Davah could see what Aeyun saw. He didn't have time to debate it, however, since Davah decided to walk further into the shrine.

Feeling disconcerted, Aeyun followed, kneeling carefully beside a shrivelled casualty. Gently, and not without apprehension, he reached out. He felt a deep despair, unwanted motions coursing through his body, then a piercing in his gut, matching the plunge of his own weapon in a solid form, then a force wrenching him away.

Aeyun blinked himself back to reality, confused. Beside the body he'd knelt next to was another, a sword embedded in her chest. Morbidly, he reached out to her, and he experienced the same stilted sensation, a trapped vision of their last moments, facing one another. His troubled mind overriding his discomfort with the dead, he tried the same with several other felled, and they were all the similar. Even without a full understanding, their soulsongs' anguished cries and agonised limbo made more sense. Just not enough quite enough to fully grasp.

"I don't get it," Aeyun muttered, feeling Davah's quiet ponder upon his back. "It shouldn't be like that."

Quickly, a courtesy drilled into him from his youthful days with Jourae, Aeyun propped a hand perpendicular to his chest, offering faint apologies to the dead for his intrusion. Aeyun darted to the entrance again, peering at the almost disappeared runes, but they offered no knowledge he could glean. He turned on his heel and looked at the altar of the shrine, a space demarcated with glowing ore and strange markings, two hallways branching off behind it.

Aeyun swept past the bodies, past Davah, and when he was met with the steps of a raised platform, he climbed them to be face to face with an obsidian mask, ancient horns welded to its crest. As he stared at it, it was as if sound dropped away entirely. No muffling, no drowned noises: just silence.

He reached out, and a quietness invaded his mind as well. The periphery faded and with great purpose, he stretched to make contact.

Slowly, his body moving in stuttered progression, he grew closer to the horned mask, an inky plane of blackness elongating on either side of him. When his finger finally met bone, he was enveloped with a youthful innocence, a fascination for flowers and the small creatures that flitted between them; then came discipline, forming muscle memory and artful movements that complemented trainings, then there were flickers of smiles, warmth, friendships, and then came the burn of passion and devotion, then pain, death, war, his own clawed hands ripping through lines of soldiers, his own clawed hands calling upon energy in its purest form, his own clawed hands claiming soulsongs – love, and bittersweet joy, a pact, then loss – loss, loss, loss, so visceral it ripped him in two, pain, numbness, nothing.

Aeyun inhaled like he was surfacing from water, and a remnant of a song sung long, long ago lingered. He caressed the faded soulsong's echoes, drawing it into a close embrace. When he opened his eyes, he was in a form not his own, both unfamiliar and familiar, and his vision steadied to focus on a velvet canopy above.

"*Aeyun?*"

Aeyun froze, mind and body.

"*Aeyun? Aeyun. You need to let me know you're there and that this isn't some trick. I haven't been able to think clearly for months. Please, I am – of all things in the damned realms – begging you–*"

"Seraeyu," Aeyun found himself saying, and he couldn't differentiate between his own voice in his mind and Seraeyu's imitation of his call out loud.

"*It's you, right? Aeyun?*"

Seraeyu sounded rushed and manic and . . . frightened. It was bizarre and baffling, and Aeyun finally shifted his – or was it Seraeyu's? – gaze from the canopy.

He was in a once-lavish room, now a wrecked impression of glamour. Tattered belongings were scattered everywhere; it looked as though the place had been ransacked. An unnerved feeling grew within him, and he slid himself off the bed and walked towards the en suite, almost stumbling due to his poor coordination of stolen legs.

"*Aeyun . . .*" said Seraeyu. A wounded, warbling sound that was much too fragile for the man Aeyun knew, and it tugged at something within him.

"It's me," Aeyun said, not yet willing to divulge more.

He pushed open the door, cringing at the sensation of his claw-like nails scraping against the wood, and padded across the tiled floor. Light was streaming in through the muted glass window, and it made him squint; had the curtains been drawn in the other room?

He turned to the mirror and paused.

Seraeyu looked gaunt, dark circles under his eyes. The softness of his youthful twenties was lost under a weariness that looked out of place, his otherwise elegant features dulled and nearly sickly. It was surreal, to ponder a face so familiar, yet so different.

"Must you stare? I don't want to see. After everything I–"

Seraeyu grew quiet. Aeyun blinked Seraeyu's eyes, noticing how dim they reflected. His stomach churned and his chest tightened. He remembered the easy fire they used to hold. Where had it gone? Who was this imposter staring back, wearing Seraeyu's face?

"Seraeyu," Aeyun said, respecting the other's wishes and looking away in spite of his own curiosity. "Why?"

His mind was silent for too long.

"I was . . . angry. I wanted more. When I came across it, I was offered it." There was a break in continuity, like static, grating. *"I was naïve."*

"When you came across what?" Aeyun asked, a weird sort of misplaced panic building up inside him. He walked to the window to try to open it, but it seemed bolted shut. From the outside. He led Seraeyu's hand to the pane and tried to push harder. "Don't you have anything to tune with?"

It seemed wrong, unfitting that he couldn't feel any alicant on Seraeyu's being.

"Can't you see the jewels dripping off me? No? No. I don't, obviously," Seraeyu said in a tone that reminded Aeyun more of the snippy brat he knew him to be. *"The only thing in here is that*

damn cursed alicant. That's what I came across, the pair to my sister's. Is she . . . is she okay?"

"What?" Aeyun asked, instinctively lifting Seraeyu's arm, expecting to find Essence scars. But the skin there was bare, with the exception of a few faded marks that were not dealt by raw Essence. They looked like healed scrapes, maybe scratches. "Where?"

"It's not – go back to the mirror."

Despite himself, Aeyun followed the directive. He gazed upon Seraeyu's reflection again. It was just as startling as the last time, to see him look so unwell.

"On my chest. You'll see it."

Aeyun paused for a second, hesitant, then he hooked one of Seraeyu's fingers under the hem of his shirt and pulled up. His midriff was free from any mars, so Aeyun urged the material higher. Dark, jagged spindles started showing their edges, appearing angry and gouging, the worst of them culminating on Seraeyu's left side. Feeling a foreboding alarm at its locale, Aeyun nearly pulled the material off Seraeyu's shoulder so he could observe the awful inky radials that gnawed into his skin, right above Seraeyu's heart. Without thinking about it, he lifted Seraeyu's hand to rest over it, covering it from sight.

"Don't wake her!" Seraeyu said urgently, and Aeyun ripped his touch away, shirt's material dropping with the movement.

Aeyun acknowledged that *he* hadn't actioned that.

"Why can't I feel that alicant? And who's *her?*"

"I don't know, but to be entirely honest, I don't even know how you're talking to me." Aeyun kept staring at Seraeyu's reflection. Why did it feel so disconcerting, to see him so . . . drained? *"And her, the other daemon. The companion to the one that lingered in Raeyu's alicant."*

"The other daemon?"

"Oh. Did Raeyu not tell you? Or did she just not realise?" A pause. *"How are you even here, Aeyun?"*

"Seraeyu," Aeyun said, watching Seraeyu's mouth form his

365

own name. "Are you telling me that this alicant, this thing shoved over your heart, has overtaken you? Possessed you?"

"*Well, currently* you *seem to be doing that, but . . . yes. That's an accurate enough way to put it. I can break her hold sometimes, but it's never long enough. This is – this has been a long time, with you.*"

"With me?" Aeyun repeated, because it was Seraeyu who had killed his father. It was Seraeyu who had committed heinous acts. It was Seraeyu who had instigated it all.

Wasn't it?

"Who is she? This daemon?"

"*Sirin. Not the mercenaries, but the actual holder of the namesake. An ancient Yun.*"

Aeyun searched the reflection in the mirror to find signs of lies. As if they would surface. As if they would gurgle to life, ripping themselves from the frigid void itself. As if Seraeyu's piercing gaze was not one with Aeyun's own.

"*Oh–*" Seraeyu gasped something painful, and Aeyun could see energy wisping from that gnarled focal point on his chest. "*You have to leave. However you might do that. She can't know you're capable of this – but please, Aeyun, don't leave me to her whim. I can't – the things I've done. The things she'll do – it has to end – you have to go. Please, now!*"

On the last plea, Aeyun felt himself forced away and he was again warping through time itself. Striations filtered through blank space, compressing and decompressing, and he struggled to find air, drowning within it.

Like a trance fading, he stumbled from the altar, Davah's hand behind him to steady his teetering balance.

"Starry sea," Aeyun said, confounded. "What the *fuck*?"

"Friend, what's going on? You touched that creepy mask then you kinda just zoned out for a bit." Davah's question went ignored while Aeyun gazed upon the mask.

Sirin.

Sirin. Sirin the Yun. His eyes drifted up to the horns welded to the obsidian again.

Sirin. He whipped his head around to look at the scattered, half-mummified corpses.

Sirin.

All dead, the communication he'd registered after picking up the stray stone in their plundered sea-skimmer rattled around his brain. *Don't come back.*

But she must have. Because she had both pairs.

Bewildered, conflicted, and entirely depleted, Aeyun's eyes rolled back. The last thing he saw was the glare of the horned obsidian mask.

"It's okay to be scared."

But it wasn't. Fear was dangerous. Fear was the beginning of the end. A charm to call death.

"You don't have to lash out. You have time, kid. You have nothing but time."

Time gave him nothing but heartache. He needed results. He needed to do better. Be better.

"You're my ward now. You know what that means, right? That means I look after you."

That wasn't right. It was his duty, and he failed. He failed, he failed, he failed, he failed . . .

CHAPTER THIRTY-SEVEN

Aeyun awoke in an unfamiliar room, gilded in tarnished filigree and peeling murals. He pushed himself up and immediately became aware that he couldn't use his right limb; not in the slightest. Placing all the pressure on his left palm, he hinged his waist and cradled his deadened arm once he was upright.

A crisp, floral breeze blew in from the open-air windows lining the walls, and Aeyun shivered as it ran down his spine. Looking down, he saw that one of the blankets Davah had brought with him was draped across his body. Davah's own blanket was folded neatly on the cot to his left. So, he had looked after him? For how long?

Aeyun got up and was punched with lethargy, as if he were recovering from a long sickness. With a frown, he steadied himself on his wobbly feet, then glanced around, noting dozens of cots, long abandoned.

A dormitory? Aeyun walked on, grasping onto beams and bedframes as he went to keep his footing true. What was wrong with him? To be this unsteady . . .

The hall was quiet, only stray birds chirping a soft melody to guide him. He looked to the left – a narrow stretch that branched, arches peering over the valley below – then to the right – a path to black marble floors. Aeyun followed that one.

His left hand guided him as he trod, tracing a path on the carved wall. Eventually, after what felt like too long, Aeyun came upon the main chasm of the shrine, where he'd first entered. His immediate observation was that it was baren; cleared of the felled Sirin. Knitting his brow, he kept going, sparing a wary glance towards the obsidian mask hung on the wall.

"Davah?" Aeyun called out, voice hoarse.

It echoed across the ceiling, and he looked up, curious. The tap of footsteps drew his attention back to the entrance. There, Davah stood with a bag made of twine, full of tree-borne fruit.

"You're awake," he said. "You want some water? There's a well out there."

Aeyun slowly nodded, hit with how parched he was. Davah started to turn to the courtyard again. Aeyun stumbled forward to follow him, narrowly avoiding tumbling over entirely, instead ramming the junction of his shoulder against a beam.

"Woah, friend. Easy there," Davah said, already doubling back to offer his support.

They made their way out to the greenery, vibrant under the sun's blessing. Aeyun had to squint at the sudden adjustment of light, then he allowed Davah to guide him to a well hidden behind one of the ruins.

"How long was I out?" Aeyun asked scratchily, becoming more eager to quench his thirst as the bucket was lurched upwards by Davah's hoists.

"A few days," Davah answered. "I think you pushed yourself

too hard in one go."

Aeyun allowed himself a palmful of well water once in reach. "Yeah, you're right."

He greedily drank more until his innards felt less shrivelled.

"You should probably have one of these, too," Davah said, offering a round, waxy fruit from the bag that hung on the crook of his arm. Aeyun eyed it and his stomach turned.

"Maybe in a bit. I'm not really . . ." He blanched at the very thought of a bite. "Yeah." He took a last handful of water to splash across his face.

Davah nodded. "Fair enough."

He eyed Aeyun then with restrained inquisitiveness.

Aeyun looked back, feeling sheepish. "Ah, thanks for looking after me. You're probably tired of it by now," he said, trying to figure out what Davah's eyes were saying.

"No," Davah said, his tone conveying that his mind was elsewhere. "You look bad."

The statement took Aeyun aback, and he chuckled depreciatively. "Thanks?"

"No, like you look shattered." Davah considered Aeyun's limp arm. "Can't move that, can you?"

Aeyun shook his head, grimacing.

"Maybe we should find something for you to fix that." He tugged Aeyun along with him towards vines that clung to the mountain face. "That happening more often?" Davah asked, failing to sound casual.

Aeyun took a moment to think before answering, "I don't know?"

When they reached the rocky wall, Davah helped lift Aeyun's right hand to rest on a bloom-riddled vine, looking at him expectantly. Aeyun descanted his mantra, and Vitality thrummed through his body, invigorating him with energy he hadn't realised he'd lacked until it returned. As he muttered his chant, the vines began to dry up, and the flowers withered, their petals flitting down and brushing past him, some getting caught on his arm or in his hair. Something about the scene sowed a sadness in his slow-beating heart. He shook Davah's hand off and stepped away, steadier than before.

Aeyun wandered back to the well, filled the bucket, then unlatched it. He waddled back to the vines, tugging at the dehydrated ends and fitting what he could in the water.

"Sorry," he said to the creeping plant.

"Bleeding heart," Davah teased him, and Aeyun gave him a wry grin. "Feel better?"

"Much," Aeyun said truthfully.

His body felt less stiff, and his mind less clouded. In his recovered state, his memory recalled the other day's events. He wasn't sure what he wanted to say, or even what he wanted to think. There was something he did want to know, though.

"You moved the bodies."

Davah hummed as they started back towards the centre of the courtyard.

"Yeah. Couldn't leave them there. Gave them a burial ground in the corner, over there." Davah pointed to a series of mounds set in rows at the far end of the green space. "This might sound weird, but I think they might've been part of Sakaeri's crew? You know, like, the Sirin?"

Aeyun couldn't tear his eyes from the dozens of soil heaps.

"Oh?" It left his mouth before he could think about it. He *knew* they were Sirin.

"Yeah. The way they were dressed, and the weapons they had. This weird place, hidden away like this. They were all missing their eyes, actually. And I don't think it was from natural causes. There were these . . . scrape marks."

Davah's statement caused Aeyun to finally look away from the new gravesite, though he didn't respond until a rustle of leaves above broke the quiet.

"Someone stole their eyes?" Aeyun asked, receiving a nod. "Why?"

"Why does anyone do anything?" Davah said obscurely,

taking it upon himself to move their conversation back inside the shrine. "You know that mask there?" Davah indicated with a jut of his chin towards the horned artefact hanging behind the altar. "I get a really weird feeling from it."

"Oh?" Aeyun repeated himself; it sounded asinine, even to his own ears.

"Yeah. Can't really describe it. Not really good or bad, just something jarring that's present. And you just touched it, without hesitation." Davah turned his attention to Aeyun. "Wanna talk about that?"

Aeyun matched the mask's stare, allowing himself to study it from afar.

"You know how I can *feel* Azura?" Aeyun started, briefly wondering how his aerofoil was back in the dormitory – barracks? He didn't wait for a response, knowing that Davah was aware of what he was referring to. "Those horns are Yu-ta. Someone welded them to that."

Davah's lack of reaction made Aeyun wonder. As it lagged, the wonder turned sour, and he withered along with it.

"Ah," Davah finally responded when he realised that Aeyun was waiting.

"Any thoughts on that?" Aeyun asked, pushing.

Davah shrugged. "What am I meant to think about it? It's an old mask with the horns of some unnamed Yu-ta," he said, and Aeyun didn't dare falter. "That means nothing to me. What? Did you *feel* something from it when you touched it? You did look disconnected for a moment."

Aeyun's insides felt cramped; itchy, almost.

It was the first time that he'd felt that way in a long while, and it was the first time he'd felt that way with Davah in even longer. While he had been so assured that he was making the right progress, on the right path, only days ago, he now felt as though something had shifted. Sand moving against the grain.

Da'garu, last he saw her, had looked terrified of his presence, and she couldn't speak. Uruji sent him away, forcefully, with a descant, of all things, telling him to leave and not return. Raeyu had begged him to not come for them, saying that it would mean Aeyun's demise. Saoiri was alone in an occupied land, and they *weren't* going to her. Sakaeri was still missing, ripping people to shreds somewhere, if Aeyun's vision held any truth. And her band of Sirin, the deadly mercenaries of lore, were very real and they were very dead. And had been for a long time now.

And Sirin, according to one Seraeyu Thasian, was not only the name of these deceased warriors, but of a daemon residing in the alicant over his heart. Seraeyu Thasian, who Aeyun had loosely been planning to exact vengeance against, if he were truly honest with himself, was . . . afraid, and trapped. And Aeyun didn't know how to communicate *any* of that.

Davah, surely, would not feel any loyalty towards Seraeyu, and Aeyun couldn't fault him for that. But it also scared him, especially when he kept glaring at the horns on the mask. Aeyun found that, just like he wasn't ready to divulge his tethered connection to Raeyu, he wasn't prepared to speak about his recent revelations on Seraeyu's status either. Instead, he voiced something based in a sinister, betraying notion; a fearful reckoning.

"You know that my brother is Yu-ta, right? And that Raeyu is as well?"

Davah gave him a scornful look, as though it were a stupid question. "Of course I do."

"No," Aeyun said, shuffling his feet to dispel his discomfort. "I mean, you realise that I am trying to bring them back; keep them safe. The two of them. Yu-ta. Not like Sakaeri. Not like someone who's rejected their heritage. They *are* Yu-ta."

Davah stared at him. "I know," he said, but there was something held there.

"And while I am not Yu-ta, Jourae was. I lived with Yu-ta for more than half my life. You realise that, right?"

"I know," Davah repeated, his mouth thinning to a line.

A bell chimed in the distance and the breeze picked up outside.

"I don't hate the Yu-ta," Aeyun said, wanting to make it clear.

"I know." Davah paused. "I hate oppression, Aeyun. Sometimes it's hard to differentiate the two, because the Yu-ta, especially the Thasian, are tied pretty closely to the concept. But, sure, look, while I might have my misgivings about them, I guess you are kind of Thasian-nee, even if you don't look like it, and we get on well enough. People like Seraeyu Thasian are different. Built to reign terror; he should have stayed Untuned. Power in hands like his was bound to be a catalyst for destruction. People like him, all they crave is more. It's never enough."

Aeyun didn't know what to say. In his mind, fluttering to life in his recent memory, he saw the reflection of Seraeyu in the mirror, drained and grim, a festering tattoo of rotten Essence eating into his heart.

She can't know you're capable of this – but please, Aeyun, don't leave me to her whim. I can't – the things I've done. The things she'll do – it has to end.

Seraeyu Thasian wasn't a mastermind of ruin, but a tool for it. Trapped in his own mistake. Which Aeyun and Raeyu had unwittingly spurred when they denied him his right to tune, when they'd silenced his will. When *Aeyun* had snuffed his song to a murmur.

Did Seraeyu know? Did Seraeyu know what they'd done? That it had been Aeyun's doing? That Aeyun had taken away his choice as to who he wanted to be? Did he know, and did he forgive him? Did Aeyun even forgive himself, now that Seraeyu was a puppet in the hands of something foul?

"Even before he snapped, he was a shite person. He never gave a rat's arse about anyone but himself. He didn't even pretend to care."

Aeyun thought about when Seraeyu had told Uruji that his training needed to include lessons on how to make elixirs. A time that suspiciously coincided with a bout of sickness the younger Thasian-nee suffered. He thought about how Oagyu used to scream at him for being incompetent, a waste of space, someone unworthy of the Thasian name. He thought about how, when he was younger, Aeyun had come across him sobbing by a bush. When he'd hesitantly gone to check on him, Seraeyu hid his eyes, embarrassed, and Aeyun spotted a small, fresh-dug mound.

Seraeyu said he'd found a runt on death's door, left to perish by its mother, and that he'd buried it after its last whimper, refusing to let it succumb without someone by its side. And Seraeyu said he promised himself he wouldn't forget it, because it hadn't been useless; it shouldn't have been abandoned.

Aeyun's eyes prickled, glazing over. He was a *fool*.

"Ridding the realms of Seraeyu Thasian is enough," Davah said with a tired sigh, walking further into the shrine. Aeyun watched his retreating back.

But please, Aeyun, don't leave me –

"And then we can move past this terrible chapter in history. Maybe it'll be a good thing, too. Haebal and Raenaru having to figure out what to do without the Thasian."

Aeyun wanted to turn back time. He wanted everything to stop.

"Maybe things will get better, for everyone."

Aeyun couldn't sleep. Davah was snoring lightly on the next cot over, and Aeyun stared at the chips on the ceiling, thoughts running in countless directions.

He swung his feet over the side of the bed and wandered over to Azura, giving the ivory a fond pet before he walked past it and returned to the hallway he'd entered earlier that same day. Instead of heading towards the main chamber, he took a curious turn left, quietly padding down the grooved wood. He hadn't bothered to put on shoes, and his cloak was left behind with the blankets. They didn't feel important enough as his mind ached to be anywhere else.

As he continued on, the night air tickled his exposed, bare

expanses of skin, and Aeyun subconsciously trailed his fingers down his scarred arm.

When he was met with his first fork, he turned right, his focus flitting between one open arch to the next. The valley beyond was quiet, and the shadow-silken sky blinked down at him with a smattering of stars, looking brighter than they ever had from his vantage. Just beyond that, the moon beamed luminously, washing the mountaintops with an ethereal glow. In the still of the night, Aeyun tried to coax his anxious mind to rest.

Soon, he found a stairwell that led outside, cascading down the mountain's face, and he could see a terrace below, glowing ore and bioluminescent flora – *lunarius*, his mind provided – clinging to its enclosure. Intrigued, Aeyun followed the steps down. When the ground plateaued, he walked over to a carved bench and sat upon it, looking up.

He figured he should tell Raeyu about Seraeyu. It only made sense. And she would want to know that her brother wasn't–

Or maybe it would hurt her more to know that Seraeyu was trapped, doing deeds against his will, manipulated by some other presence. Hadn't Seraeyu said it was the companion to Raeyu's alicant? For the life of him, Aeyun couldn't recall Raeyu mentioning something living in the ore, just that it held a great power, and that it had been passed from Thasian to Thasian for a long time.

Was Seraeyu lying?

Aeyun felt guilty, and he couldn't pinpoint exactly what for. His mind just kept jumping to Seraeyu's face and the worry in his voice. It had been a cry for help. He was asking Aeyun, the man who had doomed him to a silenced life, for help.

Aeyun took a deep breath and sighed. His head was spinning, and no one direction felt *right* anymore. What would he do now? Even if Seraeyu was a victim in this – *he's your victim*, Aeyun thought bitterly – trying to remove that alicant would surely kill him. He couldn't pretend to know the circumstances around that fusing, but he was sure that Seraeyu wouldn't have tied something to his very lifeforce like that without some serious manipulation. Seraeyu was rash and *too much* at times, but he was never stupid.

So, what would Aeyun do? Was there no other option but to slaughter the being controlling Seraeyu along with Seraeyu himself? The thought made Aeyun want to hurl. He'd known distantly what might have to happen, but he'd not thought about it at length. Now confronted with it, having *seen* Seraeyu for the first time in what was nearing two years, he couldn't reconcile the idea.

Strangely, Seraeyu had known it was him right away. How had that happened? Aeyun was sure that the man paid him next to no mind, but he called out his name immediately. It hadn't been a trick, right? Seraeyu was being genuine? Aeyun had no real way to know. Right?

Right?

Suddenly impulsive, Aeyun closed his eyes and focused. He evened his breath, and he tried to embrace the energy around him and reach beyond. After long moments of quiet, he could feel the realm stretch out around him. When he opened his eyes, he saw a sea of black, interspersed with bright pockets of colour that ebbed and flowed. Aeyun drew a deep breath, centring himself, then he reached out a hand, the movement stuttering yet somehow fluid.

"Seraeyu," he called out, but it came out like a delayed echo, swerving from one side to the next, then far beyond. Aeyun waited, then he said again, "Seraeyu, *cah, ou'uo ca.*"

Something dim formed before him: just a silhouette, but it felt familiar, if dampened. Aeyun took a step forward and the space below his bare feet rippled. The figure, drawn in on themselves, startled and began to tilt their face up. Aeyun knelt down and, careful as he was hesitant, propped his fingers under their chin.

It started with the eyes. They gained a starry-dotted glimmer, and the recognisable form of Seraeyu filled out from there. Seraeyu stared back at Aeyun, baffled, then he took a shaky breath and shook his head, as if trying to dispel the vision.

"I've lost the plot. This must be in my head," Seraeyu claimed aloud, aiming his gaze away from Aeyun. "I've actually gone mad, fooled myself into thinking that–"

"Seraeyu," Aeyun said, retracting his hand. "I called you to me."

Seraeyu looked back, puzzlement drawn clearly across his features. He weaved lightly to the left to peer over Aeyun's shoulder, taking in the endless Essence and pockets of energy.

"But that's not how this works?" Seraeyu shook his head again. "Why would you call me to you?"

"Because," Aeyun said, ignoring the first question, "I need to know – you need to know that you're not alone."

Aeyun then realised that he'd never seen anyone cry in this odd expanse. As water slipped from Seraeyu's eyes, it bubbled sideways, floating aimlessly away from his cheeks. The next revelation Aeyun had was that an embrace felt just as real here as it did in the corporeal plane.

Seraeyu had inclined forward, fingers digging into Aeyun's shirt and forehead slamming against the crook of his neck. Aeyun's arms stayed frozen at his sides, then he slowly, cautiously, wrapped one of them around Seraeyu's back. He could feel silent sobs wrack the so-called mad Thasian, and Aeyun felt his own eyes prickle with emotion.

He'd messed up. He really had.

Aeyun put his other hand behind Seraeyu's head, patting lightly. Seraeyu let out a fragmented and mournful lament, and Aeyun's heart clenched.

Aeyun looked up, or whatever direction was above them, and bit his lip to steady his own voice. "I'll figure it out," he managed to say.

"I'm so sorry," Seraeyu sobbed out, gripping tighter at the fabric of Aeyun's shirt. "For so much – for everything. I have so many regrets. I'm so sorry." Seraeyu gulped back a strained sob and leant away from Aeyun. He dropped his hold, leaving only trace touches behind. "Is she alive? Is she okay?"

"I–" Aeyun paused.

A stray idea betrayed him, wondering: what if it's still a ruse? What if this is a creative ploy to find out where Raeyu is?

"Oh, I see. You, ah, you don't have to tell me," Seraeyu said brokenly, almost if he had read the thought on Aeyun's face. "I understand, it's fine." He sniffled and pulled away. "Whatever you think, whatever you might believe – don't let me do her bidding. Don't let me be a slave to her agenda. I'm so tired. I don't need to fail any more expectations. I can't handle it; I never wanted to be this kind of monster."

A resolve scorched brightly within Seraeyu's determined gaze, the depths of it battening up all the terror and sorrow.

"Kill me, if you have to."

"Seraeyu," Aeyun said, and it was like a barrier falling away. "Seraeyu, you – dammit. I'm sorry, you didn't fail. *I* screwed up. You have to fight. Fight it, and I'll figure it out. Just – just fight it, keep fighting, and keep living." A lump formed in Aeyun's throat, and he couldn't dare look Seraeyu in the eye. "Don't stop fighting. I won't leave you to be on your own."

"If it comes down to it, Aeyun," Seraeyu said, a quaver preceding the unfinished request. Aeyun knew what he meant. But he couldn't now. He couldn't. He didn't think he had it in him to doom Seraeyu. *Again.* "I'd, well, I'd rather live." Seraeyu chuckled wetly, morbidly, and sniffled again. "But . . . I'm not even sure how I would now."

"I'll figure it out," Aeyun said, trying to convince himself as well. He could feel a thickened bloody trail escaping from his eye, and Seraeyu's expression contorted with concern. "For now, I can't stay. Can you tell me something, anything that might help?"

"You're bleeding. Aeyun, you're . . . you're bleeding," Seraeyu said, fingers timidly extended, tracing a distant path alongside the crimson rivulet. Aeyun nodded, trying to convey that he was aware. Seraeyu seemed to get the message, though he was still shaken. "She's wickedly vengeful. She wants to take down everyone and everything associated with whatever wronged her. Yu-ta, and . . . I don't think she'll stop. She just keeps drawing others in and – I can't, it's–"

"It's enough, Seraeyu. I have to go," Aeyun said as a sharp pain started forming in his head.

He stood and reached out a hand. Seraeyu blinked at it as though it were some strange offering, then carefully slid his hand into Aeyun's and allowed himself to be pulled up. Aeyun watched as the man gave him a small, sad smile in return.

Suddenly, Aeyun was thrown back onto the terrace, feeling as if he'd dropped from the shimmering heavens themselves. The realm felt pressurised and surreal until he was able to centre himself. Once he had, he looked down at the hand that had only just been holding Seraeyu's.

Aeyun had made a mess of things, and now he had to clean it up.

The view beyond his outstretched fingertips was mesmerising, spanning on and on until the horizon swallowed it up. Giants kissing the sky, itself a blue ever-expanding river. This vista was a fantasy he'd never deigned to dream of, both marvellous and terrifying.

Those monoliths that careened up in a static growth were wrapped in pathways and bypassed by a leagues-high bridge that welcomed the motion of a metal monster, fleeing from something so quickly that it must have been promising horrors unknown.

The realm did not shift with his feet. It did not bend for him, carrying him. Instead, he fumbled on, sights and sounds and smells unfamiliar, but all at once enrapturing.

CHAPTER THIRTY-EIGHT

Aeyun was sat in the courtyard the next morning when Davah found him. He couldn't sleep after his jaunt into the in-between, and he'd gone to the knoll before the shrine to listen to the birdsongs. It had been healing, in its own way, to delight in the chirps and whistles one bird sent to the next, the collection of them singing a tune only they understood.

Aeyun was troubled, however. He didn't know how to move forward. He couldn't make sense of his own priorities.

What next?

"Hey, friend," Davah called, plopping down on the grass beside him. Aeyun gave a wry smirk at nothing and hummed. "You doing okay?"

381

"Honestly?"

"Honestly," Davah responded.

"No," Aeyun decided. "Not really. I feel lost."

"That's understandable. We are in the middle of nowhere–"

"That's not what I meant."

"I know what you meant," Davah assured him, then sighed. "Look, everything's gone a bit mad, right? So, let's remember what our goal was. You wanted to find Sakaeri, since you're convinced she's in trouble out there, somewhere. Right?"

"Right," Aeyun said, frowning.

He needed to find Sakaeri. But he also needed to contact Raeyu and Uruji. To talk to his sister. And to liberate Seraeyu from the chokehold this Sirin daemon had on him. And, lest he forget, Saoiri was still trapped in an occupied land.

He knew where Seraeyu was, or at least where his body was. He was in Haebal City, and presumably hadn't left. He was in the Tower when Aeyun . . . possessed him? And wasn't that just a terrifying thought he hoped he never had to circle back to. What if Aeyun marched straight there? What would happen? He'd find Seraeyu, surely, and then he'd – what?

He knew where Raeyu, Uruji, and Da'garu were too. Holed up in that ancient a'teneum, getting friendly with Gama-of-Yun, an acquaintance who seemed more odd with each passing day. That was another conundrum. Sirin, a Yun? What did that even mean? Aeyun groaned, frustrated.

Saoiri he could also place, but Sakaeri was missing. Just *missing*, untraceable. Aeyun had tried to seek her out in the unknown, but it was like banging against a locked door, and Aeyun happened to lack the key. His eyes roved across the courtyard, veering back towards the entrance of the shrine.

They were in whatever this Sirin compound was, and the Sirin had been targeted. Sakaeri was a Sirin. Did whoever orchestrated this massacre seek her out, too? Is that where she'd disappeared to? Spirited away, somehow landing in Kaisa's hands? Or maybe it was Kaisa himself, though Aeyun didn't understand how the man would have annihilated an entire band of Sirin. Whatever the case was, if Aeyun could find whoever did this, he had a hunch it would lead him to Sakaeri.

And he needed . . . They all needed another ally.

Aeyun's abrupt stand made Davah jump.

"I think I have a plan," Aeyun said.

It was half-baked, and it only addressed one problem, but it was something he could put into action. He made a beeline for the shrine and Davah was quick on his tail, keeping pace with his hastened steps. Still shoeless, Aeyun's footfalls landed silently on the marble, and he proceeded all the way to the obsidian mask, adorned with the horns of what Aeyun could only assume was what remained of Sirin.

He snatched the mask off the wall and held it, waiting.

Nothing happened. No pull into the nether, no revelation of great insight, just a faint buzz of a life once lived, now a soft murmur among the grand symphonies. The obsidian stared back at him, and the horns weighed heavily on its crown, dulled from years exposed to the mountain air.

"Friend," Davah said, peering down at the mask. "You're taking that, then?"

"Yep," Aeyun affirmed. "Sakaeri is a Sirin. These people were Sirin. We draw out what came for them, and I think they'll lead us to her, and Kaisa."

"You *want* someone – some*thing* – that murdered a group of deadly Sirin to find us?" Davah asked, and he dragged a hand down his face, like he already knew the answer. "Alright. Okay. Sure, if that's the plan, that's the plan. Maybe you're the mad one here."

Aeyun was starting to feel the same, but he wouldn't admit that out loud.

Half an hour later, they were headed back down to their abandoned sea-skimmer by the shoreline. Aeyun felt like the strangeness of that sanctuary still held intrigue that he wanted to satisfy, but he also didn't want to waste more time. He'd already been comatose for days. Promising himself to look into it again, when time was more forgiving, he and Davah descended the weatherworn stairs. This time, there were no whispering banshees.

When they reached the craft by the water, Davah asked if Aeyun wanted to see if there were alicant to pilfer, given it was a gate. But Aeyun refused.

"We might need to return," he said, and Davah gave him a peculiar onceover.

To Aeyun, Lu-Ghan still felt like a good bet. It was their first lead, and he didn't see a reason to adjust it now that he had some semblance of a plan. When he'd instructed Davah to join him in the hull, his companion just gave him an exasperated sigh.

"Aeyun, friend, I know that you managed to get us here, but how do you intend to use a broken, tiny gate to get us out? You have limits." Davah mumbled the last part, placing the used blankets back in their designated spot.

"I have to try, and there's no way we'd be able to go through Raenaru's gate." It was absurd to think they'd be able to bypass the security there, that Seraeyu – Sirin? – had put in place. "I have to try," Aeyun repeated, then sat down and tried to get himself in a similar state as the previous evening. When he'd been able to reach across the inky expanses.

Davah watched quietly, arms folded as he leant against the side of the hull.

Aeyun first reached out to his Vitality, the breathing force of existence. He could feel the realm around him anew. The waves lapped the shore, expelling their energy and crashing on the sand, little critters below the grains digging and bubbling to the surface. The wind blew through the valley, carrying upon it feathered wings that soared, dipping and diving among invisible air pockets. On the foothills, foliage swayed as mushrooms burst to life above the gloom below; a new beginning for a sudden end.

He felt Davah's pulse across from him, faint, but excited, and he felt his own energy, summoning the realm around him. Welcoming it and greeting the flow of it all like an old friend. He felt the distant tugs of those far off, and the constant ebb of that incorporeal web around his heart.

His vision having gone radiant, Aeyun was satisfied that he'd sung the right tune.

Only then did he beckon Essence. He called it to him, just as he'd called Seraeyu through it the previous night, and he enticed it to carry him to Lu-Ghan. Energy culminated upon the ground, and Aeyun struggled against the pressure of it, willing the realm to lend him guidance. His vision darkened and sound dissipated with a high-pitched ring. In his mind's eye, he saw rustic sigils alight on the grassy rubble below, and bits of ore sparking to life, glowing vibrantly in the grey of the day. He held onto it, both the vision and his desire, and he cried out for Lu-Ghan.

They needed to go to Lu-Ghan.

Lightning surged up from the ground, siphoning through the alicant shards scattered there. It erupted violently around them, flashing white and black, and countless colours that Aeyun couldn't comprehend. As always happened when he jumped realms, he found himself suspended in the nothingness, surrounded by *everything*.

For a moment, the briefest of nonsensical time, Aeyun could *see* Da'garu reading beside an unmoving Gama-of-Yun, high in the uppermost tower of the a'teneum. He could see Uruji studying his own collection of books, lost among its pages. He could see Raeyu walking among a glade, and he could swear that her gaze flickered his direction.

He could see Saoiri, hidden behind heavy curtains as Orinian grunts traipsed past her window, and Sakaeri, mindlessly slashing across another man's throat, no hint of emotion on her face. And he could see Seraeyu stalking through what was left of the Tower, a presence leering over him, horned with long hair cascading down as they whispered in Seraeyu's ear.

The oddest thing was Seraeyu's sudden halt. When it seemed like the daemon's attention was about to lift, Seraeyu reached up and drew it closer, but *his* eyes did meet Aeyun's. There was no question. A connection formed, and Aeyun felt exposed in the expanding aether, a deep molten amber pinning him.

Then it all fell away, and the sea-skimmer crashed into place in a cavern, lightning flashing brightly before being snuffed out, leaving them in darkness. Only in the moments following, in the stillness that resulted, did the glowing flora open themselves again, curiously leaning towards the ruckus.

Aeyun rolled to the side, moaning in discomfort from landing on his shoulder. Davah gave his own groan, holding his head where it had presumably banged on the wall.

"We need something to strap us down, fecking Yun of the stars!"

Davah kept muttering obscenities under his breath, but seemed pleased when he pulled his hand away and discovered no sticky residue between his fingers. Aeyun, on the other hand, had to wipe away a trail of it from his cheek.

"Maybe I should have rebuilt the gate before we did that," he muttered, mostly to himself, but Davah looked up at him.

"You did that," Davah said, as if only just realising it. A wide, toothy grin spread across his face. "You *did* that!"

"I did that!" Aeyun joined in, beaming. "*Starry sea.*"

"Yeah, feckin' stars and all!" Davah agreed, gleeful. Then his delight faded, and he peered around the soft-lit cave beyond the grubby glass panels. "Where are we?"

"Lu-Ghan?" Aeyun was hopeful, but he wasn't sure.

"Are we?" Davah pushed open the hatch. It caught on a batch of puffy, slimy fungus. The bulbous growths wheezed and produced a cloud of glittering dust, as if protesting the assault. "Ah, shite," Davah muttered, tuning a soft wind to blow the particles away from his nostrils.

It took some acrobatics to manoeuvre themselves out of the sea-skimmer between its roof and the cave's ceiling, but they managed,

386

even shoving Azura out with some measured movements. They put on their masks, Aeyun rigidly considering his new Sirin guise before securing it in place. He frowned behind the cold press of obsidian, feeling unnerved with a pair of stolen Yu-ta horns on his head. As they waded carefully through the shallow waters of the cavern, they avoided the odd spongey masses where they could. It was almost reminiscent of his boyhood, when he'd been carried through the current of an underground aquifer.

As they walked for long minutes without indication of an exit, Davah started complaining. Little grunts of discontent here and there. Aeyun understood; he was none too pleased himself. Finally, after what seemed like far too long, light brimmed beyond a rocky ledge, and the two of them huffed in relief.

Noticing the lack of a path up, Aeyun lodged Azura into the cave wall and let Davah climb up first, following after as Davah gave him a hand.

"Woah, would you look at that," Davah exclaimed when their locale came into focus.

They were nowhere near Bhu-Nan, by the looks of it, instead on top of a crevice in the mountainside, the gorge below bridged by an ancient-looking crossing, just beside a dried-up aqueduct. The runic script scraped across the stone where they stood didn't escape Aeyun's notice, nor did the torch-like structures that flanked the scrawl, long having lost their alicant.

Aeyun and Davah shared a look, then hesitantly kept on.

"Most people steer clear of the ancient sites," said Davah. He brushed his fingers across the wall of the crossing, hazarding a look into the depths below. "In fear of what daemons of old might be lurking there." Aeyun listened, letting Davah orate folkish beliefs that hadn't quite breached the gilded walls of Cheyun. "The realms were untamed once; wilder. At least, that's what the stories say."

"Wilder how?"

"Freer, I guess. Creatures were said to have roamed; great beings of the elements, until we tore them down. Fables of our youth, you know?"

"I don't, actually," said Aeyun.

He didn't know the lore of the realms, not like the children who heard them as bedtime tales. When he was young, before Haebal, he'd only known of that which existed inside The Veil. Everything beyond was dust.

"I suppose you wouldn't," Davah conceded, but he didn't elaborate.

"Where in the Great Starry Sea are we?" Aeyun asked once they reached the other side of the pass, rolling hills and meadows stretching out beyond in seemingly endless undulations of magenta and gold; blood-barley's natural colouring. If they were in blood-barley territory, they were probably in the Fan-Bhan region. Assuming Aeyun remembered his geography correctly.

"Which way do you reckon?" Davah asked, folding his palm above his eyes like a visor, trying to see through his mask better. "It could just be me, but I think I see something over there." He indicated to a small, unnatural-looking crest on the horizon. "Like, way over there."

"Yeah," Aeyun agreed.

Sure, he could jump realms through crumbled gates, but he'd have to hoof it through fields to get to any sort of civilisation now. The realms were cruel.

While dawn had been breaking when they'd entered the swelling landscape, the afternoon sun was shining harshly on their backs when they came into what looked to be a small country town, landlocked between the hillside and the mountains. It had a faded sign, held up on half-tumbled stones, on which was scrawled *Lan-Han* – it wasn't a place Aeyun could recall hearing about before.

Surely looking out of place, the pair of them wandered in, garnering stares and glares of all kinds. Soon enough, a brutish man, welted from too many hours in the harsh light, approached them, burly arms crossed.

"I don't know where you came from, but your kind isn't

welcome here," the man groused, and a few other villagers came to flank him.

Aeyun hadn't expected trouble so soon. And he wasn't sure what the man meant by *your kind*. He tilted his head and felt extra weight dip with it. *Oh*, he thought.

"Those aren't attached to his head," Davah said, tamping down his Mhedoon lilt as much as he could. "They're attached to the mask."

The man eyed Davah warily before he shifted his gaze to the horns, scrutinising them.

"You a Yu-ta hunter?"

The question took Aeyun aback because, one, it was odd to hear Yu-ta folk spoken of like animals. And two, the man said it so casually, as if it were a common term. Was it?

"What's it to you?" Davah asked for him, and the villager harrumphed, curling his lip.

"Wondering if you might be for hire. You both look the type," he said. Aeyun felt the penetrating gazes of the villagers over the man's shoulders. "Are you?"

"You're looking to put a hit out on a Yu-ta?" Davah asked, bypassing the man's question with one of his own.

Aeyun stood quietly, his skin crawling at the look on the villager's face as he grunted. It was cold. Detached. Angry.

"We make good coin using our bodies. We take the options we have available to us, and that's either farming or fighting. In the past months, every one of our brothers and sisters who've gone to the proving grounds has come back in a body bag, some of them not even whole. We made an honest living there for ages, but that champion is a menace. A fiend.

"I don't know why she came around, or where she came from, but that blunted freak isn't fooling anyone. We've seen her claws, like a fucking beast from the frigid depths of the void itself. Maybe she fled from the Mad Thasian or maybe she blew damned Oagyu Thasian to bits herself, and now she's come to our proving grounds to get her jollies, who knows. All we know is that she's taking our people for slaughter and stealing our coin. Are you for hire?"

Aeyun's heart was racing. His disgust for the man was overshadowed by his premonition that he was referring to Sakaeri. It had to be. A blunt-horned Yu-ta woman, clawing people to death? Hadn't that been Aeyun's vision?

"Maybe we are. Why wouldn't your little gang here go? Trying to intimidate me and my friend here, but not brave enough to entertain combating one she-daemon?" Davah asked, an edge to his voice that Aeyun wasn't sure he'd heard before.

The villager in front of them scoffed. "I may be brawny, but I've got brains. I understand that I'd be walking to my death. Those of us left figured that out when our fourth came back maimed. One is bad luck. Two is a bad match. Three is cause for concern. And four, well, that's the nail in the coffin. We know we need the real deal. Ours aren't even meant to be in those types of fights, but the prize must be some kind of beauty, if our folk keep going for it."

"When's the next call for the Pit?" Davah asked, establishing that he knew exactly what the villager was referring to. He received a nod of approval from the man and a few behind him.

Aeyun frowned. What a miserable way of life.

"A week's time. The Kaisan make their rounds. They only left here maybe a day ago. They'll be making their circles until then, recruiting." The man paused, curled his mouth into an ugly twist, then asked again, "Are you for hire?"

"What's your offer?" Davah countered like quicksilver. Aeyun failed to hush the small *tsk* that escaped him. It brought the villager's attention over.

"He talk?"

"No, but he fights," Davah said, drawing focus back to him. "Your offer?"

"A stone in coin and our silence about a wandering Doon-for-hire," the man said.

Aeyun determined that he wasn't as dim-witted as he looked.

390

Davah hummed lowly, seeming to consider. It was taking too long for Aeyun's liking, so he smacked his gauntleted hand down against Davah's back.

"Well, my friend here consents, so I guess I do, too," Davah said, a twinge of annoyance in his tone.

The villager nodded, then jabbed a thumb over his shoulder towards a run-down inn. An elderly mutt sat on its stoop, panting in the fading heat of the day.

"You can stay at Lan's free of charge until the Kaisan come. You'll have to make do on your own food though. We have no surplus to give you; we're selling what we can to the capital to make up for the loss at the proving grounds. Both in body count and in coin."

Davah gave the man a nod, shrugging off Aeyun's heavy hand. The made for the inn and the mutt lifted its head, giving them a curious glance. Davah knelt down and gave it a pet, offering soft-delivered praise. The mutt's tail wagged, smacking on the wooden planks below, and Aeyun chuckled.

Davah should adopt and animal companion, he determined. It would suit him. For now, they left the contented canine be and continued on, going to their accommodation as directed.

"Convenient," Davah said once they were alone their provided attic room. "Convenient that we run into someone looking to send fighters to a Pit, eh?"

"Yeah," Aeyun said, still too on edge to remove his mask.

The room was dusty and disused, and he was sure that travellers didn't often cross these lands. There was never much reason to go inland when journeying across realms. If anyone needed to, they tended to use whatever rail or hyperline serviced the landscape. As far as Aeyun could tell, this forgotten town was in the middle of nowhere, its sole economy based on production. And battle tournaments, apparently. Aeyun wondered if most of Kaisa's fighters came from towns like this. The townsfolk were being pawned, used like a resource themselves. He felt for their plight, in a way. From what he'd heard about the Kaisan Pits, though, he doubted it was only novice fighters and alicantists.

One thing the man said rung true: these men and women shouldn't be pitted against Sakaeri by any means. Aeyun wondered why they were. Following a morbid train of thought, he considered that it was bad business, and Kaisa, while he was many wicked things, wasn't a bad businessman.

"It probably would have happened at any backcountry town we came to, to be honest. I suspect it's not just this place's men and women being butchered," Davah said as he dug through his bag to toss Aeyun a tree-borne fruit, then fished out another and bit into it himself.

"Why, though? It doesn't make sense," Aeyun muttered, shifting his mask further up his nose to sink his teeth into the fruit's flesh.

"Why don't you take that thing off? It's creepy," Davah said, gnawing loudly.

Aeyun considered the idea, then said, "I don't know. This place is creepy. I feel creeped out myself."

"Really?" Davah asked, an amused snort leaving him. "Right, we only recently had this conversation. Lots of people live in places like this; you just don't come across them on the main thoroughfares."

Aeyun debated a moment, then removed the obsidian mask and laid it beside him, setting it upon the motheaten blanket.

"We never came somewhere like this when we were hunting ore," he defended, and Davah scoffed.

"Why would we? These people have fuck all, and I wouldn't want to steal from them anyway. I mean, listen," Davah said, leaning forward to rest his elbows on his knees. "These poor lads are systematically sending their loved ones off to the Pit not for glory, but for coin. Because they need it. It's depressing."

"Yeah, I guess you're right," Aeyun said, the fruit pulp gritty in his mouth.

Swallowing thickly, he knew that the next week was going to be a brutal wait.

"I can't do it." The sentiment was followed by a sullen frown.

He offered a gentle smile, recognising the fragility of a task unattainable. "Sure, you can. Don't give up hope."

For a moment, it seemed like something else would be said, some sort of response that felt important, but unwelcomed. A notion, hidden in the depths of something buried, bristled in preparation. But it never came. Instead, he was met with a look of determination.

Claw-nailed fingers gripped tight around a stem, held over the smallest of scrapes, a concentration marring the smoothness of youth. The reciprocating hand, the one that dug into the meadow's blades, curled in concentration.

But then the pinched bud was gone, disintegrated, and wide eyes had turned white-spotted obsidian, only a momentary flash. Grass had browned and wilted, and under the staggered lift of a palm, there sprang a crushed flower that hadn't been there before unfamiliar words were sloppily spoken.

CHAPTER THIRTY-NINE

It hadn't been a week. It hadn't even been three days, and four Kaisan were storming into the village at dusk, shouting for the wayfarers to come out.

Aeyun and Davah collected their things and exited Lan's Inn at a far more leisurely pace than Aeyun's own heart. As soon as one of the ostentatiously dressed Kaisan spotted Aeyun's mask, he pointed and said, "That's the one."

The claim prompted a flurry of action, including the two non-Eye Kaisan darting forward to latch onto Aeyun's arms. With no warning, Davah snatched his harpoon off his waist and elongated it, swinging it deftly to ward off the assault.

"Okay, we'll play nice," said the Kaisan on the right, a slender woman with sharp features and sheared raven hair, her hands up as she backed away.

The Kaisan on the left, a bony man with poor posture and a suture-split, lopsided grin, seemed more stubborn. He held his ground and stared Aeyun down. The two in the back, stone-faced and dull, watched on, surely playing a live feed for Kaisa's enjoyment.

"Where'd you get that mask?" the Kaisan on the left asked, ignoring the sharp point of Davah's blade. Aeyun stayed silent. "Peculiar-looking, that one. Where'd you get it?"

Aeyun didn't dare breathe.

"Kaisa would like to see you," one of the flanking Eyes stated.

Aeyun found himself frowning. This was his plan, wasn't it? But it felt like a piece was missing.

"They were looking to go to the Pit," the villager from the first day spoke up, too far from the group to sound assertive.

"Oh yeah?" the Kaisan on the left piped up again, folding his arms. "Were you now?" He looked back at his colleague behind him with a smirk. "That can be arranged." One of the Eyes looked down at a stone in her hand – a communication stone, clearly – then nodded her consent. "Wanna get warm and cosy in the land-skimmer, boys?"

The man smiled something curled and twisted. When neither Aeyun nor Davah responded, he tutted and turned on his heel, heading back towards the entrance of the town.

The other Kaisan followed the first, tentatively glancing behind her as she did, and the two Eyes waited until Aeyun and Davah formed a line in the middle of the pack. They then followed the pair of them up, gazes burning a hole into the back of their heads.

In the land-skimmer, Aeyun and Davah sat flush, side by side.

As far away from the other inhabitants as possible. Those crossed irises had yet to look away, and it was making Aeyun antsy. Beside him, Davah wiggled his foot, the one on top of his crossed ankles, clearly feeling *watched* himself.

"You're a weird pair, aren't you?" That same loud-mouthed Kaisan asked, gazing at them, amused. The woman to his right, the other non-Eye, smacked his knee in an attempt to get him to shut up. "Quiet, yeah?"

"Leave them be, Jjenka. They'll be answering to Kaisa soon enough anyway," the woman chided, seemingly not at all interested in engaging with their 'guests'.

Jjenka scowled and raised his arms up to cross them behind his head. An attempt to get comfortable.

"You make life boring," he told the woman, kicking his legs up on the table before him.

The Eye on the other side of him glanced down at the stone in his hand. "You may interrogate them," he said monotonously.

Jjenka's smile grew serpentine. He grabbed the Eye's face and angled it towards him, blowing a kiss in the air.

"Kaisa, you're a blessed being, did you know that?" Jjenka smacked the Eye's cheek playfully when he'd conveyed his message – the Eye didn't react – then he leered at Aeyun and Davah. "So, are you mute by choice? Or can you speak?"

Silence continued. Jjenka scowled.

"Okay, let's assume you're actually mute. You can hear, though, right?"

He pointed to his ear, the motion derogatorily slow. When it still failed to produce a reaction, Jjenka swung his feet down from the table and growled.

Aeyun did not want to deal with this lot; any of them. The constant surveillance was making him desperately uneasy, and Jjenka's jeers were pissing him off. All he wanted was to save Sakaeri and then figure out how to get to Ca'lorus. Because maybe Gama-of-Yun could sort out this mess with him, given it was apparently another Yun – whatever the *fuck* that actually meant – who held Seraeyu's soulsong. Nothing was moving fast enough, and that included the damned land-skimmer.

"So, why were you wanting to hop into the Pit?" Jjenka asked, looking like a new ploy was dancing in his head to get them to speak. "Is it that Sirin? You want to recover her, your lost sister-in-arms? Or maybe you wanted to off her yourself, for having been led astray? Or maybe–" Aeyun didn't like the look in Jjenka's eyes. "–Maybe you wanted her as your own toy?"

As it turned out, Jjenka had found a button to push, since Aeyun involuntarily clenched his fist to keep it from flying.

Jjenka watched it play out triumphantly.

"Ah, how sweet. Is she your love? Why'd you take so long, then? I'd say she's nearly broken by now. A mindless thing, that woman. Just a creature."

Livid, Aeyun could feel his anger boil down to his core and his next action he did by accident. A radiance grew behind his obsidian mask and Aeyun could feel Vitality flowing through the air. He could feel where it wound around Jjenka's soulsong, and he grabbed at it, imposing his deep sense of loathing upon it. It wasn't until Davah roughly elbowed him that he realised what he was doing. He dropped his hold, seeing that Jjenka had retreated back into his seat, eyes wide.

The remainder of the trip was spent in tense silence, Aeyun keeping his head down to not look at the Eyes who watched him. He didn't know what the rest of them were doing, and he didn't care to find out. The only person he held any penchant for was Davah, whose foot relentlessly wiggled until the land-skimmer finally came to a stop.

"Out," the Eye to the far side intoned.

Aeyun wasted no time exiting the craft. Davah landed beside him, and the two of them backed away from the four Kaisan as they emerged. Seemingly over his short-lived terror, Jjenka motioned for the two of them to spin around. They did so begrudgingly and saw the exterior of a massive arena, shrouded beneath a large overhang clinging to the topography above. It looked like a repurposed build, supplemented with modern architecture and technology.

Aeyun sensed the Kaisan approaching from behind. To avoid their touch, he placed a hand on Davah's back and pushed the pair of them forward. They walked towards the arena's entrance, the promenade lined with statues of fearsome figures and impressions of prizes won. Glowing alicant lined the path, and a generous draping of fluorescent particle ore danced near the ticket counter.

Aeyun hated it. All of it. The ostentatiousness, the spectacle of it, the promise of glory – it was all awful. The brainchild of someone too keen on presentation.

"You go that way," Jjenka announced smugly from behind, indicating to a darkened side entrance.

Aeyun inwardly bid the man good riddance when he offered a short, cheerful wave and veered away, pulling the other non-Eye Kaisan with him. Now left with their two hawk-eyed keepers, Aeyun and Davah dipped towards the shadowed door, nudging it open when one of the Eyes instructed them to do so.

They were led to a waiting room, painted in grey and lined with leather seating. A melody was playing from a music box in the corner, something soft and jazzy, and Aeyun glared at it in disdain. Of course, Kaisa would butter up his clients and combatants with some sensual ambiance.

Davah was nearly bursting to speak; Aeyun could tell he was holding himself back, though. All for the sake of anonymity. Eyes still stood watch just outside the door.

Cheers sounded in the distance, along with a jubilee of victorious music that clashed terribly with the notes from the music box.

Aeyun wondered if someone had just been murdered.

"What a beautiful match, a beautiful match, honestly!" Kaisa gushed as he burst through the doors, the Kaisan outside pulling them shut behind him. "Ah, you should have seen it. A dodge left, a leap right, then *rip*, right through the ribcage." Kaisa hummed appreciatively as he plopped himself down on a plush chair across from them. "I never tire of it." His distracted gaze finally trailed over to the pair of them and something in his eyes darkened. "How interesting. Last I saw that mask, it was hanging in a room full of dead bodies."

So, Kaisa had been there. He'd seen it.

"Are you a Sirin? Too little too late, I'm afraid." Kaisa tutted, feigning disappointment, then smiled smarmily. "You've come here with a friend to participate, have you? Have some fun in my little arena of death and joy?"

Aeyun couldn't believe he'd once offered this man one of his wares.

"Are you perhaps a Sirin as well? I doubt it," Kaisa said, looking Davah up and down. "No matter. I'll gladly let you compete. Will you enjoy seeing your comrade? I wonder. Here now, here."

Kaisa pulled his shirt collar aside, indicating that they do the same. A symbol was branded on his skin, an old calligraphy, and Aeyun stifled a gasp.

It was a rune. There was a rune seared into Kaisa's *skin*.

"If you want to join the club, you have to get one of these," Kaisa said, brushing over the skin just beneath his clavicle. "Just some excitement." He waited, seemingly growing impatient when neither Aeyun nor Davah moved. "Come on now. Else I regrettably cannot let you participate. Come on."

Filled with trepidation, Aeyun pulled down his collar and lengthened his neck, allowing Kaisa access to the indicated area. The pitmaster grinned foully, toeing up to Aeyun. He took his time carving the shape of the symbol there, and it sizzled into place painfully with the help of Kaisa's pyre-ringed finger. Once he was done, he smiled and patted the tender, scorched skin.

"There now, not so bad," he cooed. Aeyun took three steps back to gain some distance between himself and the man. He repeated this with Davah, then proudly appraised them, like gems on display. "Ah, I won't be the only one excited for these coming bouts. Don't let me down."

Kaisa exited as breezily as he entered, and the door latched closed behind him.

Once alone, Davah yanked down his collar and spun towards Aeyun. Aware of their guards, Aeyun lifted a finger to his mouth to indicate silence, then dug into his satchel and pulled out some moss he'd smuggled from the shrine's grounds before they left. As quietly as possible, he descanted a stitch on Davah, erasing the putrid mark, then did the same to himself. He didn't know what it was for, but whatever it was, it was gone now.

Their waiting ended an hour later when the door creaked open again, a muscled woman with a long scar down her face standing on the other side.

"You first," she pointed at Davah.

Reluctantly, Davah stood up. He offered one last look at Aeyun, then he was swept away beyond those heavy metal doors.

Aeyun was alone.

Every jeer, boo, and cheer of the crowd made him jump. He was listening on the edge of his seat, straining his ears for any indication of Davah's pain. The crowd finally roared to life, drowning out that callously ambient score inside the room, and Aeyun stood up, unwittingly at their mercy. Endless minutes later, Davah was shoved back into the room. Aeyun rushed to him, holding him steady after the woman's push had him teetering. The door latched again and Aeyun panickily poked and prodded.

Davah pushed Aeyun's wandering hands away and limped towards the sofa, falling down onto it. There, he indicated towards his knee, and said, "Torn."

Aeyun ripped out some more moss, thought about it, then doubled the quantity and crushed it in one hand. He knelt down and laid his palm on Davah's ripped ligament, descanting as quietly as he had done before.

When the sound of the metal dislodging resounded from the entryway, Davah forcefully shoved Aeyun away, and Aeyun tumbled back, catching himself on his elbows. The scar-faced woman flitted her attention between the two of them, then snorted, and Aeyun had the distinct impression she'd come to the wrong conclusion.

She indicated to Aeyun, waving a hand towards the hallway. He got up and snatched Azura from where he'd leant the aerofoil on the wall, then offered a look back at Davah, mirroring his friend's departure. That wooden mask gazed back until the door latched closed.

The atmosphere outside the room was cold and clinical. Aeyun kept on, each step feeling more damning than the last. When he finally reached a set of gates, another Kaisan was there, waiting impatiently among the washed-out glow of snowy particle ore.

"You're up, buddy. Dunno who you are, but good luck, I guess," the Kaisan said, unlocking the gate and urging it open.

Aeyun took another hesitant step and was instantly slammed with the cries of a greedy crowd, ready for more gore as they noticed the gates welcoming the next warriors. He dropped a hand over his mask to make sure it was secure, then walked out fully, passing by stands full of onlookers. Where had all these even people come from?

He scanned the sea of heads, and he was disgustedly nonplussed to find some high-ranking representatives from the realms among them. Mostly sat in what seemed to be extravagant viewing boxes. Aeyun's boots left tracks in the dirt-laden ground, and he felt Azura's perturbed buzz, an aversion to the masses. He scrubbed his bare hand down it, hoping to calm its energy.

"A wanderer most peculiar!" an announcer cried, startling Aeyun enough that his head snapped in the direction of the shout. It was a woman adorned with clashing colours and wrapped in jewellery that looked as though it were pilfered from Thasian storehouses. "A wild sight that we've yet to witness: the Bone Soldier!"

Another deafening roar resounded throughout the arena, and Aeyun felt crushed beneath it.

"Against this bonified brute we have the one, the only: the Pyromancer!"

From the other side of the arena, a woman walked towards Aeyun. She was dressed flagrantly, her clothes fitting her motif. Aeyun squinted. It wasn't Sakaeri. He took a deep breath. But she was in his way to finding Sakaeri, so he would have to fight.

The woman raised her hands, egging on cheers. Aeyun sneered at the gaudy showmanship.

The announcer's voice rung out again. "This preliminary is a special bout, and a step towards qualifying for our grand prize. And today, my dearest pals, we have the rapt attention of the realms! We have viewers from all of our beautiful destinations, including the Dracon of Orin!"

An image of the sitting king of Orin appeared in the dedicated holocaster, her reflection looking regal and ill-suited to this brutality. Aeyun scowled at it.

"And we have our very own Praetor of the Thasian Legacy—"

Aeyun's heart skipped a beat, and he turned to the holocaster on the opposite side of the arena. There, the dead-eyed impression of Seraeyu sat, adorned with all the crystals and jewels royalty draped upon themselves, his attire similarly much too refined for this kind of low-brow entertainment.

A quiet desperation overtook him, and he searched the stands for where the Eye was broadcasting the image from. To his dismay, he zeroed in on an uppermost corner, an area filled not with Sentinels but with Draconguard. Yet there Seraeyu sat, a mere impression at this distance. Even still, a phantom presence hung just out of sight, and Aeyun could see – or perhaps feel – whispers of another by Seraeyu's ear.

His gaze flickered back to the holocaster. He couldn't tear his eyes away from the cold dissociation, the image so disparate from the man he'd called to him in the in-between.

Seraeyu.

"Fight!" the announcer cried.

Aeyun barely had enough time to lunge left to avoid a blast of fire. The burst of warmth that followed felt like it grazed his skin, heating the air in the arena. He feinted right, then crossed

401

left again and sized up his opponent.

He could get through this.

Yet to take action, Aeyun could feel the crowd's unrest long minutes later. But he was taking his time, learning his adversary's moves. She was self-taught, that much was clear, but she was disciplined in her own technique. Her movement was fluid, like flowing lava. Then came the ignition. Bright, loud, and sudden. And gone just as quickly as it appeared. It had to be finite.

The woman, the Pyromancer, had more ore stashed away, plucked out as needed. Aeyun wondered how often they were left to rest or replaced altogether. He spotted a bag attached to her hip, so he guessed she had even more hidden there. Waiting it out likely wasn't an option.

While the woman was quick, she was rash in her movements. Much like a licking flame, her feet would carry her forward, then back, then to the side, then the other. It was a haphazard pattern, yet a structure remained. If Aeyun could use that to his advantage, he might make things easier on himself. He did his best to maintain a distance, enough that he could twist out of the way from a burst of flames, and enough that he could take action when the time was right. He jumped back once, twice, another time, and he could see the frustration on her face as she lurched forward.

Now, he thought, and he pulled Azura off his back, giving the aerofoil a great swing before flinging it forward. Azura glided through the air, impacting the woman with a resounding smack. She flew backwards and Azura triumphantly returned to Aeyun's awaiting hand. The crowd erupted around him, but he watched the Pyromancer right herself with bared teeth, clearly displeased at the new development.

It continued like that for a few rotations around the arena, and the viewers were starting to vocalise their discontent of the endless chase. The woman paused and swivelled her head warily. For some reason, she almost looked panicked, then she seemed to build her own resolve. With it, she ran straight towards Aeyun.

Unused to the direct approach, he moved to the side, but her direction followed, unhindered, so he shoved Azura into the dirt before him. Just in time to guard against a vortex of flame.

He thanked whatever built the fabric of the Great Starry Sea that Azura was made of durable acid-whale bone.

The woman had not abated. She twisted around Azura's barrier, bracer-bearing wrist too close to Aeyun's face, so he raised his gauntlet-covered hand in retaliation. An explosion burst open from her fist, flinging his body across the field. As Aeyun rolled to a stop, he feared the worst, that he wouldn't be able to see due to injury. But his vision was fine. It was his hearing that was impaired, a shrill ringing piercing his eardrums. His hand drifted up and he felt the surface of the obsidian, hissing when he touched its heat. But the inside was fine. Cool and fine.

He stood, slowly, and the woman, now far from him, stared shocked. He glanced down at his gauntlet, where an odd energy had pulled and culminated; he could feel it accumulating where the seed lay embedded. Aeyun stretched his fingers – had it absorbed the blast?

Curious, he held his hand out and expelled what had gathered. Likely compounded with other leeched energies, the result was as generous as it was frightening. Vines burst forth, growing first up his arm and clinging around it, then plunging violently into the ground before they speared up around the woman, caging her between thorny masses. Energy rolled off the growths before it zipped around the arena. A rush of blue-hot flashfire erupted, roaring up in cyclonic bursts. In the aftermath, smoke rose in its wake, clouding the trough of the arena in a thick haze. Aeyun stumbled back a step, a little overwhelmed at the result.

The Pyromancer looked leg-locked, staring at him in awed dread. She crashed to her knees and held her hands up, a sign of surrender. Aeyun receded the seed's tune, then began walking back to Azura. When he reached the pair of them, his aerofoil embedded by his downed opponent, the woman didn't look up, but she did speak.

"What kind of daemon are you?"

"What's the grand prize?"

"A . . . place in the Stimfal," she murmured, and Aeyun could see her attention dart to the coming Kaisan. "Retirement from this. Honour. Pension."

Even as a Kaisan led her away, Aeyun found himself mulling over her words. The Stimfal? What was the Stimfal? How did it offer honour, and what service was provided for its pension?

Aeyun spared another glance at Seraeyu's holocaster. He had the same empty stare, but when Aeyun looked towards the viewing box high in the stands, the wraith-like parasite that clung onto Seraeyu's shoulders looked clearer than before, her features more distinct to his eyes.

Aeyun couldn't shake the sense of familiarity.

She never liked the way he looked at her.

He sported horns cradled in messy hair, like he either didn't know how or didn't bother to make it less unruly. He wandered around with this reverence that made little sense, not for a child plagued with the task of bodyguard and tool of ceremony.

When he looked at her it felt uncanny. It felt intrusive and belittling. It felt cruel, and it felt subjugating.

Mostly, though, it vexed her because when he looked at her, standing in the shadow of a father who often raised a brow but nothing more, she could feel him reaching out. Trying to connect without knowing why, and without knowing how.

She wanted none of it, so she always turned away.

CHAPTER FORTY

Sakaeri stumbled down the hall, only half-aware of what she was doing. When she knocked into the corridor wall, off balance, no one helped her. They never did, the bastards. They simply stood back and waited for her to right her footing. She kept on, the lights above bearing down angrily, bitter with their smiting glare.

Something in her stomach felt damaged. Or was it her chest? Whatever it was, it hurt. *Bad.*

"That was a good match," Kaisa said, standing at the end of the strait, just beside the door she was meant to return to.

Whenever there were matches like this, they put her in one of the general waiting rooms. It disgusted her that she looked forward to the plush couch within it – a gruesomely welcome change compared to her cell – since it also meant she'd be ripping people's throats out.

That's what Kaisa liked to do, it seemed. Have her rip into her opponents' jugulars, using her battle-ready fingers for sick entertainment. It was feral and animalistic. Somehow, she'd become his trained mutt. It made her *sick*.

She wasn't a stranger to death, and she wasn't a stranger to being its harbinger. Sakaeri, however, didn't kill for sport. This was grotesque, the show that Kaisa put on. And Sakaeri had become nothing more than a puppet in his hands. Those pitted against her weren't even warriors of any valour, just cannon fodder. Poor souls so desperate to get their hands on the promise of wealth – and whatever that promise was, she was sure it wasn't worth it – that they corralled their fear and took on the foul creature Kaisa commanded her to be.

If she had known what he could do, what he was capable of, she would have steered far, far away from him a long time ago. Kaisa, she figured, could very well be the most powerful man in the realms. Aside from Seraeyu, who spectated these games.

The glimpses of her memory while in the arena told her that Seraeyu watched, stone-faced and steely-eyed. He didn't look like the child he once was, years ago. Raeyu's sly, troublemaking younger brother.

She never *really* found issue with Seraeyu. She even understood him, to some extent. So what if he indulged too much or wasn't quite what Raenaru wanted to see in a leader? So what if he didn't lay down his autonomy for the populace's every whim and want? She hadn't given it a second thought, only thinking him reckless – not that she could talk, she considered – at least until his fist punched through her father's chest. Then his recklessness turned into power lust, and that's when she saw what others did.

An angry, spiteful, self-centred brat, wanting for everything he didn't have, simply because he didn't have it. Someone so consumed by their desire for *more* that it overtook them, turning them into a beast of their own making.

Seraeyu didn't have to be that way, but he chose it. The snarky second sibling she knew from the Tower was replaced with someone cold and cruel, wanting to rule the realms with an iron fist. At least, that's who stared down at her from his private box. That's who had been flanked by Orinian Draconguard, callously watching as another of her victims perished in a gush of crimson viscera.

It didn't make *sense*, yet that was the reality of it. Praetor Seraeyu Thasian, head of the Thasian Legacy, was no longer the boy who asked if she was okay through his sobs, shaking out of his own skin. He was something new and terrifying. There wasn't a drip left of the empathy Sakaeri thought he couldn't turn off. But *why?*

Kaisa opened the door for her, and she winced as she sat down on the couch.

"Mm, you've been in better shape, haven't you?"

She ignored him.

"I have a very special surprise for you," he gloated. She still didn't look up, instead nursing her sore left side. "It seems your friends have decided to pay a visit. Odd, considering they should all be dead."

That got her attention.

Sakaeri looked up and Kaisa smiled charmingly at her. She fought the urge to spew her barely digested rations. If only she could rip *his* throat out, but even as the longing thought filtered through her brain, she could feel the burn of the mark below her clavicle. If she could, she would. He'd be one of the very few that deserved such a gruesome way to go.

"You know what's even more odd? They showed up in that mask – you know the one." Kaisa indicated with two fingers over his head, making them look like horns.

Horns? A horned mask? Her heart dropped with one loud thump. *The Sirin mask? How? Anyone who survived that massacre went into hiding . . .*

"Oh, you think it's odd, too?" Kaisa laughed airily. "Interesting.

407

All of this is so intriguing. So much fun, really! I just – ah, thank you, for making my life so entertaining."

"You're disgusting," she ground out, rebelling against the strain in her throat.

Was something swollen?

"No, dear, no. I'm just making the most of the realms we live in. Eat or be eaten, isn't it? I just happen to have some very sharp teeth." Kaisa smiled. "Lucky me!"

The tell-tale burn at the base of her neck sizzled and she gave him a glare that she hoped promised death in the most vulgar, obscene way imaginable.

Kaisa just grinned back, as he always did. "It's time for some fun, darling."

By the time she was stumbling back into the welcomed embrace of soft cushions, she was halfway certain that her rib was broken. Spitting out blood on the shaggy carpet – and wishing whichever Kaisan it fell to a very fun time trying to get that stain out – she was heaving in shallow breaths. At this rate, she wasn't even sure she'd have the chance to meet this mysterious Sirin persona. But maybe that would be a good thing.

Who would have been stupid enough to go back there? Well, Sakaeri had, but that was foolish then as it was now. But after getting a message like that, from well-mannered Yujuna, of all people, she had to return. Just to see. And she saw all of it. All the remnants of mayhem, the corpses littered in the main hall.

At the time, she didn't understand why they'd turned on one another, only knowing by Kaisa's calling card – a coin with an emblem of his own design, used for betting at his racketeering stands – that he'd played a part.

Sirin weren't a loyal bunch, but there was an unspoken agreement between themselves. They took care of their own, and that included the more nefarious *take care* command when one of them flew astray. But an all-out bloodbath at the temple? That never sat right with her. But now, after months of torment, she got it.

They hadn't turned on each other. Kaisa had. Kaisa did it all.

"Hey, I have medicine for you."

Sakaeri didn't bother moving when Wen entered. She knew it made no difference now and, of all of them, Wen was the least of her worries.

"I'm so very grateful," Sakaeri bit out, but Wen didn't take the bait. She never did.

"They're both men, if that means anything to you."

It took a second, then Sakaeri cracked an eye open. "Hm?"

Wen paused where she sat on the table in front of Sakaeri, having halfway twisted open the tincture's cap. "The other Sirin. But . . . I'm not sure they're Sirin at all."

"No?" Sakaeri asked, despite herself.

Wen started at the cap again, and it came loose with a pop. She urged Sakaeri up in a sitting position, her eyes scanning across her for the worst of the damage. Unfortunately for Sakaeri, it was likely the majority of it was internal rather than external, and there was no way Wen would be able to fix a fractured bone with a salve.

"One of them has that creepy mask, the one Kaisa said is from your compound. But the other has a wooden one. Their weapons aren't an assassin's weapons, either. They just . . . don't seem the right type."

Sakaeri couldn't let herself hope. There was a comically slim chance that any of this would work in her favour.

"They were trying to head to the Pit anyway, when we picked them up." Wen paused, a look of concentration on her face as she covered a particularly deep gash. "The one in the obsidian mask did something weird to Jjenka, too. I don't know what, but he was trying to goad the guy about you and then there was this really tense moment and Jjenka looked like he barely survived a living nightmare. I've never witnessed him rendered speechless before."

"Why are you telling me this?"

Wen leant back but refused to look up. Instead, she quietly set the tincture aside. Her hands hovered above the table's edge, as if she wasn't quite sure where to put them.

"I've played a part in some awful things, Sakaeri. I can't claim otherwise." She sucked in a breath, finally peering up regretfully at Kaisa's prized prisoner. "But you didn't deserve this."

"I probably deserve a lot of things," Sakaeri admitted, wheezing against her rib. "But *no one* deserves this."

It wasn't quite charged, the moment that passed, but it was certainly loaded. It ended with Wen glancing away ashamedly.

"If they manage it, I hope I never see you again," she muttered. Somehow it came across as one of the kindest things anyone had said to Sakaeri in this wretched place.

"Will you take care of Goeth, if I'm suddenly gone?"

Sakaeri wasn't sure where the question bubbled up from, but it felt important. She wanted some assurance that the man wouldn't be left to shrivel in her absence. Although perhaps that would be the kinder fate.

She wasn't expecting Wen to cock her head sideways with a confused furrow of her brow. "Goeth?"

Sakaeri blinked at her. "Goeth. You know, the old, tattooed miscreant a few cells down from me?"

The line between Wen's brow deepened, and Sakaeri tried not to read it as concern.

"Sakaeri, you were the only one in that block."

That didn't make sense.

"You were always the only one in that block. Kaisa wanted you isolated." Wen's attention flittered upwards, as if recalling something, then she carefully brought her gaze back to Sakaeri. "But Goeth was—"

The metal door across the room slammed open and Kaisa strode in, all smiles and anticipation. He ushered Wen away – though she managed to give Sakaeri one last glance that communicated *something* that couldn't quite be decoded – then pressed his index finger to the mark against his own skin.

"Okay, my little flightless bird. The final show is about to begin."

"I think you play everyone for a fool."

The statement had him whirling around, looking into amber eyes that didn't shy under the scrutiny. Instead, he found a scowl, but it wasn't necessarily accusatory like the sentiment it followed.

More disillusioned.

"Some sort of guardian; a pining steward, are you?" Now the words were harsh, punctuated with a scoff, aiming to stab a few holes in his façade. "I think you're just a lost lamb. You've no clue what you're at any more than the rest of us, least of all me in this fucked-up Tower."

"I don't know what you're trying to say."

But he did. He could sense it. Worse still, he could see it.

"I think you're just squishy nonsense under all that glaring intimidation you try to pull. I think you're turned upside-down and backwards in a realm where you feel you don't belong–"
A gesture was made to marble halls and tufted curtains. "–and burrowed beneath all that full hearty determination is just one man who can't accept his own weaknesses."

There was a pause, just a short breath.

"Take it from someone well aware of his own. Unless you face yourself head-on and accept your puny, pathetic mortality instead of regurgitating this joke that the realms call order . . .

"One day, Aeyun, you'll get yourself killed fighting for something that you don't even believe in."

CHAPTER FORTY-ONE

The matches kept going, and Aeyun was exhausted. He would heal up his and Davah's wounds when he had the chance, then one of them would be sent back out. Every time Aeyun entered the arena, his attention was drawn towards Seraeyu's position, as if he expected to see something change. It never did. There he sat, a regal reflection of the Orinian king only a few paces over, posture too rigid to label as recognisable.

Eventually, Davah returned from his last match and motioned across his neck. He was out, and his arm was broken. Aeyun made a move to try and stitch up his injury – his supply was running low, and his energy was depleting along with it – but the door opened too soon.

Aeyun was ushered out into the hall, and an odd air of finality hung in its corridor, lingering like petrichor. When he reached the gate, the Kaisan there nodded.

"Last round today, buddy. I hope you make it. You're a unique one, I'll give you that," he said, pushing the metal latch apart.

Something was different. Something was *there*. Aeyun could feel it as soon as his boot hit the dirt. The atmosphere was oppressive, and it crept into him like an illness, crawling up his insides in a sick preparatory dread. He kept walking, and when he turned the corner, a figure was stood in the centre of the arena, head down.

"Friends of Kaisa!" the announcer called out. A hush fell over the audience. "We've come to our final event for the evening. It's time to welcome our very own terror, the nightmare that stalks your dreams: the Widowmaker!"

The crowd didn't scream. They didn't cheer, and they didn't shout. Instead, there was a slow build of fists and feet pounding, and an elevating chant of *kill them dead, kill them dead*, again and again and again.

Aeyun looked on, horrified.

What in the entirety of the frigid void was happening?

"In this very special and unprecedented match, our favourite morbid machine will be up against tonight's reigning champion: the Bone Soldier!"

A roar of cheers rang out, but Aeyun was focused on one thing. The Widowmaker. Her familiar stature, twisted into something gnarled. Her proud shoulders hunched, unnaturally so, and her expression shallow and unfeeling. A cold, emotionless brutality stood stalwart there, mocking the fiery frenzy that it had replaced.

Sakaeri stood there. Or what was left of her did.

Aeyun walked slowly, making his way to the centre of the arena. Sakaeri didn't look up the entire time, her gaze angled down, and Aeyun noticed how unkempt she appeared. Hair matted, clothes ripped, a long scar trailing down her leg. Where was her cloak? Where were her weapons? Where were her alicant?

She just stood there, bloodstained and vacant.

His gaze latched onto one thing. Around her arm, that ring of metal that was once so pristine did not gleam as it used to. It was tarnished and sunk into her skin, the imprint of her own hand wrapped around it, distorted as one would expect when a burning touch met molten metal.

She had refused to let that one *stupid* gift go. And dammit, she didn't have to have done that. Aeyun could have made her another. Raeyu could have given her another. They could have made and given her a hundred more.

She hadn't needed to cause herself more pain.

When Sakaeri did finally look up, her eyes were dull, not unlike the uncanny and empty look Seraeyu held, yet somehow different. When she lumbered a little unnaturally to the side, Aeyun saw the small marking below her clavicle. The little rune looked scabbed painfully into her skin. As he stared, it seared to life, burning deeper into her flesh.

Before the announcer even had the chance to start the fight, Sakaeri lurched forward, claws aiming for his throat. Aeyun hopped back, wide-eyed through the slits of his mask.

414

Sakaeri looked absolutely feral. She reared her teeth and snarled, knuckles curled, poised to attack. Aeyun stumbled back again.

What happened to her? It was the rune, right? Somehow, the rune–

Sakaeri dove towards him again, now aiming for his ankles. She managed to catch him, fingers wrapping around a boot, tugging, and Aeyun fell. Sharpened nails dug into his shin and tore down, drawing raw and bloodied chunks with it, and Aeyun choked out a pained gasp, trying to scramble back more. Sakaeri continued to crawl, piercing into his body with each gain, until finally she sat over him, and he was looking straight into her eyes. She drew back her arm, ready to strike–

Sakaeri! Aeyun called, reaching across a radiant aetherscape, crying out to a girl in an ill-suited housemaid's robe to let him lead her back to safety.

At the same time, he could swear that he heard Raeyu's cry of *Aeyun* ring out.

Sakaeri hesitated, just for a moment, and Aeyun used it to his advantage to dig a hand into his satchel. Gripping onto what was left of the moss there, he placed his other hand over the ugly runic scar. He wanted nothing more than to rid her skin of Kaisa's nightmarish claim.

Kaisa couldn't be allowed to keep her.

Not Sakaeri.

No one owned Sakaeri. No one would ever be allowed to own Sakaeri but Sakaeri herself.

"*Ca'ou ju, cah e'ju, ou'ju.*"

Beneath his hand, a white radiance grew, seeping into the abused flesh. There was a limit to what could be healed, and Aeyun truly was no god. He could not remove damage done so fiercely, so repetitively. He could not erase it, but he could, perhaps, overwrite it.

It was an ugly realisation. Exchanging Kaisa's mark for his own. Forever leaving Sakaeri with damage that would never be erased.

Above him, the husk of the woman he knew growled. Something low and primal and utterly *wrong*.

He could only hope she'd forgive him, then he forced caustic power into his palm. Potent Vitality spoiling layers of flesh where the scarring was too hardened to heal.

The recognition returning to Sakaeri's eyes was the most gruelling part. The anguish that was held there ripped into Aeyun's heart, creeping into his soulsong, and he wanted to weep for her. With her.

"You," she breathed, voice rasping, like the word fought to be spoken in the first place. Aeyun just nodded dumbly, not shifting in the slightest lest he blunder the hex's removal. "You're here."

"Of course I am."

"You *stars-damned* idiot!" she spat, but it lacked all malice and was instead wrapped in what Aeyun didn't dare to dream was affection.

Ignoring the pain in his punctured leg, Aeyun shuffled his body upwards and looped his arm under hers, urging them into a standing position. Confused shouts floated through the audience. Aeyun nearly burst out laughing when Sakaeri visibly stopped herself from gesturing rudely to the Eye feeding his focus to the main holocaster.

Aeyun flickered his gaze over the crowd. Kaisa, up on his balcony, looked none too pleased. But, concerningly, also not particularly confounded. His expression settled somewhere between disappointment and exasperation. The only attention Aeyun spared elsewhere was towards Seraeyu, who had stood and bellied up to the edge of his viewing box, taking a keen interest in the goings-on below.

But was that Seraeyu, or . . .

"Hey – hey! What do you think you're doing?" the Kaisan at the gate shouted.

Aeyun was about to tune with something, anything, but Sakaeri slammed a hand over Aeyun's ear. Right where a studded pyre alicant was pierced through his lobe.

"Fuck *off*!" she shouted. The gate was blasted apart by the fiery shockwave sent forth from her thrusted palm, the guardsman smashing against the wall, unconscious.

Aeyun cursed under his breath but took the cue and launched them towards the opening.

"Where are we going?" Sakaeri wheezed, holding onto her side. "My lung better not be punctured after all this."

Aeyun glanced worriedly to the side. "You gonna make it?"

"Yeah, I'm gonna fucking make it," she growled.

He wasn't sure which one of them she was trying to convince.

Breaching the hallway, Aeyun spotted the two Eyes stationed in front of the waiting room door. They both snagged on his gaze. He reached out, but Sakaeri beat him to it again and blasted them away with enough force to blow a crater in the wall, negating the need to force the door open. As soon as Davah saw them, he looked up and got to his feet, loosely cradling his own broken bone.

Sakaeri tensed but Aeyun whispered, "Davah," and it placated her enough to stand down. Now a battered and bruised triad, they ripped down the hall like a hurricane.

"Ore?" Davah called out, breathless in his hastened gait.

Aeyun shook his head in one sharp move. "No time!"

When they finally reached the threshold to outside, Sakaeri blew the door open with just as much fervour as she'd displayed on the way there. Just paces beyond, Kaisa stood, looking like he couldn't decide whether he wanted to be angry or amused.

"What a development," Kaisa said, watching the three of them as they skirted around his presence. "This looks oddly familiar," he commented, and Aeyun tried to calm his erratic heart.

Sakaeri was grumbling profanities while Kaisan collected on the path, blocking their way out. In the distance, Aeyun could spot a pair of horns he recognised all too well. His pulse picked up, thrumming harsh and wild. He was *not* prepared for this.

"This is bad," Davah whispered, and Aeyun nodded.

He didn't know how to get them out of this. He was drained, and he wasn't sure he could even call on Essence with his Vitality as dried up as it was. Surely, if he did, it would result in something erratic, and Aeyun didn't want to risk killing both himself and his companions when they'd only just escaped. Last time he had so little control over his attunement with Essence, it had resulted in innocents' deaths.

He couldn't shoulder that again. He still couldn't cope with what had happened before.

Ideally, they'd bypass Kaisa and his small legion of Kaisan. But as the numbers gained on the pathway, it wasn't just Kaisan they'd have to navigate. Crowds were funnelling out from the arena, curious and flustered by the last fight. When they found the Kaisan pitmaster himself standing on the walk, they formed a crescent around the scene, chattering to their neighbours and eyeing the three battle-weary fighters pinned between the arena and their entertainment orchestrator.

Seraeyu – Sirin? – was also nearly upon them, forcibly removing people from his path. Aeyun couldn't decide whether to focus on him or Kaisa.

Aeyun just wanted to get back to the sea-skimmer stranded in the cavern. He wanted to take Davah and Sakaeri and get out of this nightmarish land. Lead them to that crumbled gate and harmonise with the assistance of the alicant and sigils there, as he suspected he might be able to do, if he still had a damned conduit.

He felt stuck, lost.

Then a reckless idea struck him.

Perhaps he had no gate. Perhaps he had no runes. Maybe his Vitality had waned, and his control of Essence was dismal, but he still had it. Hanging from his neck, tucked in a velvety pouch, Ca'lorus was calling him home. His mind was drawn back to that moment in the arena, when he could have sworn he heard his name.

Raeyu, I need you, he thought, begging for the first time in a long while.

His appeal reached out and a warmth enveloped him, the realm quieting for fleeting seconds. He could feel her there, with him, present. Taking a hollow breath, he lifted his hand to the pendant, clutching it tightly.

There was a moment where time felt like it stopped. Sound petered away, and even Sakaeri stopped her muttered tirade, looking around quizzically. Moisture rose up from the ground, floating in little spheres, and Aeyun watched one rise.

It wasn't possible, was it? Was this enough?

Around him, the sea of faces grew sceptical, confused in their perverse stupor, and Aeyun held his breath as a barrier broke. Just as Seraeyu breached the throng of onlookers, flanking Kaisa's right, a rip tore through the air, the scar of which Kaisa stared at. His expression turned both perplexed and intrigued as his footing left the pathway, his form drifting up alongside those near enough the rift. Beside him, Seraeyu stayed grounded. And that was decidedly more terrifying than even his look of livid disdain.

"*Ca'ou o, ou'e'uo, A'vor a'Ca'lorus.*"

The light that shined from the pulsing tear was imperceptible, but Aeyun could *feel* it shifting, searching. Finding. It beckoned him, and Aeyun answered, propelling himself, Davah, and Sakaeri towards it. In that moment, he was all too happy to forsake those who stood idle, watching. Kaisa's eyes followed him, but soon they latched onto Seraeyu's back as he stalked menacingly towards them.

Aeyun stared at his approach, panicked, then the feeling compounded when Seraeyu snatched at the person closest to his position: Sakaeri. In slow motion, Aeyun watched as Sakaeri struggled against the vice grip. But inky, miasmic Essence dragged her down, drawing her into Seraeyu's grasp. Aeyun called to her, but his voice was drowned in the rift's sinking roar. Sakaeri gazed back at him, something bittersweet flashing there.

Thank you.

The words didn't reach him, but he read them clear as day.

Sakaeri ripped at one of Seraeyu's many jewels and held out her hand. Not towards him or even Kaisa, but back towards Aeyun. She had the audacity to smile, and Aeyun wanted to scream. She couldn't do this. Not after everything.

And yet.

She did.

Both Aeyun and Davah were forcibly tumbled into the rift by a fate-sealing gale. Before he could take a breath, before he could wail and shout because he failed – *again* – they were dropping out from air, landing in a bed of wildflowers that Aeyun hadn't seen since he was a child. As he hit the ground, Davah rolled away from him on impact, sputtering out a groan.

Aeyun could *feel* it. All of it.

The air, the ground, the shifting forests beyond, the city hidden among meandering dirt paths, and the grotto that led to the a'teneum no one could find.

He could feel Ca'lorus in his very bones.

When he opened his eyes, he could see the cusp of The Veil as it arched over his homeland and the odd distortion of light it caused. Flickering translucent, pastel hues across its expanse. He moved to sit up, and the fragrant smell of wilderlilies greeted him, wafting up from where he'd crushed a few beneath him. It was, for all the trouble, surreal.

Finally, he rolled forward to his knees and looked up, seeing–

Raeyu. She was standing far away, her one arm wrapped around herself, looking wistfully aggrieved. Her mouth opened, as if she would say something, then it closed again, and she shook her head, fearful. Aeyun, unable to comprehend *why* she was acting that way, started to reach out a hand. Then he saw the little sparks of inky particles that flitted from his fingers, multiplying as each second passed. In his periphery, he registered Uruji running out from the a'teneum's door, its edge violently smacking the adjacent wall.

"No!" he shouted, shoving past Raeyu, who stumbled to the side to allow him by.

Baffled, Aeyun's hand started falling, as did his energy. His insides felt ashen and his muscles molten. As if there wasn't enough determination in the realms to keep him steady. His eyes drew to the doorway again, past Uruji's nearing form. There Da'garu stood, in the flesh, half-hidden behind the stone.

"What's wrong with the two of you!? I said to *stop*!" Uruji cried out.

As Aeyun listened to his brother's distraught reprimand, he felt it culminate.

His heart thumped unevenly, then it suffered a distorted pain, feeling like it was crushing in on itself. A gasp left him in the lurch of it, and soon he was clutching at his chest. A pressure grew there, then it pulsed, and he was being ripped apart. Shredded into a million pieces. All the while the darkness grew, his vision turning spotty with it.

He wasn't sure, his senses were failing him, but he felt as if he had toppled over. The ground was no longer welcoming but hard and punishing.

"Aeyun!" Uruji called somewhere beyond him, but Aeyun couldn't shout back. Blood surged up his throat, garbling his breath as it dribbled down his chin.

"Not again, feckin *stars*," Davah said, sounding closer than he had been before.

"Aeyun!" Uruji cried out again. It seemed like he was in front of him, but Aeyun's perception was spinning. He felt his mask get thrown off, then there was a strained sob from where he thought Raeyu was. A piece of his heart tore with it. "I told you to stay away! Now the exchange – dammit!"

"Uru–" Aeyun hacked. When his eyes focused, he saw a sprinkle of crimson on his brother's cheek. "Uruji," he managed to murmur between strangled breaths.

Uruji, however, wasn't paying attention to his unspoken apologies. Instead, he planted his thumbs on the sides of Aeyun's head, his eyes starry and mesmerising.

The realm became a layered mess of hazy white, a fractalised aetherscape mixed with the a'teneum grounds. There, in that confused plane, Aeyun trailed his eyes across the tether that tied him to Raeyu.

It will be the end of you, she'd said.

What was once a milky, colourless thread was now a surge of energy tinged with black, Essence washing up towards her. Raeyu was batting it away, her struggles reflected in that broken distortion. She was crying out a sob, but it did no good. It still flowed to her, ripped from Aeyun's very soulsong, steady and fearsome.

Aeyun intuitively knew what it meant when he saw it. The unfinished end to that scene, all those years ago. The way it was meant to go. How it should have gone, if he could have sung a duet with Essence, back when Raeyu lay cold in his arms.

Uruji didn't say a word. He just stared, eyes glassy and unrelenting, and Aeyun stared back. Uruji's thumbs pressed harder, and he set his jaw, speaking words in a cadence Aeyun couldn't follow. Something burning freely became a soft simmer, sparking once before being extinguished entirely. Then everything before him faded, including the stern determination on his brother's face.

Around him, a maze of smoky black arose, punctuated with distant reflections of colours spinning in and out of existence beyond fissured planes. It wasn't right, partitioned off like a prison, and Aeyun felt caged within it. Half complete, Aeyun's vision grew radiant, and a whisper of something called to him, singing a familiar tune.

Shakily, he stood, feeling both weightless and heavy on rubber legs. Willing himself to move, his foot fell, and the bodiless plane rippled. Then he stepped again, and again. Everything left his mind. All that mattered in that moment was finding the origin of the tune; that melody that sought him out in the darkness.

When he was met with a wall, he pivoted and turned down the next path, feet unsteady. His bright eyes would latch onto a glimmer of light every once in a while, but it was gone just as soon as he looked for it. Still, in the distance, somewhere, the call remained. He kept on, twisting around the maze without shape, trying to find it. Seeking its source.

After endless moments, he could sense a change, something among the blackness. The vast unknown. He fell to his knees. It only made sense, didn't it? This was something Aeyun had written in the stars by his own hands, only then he hadn't known what he'd done.

There Aeyun crumbled, sat before the man he'd silenced. Prostrated mournfully before the shadow of a young child, one whose shoulders should never have been expected to hold the weight of a dynasty. One he'd doomed to be judged inadequate by not only the Thasian patriarch, but all of Raenaruan society. All it took was an inhale, and Seraeyu awoke into existence in front of him, gasping, his eyes glowing with blinding brilliance.

"Aeyun," he whispered, and it felt like a necrotic blessing, full of misplaced security. Unearned trust.

Aeyun felt it leave him. All that raw power, all that Essence he sang with. The force that was too great to be one's alone, and he finally understood.

He understood as he watched that intense, enigmatic force build around Seraeyu, seeping into him. Two manifestations of Essence that were woven together as one, inseparable and reunited. Returning to their first host. Slowly, the edges of Seraeyu's eyes bled black into the white, consuming it, and soon all Aeyun could see was inky obsidian reflected there.

Reciprocally, the glowing brilliance of Seraeyu's Vitality wound into Aeyun. It became one strand of power once more, banishing Essence from his being, and his own focus became blindingly radiant. He felt Seraeyu's lifeforce so strongly it was overwhelming. And it was *familiar*. Interwoven inside him, twisting tightly among his own Vitality, it felt as if something he'd lost – something he'd long held – finally came home, settling around his soulsong like a satisfied sigh.

He understood now. No ritual, no exchange, was free.

That was what he'd given up. And this was what he'd gained.

"Aeyun," Seraeyu said, stronger, brow drawn down, a bewildered tension building.

Aeyun gazed up at him, shame curling within.

"I won't let you suffer for my mistake," he said. It sounded brittle to his ears. He didn't want to know what it sounded like outside them. Seraeyu looked down in Aeyun's direction, then he gazed at his own hands, seeing something Aeyun could no longer comprehend. "I promise."

"Why–"

Hands, disembodied and sharp, wrapped around Seraeyu's head, covering his eyes with their ghoulish snare. The ominous shadow of a presence loomed just beyond. Dread, frozen and venomous, filled Aeyun as scarlet trails rolled down Seraeyu's cheeks, obscured behind spindly, deamonish fingers.

"Blood of Ka'la'drius," her voice echoed.

"I hear you."

ACKNOWLEDGEMENTS

To those who have been on this journey with me from the start: thank you, from the bottom of my heart. To those who joined along the way, your encouragement and insight has been truly invaluable. To Nicola Hodgson, this title's editor, thank you for your guidance. It would be near impossible to convey the appreciation I have for everyone who's helped, in one way or another, this book come to fruition. Thank you to those have been, are, and will continue to be a part of the adventure.

Lastly, thank you, dear reader.

This story comes to life with you.

If you enjoyed this story and would like to support independent publishing, please consider leaving a review of this title on your preferred retail or review outlet.

If you would like to read more about *Where the Silence Sings* and The Symphonic Masquerade series, including an online pronunciation guide, visit:

www.emeryblaine.wordpress.com

More by Wild Door Publishing can be found at:

www.wilddoorpublishing.com

See you next time!

Milton Keynes UK
Ingram Content Group UK Ltd.
UKHW010751170624
444254UK00002B/32

9 781738 506002